OKLAHOMA!

The twenty-third brand-new tale in the Wagons West series—a thrilling adventure of the men and women who dare to stand tall against all odds— unflinching in the face of rifles and six-guns, unyielding in their defiance of the lawbreaker, as they fight for this wild, free land.

★ ★

WAGONS WEST

OKLAHOMA!

Insatiable hunger for land has led to a stampede of young pioneers into the Oklahoma plains—as mighty as the whistling wind and as unstoppable as the American heart

TOBY HOLT—
A man who answers his friends' cries for help with his fighting skills and his own blood—even if he must leave his fiancée to wait for his return as he straps on his six-shooter and makes a date for high noon.

ALEXANDRA WOODLING—
A bold Southern beauty who is more woman than any man can handle challenges Toby Holt's family with her iron will . . . and fights for his heart.

CAPTAIN HENRY BLAKE—
A magnificent soldier ordered to use his military prowess on the lawless streets of Fargo . . . unaware of the tragedy fate has in store or the cruel twist that will send him to Custer's Seventh Cavalry.

CINDY HOLT KERR—
The sassy blonde sister of Toby Holt, an independent woman headed toward an exotic land where danger and a diabolical enemy await.

BARONESS GISELA VON KIRCHBERG—
The regally beautiful aristrocrat who lives only for the kisses of Henry Blake . . . and who may die because he puts duty before love.

★ ★

HERMANN BLUECHER—
No greater villain lives than this former German spymaster who now plies his trade of blood and greed on Turkey's soil as his hate for Henry Blake becomes a murderous obsession.

EDWARD BLACKSTONE—
The rakish New Orleans gentleman turned Oklahoma rancher who breaks all the taboos of a faraway country to bring back breeding stock to save his land.

RAMEDHA—
A seductive child-woman of the sensual East who wants to experience Edward Blackstone's passion even if she jeopardizes his future and his life.

PERCIVAL SLOAT—
The shifty-eyed owner of an Oklahoma Territory newspaper who has a scheme to make himself rich . . . if he can gun down Toby Holt.

TIMMY HOLT—
The irrepressible young son of Toby Holt, whose curiosity will lead him into a terrifying flight in a balloon sailing toward adventure . . . or death.

EULALIA BLAKE—
The strong-willed matriarch of the Holt-Blake clan, she wants Toby to take a wife . . . but she's ready to do almost anything to keep it from being the wild-willed girl he loves.

Bantam Books by Dana Fuller Ross
Ask your bookseller for the books you have missed

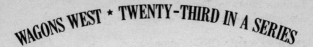

WAGONS WEST ★ TWENTY-THIRD IN A SERIES

OKLAHOMA!

DANA FULLER ROSS

TM **BCI**

Created by the producers of
**White Indian, Stagecoach,
Abilene,** and **San Francisco.**

Book Creations Inc., Canaan, NY · Lyle Kenyon Engel, Founder

BANTAM BOOKS

TORONTO · NEW YORK · LONDON · SYDNEY · AUCKLAND

OKLAHOMA!

*A Bantam Book / published by arrangement with
Book Creations, Inc.*

Bantam edition / May 1989

*Produced by Book Creations, Inc.
Lyle Kenyon Engel, Founder*

ISBN 0-553-27703-0

Published simultaneously in the United States and Canada

PRINTED IN THE UNITED STATES OF AMERICA

O   0 9 8 7 6 5 4 3 2 1

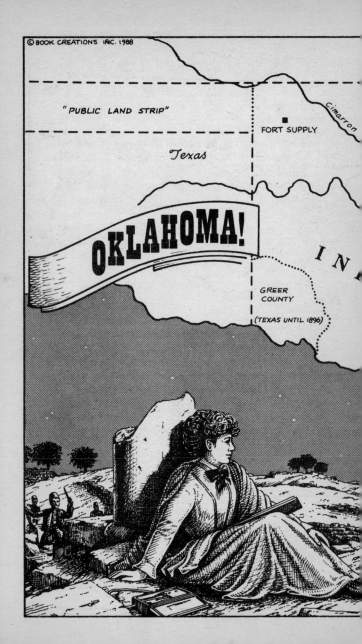

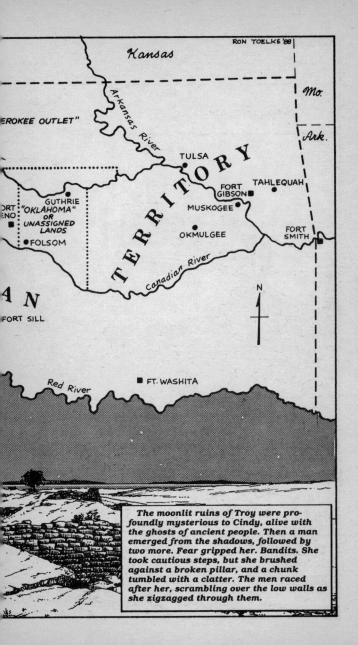

RON TOELKE '88

Kansas

Mo.

Arkansas River

EROKEE OUTLET"

Ark.

TULSA

TAHLEQUAH

FORT
GIBSON

T E R R I T O R Y

MUSKOGEE

ORT
ENO

"OKLAHOMA"
OR
UNASSIGNED
LANDS

GUTHRIE

OKMULGEE

FORT
SMITH

FOLSOM

Canadian River

A N

N

FORT SILL

Red River

FT. WASHITA

The moonlit ruins of Troy were profoundly mysterious to Cindy, alive with
the ghosts of ancient people. Then a man
emerged from the shadows, followed by
two more. Fear gripped her. Bandits. She
took cautious steps, but she brushed
against a broken pillar, and a chunk
tumbled with a clatter. The men raced
after her, scrambling over the low walls as
she zigzagged through them.

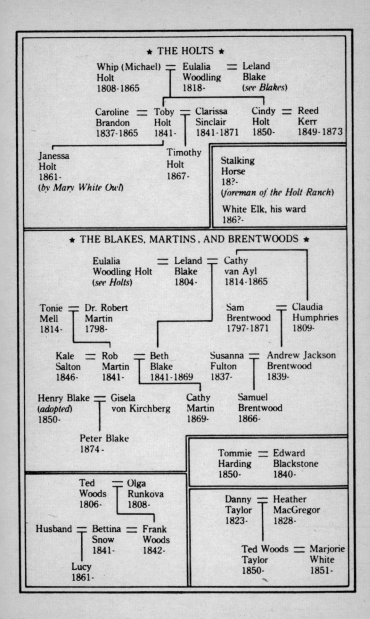

★ THE HOLTS ★

Whip (Michael) Holt 1808-1865 = Eulalia Woodling 1818- = Leland Blake (see Blakes)

Caroline Brandon Holt 1837-1865 = Toby Holt 1841- = Clarissa Sinclair 1841-1871

Cindy Holt 1850- = Reed Kerr 1849-1873

Janessa Holt 1861- (by Mary White Owl)

Timothy Holt 1867-

Stalking Horse 18?- (foreman of the Holt Ranch)

White Elk, his ward 186?-

★ THE BLAKES, MARTINS, AND BRENTWOODS ★

Eulalia Woodling Holt (see Holts) = Leland Blake 1804- = Cathy van Ayl 1814-1865

Tonie Mell 1814- = Dr. Robert Martin 1798-

Sam Brentwood 1797-1871 = Claudia Humphries 1809-

Kale Salton 1846- = Rob Martin 1841- = Beth Blake 1841-1869

Susanna Fulton 1837- = Andrew Jackson Brentwood 1839-

Henry Blake (adopted) 1850- = Gisela von Kirchberg

Cathy Martin 1869-

Samuel Brentwood 1866-

Peter Blake 1874-

Tommie Harding 1850- = Edward Blackstone 1840-

Ted Woods 1806- = Olga Runkova 1808-

Danny Taylor 1823- = Heather MacGregor 1828-

Husband = Bettina Snow 1841- = Frank Woods 1842-

Lucy 1861-

Ted Woods Taylor 1850- = Marjorie White 1851-

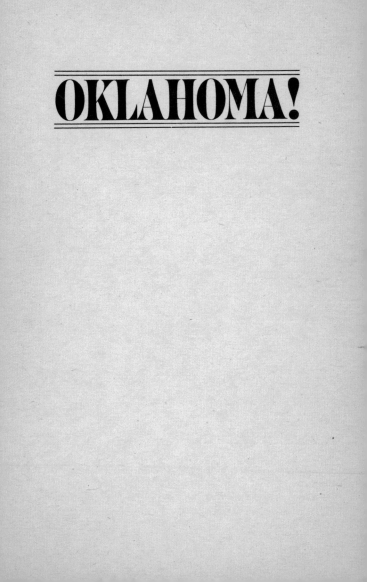

OKLAHOMA!

I

On the M Bar B ranch in the Oklahoma Territory, Rob Martin, a tall, red-haired man in his thirties, with muscles hardened by labor, was piling wood on the carcasses of four cows, dead of tick fever. He frowned as he attended to the disagreeable task.

Suddenly hearing a metallic clatter in the far distance, he stopped and turned. The signal bell at the ranch house was ringing furiously, indicating some emergency. Rob ran to his horse and, leaping on it, spurred it forward.

He was far away from the house, and the minutes seemed agonizingly long as he rode at a dead run across the rolling hills of the sprawling ranch. Finally spotting the house and barns, he saw no sign of activity. His horse pounded past the barns, and Rob pulled hard on the reins as he took the turn to the front of the house.

His wife, Kale, was ringing the bell on the porch, her free arm around Sally Collier, the wife of a neighboring homesteader. Barely more than a girl, Sally was clutching an infant and weeping hysterically. Rob's young daughter, Cathy, was also trying to comfort Sally.

"Lummas and some of his men are at the Colliers' place, Rob," Kale called as he reined up. "They're threatening to burn the house and kill Billy!"

"Lummas said that Billy rustled one of his steers from the Circle S!" Sally wailed. "Billy did no such thing, but Lummas won't listen!"

1

Wheeling his horse, Rob started toward the Collier homestead but reined up again as Kale shouted, "Rob!" She pointed a finger at him, and her violet eyes narrowed. "Lummas has gunslingers with him, so you be careful. Do what you can to help Billy, but make sure you come back here on that saddle, not across it."

Rob nodded, then spurred his horse and rode away.

The young couple's homestead was on a creek to the east, between the M Bar B and the Circle S. Within minutes, Rob could see that the men from the other ranch had fulfilled at least one of their threats: A column of dense smoke rose from the barn and the cabin. Rob feared he would find Billy Collier hanged from a tree—the common retaliation for cattle rustling. But as he rode nearer, Rob felt vastly relieved: Billy was being tormented, but he was alive.

The tall, heavyset Lummas was sitting on his horse in front of the burning buildings, along with his three gunslingers and two of his ranch hands. Billy, white-faced with terror, was lying on the ground among the horses. A lariat was wound tightly around him, and one of the gunslingers clutched the end of the rope.

"What do you want here?" Lummas demanded as Rob rode up. "This is none of your business."

"There's a young mother at my ranch," Rob answered coldly, "crying her heart out because some men were threatening to kill her husband. If there's a man who can listen to that and think it's none of his business, I'll look him in the eyes and tell him he's not fit to be alive."

Lummas flushed hotly as he looked away. The two ranch hands were also discomfited, but the three gunslingers laughed. "Now we know why he's here," one remarked derisively. "He's a hero."

"Naw, you're the heroes," Rob shot back sarcastically. "Three armed men roping an unarmed boy . . . now that's what I call real men!"

"That's enough talk!" Lummas barked as the angry gunslingers moved their hands closer to their pistols. He stabbed a finger at the one who had spoken. "You're paid to use your gun, not your mouth! We've done enough here. Let's go on back to the ranch."

"I'll be along, Mr. Lummas," the gunslinger holding the lariat said. "I'll drag this rustler back and forth for a while so he'll remember to leave your steers alone."

"No, you won't!" Rob snapped.

"Who's gonna stop me?" the man challenged, his hand poised over his holster.

"I will!" Lummas shouted, riding his horse between Rob and the gunslingers. He took the rope from his man and threw it down. "We're going back to the ranch, all of us, and we're going now!"

"That's the problem with hired gunmen, Mr. Lummas," Rob said. "They're like dogs with rabies. They'll bite for you, but it's hard to get them to stop. Men who kill for a living should not be roaming about."

"Go on, reach for your guns!" one of the men challenged.

"You climb out from behind your gun and see what happens!" Rob countered. "Without a gun to hide behind, you're all alike—sniveling cowards. The three of you put together wouldn't make one good man."

"I don't need a gun to take care of you!" the largest snarled, unbuckling his gunbelt as he dismounted, then flinging it into the dust. "Let's see if you've got anything to back up that talk!"

Lummas tried to stop the fight but was ignored.

Smiling in grim pleasure, Rob dismounted and unfastened his own gunbelt, then hung it over the horn of his saddle. Billy Collier scrambled out of the way. The gunslinger charged forward, fists cocked, as the other two cheered him on. Rob circled, dodging blows or fending them off with his forearms as he waited for an opening. The man facing him was about his size but had a longer reach. He was also too confident, for he swung wide blows, leaving his stomach unprotected. Seeing a good opportunity, Rob jabbed a hard right to the man's midsection. The gunman was stepping forward at the same instant and appeared to have run into an invisible wall. His body stiffened as his sour grin faded into a grimace.

The man moved back, then with a snarl lowered his head and charged Rob, butting him hard in the stomach. Rob's feet flew up, and he was hurled several feet before landing hard on his buttocks. He looked up to see his adversary coming at him, grinning wickedly.

Rob scrambled to his hands and feet and scuttled to the side, narrowly avoiding the gunslinger's kick. He launched himself at the big man, driving him back against a protesting horse. Both men moved quickly away from the mounts.

The gunman began protecting himself, raising his fists as Rob feinted toward his face with a left, then swung a long, hard right into the man's stomach. The breath burst from his lungs as he staggered back. Rob followed him, swinging a right to the man's nose.

As his fist connected solidly, Rob twisted it, grinding it into his adversary's face. Blood exploded from his mouth and nose. The man fell heavily and sprawled on his back. The fight was finished.

The other two gunslingers looked in silent astonishment at their companion. "How about you, boys?" Rob invited them.

One gunslinger spat an oath and reached for his pistol. Lummas reined his horse around, reached over, and gripped the man's wrist. "You leave that gun where it is!" he bellowed. "Now ride out, like I said, or you start looking for other jobs!" He beckoned the two ranch hands and pointed to the third gunslinger. "Get him on his horse and get out of here. Now!"

The hands dismounted and pushed the gunslinger onto his horse; then the five rode away, but Lummas remained behind.

Lummas turned to Rob, who was buckling on his gunbelt. "There are times for a man to take a hand in things, Martin," he growled, "and times when a man should just let things be." The rancher turned his horse and rode away after his men.

Billy rushed over to pump Rob's hand. "Somebody killed a Circle S steer and hung it in those trees," he said, pointing to a copse up the creek. "But it wasn't me. It's on my land, but I don't know how it got there." He looked at his burning cabin and barn and shook his head, almost in tears. "Now I'm finished, Mr. Martin."

"No, you aren't, Billy," Rob soothed. "You and your family are safe, and that's the important thing. You and Sally can make a new start." Rob mounted, then kicked his left foot out of the stirrup and beckoned. "Come on, Billy. Your wife's worried about you, so let's set her mind at rest."

Billy put a foot in the stirrup and swung up behind the saddle. Then Rob turned the horse toward his house. The young fellow continued to profess his innocence.

Knowing Billy fairly well, Rob believed he was too honest to rustle a steer. That the animal was hanging in the trees was a puzzle, but no more strange than other things that had happened during the past few months: Watering holes had been ruined; pastures and crop fields had been burned; houses and cabins had been randomly shot at; and unexplained mishaps had befallen local residents.

In no instance had blame been pinpointed, so the end result was an atmosphere of hostility, with each suspicious rancher and homesteader ready to battle all others. Ranchers had hired gunslingers, while homesteaders' cabins had become small forts. Rob had been untouched thus far, and he was at a loss to explain what had precipitated the situation. He knew only that the entire area was poised on the brink of open warfare.

Rob was certain it was only a matter of time before the M Bar B became directly involved in the trouble, and he was equally certain that the ranch was unsafe for Kale and their five-year-old daughter. He had talked to Kale about taking Cathy to stay with friends in New Orleans but met with a blunt refusal. This latest incident convinced him, however, that they must go.

Upon returning to the ranch, Billy was greeted with tearful relief by Sally, who assured him that the cabin and barn were unimportant because his safety was all that mattered.

"Well, they didn't do nothing much to me," Billy said, "but they might have if Mr. Martin hadn't showed up. He was more than Lummas and his gunslingers could handle. Right to their faces, he said them gunslingers was like dogs with rabies. He whipped one of them. You should've seen it, Sally."

The young woman gasped with awe as she looked at

Rob, but he cringed inwardly, knowing what Kale's reaction would be. As he glanced at her, he saw what he expected: She was enraged.

"Well, you and Sally can stay here with us, Billy," Rob said, quickly turning his horse. "I have a job I need to finish."

As the young couple followed Kale into the house, Rob rode away, wishing that Billy had been less specific in his praise. Although disposing of the cattle carcasses was extremely unpleasant, Rob consoled himself with the thought that enough time might elapse for Kale's temper to cool.

Rob resumed dragging mesquite logs and branches to the pile of carcasses. The death of the cows was a far greater loss than twenty times their number of steers, because they were expensive breeding stock. Other ranches bred and raised cattle to sell, but the purpose of the M Bar B was to circumvent tick fever, a disease that was the scourge of southwestern cattlemen. Rob and his partner, an Englishman named Edward Blackstone, had hit upon the idea of developing a strain of cattle that was immune to the disease. They had pooled the last of their money to buy the ranch and breeding stock for it.

Longhorns were immune to tick fever, plus they could subsist on very sparse graze and go for long periods without water. But they were relatively small, bony cattle. Rob and Edward had intended to crossbreed longhorns with Herefords to obtain a breed of large cattle, immune to tick fever and as hardy as longhorns.

The venture had been plagued from the beginning: The expensive thoroughbreds contracted the disease and one by one succumbed to it. Then tragedy had struck when Edward's wife, Tommie, fell ill and died. After that, Edward had gone to visit their friend, Toby Holt, at his logging camp in Wisconsin.

Sometime later, Edward had learned that the Brahman cattle of India, which were huge, hardy animals, might be immune to tick fever. Presently, he was going to India to investigate the possibilities of obtaining some Brahman for the M Bar B. In the meantime, lacking the money to hire ranch hands, Rob had been struggling to manage the ranch by himself.

After tossing a last log onto the pile, Rob struck a match and lit a handful of dry grass. Watching as the flames crept through the branches and logs, he pondered moodily. He had never accepted defeat, but his family's safety was at stake. If he was unable to get Kale to take Cathy to New Orleans, he would have to abandon the ranch. As the woodpile became a mass of fire, Rob rode back to the house.

He hoped that Kale's temper had settled, but the odds were against it. After putting his horse into a corral, he carried his saddle and bridle to the tack room inside the barn. Then, through the wide front door of the barn, Rob saw Kale storm angrily out the back door of the house and march into the barn to confront him.

"Did you go over there to help Billy or to get killed?" she demanded.

"Don't be silly, Kale," he said. "You know that—"

"Silly?" she cut in furiously, stepping closer and lifting to her toes to shout in his face. "You dare call me silly after what you did? That was foolish! It was idiotic!"

"Now stop this," he ordered. "What happened is over and done with, so let's have an end to it!"

While he was saying the words, he knew they were a mistake. Nothing made Kale angrier than his taking a domineering attitude. Her eyes wide and her face turning pale, she tried to reply, but she was speechless with rage.

"Kale, honey, I'm sorry," he said earnestly. "Lummas is basically a decent man, and I had it all over his gunslingers. I wouldn't have risked my life. Honest."

Rob watched her expression soften as he pulled her to him. Then, as often happened between them, emotions altered swiftly. His body pressed to hers, Rob ran a hand through thick, blue-black hair and pulled her head back, then kissed her. She put her arms around him, and the anger between them turned into an explosion of passion.

Lifting Kale as they kissed, Rob moved toward an empty stall. Its door opened too slowly for him, and a hinge broke as he shoved it. The door flew open and sagged on one hinge as

Rob and Kale fell into the soft hay, pulling at each other's clothes. A moment later, they were making love.

Afterward, Kale lay in his arms as he kissed and caressed her. "You must do something for me, Kale. You must take Cathy and go to—"

"No, Rob," she cut in quickly. "I won't leave you alone here."

"You won't be. Billy and Sally will be staying here for at least a few months. Think of Cathy's safety."

Kale was silent for a long moment, then she sighed and nodded. "Very well, we'll go to New Orleans on one condition, Rob. You must send a telegram to Toby and ask him to come here."

"But I'm not sure exactly where he is at the moment."

"You can contact him by sending a telegram to Portland. If he isn't there, his family will forward it to him. On the day you get a telegram from him, saying that he will come here, I'll leave for New Orleans."

Rob hesitated, then nodded. "All right. We'll see what he says, then discuss it again."

"My answer will stay the same. When will you send the telegram?"

Rob smiled and pulled her closer. "Soon. But while we're here, I want to take full advantage of it."

"So do I," Kale murmured, a sultry smile on her beautiful face as she put her arms around him and lifted her lips to his.

As the headlands of San Francisco Bay fell behind and the steam- packet picked up speed, turning north toward Portland, Oregon, Toby Holt enjoyed a warm sense of heading for home. The tall, rangy man's adventures had taken him to many distant places, but now, in the summer of 1874, he was returning to the place where all his journeys began.

This trip home was even more special because of the young woman beside him at the rail. Women moving about the deck glanced at the tall, handsome Toby in his neat, tailored suit, but Alexandra Woodling drew more attention, from both men and women.

The small, slender woman's silk dress, its fitted bodice

trimmed with European lace, was a shade of emerald that accentuated the flecks of green in her large, hazel eyes. Her auburn hair was tucked up into a fetching hat, its wide brim bedecked with yards of patterned tulle, which matched the lace on her dress. She had an air of sparkling vitality, as well as the poise and self-assurance of a woman much older than her nineteen years.

Her mother had been a Bradford, a direct descendant of the governor of the *Mayflower* settlers at Plymouth Colony in 1620. On her father's side and through her upbringing, she was a Kentucky bluegrass aristocrat, born into the exclusive hunting club circles of Lexington society. She possessed steely physical courage from riding to hounds at breakneck speeds on perilous cross-country courses from early childhood.

"Then your family will probably meet the steam packet when we arrive," she said in her soft Kentucky accent, continuing her conversation with Toby.

"Yes, and others," Toby replied.

"Well, I must give some thought to what I'll wear on the day we arrive," Alexandra mused. "I do want to make a good impression."

Toby laughed. "Wear whatever you wish, Alexandra. When did you start to worry about what people think of you?"

"I'm not worried," she corrected him, "but I must give the matter some thought. Speed and wind are of little use to a horse that shows like a mule. First impressions are important, Toby."

Looking out across the water, Toby thought about Alexandra's introduction to her future mother-in-law. He knew his mother, Eulalia Blake, would have reservations about Alexandra, which would have nothing to do with the young woman's appearance. Above all, Eulalia was a devoted grandmother, and she would want a daughter-in-law who would be a good stepmother for his daughter, Janessa, an intensely intelligent girl who was very mature for her thirteen years, and his mischievous son, Timmy, seven years old.

Even Toby doubted Alexandra's capacity for mothering. In addition to being only a few years older than Janessa, Alexandra had absolutely no homemaking skills or experience in caring for children. She had a keen mind and was adept at quietly taking control and organizing things, but Toby was unsure if those attributes would prove helpful. He only knew that he loved Alexandra and was unable to contemplate life without her.

The conversation turned to the duration of the voyage. "The packet maintains the same speed, regardless of the weather," he explained. "It doesn't deviate from its schedule."

Alexandra started to reply, but her smile faded as she looked along the deck.

Toby turned to follow her gaze. Several yards away he saw a stocky, muscular man who was taking swigs from a whiskey bottle as he leered drunkenly at women passing along the deck.

"He should be in his cabin," said Toby disgustedly.

Alexandra shrugged as she turned back to the rail. "Perhaps he has friends who'll take him in hand. So we'll arrive in Portland on Thursday afternoon?"

"That's right," Toby replied. "With plenty of time to look around the ranch and to check on your horses before we go across the river to my mother's house at Fort Vancouver. She and the general live in a house provided by the government. I'm sure you and Juanita will be very comfortable there."

At the mention of her maid, Alexandra smiled wryly. "I told Juanita to rest and enjoy the voyage, but she's probably fussing about in the cabin."

Toby chuckled. "Is she pleased with those books you bought for her in San Francisco?"

"Delighted," Alexandra replied. "She does love those romantic novels. I'd better go and see what she's doing, Toby. I'll make her sit down with a book, then I'll rejoin you."

As Alexandra walked away, Toby reflected with satisfaction on how smoothly Juanita got on with his fiancée. Juanita was from the New Mexico Territory, where he had eliminated a band of comancheros who had been ravaging the territory.

Juanita, trained from childhood as a lady's maid, had been a captive until Toby rescued her. Her employers had been killed by the comancheros, so Toby had brought her to Alexandra, who was accustomed to doing things for herself. But Alexandra had immediately welcomed Juanita after hearing about the young woman's ordeal.

Suddenly there was a commotion nearby. A small man, walking unsteadily on the heaving deck, had accidentally bumped into the drunken man, causing him to spill some of his liquor. He was bellowing profanities.

The small man, accompanied by a girl, spoke with a strong Italian accent as he apologized.

"I am very sorry, *signor*," he said. "I deeply regret what happened."

"Damn your regrets!" the drunk yelled, pushing the man roughly. "If you don't know how to walk without running into people, it's time you learned!"

Facing the younger, much larger man, the Italian was intimidated, but the small girl had enough pluck for both herself and her father. She darted forward and kicked the drunk.

The girl's heavy boot thudded solidly against the man's shin, and he yelped in pain and almost fell. He reached for the girl, but her father stepped forward to protect her. The drunk knocked him to the deck, then seized the girl by her hair and shoved his bottle into his coat pocket, freeing his other hand to slap the child.

The blow never landed. Already moving to put a stop to the trouble, Toby caught the drunk's wrist. Then he grasped the man's other wrist, which held the child's hair, and held it in a crushing, viselike grip.

Releasing the girl's hair, the drunk yelped in surprise and pain. In a single, smooth motion, Toby turned loose the man's wrists and drove his fist into the drunk's stomach. The man was hurtled across the deck and slammed into the bulkhead, where he held his stomach and gasped for breath.

Striding to his adversary, Toby ripped the bottle from the man's pocket and flung it over the rail, then pushed him upright against the bulkhead.

"I didn't hurt that girl," the drunk grumbled in his defense. "She kicked me, and I—"

He broke off with another yelp of pain as Toby pulled

him from the bulkhead. "She had every right to do that!" he barked. "And if you had slapped her, I'd have broken every bone in your body. Now apologize to this gentleman and his daughter, then get out of here."

"All right, all right," the drunk muttered, moving away and glancing at the small man. "I'm sorry for what I did."

The Italian, amazed by how quickly Toby had dealt with the situation, merely nodded in reply. As the people who had gathered to watch the confrontation began dispersing, the small man collected himself and thanked Toby.

Toby extended his hand. "I'm glad I was able to help," he said. "I'm Toby Holt."

"I am Enrico Fossi," the man replied, shaking hands. "This is my daughter, Gabriella."

Toby smiled warmly, coaxing a timid smile from the solemn child as she curtsied. "Gabriella certainly has a lot of spunk," he commented. "She reminds me of my own daughter, up in Portland."

Fossi laughed and said that the girl had ample courage, even if she did sometimes lack judgment.

Alexandra returned, and she glanced around curiously at the people who were still moving away. "What happened, Toby?" she asked, then nodded politely at the man and his daughter.

"That drunk began making a nuisance," Toby replied, dismissing the matter. Then he introduced Alexandra as his fiancée to Fossi and Gabriella.

Fossi lifted his hat and bowed. "I wish you every happiness. My daughter and I plan to make our home in Portland, if I can find work."

"What business are you in?" Toby asked.

"I am a construction engineer," Fossi replied. "I had more than ample work in San Francisco, but it is not a good place to raise children. From what I've heard about Portland, it will be much better."

"Well," Toby mused, "Portland is far more settled, although it isn't growing as fast as San Francisco. Once the railroad gets there, it should begin growing more rapidly. That's still a few years away, but you certainly won't have any shortage of work then. Portland is a good place to raise children."

Fossi commented that as a widower, he considered his daughter to be more important than his work. Then he thanked Toby again and moved away with Gabriella.

As Toby and Alexandra stepped to the rail, he said, "I didn't want to discourage the man, but most people in Portland do their own construction or hire a couple of carpenters. With very few exceptions, the construction isn't all that complicated—just simple houses."

"Speaking of houses," Alexandra said, "I can't wait to see yours."

"I know you'll love it," Toby answered. "Part of it dates back to the first settlement in Oregon, but it's been expanded over the years. Each woman who has lived there has added her touches. It's large, very attractive, and one of the most comfortable houses you'll ever find." He smiled. "Yes, I know that you'll love the house as soon as you see it, Alexandra."

Late that night, Timmy Holt was torn with indecision as he crawled under his road locomotive with a carbide lamp and looked at the steering linkage. Horses outside in one of the corrals stirred, and Timmy froze, wondering if a ranch hand had seen the light in the barn, where the road locomotive was kept. He listened fearfully, but the horses settled down after a moment, so he continued his inspection.

Timmy crawled around the wide, solid-steel front wheel. It was a tight squeeze. When his father had first bought the huge machine for him, he had been able to scramble under it easily, but that had been some time ago. Now seven years old, and large for his age, he had difficulty in sliding under it.

His father had bought it, knowing that it would never run; indeed, it had been nothing but a rusty hulk when oxen had towed it to the Holt ranch near Portland. A steam-driven machine designed to take the place of draft animals, the road locomotive had been allowed to go to ruin by the farmer who inherited it.

Now the machine looked as good as new. Calvin Rogers, an engineer who had been crippled in a hot-air balloon accident, had worked with Timmy, explaining the function of each part while they had disassembled the machine a piece at a time, removing rust, repairing, and painting it.

Now the road locomotive should run. According to Calvin, however, the steering linkage was worn and loose. But as Timmy checked the linkage, finding no play that he considered excessive, he had a suspicion that Calvin had stretched the truth to serve a purpose.

Everyone, including Calvin, considered the machine dangerous. Timmy's father was due to arrive in two days with the woman he planned to marry, and Timmy wondered if Calvin was delaying a decision until then. Calvin might intend to present Toby with the fact that the machine was now repaired, and what was to be done with it?

The answer that his father might give troubled Timmy. He feared that his father, distracted by wedding plans, might simply decide to dispose of the road locomotive.

As he crawled from under the machine, Timmy reflected that his only opportunity to drive it might be right at that very moment. A brass whistle on the boiler gleamed in the light of his lamp. Calvin had installed the whistle as a safety device to prevent Timmy from starting up the machine by himself. It blew shrilly whenever the boiler was pressurized, and if it was removed, the head of steam would escape through the hole.

Having long since figured out how to overcome that problem, Timmy told himself that he was simply seeing if his idea would work. Moments later, the telltale whistle had been replaced by a short length of pipe with a cap on its end.

Assuring himself that he was checking to see that no steam escaped around the pipe, Timmy went for wood and straw. He put them into the firebox, lit the straw, then closed the door and blew out his lamp. The firebox door was warped, so light from the fire dimly illuminated the cab of the locomotive as Timmy perched on the seat and monitored the needle on the steam-pressure gauge.

Instead of the usual shrill blare of the whistle, the only sound was that of the wood burning in the firebox as the needle crept upward. Smoke billowing from the stack quickly filled the barn, and Timmy rationalized that he was merely letting the smoke out as he climbed down from the cab to open the barn doors.

The barnyard, bunkhouse, and ranch house were quiet in the moonlight. The horses in the corrals milled about but settled down after a moment. Timmy returned to the road locomotive.

The needle on the gauge was edging past the operating pressure. Timmy quickly opened a valve to let steam into the piston chamber, which would cool the boiler and stabilize the pressure. When the chamber was charged with steam, it made a faint, ringing noise, which had heretofore been drowned in the blaring of the whistle. The sound was one of powerful, contained energy, which needed only a tug on the throttle to be released. Timmy felt a surge of keen excitement as he listened to the inviting sound.

The boy slid up onto the seat, then checked the transmission lever to make certain it was in the forward position before reaching for the throttle. As he pulled the throttle out an inch, the engine snorted rapidly, and the wide rear wheels kicked up dirt against the back of the barn. The machine jerked forward. The road locomotive angled toward the left side of the barn door. Timmy tried to turn the machine to the right but found that Calvin had been truthful about problems in the steering linkage. The steering bar traveled several inches before it met any resistance; then its effect on the front wheel was too little and came too late.

The road locomotive rumbled out of the barn, and the left rear wheel slammed into the thick beam at the side of the door, snapping it. The huge, heavy machine barely faltered from the impact, but the barn door crashed down, and the entire corner of the barn collapsed.

Lifting an arm to protect his head, Timmy looked back as sheet-metal roofing and heavy boards toppled behind the road locomotive. Part of the door was caught on the rear wheel, but it broke into splinters of wood as the machine chuffed and clanked across the barnyard, picking up speed.

The horses in the corrals whinnied and danced about in panic as the road locomotive rumbled toward them. Timmy tried to close the throttle, but it was stuck. He pushed frantically on the steering bar to turn the machine away from the corrals. It continued picking up speed as it gradually veered to one side.

Ranch hands ran out of the bunkhouse, shouting, but their cries were almost drowned by the noise of the road locomotive. The machine angled away from the corrals, but a rear wheel slammed into a corner and sent the thick rails flying. Thirty quarter horses streamed through the opening, bucking and kicking as they raced about the barnyard.

The ranch hands leaped out of the machine's path as it clattered toward the long, low bunkhouse. Timmy threw his weight against the steering bar, and the front wheel slowly responded as the machine turned onto a path parallel to the bunkhouse. But a rear wheel caught the front edge of the porch as the road locomotive traveled the length of the building, peeling the porch from it. Floorboards splintered as support posts collapsed, and the porch roof crashed down behind the machine.

As the road locomotive approached Calvin Rogers's room at the end of the building, he threw his window open. "Close the throttle, Timmy!" he bellowed.

"I can't!" Timmy shrieked. "It's stuck!"

The man shouted something else that was lost in the noise of timbers splintering as the road locomotive passed his room. Dragging pieces of the porch, it headed toward the ranch house. The barnyard was in chaos as ranch hands in hats, boots, and longhandle underwear tried to herd the panic-stricken horses back into the corral.

Stalking Horse, the Cherokee foreman of the ranch, shouted to his ward, "White Elk! Try to stop that infernal machine! I'll get everyone out of the ranch house!"

The Indian youth was already running toward the road locomotive. The firebox door had jarred open, and the fire cast a ruddy glow over the cab as White Elk bounded up to it in a long, agile jump. "How do you stop this thing, Timmy?" he shouted.

The boy pointed to the throttle. White Elk began trying to push it back in as Stalking Horse ran past the machine and toward the house at a pace that belied his advanced age. The foreman shouted as he ran, but someone in the house had already been awakened by the uproar, and a light was shining in the kitchen windows.

The back door opened, and Janessa stepped out in her nightgown and wrapper. The tall, slender girl took one look, then ran back into the house, calling a warning to the housekeeper, Clara Hemmings, and her children. Stalking Horse ran into the house behind her as White Elk gave up on the throttle. He gripped the steering bar and tried to turn the road locomotive from the house.

Muscles knotted in White Elk's arms as he planted his feet firmly and strained on the steering bar, his teeth clenched. Just as the road locomotive began turning toward the road beside the house, something snapped with a metallic clatter, and the steering bar suddenly became slack. White Elk fell heavily. He crashed against the hot firebox door, then rolled away from it and climbed to his feet.

The road locomotive hissed and clanked relentlessly toward the house. When it was only a few yards from the building, Janessa and then Clara Hemmings and her children ran out the door, with Stalking Horse right behind.

White Elk cupped his hands around his mouth. "I can't stop it or turn it, Stalking Horse!"

"Get off, then!" the foreman shouted back. "Grab Timmy and jump!"

The youth picked up Timmy and leaped, turning in the air to cushion the impact for the boy. They hit the ground hard, with White Elk sprawled flat on his back and Timmy on top of him.

An instant later, the road locomotive plowed into the Holt residence with a deafening crash. The house shifted on its foundations and listed to one side as the rear wall buckled. The machine buried itself deep in the house, with only its rear wheels visible, and the roar of escaping steam joined the bedlam as a steam line broke. The rear wheels continued turning, gradually slowing as the boiler lost its head of steam.

The ranch hands, Calvin Rogers among them, had followed the machine to the house. Everyone stood and looked in shocked silence except Janessa, who picked up a lawn chair and ran to a window. Standing on the chair, she peered into

the kitchen, then jumped back down. "Get the fire buckets!"
she shouted.

Loose horses scattered ahead of the mad rush toward the
barn, where the canvas fire buckets were stored. Calvin
limped to the pump that fed the watering troughs in the
corrals, while the others, carrying buckets, formed a line
between the barnyard pump and the house.

Smoke and flames shot from the broken kitchen windows
while the bucket brigade was formed. The people worked
furiously to save the house.

When dawn broke, the fire had been extinguished. In
the bright light flooding across the sky, ranch hands, still
wearing only hats, boots, and longhandle underwear, hastily
retreated to what was left of the bunkhouse to put on trousers, then joined the others gathered around the kitchen
windows and door.

The road locomotive filled the demolished kitchen. What
remained of the floor was canted to one side, while the
furniture was a mass of fire-blackened rubble. Even the foundation had been destroyed.

Clara Hemmings was the first to speak. "I had everything all ready for Mr. Holt and his young lady to make their
home here after they're married," she murmured sadly. "And
now this. . . ." She choked back a sob and wiped her eyes.

"It isn't your fault, Clara," Janessa consoled, putting an
arm around the woman. "Dad will know that. I suppose I'd
better go tell Grandmama and see if she wants to look at it."

"That would be a very good idea, Miss Janessa," Stalking
Horse commented.

"All right, I'll get dressed," Janessa said. She turned to
Timmy, her Holt eyes a cold blue as she pointed a finger at
him. "You go to what's left of your room and stay there! You'd
better not give me any more reason than I already have to
thrash you because I might not stop until I wear out every
switch on this ranch!"

The boy, needing no further warning, hurried toward
the front door to go into the house.

Eulalia Blake stood in her parlor at Fort Vancouver and
looked out the window at her flower garden. At fifty-six, she

was an active, vibrantly healthy woman with matronly beauty and poise. She was a determined woman, who dealt with difficulties by confronting them head-on. Something was creating havoc in her flower garden each morning, and she intended to put a stop to it.

Hearing her husband coming downstairs for breakfast, Eulalia stepped into the entry hall. Major General Leland Blake, the commander of the Army of the West, had the athletic bearing of a man much younger than his seventy years, and snow-white hair made his complexion seem even more tanned and ruddy. He smiled warmly at Eulalia. "Good morning, m'dear."

"Good morning, Lee. Your coffee is ready in the dining room, and I'll join you for breakfast in a moment."

Lee nodded amiably, then kissed Eulalia, and she smiled affectionately as she watched him go into the dining room. As she returned to the window, her smile faded, and her chin assumed its determined angle once more. A moment later, she saw what had been causing the damage in her flower garden; it was, as she had suspected, the fort mascot, a bulldog named Spike.

The dog was cared for by a retired corporal named Ben Craddock, who had spent some fifty years in the army. He lived in a room over the stables and did odd jobs around the fort, but the absentminded old man was nowhere to be seen as the dog trotted along the road. Eulalia watched it make a beeline for her flower garden. Then she quickly and quietly stepped toward the front door.

She went outside and down the steps, stopping to pick up a stick. The dog was already beginning to dig in the soft soil of the flower beds, uprooting the flowers.

"You stop that, Spike!" Eulalia shouted.

The dog, accustomed to doing as it wished, bared its teeth as Eulalia ran toward it. She feinted with the stick. The dog snapped at it. She brought the stick down sharply across the animal's rump. The dog yelped, surprised; then, snarling in rage, it charged at Eulalia.

Holding her skirt aside to keep the dog from tearing it, Eulalia nimbly evaded the animal. At the same time, she plied the stick furiously, raining stinging slaps on the dog's rump. Unused to being disciplined, the dog yelped in frustration as it snapped at Eulalia and the stick.

Finally the animal wheeled and ran. Eulalia kept up with it for a few steps, still drubbing it as it raced away. Craddock was ambling along the road, carrying the dog's leash. He looked in surprise at the animal running toward him, then at Eulalia standing at the end of the path in front of her house with the stick.

"Has Spike done something wrong, Mrs. Blake?" he asked.

"He certainly has, Corporal Ben," Eulalia replied. "He's been rooting in my flower garden every morning."

"I'm mighty sorry about that, Mrs. Blake!" Craddock exclaimed, appalled. "I really am. The last thing I need is for the general to be mad at me."

"I see no reason for the general to know about this, Corporal Ben. But when you take Spike for his morning walk, please keep him on his leash until you're past the houses. Good day."

"Good day, ma'am," the man said, lifting his hat and leading Spike along the road. "And thank you."

As he passed with the dog, it bared its teeth at Eulalia. She pointed the stick at it threateningly, and the dog scuttled around to the other side of Craddock for protection. Then Eulalia dropped the stick and stepped back along the path, patting her hair and straightening her dress.

By the time she was back inside the house, Eulalia was completely composed. She went into the dining room, where Lee stood and held her chair as she sat. The maid brought in breakfast.

Ever since Eulalia had received a letter from her son the previous week, the Blakes' discussions had centered around Toby and Alexandra. The letter had mentioned nothing about arrangements for the wedding. That troubled Eulalia, making her wonder if Toby and Alexandra planned on a quiet wedding, which she disliked because the people excluded from the guest list would be offended.

Lee simply looked forward to seeing his stepson. When the subject of the wedding came up, Lee reassured Eulalia.

"I think you're concerned for no reason, my dear. If she

even contemplated a quiet wedding, I should think that her maternal ancestors would spin in their graves."

"Well, there's nothing wrong with her paternal ancestry," Eulalia put in quickly. She was a Woodling herself, and the young woman was a distant cousin. "If the Bradfords weren't overly pleased with my cousin Alexander, it wasn't because of his background."

"No, certainly not," Lee agreed. "With the Bradfords on one side and the Kentucky hunt club set on the other, Alexandra has a pedigree like her horses at the ranch. In my opinion, there was no mention of wedding arrangements because they plan on having a very large one that will take time to organize."

"Perhaps," Eulalia conceded hopefully. "In that event, Alexandra will be staying here with us for some time."

"It doesn't make any difference exactly when they get married, does it?"

"It does to Clara Hemmings," Eulalia replied. "She has planned to be married as soon as Toby and Alexandra are settled. She's very loyal to Toby, and I'm sure she'll offer no objection if she has to postpone her own marriage to accommodate Toby's plans."

"And I'm sure that everything else will work out equally well," Lee added cheerfully. He took a last sip of coffee, then stood.

Eulalia smiled and lifted her lips as he bent to kiss her, but her smile faded when he left.

What she knew about Alexandra was less than reassuring. The girl had grown up on a Kentucky horse farm without the benefit of a mother's guidance. When her father had been killed, Toby had sent her horses to his ranch. They were hunters and show horses—extravagantly expensive and totally useless, as far as Eulalia was concerned. Moreover, a still had been sent to the ranch from Kentucky, and Eulalia had been shocked to learn that Alexandra used it in making bourbon whiskey.

For years Eulalia had hoped that Toby would remarry. But now she had reservations about his choice. She was more than willing to accept Alexandra on whatever merits she had, but it would take more than a young woman of nineteen who could ride and make whiskey to be a good stepmother for Timmy and Janessa. Perhaps Alexandra would realize her own shortcomings and seek advice in dealing with the children, which Eulalia would be more than glad to give.

There was a knock at the door. A maid started to answer it, then walked back along the hall when she saw Eulalia going to the door. Opening it, Eulalia was delighted to see Janessa. "Why, come in, my dear, come in!" she exclaimed. She kissed the girl and smiled at her fondly, then closed the door. "Let's go into the parlor, Janessa. It's a pleasure to see you, as always, but you're here very early. Nothing is wrong, is it?"

"Yes, ma'am," Janessa replied bluntly. "Timmy started up his road locomotive."

Eulalia wheeled in sudden terror. "Has he been injured?"

"No, ma'am. There's not a scratch on him."

Eulalia breathed a deep sigh of relief. "You gave me such a fright, Janessa," she said. "I could just see that boy lying under the wheel! I thought Calvin Rogers had it fixed so that Timmy couldn't start it up by himself."

"He did, but Timmy figured out a way around that."

"That doesn't surprise me in the least," Eulalia said grimly. "Tell me about it, Janessa."

As she led Janessa into the parlor, Eulalia knew she would have to take an active part in the conversation. Janessa strongly resembled Eulalia's daughter, Cindy, at the same age, but Cindy was outgoing, while Janessa was reserved.

"I thought you might want to come over to the ranch and see what happened."

"No, not as long as Timmy and everyone else is all right. There would be no point in my going there, and I'll have a busy day today."

"All right, then," Janessa said, standing up. "I'd better get back to the ranch because we have a lot of work to do."

"Work at the ranch? Timmy didn't run into anything, did he?"

"Yes, ma'am."

"Please sit down, my dear. What did he run into?"

"Well," Janessa replied, "he knocked down one corner of the barn."

"That will probably cost a lot to repair."

"Yes, ma'am. Then he hit a corral and the bunkhouse."

"Oh, no! It's too bad that your father will have this facing him when he gets home, isn't it?"

"Yes, ma'am. Then he drove it into the house."

"What?" Eulalia exclaimed, leaping from her chair. "That was my first home in Oregon, Janessa, and your grandfather built it with his own hands. Is it badly damaged?"

"Yes, ma'am. I thought you would want to look at it."

"Absolutely," Eulalia said firmly, stepping toward the door. "I'll send for a carriage and get ready, then I'll go to the ranch with you."

Eulalia's maid summoned an orderly and sent him for a carriage, while Eulalia put on her hat, gloves, and a light shawl. A carriage from the fort drew up in front of the house, and Janessa tethered her mare to it and stepped inside with Eulalia.

During the drive to the dock and the ferry trip across the river, Eulalia questioned Janessa about the damage. The more she heard, the worse she felt. Finally she resigned herself to what she was going to see and fell as silent as her young companion.

As the carriage moved away from the Portland docks, Eulalia noticed that Janessa seemed nervous. Eulalia knew what was bothering her: Janessa wanted a cigarette, but because Eulalia strongly disapproved of her smoking, she was waiting until later to have one.

The girl, trained by her mother in herbal medicine, planned to be a doctor and had worked with Dr. Robert Martin in Portland for years. In view of the nature of that work, plus her smoking and other things, Eulalia firmly believed that Janessa needed guidance that Alexandra Woodling would undoubtedly be unable to provide. And a mature, experienced woman was certainly needed to control Timmy.

As the carriage passed the telegraph office, the delivery man was coming out the door. He called to Janessa, "Did you decide whether or not to send those two telegrams on to your dad, Miss Janessa?"

"Yes, sir," Janessa replied. "I decided to hold them until he gets home, since he'll arrive on Thursday."

The man nodded and waved as the carriage rumbled on past him. Eulalia lifted her eyebrows, curious. "Toby has telegrams waiting for him at the ranch? Where are they from, Janessa?"

"One is from Washington," Janessa replied, then looked away, her pretty face flushed and her eyes burning with anger. "The other one was sent from Germany, Grandmama," she added quietly.

Frowning, Eulalia knew that the only one who would have sent the telegram from Germany was her and Lee's adopted son, Henry Blake, an army captain stationed there. His name had become anathema to her some three years before, when he had jilted her daughter, Cindy, in favor of a German baroness. Janessa felt the same about him, because she and Cindy were as close as sisters.

"I wonder what he could want from Toby," Eulalia commented.

"I've tried not to think about it, Grandmama," Janessa replied, pushing at her hair nervously and looking out the window.

Eulalia smiled at her granddaughter. "Go ahead and smoke a cigarette, if you must, Janessa. It isn't that I approve. The fact is, you're fidgeting about so much, my dear, you're starting to make *me* nervous."

Quickly taking her cigarettes out of her pocket, the girl gave one of her rare, wide smiles. She lit a cigarette and relaxed in satisfaction. The reference to Henry Blake made her think of Cindy. She was living in Paris, studying art. The previous month, she had returned to the United States to assist her friend, Marjorie White, a well-known photographist. Marjorie had been captured by the Maoris of New Zealand, and her husband had been killed while rescuing her. Cindy, whose husband had also died violently and before her eyes, had spent a few days in Maine with Marjorie, then convinced the woman to return to Paris with her.

Janessa finished her cigarette and sighed regretfully. "I wish Cindy could have come here for a few days. I miss her so much."

"I know, my dear," Eulalia replied sympathetically. "We all do. But Cindy has responsibilities elsewhere. That's what keeps your father away so much, and now we have the same thing with Cindy."

Janessa replied that Cindy had said the same thing in her last letter. She had also mentioned that Marjorie's photographic record of captivity by the Maoris promised to bring her worldwide fame and she planned to begin a European lecture tour. Her fame, of course, would be no consolation for the loss of her husband, and Janessa assumed that the lecture tour was an attempt to distract her from her grief.

When the ranch house came into view, Eulalia was speechless with despair. The original log cabin, which had been enlarged into a rambling, rustic structure over the years, was far more than a house to her. She and her first husband, Whip Holt, had been on the first wagon train to Oregon, and this was where they had put down their roots. Toby and Cindy had taken their first steps, then grown to adulthood in that house. It was the focus of her life, the symbol of her hopes and dreams.

Eulalia and Janessa got out of the carriage, and Eulalia walked around the barnyard, looking at the destruction. Seeing the damaged barn and bunkhouse, she felt even more disconsolate. Stalking Horse, Clara Hemmings, and others gathered around her, but their attempts to make Eulalia feel better failed.

The worst moment came when Jonah Venable, the groom who had accompanied Alexandra's horses from Kentucky, remarked that two of the hunters had leaped out of their corral during the excitement. "But we catched them back up," he assured her, "and neither of them skinned a leg or anything, so there's no worry on that score."

Eulalia almost had to bite her tongue to keep from retorting that nothing had been farther from her mind than worry about the hunters. She also noticed that the building constructed for the young woman's whiskey still, with a cellar full of bourbon under it, was untouched. Having seen more than enough, Eulalia turned back to her carriage.

The housekeeper stepped to the carriage with Eulalia and mentioned that Toby and Alexandra might delay their wedding after what had happened. With an effort, Eulalia put her own concerns aside. "They may," she agreed. "I know you want to leave as soon as possible, but Alexandra can't take over the household until they are married, of course."

"My plans can be changed," Clara offered. "That's the least I can do, after what Mr. Holt has done for me and my children. When I do leave, my eldest son, Clayton, would like to stay. He plans to quit school and work with Mr. Venable with those hunters, learning to be a groom."

"But he needs to get an education, Clara," Eulalia said, frowning.

"Being a groom is what he wants to do, Mrs. Blake, and he has a head like a brick when his mind is made up."

"Well, if that's what he wants to do, I don't foresee any problems," Eulalia said.

Clara nodded and turned back to the house.

Eulalia had rarely known a more gloomy moment. What worried her most of all was that if an experienced woman like Clara had difficulty controlling Timmy, what would happen when Alexandra became responsible for him? And Alexandra might actually be a bad influence on Janessa. Her grandchildren meant everything to Eulalia, and their future appeared to be very much in doubt.

II

The squalor and congestion of the side streets of Constantinople surrounded Hermann Bluecher's hired palanquin. Ignoring the din coming through the curtains, he waved a perfumed handkerchief under his nose to counteract the offensive odors. Presently, he realized that he was on the avenue leading to the ministerial building. He checked his papers a last time.

The bearers set the palanquin down with a bump, and then the head bearer opened the curtains and salaamed. In the past Bluecher would have needed assistance to climb out of the palanquin, but now he weighed a mere two hundred twenty-five pounds. The food on the freighter that had brought him to Turkey was abominable, and he had shed many pounds as a result.

The imperial seal on the papers brought a deep salaam from the guard, and Bluecher passed through the gate into the vast plaza around the ministerial buildings. At one time he had been the head of internal security of German military intelligence, with a large network of personal agents, but the ways in which he had misused those agents had forced him into exile. His bank accounts in Switzerland made it a comfortable exile, but his most valuable asset was his keen mind, which had been honed by the finest universities in Europe.

During his voyage to Constantinople, Bluecher had concentrated on learning Turkish. Two of the sailors on the ship had been Turks, and Bluecher had paid them well to coach him in their native language. He had also forced himself to think in Turkish, a familiar process to him, since he was fluent in several languages. When he arrived in Constantinople, he considered himself to be fluent in Turkish.

Upon his arrival he had applied himself to learning the customs and subtleties of dealing with officials of the Ottoman Empire, and now he proceeded with full confidence. His papers, a reply to his application for a government post, granted him an audience with the minister of internal affairs. Bluecher presented the papers to the vizier's secretary, at the same time pressing a gold coin into the man's hand.

The coin was a substantial sum, and it brought a smile to the secretary's face. He led Bluecher into an anteroom, where the German was kept waiting only a few minutes until being ushered by the secretary into the vizier's opulent office. The vizier, reclining on silk cushions, was an aged man with a white beard and deeply wrinkled face. From his first glance at the man's dark, penetrating eyes, Bluecher knew he had found a kindred spirit, a man obsessed with power.

Bluecher salaamed deeply as the vizier leafed through the German's papers. Then he spoke quietly. "Why did you leave your position in the German government?"

"Because my exercise of authority among common people was considered too vigorous, effendi," Bluecher replied. "The present policy of the German government is one of coddling such people."

"And what do you consider wise government policies?"

"Those which, regardless of their nature, increase the stature of a nation in respect to other nations, effendi."

The answers satisfying the vizier, he put Bluecher's papers aside. "The ministries of the sultan welcome talented foreigners."

"I am eager to serve, effendi."

The vizier began talking about Serabatan Province. The provincial governor was a relative of the sultan, his status making it inappropriate for him to be concerned with mundane details. The province was overrun with bandits, commerce was at a standstill, and—of primary importance to Constantinople—tax revenues had plummeted. As a result, there was a need for a capable lieutenant governor.

Serabatan, Bluecher knew, was on the Aegean Sea, with the provincial capital at Balastafa. For an ambitious man like himself, it was in the hinterlands, far from the seat of power in Constantinople, but an official post there would be a step toward a position of greater authority.

The secretary whispered something in the vizier's ear, then helped the old man to his feet. The vizier beckoned Bluecher toward the side of the room, where a door opened out onto the balcony. Below was a courtyard where four men waited. One was kneeling, his head on a block, and two others were holding him down. The fourth man, holding a large scimitar, looked up at the balcony and awaited the command to use it.

As the vizier motioned, the scimitar flashed down and chopped through the hapless man's neck, the headless body twitching. The man's head, blood spurting, rolled across the courtyard stones. The other three men salaamed deeply to the vizier, then walked away.

"A bandit, effendi?" Bluecher asked.

"No," the vizier replied. "He was the former lieutenant governor of Serabatan."

Fear raced through Bluecher as he took another look at the headless body. Then he followed the vizier back inside. Unlike the effete nations of Europe, the rewards for success here were immense, but the penalties for failure were drastic.

The vizier settled himself on his pillows, then explained that the duties of the lieutenant governor were simple: to provide a steady and ample flow of tax revenues and to ensure that no problems in the province came to the attention of Constantinople.

"The post," the old man continued, "carries with it the title of pasha and a force of personal guards, along with a comfortable salary and whatever gratuities may be presented." He pointed to a hardwood box decorated with gold and silver scrollwork on the table. "The official seal of the province is in that. Either take it with you and leave here as a pasha, or simply leave here and never return."

Bluecher picked up the box. The vizier gave him a small smile that seemed to warn against failure, then dismissed the

German with a wave. After salaaming deeply, Bluecher followed the secretary out, carrying the small box.

A few minutes later, Bluecher was closeted in a small anteroom with the secretary to work out the details of his assignment. Knowing that the secretary would expect another bribe, Bluecher gave the man a lavish sum. Delighted, the secretary wrote out a requisition for spare horses for the guards, as well as other items Bluecher wanted.

"How many slaves do you want as bearers for your palanquin, Pasha?" the secretary asked.

"None. I want a coach, not a palanquin."

"A coach is a very uncomfortable means of travel."

"It is also fast, and I care more for speed than comfort."

The secretary shrugged and nodded, writing. A short time later, Bluecher returned to the plaza gate, where a hired palanquin took him to his lodgings to pick up his personal effects.

The sun was near its zenith, and the giant, ancient city, astride the Golden Horn where Europe and Asia met, shimmered in the blistering heat. It was the quietest hour of the day, and the streets were almost deserted as the palanquin bearers, panting and sweating, took Bluecher to his lodgings. He gathered up his belongings, then told the palanquin bearers to take him to the military garrison, where his coach would be waiting.

At the garrison, in the shadow of the Byzantine hippodrome on the outskirts of the city, the guards had assembled, and other preparations were being made. With rifles in their hands, scimitars at their waists, and crossed ammunition belts on their shining chests, the guards were a formidable force. They stood rigidly at attention in ranks as the captain of the guards salaamed deeply to Bluecher and asked for instructions.

Bluecher pointed toward the slaves who were moving listlessly around his coach, preparing it for the departure. "I want to get to Balikesir as quickly as possible," he said. "See that it is done."

"Your wish is my command, Pasha," the captain replied.

The captain barked an order to the guards, who descended on the slaves and began beating and kicking them. This resulted in a frenzy of activity. Loaded supply wagons were brought out, along with teams and spare horses. A few minutes later, Bluecher's coach set out, guards riding ahead and behind it.

Making himself as comfortable as possible as the coach jolted along the rutted road, Bluecher looked at his papers and planned his course of action. The Ottoman Empire, a backward nation without railroads or other modern conveniences, was rotten with corruption at the center and disintegrating at the edges. It was perfect for Bluecher. He would make Serabatan into a model province.

Bluecher pondered other plans. The individual who had caused his exile from Germany had been an American army captain named Henry Blake. Bluecher burned for revenge. He had decided that Blake had to suffer, then die, and the best way to punish him was to kill his wife, Baroness Gisela von Kirchberg. An informant had recently written that Blake and von Kirchberg had married and left Germany for England, along with a retinue of servants and other employees.

Late at night, Constantinople far behind, the cavalcade stopped at a village to rest the horses, then set out again before daybreak. On the following day, the procession crossed the border into Serabatan.

At the first district capital he reached, Bluecher stopped to make his presence felt. At the army garrison on the edge of the town, where a lieutenant was in command, the rolls listed sixty soldiers. Bluecher had the lieutenant assemble the soldiers, and there were only twenty-two.

Bluecher glared at the lieutenant. "You have been collecting the salaries for sixty soldiers and pocketing the rest!"

The lieutenant, having expected Bluecher only to demand his share of the graft, was confused. "If you will come to my office, Pasha, I am sure you will—"

"You no longer have an office!" Bluecher interrupted, ripping the insignia off the man's shoulders. "You are now a private! Join the other soldiers!"

As the astounded man slinked to the ranks, Bluecher beckoned a tall sergeant, appointed him as the new lieutenant, and ordered him to start recruiting soldiers. The man beamed with delight and assured Bluecher there would be sixty soldiers when he next visited the garrison.

"They aren't to sit in the barracks," Bluecher growled. "They are to patrol the roads and arrest bandits. Within ten days, I expect you to send twenty-five bandits to Balikesir for execution!"

The new lieutenant's smile faded. "But I may be unable to capture that many bandits by then, Pasha."

"Then be prepared to be brought to Balikesir yourself," Bluecher snarled, "ready for execution."

The man blanched, then set his chin firmly and salaamed. "Twenty-five bandits will be delivered within ten days, Pasha."

Bluecher stepped into his coach, and as the cavalcade rode out of the town, he relaxed. He knew that the news would spread among the army garrisons, recruiting would begin all over the province, and soldiers would start patrolling the roads.

When he reached Balikesir, Bluecher found that the governor, an opium addict, was in a constant stupor. Bluecher was intensely gratified; he was, for all practical purposes, the provincial governor.

At the lieutenant governor's home, a luxurious villa on a wooded hill overlooking the city, Bluecher assembled the official staff. He explained that all of them would be expected to perform efficiently and no gratuities were to be accepted under penalty of death. Then he ordered his secretary to summon the provincial treasurer.

The treasurer arrived while Bluecher was relaxing in his bath. The man salaamed deeply, placed a small chest on the edge of the tub, then retired to a respectful distance to express his pleasure over Bluecher's arrival.

"You won't be pleased very long," Bluecher said bluntly. "Inform the district tax collectors that I will be visiting each of them in the near future to examine their accounts. I also intend to examine your books, so have them ready."

"Be assured, Pasha," the man said smoothly, "that all the accounts are in order." He pointed to the chest at the edge of the tub. "There is the appropriate amount due you from the last tax collections."

"Then it should be in the treasury at Constantinople!" Bluecher bellowed. "In the future, if one copper coin is held back from tax collections, the official responsible will be beheaded! Now get out of here!" He jabbed a finger at the chest. "And take that with you!"

The treasurer picked up the chest, salaamed deeply, then scuttled out. Bluecher had a good laugh over the righteous ethical stance that he had assumed, reflecting that virtue was indeed an interesting change.

After enjoying his bath, and a repast that servants brought in, he summoned his secretary, an escort of guards, and his coach, then set out for the nearest district capital.

Bluecher began spreading a reign of terror among the district capitals, reviewing tax accounts, inspecting soldiers, and setting quotas of bandits to be captured. It was a grueling schedule, but he enjoyed what he was doing.

When his coach passed people working in fields or in towns, he could point to any of them and order their execution. Acutely aware of that, the workers salaamed deeply as the coach went by. The heady feeling of power gave Bluecher a deeper, more lusty pleasure than he had ever known before. He had found his place in life.

Only one thing interfered with his enjoyment: A possible source of trouble in the province was a foreign archaeologist working near the coast. The vizier had specifically said that any problems in the province should be dealt with there, but the archaeologist enjoyed special status with Constantinople and might complain about something.

Bluecher had already identified one of his staff who would make a good informant and had dispatched the small, furtive man to Karahisar, a town near the archaeological site. When he received a prompt report from the man, Bluecher felt less concerned.

There was little bandit activity in the area of Karahisar, and the foreigners seemed content enough. One, a Frenchman named Choubrac, had recently left because of illness. A replacement for him was expected to arrive soon, but nothing else of note was happening there.

Pleasant background music from a string ensemble muffled the murmur of conversation and soft rattle of dishware that surrounded Cindy Holt Kerr and Marjorie White as they had dinner in an expensive Montparnasse restaurant. It was a sedate atmosphere, yet there was an undertone of excitement among the diners in costly, stylish evening dress and glittering jewelry.

Although Cindy should have enjoyed dining with her friend, she was thoroughly miserable. During the past two weeks, Marjorie had subsided into the grief that had gripped her after her husband had been killed. In addition to remorse for her friend, Cindy felt the same for herself. She had recently finished a series of etchings of the battle in which her own husband had been killed but had been unable to start on another project.

Listening to Marjorie talk about her feelings had resurrected Cindy's grief, because the two of them had much in common: Both their husbands had been killed while rescuing them, and both felt wretchedly guilty over their shortcomings as wives while their husbands had been alive.

Picking at her food, Marjorie apologized. "I'm afraid I've ruined our dinner. I'm sorry, Cindy, and this is such a nice place."

"Well, it doesn't seem the same this evening," Cindy observed moodily. "But that's because of the way I feel, rather than the restaurant. You haven't ruined anything for me. We probably should have stayed at the apartment to have dinner with Madame Kirovna."

Marjorie agreed. "I thought I was starting to adjust to Ted's death, then it all came back to me during the voyage. I suppose I had too much time to think."

"Having time on one's hands isn't good," Cindy said. "And I should know."

"But you help Madame Kirovna manage her art gallery, and you have friends here. In addition to Madame Kirovna, there's Pierre Charcot."

Cindy began telling Marjorie all about Pierre. A tall, handsome sculptor in his early thirties, he worked with Frederic Bartholdi, who was casting the Statue of Liberty. Cindy liked Pierre and enjoyed his companionship but did not return his romantic feelings.

"On the subject of Madame Kirovna," Cindy said, "I love her dearly, but she has such an austere outlook on life."

"Well, I've wasted my time by coming to Paris," Marjorie mused sadly. "I've decided to give up the idea of a lecture tour." She put her knife and fork aside. "The fact is, Cindy, I was a terrible wife. I was gone all the time. At least you were with Reed."

Cindy felt too depressed to try to help her friend. She touched her napkin to her lips as she sat back. "No, not in the way that I should have been, Marjorie. I didn't love Reed. And I'm sure he suspected it."

"There's more to expressing love than mouthing words," Marjorie insisted. "I loved Ted with all of my heart, and I told him so many times. But when it came to showing him, I did the opposite. Instead of making time for us to be together, I always put my work ahead of him. And in doing that, I brought about his death."

The reply that sprang to Cindy's lips brought tears to her eyes. Not trusting herself to speak, she blinked away her tears as she beckoned the waiter. Cindy and Marjorie paid for the meal and left. Then, when they were in the darkness of a hired carriage, Cindy was able to tell Marjorie what she had to say.

"I never once told Reed that I loved him," she confessed quietly, her voice almost breaking with a sob. "And when he lay dying in my arms, I could have told him then. But I didn't. He died, never having heard me say it."

The two women remained silent, each too lost in her own grief and guilt to be of any help to the other. The carriage drew up at the curb on Rue du Faubourg. Gaslights made bright splashes of light between the deep shadows under the trees that lined the broad avenue of jewelers, expensive clothiers, and art galleries. In the apartment upstairs from the Kirovna Art Gallery, Marjorie and Cindy went to the kitchen and made coffee, then brought the tray into the large, well-furnished parlor, where Madame Kirovna sat in the light of an old-fashioned candle, reading through thick eyeglasses. In her eighties, she was small, gray-haired, and shrunken with age, her sharp, deeply wrinkled features revealing the limited tolerance over her quick temper. Herbs that Janessa sent periodically had restored the use of her fingers so she could resume etching, but her bony hands remained gnarled with arthritis.

Marjorie spoke adequate if heavily accented French, and out of courtesy to the old woman, she and Cindy began conversing in that language. Madame Kirovna took off her glasses as the two younger women stepped in with the coffee, and the smile on her thin, wrinkled lips faded as she peered at them sharply.

The old woman nodded in thanks as Cindy put a cup of coffee on the table beside the candlestick. "I was going to ask if you enjoyed dinner because I thought that was where you went. Now I see that I was wrong—which is understandable, because evening is a very strange time to attend a friend's funeral."

Summoning a wan smile in response to the old woman's acid remark, Cindy sat down and said, "We went to dinner, but we weren't in the mood, Madame Kirovna. It would have been better if we had remained here."

"I'm glad you didn't," the old woman replied bluntly. "I dined alone, but at least I was able to enjoy my food. What is wrong with you?"

The two younger women began taking turns explaining, but Madame Kirovna cut them off after a moment. "When a loved one dies, everyone can think of things they should have said or done for that loved one. Or, indeed, left unsaid or undone. Everyone uses that to flog themselves in their grief. That is normal but must be resisted if it interferes with one's life."

"But it isn't that simple," Cindy protested. "Even though I didn't love Reed, I could have said that I did when he lay dying in my arms."

"Then be satisfied that you didn't lie to him," the old woman shot back. "It's evident that he was reasonably happy with you, isn't it? That was worth far more to him than a lie, Cindy." She turned to Marjorie. "When you married, your husband didn't expect you to give up your career, did he? So why bemoan the fact that you acted in the manner your husband anticipated?" She sat back, shaking her head in disgust. "Both of you are acting like schoolgirls."

"I won't deny the logic of what you say," Cindy replied firmly, "but many emotions can't be logically explained away. Perhaps you've never suffered the loss of a loved one—"

The old woman's head snapped around, and her dark, penetrating eyes glared in outrage. Cindy had seen Madame Kirovna angry many times, but this was the first time that the woman's quick, fiery temper had been turned on her. She cringed, waiting for the explosion.

It never came. Composing herself with visible effort, the old woman picked up her cup and sipped her coffee. Cindy and Marjorie exchanged an uncomfortable glance in the tense silence.

Madame Kirovna put her cup down and began relating events that had occurred in Moscow in 1825. She had been an art instructor at a university and married for about a year. Her husband had been a prosperous young businessman, and her two brothers had been officers in the horse guards regiment. In December of that year, when Czar Alexander I had died and Czar Nicholas I had come to the throne, Madame Kirovna, her husband, and her two brothers had been involved with a group appealing for a constitutional government. Known as the Decembrists' uprising, it was quickly crushed. Her husband and brothers had been executed, while Madame Kirovna went into exile in Paris.

"The group I belonged to," she went on, "wanted freedom of speech, freedom of assembly, a free press, and the other freedoms that you two have as your birthright. But some demonstrations became violent, which brought both retribution and more oppression than before."

"That was dreadful, Madame Kirovna," Cindy said sympathetically. "You can be proud that they died as martyrs, to a worthy cause, even if it doesn't make up for—"

"No," Madame Kirovna said quietly. She looked away, the candlelight making shadows in the deep wrinkles on her aged face. "I took them to the meetings, then we would go home and argue until late in the night about what had been said. They ridiculed it, which made me so angry at times that I wept. You see, they were loyal to the czar, and their names were on the death lists because of me."

Not knowing what to say to that, Cindy turned to Marjorie, who was also at a loss for words. Madame Kirovna continued. "I fled and left them to their fate. They urged me to go, but that is irrelevant. The choice was mine." She turned to

Cindy. "So never say again that I don't know what grief and guilt and shame are, Cindy."

"You're being too harsh on yourself," Marjorie offered sympathetically. "Even so, I don't see how you overcame what happened."

"I haven't overcome it!" the old woman hissed impatiently. "These past fifty years have done nothing to lighten that burden. It remains as heavy as the first day I shouldered it!"

"Then how do you endure such torment?" Marjorie asked in wonder.

"How would you carry that chair you are sitting on?" Madame Kirovna barked. "You would pick it up and then carry it! If for some reason you had to carry it for the rest of your life, you would do it and go on!" She sat back, drawing in a deep breath, then continued in a quieter tone. "You are a guest in my home, and I have been rude to you. Please forgive me."

"You weren't rude to me," Marjorie replied. She stood and stepped toward Madame Kirovna. Kneeling beside the chair, Marjorie took the old woman's gnarled hand. "You've shown me what real courage is and made me very ashamed of myself."

The old woman shrugged. "I've told you about one moment of weakness, and it is far from the only one I've ever had. But it will be well worth my talking about my old troubles if you will do whatever you must about yours and continue with your life, Marjorie."

"That's precisely what I intend to do," Marjorie vowed, her chin set at a determined angle. "Tomorrow morning, I'll start working on my lecture about the Maoris. I'll tour every major city in Europe." She turned to Cindy. "And you must get back to work, Cindy."

Cindy nodded reflectively, determined to keep her grief and guilt from being obstacles. The lack of direction in her work remained, however. "But I don't have the faintest idea of what to work on."

"You lack the maturity to see the mountains of inspiration that surround you," Madame Kirovna remarked. "For now a change of scene would probably be best." She took a letter from her pocket and looked at it, then shook her head. "This is an opportunity for a change of scene, but not one that would do for you, Cindy."

"What do you mean, Madame Kirovna?"

"This is from Jules Choubrac, a friend of mine who is employed as an etcher by an archaeologist in Turkey. He has become ill and must return to France for treatment. He wants to find someone to take his place. Sketching is all that needs to be done, but the drawings must be made by an etcher, because they will be used to prepare etching plates."

The need for etchings by an archaeological expedition was obvious, since cameras were unable to provide the serial perspectives, overall views, and other visual documentation that was required.

"What are they searching for there?" Cindy asked.

"The ancient city of Troy," Madame Kirovna answered. "The expedition is headed by a man named Heinrich Schliemann, a wealthy German-American."

Cindy gasped in fascination, suddenly remembering that she had read about the expedition. Schliemann was attracting ridicule from the archaeological establishment, which considered Troy a myth, but he was doggedly persisting. The thought of the fabled city captured Cindy's imagination. "I would like to go, Madame Kirovna," she said excitedly. "Of course," she added more soberly, "that would mean leaving you alone in the gallery again."

"Somehow or other," the old woman commented dryly, "I was able to manage the gallery without you for many, many years, my dear." She smiled affectionately. "But you can't go there, Cindy."

"Certainly not," Marjorie chimed in. "Turkey is ruled by despots and overrun with bandits."

"Listen who's talking," Cindy retorted. "The one who got her hair scorched in the Great Chicago Fire and then wound up at dinner with cannibals."

After much discussion, the old woman reluctantly agreed to make the arrangements. Cindy was radiantly happy. Although Marjorie shared her friend's pleasure, her eyes reflected deep foreboding.

*   *   *

In the oppressive, humid heat of late summer in Calcutta, Edward Blackstone emerged from the relative quiet of the dockside customs building into the congested chaos of a wide street. Calcutta was a seething, vibrantly alive riot of color, motion, and noise that almost overwhelmed Edward's senses.

What immediately drew his attention, however, was a Brahman bull not fifty feet away. Like the countless others of its kind in India, the huge, sedately graceful animal belonged to no one in particular and wandered about at will, venerated as a holy animal by Hindus. This one had garlands of colorful flowers draped on its wide horns as it contentedly munched fodder that passersby had placed in front of it.

"Now there's many a beef dinner just going to waste," another man who had stepped out of the customs building commented to Edward.

The turbaned Indian porter with Edward's baggage on a handcart frowned resentfully at the remark.

"I presume that was meant to be amusing," Edward replied coldly. "But it reveals a lack of respect for others' beliefs, which is anything but amusing."

The man started to retort hotly, then reconsidered. Edward was six feet tall, with a slim, hard build, and calm assurance.

The stranger turned away. "Just passing the time of day," he grumbled.

The porter, his rigid posture thawing to friendliness toward Edward, stepped closer. "I believe, sahib, I heard you tell the customs inspector that you were going to Chandannagar."

"Yes, I have an uncle stationed at the garrison there," Edward replied. "I was told that it's some ten miles up the river from here."

"That is correct, sahib. You will need to cross the river to the Howrah station to take a train there. You could avoid waiting for a train by taking a carriage. The view would be better, and a carriage would cost somewhat less than the train fare."

The last reason appealed to Edward because he had a limited amount of money. He smiled wryly as he glanced around the teeming street. "But can I find a carriage?"

"Nothing is easier, sahib," the porter assured Edward, then added another sound to the bedlam as he whistled shrilly.

Almost as if by magic, a landau with its canvas top folded back drew up at the curb. The porter put the bags into it, and Edward paid him, adding his thanks.

The vehicle edged back into the traffic as soon as Edward was situated.

Once the waterfront district was left behind, the streets were wider and less congested. The landau crossed the Hoogly River on a wide, busy bridge, then turned north through Howrah on the Grand Trunk Road. In the open countryside, the heat felt less oppressive, although still intense. The monsoon season was drawing to a close, and the river beside the road, an arm of the mighty Ganges, was muddy and swollen.

Fertile crop fields flanked the roads, and small communities were scattered along it at wide intervals. Everywhere Edward looked he saw Brahman cattle. The main problem would be getting the Brahmans out of the country. If his reason for being in India became known, both the Indian and the English authorities would demand that he leave at once.

He hoped the money he had would be enough. The recent depression in the United States had been a financial disaster for the M Bar B ranch. Edward was hoping to stay with his uncle so his expenses would be low.

He was also hoping that Edgar Dooley, his friend at the East India Company who had first suggested the idea of using the Brahmans, would be able to offer some advice. Dooley, a traveling auditor, was a carefree old reprobate given to bouts of drunkenness, but he was also crafty and knew all about India.

In late afternoon the landau reached Chandannagar, the military garrison, with its parade ground, barracks, and other buildings north of it. As the landau moved along the quiet, shady streets of the large town, Edward gave the driver his uncle's address. It turned out to be a luxurious bungalow set back from the street behind landscaped gardens, shaded by large trees.

As the landau drew up in front of the veranda, an Indian butler came out, then summoned servants to unload the baggage. He led Edward into the house and presented him to Mathilda Cochrane, whom he had never met. An attractive, cordial woman in her thirties—and some fifteen years younger than her husband, Edward's maternal uncle—she greeted him warmly.

"So you're Penelope's son," she said. "I'm so glad to meet you at last, Edward, because your mother was Winslow's favorite sister. He's spoken about her so often, I feel I knew her. Did you have a pleasant enough voyage, then?"

"Yes, thank you. I should have written about my plans before I came here, and I hope I'm not intruding."

"Intruding?" Mathilda exclaimed. "Edward, if you had come anywhere near India without presenting yourself here, neither Winslow nor I would have forgiven you. Come, I'll show you to your room. You'll have time to relax before Winslow and the children come home."

As the woman led him through the house, she told him about her children. She and her husband had two young boys who were attending a grammar school in Chandannagar, and when they were ten years old, they would be sent to England to complete their schooling.

"I don't look forward to sending them, but they must have their education. We're also raising a cousin's daughter. Ramedha is learning to be a teacher, tutoring younger children during afternoons. Her father was James Howard Cochrane, of the Shropshire branch of the family. Did you know him?"

"No, I don't believe so."

"He was a captain in a Gurkha lancers regiment and married a daughter of the rajah of Jaipur. Such a romantic affair that ended so tragically! They were set upon and killed by dacoits." Edward looked puzzled. "Bandits," she explained. "Ramedha was just a baby, so we took her and raised her like our own. Well, here is your room, my dear. If you need anything at all, please let me know."

Edward thanked her, then entered the large, well-furnished guest room. A servant quickly unpacked Edward's bags and went to draw a bath for him. After changing into fresh clothes, he felt more comfortable.

Just as Edward finished dressing, he heard a man's loud,

happy voice echo through the house. "Penny's boy is *here*? Well, where is he? I want to see him!"

After a perfunctory rap on the door, it burst open and Edward's uncle stepped in, beaming expectantly. A burly, ruddy man with a thick, white mustache, he roared, "Edward! My word, you were just a boy when I last saw you! Has it been that long?"

Edward smiled, his memories of his uncle those of a much younger, boisterously friendly man; he had aged but not changed. "Too long by far. It's very good to see you again, sir."

"And you, my boy," Cochrane said, shaking Edward's hand vigorously. "This pleases me as nothing else could. Let's sit and talk. I want to hear all about what you've been doing."

When they were on the rear veranda, where a breeze and shade trees relieved the heat, Cochrane explained that he was the commander of a battalion of Bengal rifles, one unit of a regiment stationed at the garrison.

Edward then told his uncle what he had been doing, although he did not mention the specific reason for his trip. He explained the financial problems he and Rob were having at their ranch. "Shortly after that," he continued, "my wife became ill and died. That was a very severe blow, of course, and I've been traveling quite a lot since then."

"Best thing you could do, lad," Cochrane said sympathetically. "You need changes of scene to keep your mind occupied. But now that you're here, Edward, you're among your own. You must make yourself at home."

"That's very kind, sir, but I don't want to impose."

"Impose?" Cochrane exclaimed as a servant brought a tray with gin, tonic water, and limes. "That word isn't to be used between us, Edward. You'll be content here, because I'll take you to the officers' mess to make friends. And if you have financial problems, I can provide whatever funds you need to tide you over."

"That's very good of you, sir, but I'll be able to manage. I have a friend named Edgar Dooley I'd like to get in touch with, so I'll make a trip to Calcutta tomorrow to ask about him at the East India Company offices."

"I'll give you a note to take to Robert Toland, a friend of mine who works there. Robby will be able to find out what you want to know. You can use a horse from the garrison stables."

"I appreciate that very much, sir."

The major waved the thanks aside, then turned and smiled as Mathilda brought their sons out to the veranda. Cochrane's voice rang with pride as he introduced them, and Edward reflected that his uncle had every reason to be proud, because both were handsome and well-mannered. Then the door opened again, and Ramedha stepped out onto the veranda.

Eighteen years old, Ramedha was a strikingly beautiful young woman. The Cochrane family traits predominated in her delicate features, and her mother's bloodline had given her thick, glossy black hair and a dusky tint to her smooth skin. But most attractive were her unusual eyes. Large and expressive, they were a rich, bright gold color.

As Edward bowed over her hand, Ramedha regarded him closely, and her smile was warm.

"Well, it's almost time for dinner," Mathilda said, leading the boys back inside. "Do you want to change for dinner, Ramedha?"

"Yes, I'll be in just as soon as I've freshened Edward's drink," the girl replied. She busily straightened the cushion on his chair, moved the table beside his chair closer, then picked up his glass, smiling as she did so. As an afterthought, she glanced at Cochrane's glass. "How is your drink, Uncle?"

"I wondered if you were going to notice that I'm here," Cochrane remarked, winking broadly at Edward. "I'll have a drop more, m'dear."

Ramedha blushed as she picked up Cochrane's glass. Her golden eyes lingered on Edward before she disappeared inside. He reflected that the last thing he needed was another complication, but it appeared that the very pretty girl was definitely drawn to him.

III

The snowcapped peak of Mount Hood glistened in the sunshine as the steam packet turned from the Columbia River channel toward Portland. Toby stood at the rail with Alexandra and Juanita, ready to disembark. He hoped that the first meeting between Alexandra and his family, particularly with Janessa and his mother, would go well.

Alexandra, vivacious but composed, was looking around in keen interest. Toby exchanged a smile with her. He wondered how anyone could help but love her at first sight. She was stunning in a gold silk dress and wide hat, with brown trim on her dress and brown tulle on her hat.

Juanita moved a fold of the tulle into place. "Are you certain you don't want a parasol, Doña Alexandra? The sun is very bright."

"No, I rarely carry a parasol," Alexandra replied, then smiled. "They're very difficult to manage on horseback."

Juanita, herself looking very pretty, smiled as she plucked at one of Alexandra's sleeves and smoothed a crease from it.

A moment later, the steam packet, its horn droning and bells ringing, edged up to a pier. Outside the pier gate Toby saw his family and friends, and he waved to them, then pointed them out to his fiancée. Crewmen pulled the gangplank into place, then Toby led Alexandra down it, with Juanita following.

Toby immediately detected tension among the group; apparently some kind of bad news awaited him. Also, Timmy's subdued behavior indicated that he had been up to something. He hung back, while the others greeted Toby with their usual heartiness. Then Toby introduced Alexandra.

He saw that Eulalia was favorably impressed by Alexandra's beauty and charm, but his mother's attitude was reserved.

"Toby's letters didn't do you justice," Eulalia commented, "not that I fault him for that, because I know with all your accomplishments, how busy he's been. I had no idea you would be so young. Well, I'm pleased that you're here so we can finally get to know each other."

"Should I have included my age in my letter to you, then?" Alexandra asked.

"No, your letter was just lovely. I was only commenting on how little I know about you. As Toby's mother, I believe my interest in you is understandable."

"It's entirely understandable, Mrs. Blake, and I'll be more than pleased to satisfy it."

Summoning a smile, Eulalia nodded.

Toby continued introducing Alexandra. The general, Stalking Horse, and the other men were delighted with her, as he had expected. Timmy was uncharacteristically shy. As Toby worked his way around to Janessa, he felt misgivings, for she was silent and expressionless.

Alexandra, however, astonished everyone by immediately achieving a rapport with Janessa. The young girl saw the candidness and warmth in Alexandra's eyes and knew that she could trust her. Janessa had been in need of a friend ever since Cindy left.

Janessa's normal reserve faded for a moment. Then, as terse as ever, she asked, "What am I supposed to call you?"

Alexandra pondered the question, her eyes shining with amusement. "Well, let's see," she said slowly. "Would you like to call me Mama?"

Janessa did not usually have a sense of humor, but the suggestion was so absurd that she laughed as she shook her head.

"I don't think so, either," Alexandra said, smiling warmly. "Why don't you just call me by my name?"

"Yes, I'd like that," Janessa said, and smiled. Everyone exchanged bemused glances, and Toby was intensely pleased.

Toby beckoned Juanita, who had remained to one side. After he introduced her, he set about satisfying his suspicion concerning Timmy's behavior. "Well," he asked, glancing around, "how has everything been going?"

Silence fell. Then Lee spoke up. "Toby, there was a mishap at the ranch earlier in the week. Timmy got his steam locomotive started."

"It ran into several things," Eulalia continued. "A barn, a corral, the bunkhouse, and the ranch house."

"But we've fixed up some things," Stalking Horse chimed in. "The barn is back in shape, and the bunkhouse. The house is more of a problem, but we can do some patching up."

Toby frowned and bent down to look his son in the eyes. "I expect better of you, Timmy. I can overlook pranks, but this is something entirely different." He glanced up at Eulalia. "How much damage was done to the house?"

A momentary silence fell again, then Eulalia cleared her throat. "The machine hit the rear of the house, and not much of the kitchen is left. Poor Clara has been using the fireplace to cook."

"Your homecoming with Miss Alexandra is a very happy event for all of us, one that shouldn't be marred with problems," Calvin Rogers added, trying to mollify Toby.

"We'll see if we can keep this from being a problem," Toby said. "Alexandra wants to look at the ranch and her horses, and while we're there, I'll see what can be done about the house."

"Eulalia and I will take you in our carriage," Lee offered. "We also brought a wagon and a detail of soldiers from the fort to take Alexandra's and Juanita's baggage to our quarters."

"I appreciate that, sir," Toby replied. "Juanita can go along in the wagon and sort out the baggage at your house." He turned to the foreman. "Stalking Horse, would you have some of the hands find my baggage and bring it to the ranch?"

The foreman nodded, while Toby assisted Eulalia, Alexandra, and Janessa into the carriage, then stepped into it. Timmy and Lee joined them.

As the carriage moved away, Eulalia gave Timmy a stern

glance for the trouble he had caused, while at the same time
putting an arm around him and pulling him closer to her. She
was still worried about the size of the wedding, and broached
the subject of the arrangements with Toby. He realized she
was concerned that he and Alexandra were contemplating a
quiet, private wedding.

"No, we're planning a big wedding for all our family and
friends," Toby replied.

"That means you'll probably be here for at least a few
weeks this time, Toby," Lee Blake commented in satisfaction.

"I hope so, sir," Toby replied, smiling wryly. "Of course,
I've tried to do that before, but other things came up."

"There are three telegrams waiting for you at the house
now, Dad," Janessa put in. "One from Oklahoma arrived this
morning. The others arrived a few days ago. One is from
Germany, the other from Washington."

Her last remark created a tense silence. Toby and Lee
exchanged an uncomfortable glance as Eulalia frowned. Alexandra, who knew all about Henry Blake, turned to Janessa
and changed the subject. "So you're studying to be a doctor,
Janessa."

"Yes," the girl replied.

"That's fascinating," Alexandra continued, "and it's far
past time for us to have more doctors who are women. A
woman is loath to expose herself to a man, doctor or not. And
when the doctor is a proper old gentlemen, as many are, who
keeps coverings on the legs of the piano in his house, women
with colic may well end up with a cure for typhoid."

A flush spreading up her face from her throat, Eulalia
struggled to conceal her embarrassment, while Toby and Lee
choked back their laughter. Janessa smiled. "You can't have
suffered from many illnesses, Alexandra."

"No, but I've had a fair share of sprains and cracked
bones from bad falls from horses," Alexandra replied. "But
none to speak of recently, thankfully."

"It's good that you're being more careful," Janessa
observed.

"No, it's more a matter of good fortune," Alexandra said,
laughing. "Cross-country riding demands the most from horse
and rider, and tumbles are inevitable. One can jump free to

avoid being pinned under the horse or thumped on the head by a hoof, but luck is still involved."

As the conversation continued, Toby was deeply satisfied with how well Alexandra and Janessa were getting along. Then he noticed that Eulalia was looking at the ring on Alexandra's left hand.

A recent fashion for betrothal rings was a diamond, but Alexandra had chosen a "regard" ring instead, with a ruby, emerald, garnet, amethyst, another ruby, and then a diamond set in a line, the first letters of the stones' names spelling out the name of the ring and the sentiment. It was a conventional ring, and Eulalia was evidently favorably impressed that Alexandra preferred convention over modern fads.

A short time later, Toby was looking at the house. While he had prepared himself for the worst, the damage was even worse than he had imagined.

For a long moment, he was speechless. Then he finally found his tongue. "I can't believe this," he said numbly.

Alexandra was more awed than appalled. "Timmy did this? All by himself? I don't see how one little boy could do this."

As attention began to shift to Timmy, he raced away to his room, and Janessa followed, to get the telegrams for her father. Alexandra turned toward the corrals. "I'm going to look at my horses, Toby."

Lee, an ardent admirer of fine horses, went with her. Toby and Eulalia stepped to the rear of the house, where he peered at what had been the kitchen.

"This is one time Timmy went too far," he said.

Eulalia nodded. "But the fault isn't his alone. That machine was supposed to have been fixed so he couldn't start it by himself. Also, he didn't buy it for himself, Toby."

Toby acknowledged the point. Janessa returned and handed him the telegrams, which he pocketed as he and Eulalia continued to survey the damage. The more he looked, the more bleak he felt. When Alexandra and Lee returned from the corrals, Clara brought lemonade out to the lawn table beside the house, and Toby then took out the telegrams and read them.

On the pretext of showing Alexandra around the barns, he led her aside to talk with her in private about the telegrams. The message from Washington had been sent by James Honnold, President Grant's secretary, and he requested that Toby come to Washington. The second telegram, from Rob Martin, described a state of armed hostility between the ranchers and homesteaders in the Oklahoma Territory and asked if Toby was free to come and do what he could to settle the trouble.

The telegram from Henry Blake concerned his baroness, who had a serious illness. Henry had heard that Dr. Martin, Janessa's mentor, knew of a cure, and he wanted Toby to ask the doctor and Janessa if they would travel to the East Coast to treat Gisela there.

"This places Janessa in a difficult position, Toby," Alexandra said.

"The doctor is in a worse situation. He's very old, and a trip across the country might be too much for him. I'll have to talk to him."

About the other two telegrams, Toby said, "I'll probably be called upon to do something for the government, in which case I won't be able to help Rob Martin. In any event, this will affect our wedding plans."

Alexandra immediately accepted the situation. She always placed duty ahead of personal concerns. "Yes. That's all right. But you'll have to get more information about that meeting in Washington before you can reply to the telegram from Rob Martin."

Toby nodded. "I hope it works out in Rob's favor. It's a great privilege to be able to do something for the government, but Rob and Edward have had more than enough trouble with their ranch. Naturally, my big regret is that this leaves our wedding plans up in the air."

"Well, something must be done about the house in any event," Alexandra rationalized. "That will require at least a few months."

"I'll talk to Janessa and the doctor about going to New York, and then I'll come over to Fort Vancouver for dinner."

"Fine. The general has offered to stable a couple of

horses at the fort for me while I'm staying there. I'll pick out two and ask Jonah to bring them over to the fort."

Toby put his arms around Alexandra and gave her a long kiss. Then they returned to the lawn table. The subject of the telegrams was avoided at the table, because neither Eulalia nor Janessa wanted to hear about Henry Blake. Soon Alexandra left in the carriage with Lee and Eulalia. Janessa saddled her mare to go to the doctor's house, and Toby went with her.

At the Martin home on a quiet residential street of Portland, the doctor's wife, Tonie, met Toby and Janessa at the door. An active, healthy woman of sixty, she greeted Toby warmly and gave Janessa a quick kiss as she led them into the parlor.

A moment later, the doctor came in. He was stooped and frail, and his face was a maze of wrinkles. He greeted Toby and lowered himself into a chair with the slow, cautious movements of the aged. He explained that he had been napping.

"Has working with Janessa become too tiring for you, Doctor Martin?" Toby asked in concern.

"No, no," the doctor replied quickly. "Fatigue isn't the killer for old people, Toby. Boredom is. Janessa has given me another ten years of life." After a few minutes of conversation, Toby mentioned the telegram he had received from Rob, Tonie and the doctor's son, and the one from Washington.

Not wanting to worry them, Toby minimized the tension in Oklahoma. "Happens all the time in cattle country. If it's at all possible, I'll go to see what I can do."

When the conversation moved on to other things, Toby handed the telegram from Henry Blake to the doctor without comment. The old man put on his spectacles and read the telegram, then silently passed it to Janessa.

As usual, the reserved girl remained expressionless.

"Perityphlitic abscess," the doctor remarked gravely, "is always a very serious illness."

"Yes, but Henry apparently believes that you know of a cure for it," Toby said. "Do you?"

The doctor shrugged. "Janessa and I successfully treated

a young fellow who had perityphlitic abscess. In that instance, the site of the abscess was the veriform appendix, but I'm not sure that's always the case. The treatment involves abdominal surgery, and the danger of infection is almost as serious as the illness itself."

"This woman is evidently in such dire condition that any measure that might help her will be justified," Toby commented. "Would you be willing to meet her in New York to see what you can do for her?"

"If you ask us," the doctor replied promptly, "Janessa and I will do what we can, won't we, my dear?"

"Yes, sir," the girl muttered woodenly.

"Do you feel up to the trip?" Toby asked the doctor. "I don't intend for you to jeopardize your health."

The old doctor smiled. "With Janessa's help, I took care of the charity hospital while Anton Wizneuski was on vacation. If I can do that, I can go to New York and back."

"In that case, I'll appreciate it very much if you and Janessa will do what you can," Toby said. "Henry wants a reply sent to Bristol, England. He's taken his wife there, ready to sail for New York. If a ship leaves soon after he gets my reply, he'll be in New York before you, even if you leave right away. Do the arrangements he mentions seem all right, Dr. Martin?"

"Yes," the doctor replied, "and it appears that Hank has a doctor advising him. I like the idea of taking the woman to a country estate on Long Island rather than a hospital in New York. The chances of infection are much greater in a hospital."

Toby stroked his chin. "The estate belongs to a family named Roosevelt. They must be friends of Henry's, because I'm not familiar with the name." He put the telegram into his pocket. "I'll let Henry know your decision, Dr. Martin."

The doctor then brought up another subject. Toby had given permission for Janessa to work at the charity hospital but only in the women's and children's wards. The doctor asked Toby if he would now allow her to work without restrictions.

"I won't put her in any inappropriate situations," the doctor promised, "but I'd like you to leave it to my judgment."

Toby hesitated. His reason for the restriction had been

to prevent an explosion of outrage from his mother. At last he nodded. "All right, I'll leave it entirely to you, Dr. Martin," he said, standing. "Henry is undoubtedly counting the minutes until I answer his telegram, so I'll go send a reply to it, as well as one to Mr. Honnold in Washington."

The doctor and Janessa went to the door with Toby. Although the girl was still smoldering with resentment, she managed a smile for her father as he hugged and kissed her. She whispered a thank-you for lifting the restrictions on her work. As Toby shook hands with the doctor, he thanked him for agreeing to do as Henry had asked.

"Just don't expect too much," the doctor warned. "The prospects are very poor for someone with this type of abscess to travel such a long distance."

On that somber note, Toby left for the telegraph office. It was after sunset by the time he arrived at the docks to take a ferry to Fort Vancouver.

At the general's house Toby found that dinner was to be semiformal in honor of his and Alexandra's arrival. She had changed into a blue silk gown and was in the parlor with Lee and Eulalia.

As Toby talked with his stepfather, he listened with half an ear to the conversation between Eulalia and Alexandra.

"There was a very good article in *Godey's* last month about educational pastimes for children," Eulalia was saying. "Several of the officers' wives said it is very useful. Did you see it?"

Alexandra smiled politely. "I'm not sure what you're referring to, Mrs. Blake. Who is Godey?"

Eulalia was startled, then struggled to keep from frowning. "I was referring to *Godey's Lady's Book*, a magazine devoted to child-raising, household management, and other areas of interest to women."

"I see." Alexandra pondered. "Yes, I believe I've heard about it, but I've never read a copy."

"Well, undoubtedly you're so busy with your horses and other things that you don't have time to read," Eulalia said, her reaction becoming difficult for her to conceal.

"No, I do quite a bit of reading," Alexandra corrected. "I read every issue of *The Horseman's Monthly*, as well as

Horse, Hound, and Horn, and other magazines. I also have a fairly good library of the classics and read a newspaper almost every day."

"Yes, I also read a newspaper almost every day," Eulalia enthused, sounding relieved to find a common ground with Alexandra. "I enjoy keeping up with current events."

"I do as well. Wasn't the assassination attempt against Chancellor Bismarck of Germany dreadful? The Chicago newspapers had several articles about it, and the manager of Toby's lumber mill obtained New York newspapers that contained more information. Fortunately, it appears that all of the conspirators were either killed or arrested."

"Well . . . yes, that was a terrible thing, of course. But my interests lie mostly in matters pertaining to the United States."

"This *was* vitally important to the United States, Mrs. Blake. If the attempt had succeeded, we could very well have found ourselves at war."

"Indeed we could have," Lee agreed, the conversation between the women having drawn his attention. "Bismarck is the keystone of Europe, and our interests are very closely involved."

A lively discussion on the subject began between Lee and Alexandra as Eulalia tried to hide her dissatisfaction over being left out. They talked about all the grisly details, which Toby knew Eulalia would consider a far more appropriate topic for a man.

Soon an even more awkward moment came. An orderly brought in drinks, glasses of vermouth for the women and cognac for Toby and Lee. Alexandra looked at the glass of wine, then smiled politely. "I'd prefer to have bourbon, if I may."

Silence fell in the room. The orderly glanced around in confusion and caught Eulalia's cool nod of assent. "Yes, ma'am," he said, picking up Alexandra's glass and placing it back on his tray. "Uh . . . how do you prefer to take your bourbon, ma'am?"

"Two fingers and neat, please."

The orderly went out, then returned a moment later with the bourbon. The incident amused Toby, and he saw that Lee had a hard time hiding his grin as the petite, beautiful Alexandra took a drink of the straight whiskey without blinking. Eulalia was anything but amused, and Toby decided that it was a good time to tell her and Lee about the telegrams, Henry's first. Eulalia was annoyed because her granddaughter was involved. "Doesn't that man know anyone else? Has he alienated everyone with his depravity? Robert Martin isn't the only doctor in the world!"

"Apparently there aren't too many who can treat that illness," Toby replied. "In any event, we've been asked to help in a matter of life and death, and we can't refuse."

Eulalia fell silent, seething. But her anger faded as Toby talked about the other telegrams; indeed, she seemed relieved that the wedding would be delayed.

When the orderly announced that dinner was served, Toby escorted his mother into the dining room as Lee followed with Alexandra. After they were seated, Eulalia brought up the subject of the house and the steam locomotive.

"Timmy must be punished. Something must be done to teach him to exercise judgment and responsibility."

Toby agreed. "Timmy shouldn't need to be watched every minute." He turned to Alexandra. "What do you think I should do?"

"First you should decide whether you wish to attend to it yourself or want me to. If you intend to discipline Timmy, it will be very time consuming and confusing."

"What do you mean?"

Alexandra's hazel eyes were unwavering as she looked at him. "I mean that while you're gone, I can write and let you know all the details if Timmy misbehaves. Then I can wait for your reply concerning what to do about it. That would be a difficult way to control Timmy's behavior, wouldn't it?"

"Yes, it certainly would," Toby agreed, laughing. "All right, from now on, you're the one who attends to Timmy. You decide what to do about him, his road locomotive, and anything else he gets into."

Eulalia sat up in alarm. "I don't want to cause ill feelings, but Alexandra hardly knows Timmy, and I don't think it's proper for her to have absolute authority over him before she's the boy's stepmother."

"Perhaps not," Alexandra replied amiably before Toby had a chance to speak, "but I'm in an unusual situation. When an army officer is commissioned from the ranks, he's always transferred to another command, isn't he? He wouldn't be able to exert full authority over soldiers who had been his friends. Similarly, unless I begin with a position of authority over the children, I won't be able to exercise it later."

Lee nodded in agreement, which earned him a sharp glance from Eulalia. The subject was dropped, but an atmosphere of discord lingered. It intensified when Toby mentioned to Alexandra that he would leave her with power of attorney over his business affairs. Eulalia obviously thought that unwarranted, but she said nothing about it.

As the meal continued, Toby reflected that his mother, a proud, strong-willed woman, was not one to remain silent. Sure enough, before the meal was over, Alexandra spilled a drop of wine on the sleeve of her dress, then dismissed it with a shrug, saying Juanita would attend to it.

"You're very fortunate to have a personal maid, Alexandra," Eulalia said tartly. "If depending upon her makes you unable to attend to yourself, however, it may be unfortunate for you to employ her."

"I view it as a convenience, Mrs. Blake," Alexandra replied amiably, "and as an obligation. Juanita knows nothing except how to be a lady's maid. Everyone needs to feel needed. I let Juanita think I was in total disarray before she arrived, and I make her feel needed." She laughed. "And I'm sure I am far more tidy than before, because she's an expert maid."

Eulalia, flushing with embarrassment, began apologizing. "Alexandra, I had no right to take that tone or say what I—"

"Please, Mrs. Blake," Alexandra interrupted, placing her hand on Eulalia's. "Your feelings were perfectly understandable, and now that you know how things stand, I'm pleased to see we agree that I'm doing the right thing."

Toby observed that the exchange over the maid had cleared the air to an extent, but numerous points of disagreement remained between his mother and fiancée, and he could only hope that everything would work out between them.

*   *   *

The next morning, having thought the matter over, Eulalia decided she had been too hasty in her conclusions about her future daughter-in-law. While the young woman did indeed have some unconventional ways, they were more than offset by positive traits.

Alexandra was regal in a way, but instead of showing any consciousness of her background, she had a warm, outgoing, and egalitarian personality. And she revealed a keen mind. But having been raised by her father, it was unfair to expect her to be entirely conventional. Actually, Eulalia reflected, when all of the facts about Alexandra's upbringing were considered, she had turned out remarkably well.

Eulalia resolved to make a completely new beginning with the young woman and set about exerting subtle control over her. That was a process she had developed while helping young officers' wives adapt to army life, and it would be a pleasure to work with Alexandra. Eulalia looked forward to long hours of advising her.

The plans Eulalia was contemplating disappeared when Alexandra came downstairs for breakfast, for all the world looking like a nattily dressed youth. She wore a dark coat in the style of a man's suit coat, with a white shirt, a dark cravat, and fitted white riding trousers. The spurs on her glossy black knee boots jingling, she put a derby hat, riding crop, and gloves on the sideboard as she passed it, then stepped to the table.

She greeted Eulalia and Lee cheerfully as she took a seat. "It's a great pleasure to be a guest in such a comfortable and well-ordered home. I slept like a log last night."

Managing a polite response, Eulalia could only recall that she had been trying to get Janessa to stop riding astride her horse, but now that appeared to be an entirely lost cause. It would be enough, she reflected numbly, if Janessa continued wearing dresses.

Lee was also taken aback but did not display his surprise. "I take it that you're going riding this morning, Alexandra," he observed mildly.

"Yes, sir. I'm going over to the ranch."

"I could have one of your horses saddled and brought here to the house for you," Lee offered.

"No, thank you, sir," Alexandra said, laughing. "I asked Jonah to bring over Perseus and Apollo because they've become fat and feisty and need to be ridden down. In view of that, your soldiers would be at risk in trying to saddle one of them."

Lee laughed while Eulalia picked at her breakfast, reflecting that her intentions had evidently been doomed from the start. Alexandra was far too unconventional to change. Her bright, young face was so beautiful, yet there she sat in men's clothes.

Eulalia weighed whether or not to say something to Alexandra about her clothing, but finally decided against it. She was concerned about alienating the young woman.

Alexandra questioned Lee about when he expected summer to change into autumn. As he replied, she sighed regretfully. "Then I won't be able to grow a late crop of corn. Well, I can't change the seasons, so I'll just have to miss a year and put in a good crop next year."

"For your horses?" Lee asked curiously.

"No, sir, to make bourbon. I have a couple of bushels of choice seed from Kentucky, but it'll keep until next year."

"That's a lot of seed. How much bourbon do you make?"

"Ten gallons, plus a quart to top off the kegs because some evaporates through the wood during the first year or two of aging."

Eulalia cringed as Alexandra continued talking on the subject, but again the older woman refrained from commenting.

Alexandra sat back in her chair and touched her lips with her napkin. "Well, that was certainly delicious."

"Indeed it was," Lee agreed. "Shall we walk to the fort? I'll stop at the stables while you saddle your horse. I'm eager for a look at those hunters."

"I'd like that very much, sir," Alexandra replied, stepping to the sideboard and gathering her hat, gloves, and riding crop. "Mrs. Blake, is there anything I can bring from Portland for you?"

Eulalia managed a smile as she shook her head. Lee moved her chair back for her and kissed her. Then Eulalia

followed him and Alexandra out. Juanita materialized in the
entry hall with a clothes brush. She brushed Alexandra's coat
as the young woman put on her derby hat.

"I'll bring a saddle horse and a sidesaddle from the ranch
today, Juanita," Alexandra said, pulling on her gloves. "Then
when I go to the ranch again, you can ride with me."

The maid smiled as she adjusted the folds of Alexandra's
cravat. "Thank you, Doña Alexandra."

"Don't stay in the room and fuss about over my things.
Take one of your books and find a pleasant place in the
garden to read or go for a walk along the river."

"Very well, Doña Alexandra."

After Alexandra and Lee left, Juanita disappeared up the
stairs. As Eulalia went into the parlor, she looked at the
humidor on the table and remembered that Lee needed
tobacco. She returned to the front door and stepped outside
to ask Alexandra to bring some from Portland but saw that
the young woman and Lee were already too far away to draw
their attention without bellowing in an unladylike manner.

To Eulalia, Alexandra's clothing made her look like a boy
who was somewhat thin in the shoulders and full at the hips,
but in reality she was an attractive young woman with her
legs outrageously exposed. Eulalia sighed and went back into
the house.

As she set about doing her chores, Eulalia had difficulty
concentrating. Toby was turning over all his business affairs
to Alexandra, so it stood to reason that Toby would also place
the fate of Eulalia's first home in Oregon in the hands of a
willful and inexperienced nineteen-year-old.

By early afternoon, Eulalia had worried herself into a
nervous state and sent an orderly to get her a carriage. She
had to know what Alexandra was doing at the ranch. The
river crossing and ride through town seemed to take much
longer than usual; then, when the ranch came into view,
Eulalia felt a sense of relief—it looked the same as before.

She was surprised to see that Janessa was at the ranch
rather than at Dr. Martin's house. The girl stood beside
Alexandra and Clara Hemmings, with Clayton Hemmings
standing at a distance from them. They greeted Eulalia, who

learned that Timmy was under the house, looking at a fireplace foundation for Alexandra.

The boy crawled from under the house, dusty and shamefaced. His usual lighthearted attitude was gone. He barely remembered to greet Eulalia, then turned to Alexandra. "It's busted too, ma'am," he said quietly.

"So nearly all the chimney foundations are broken," she said.

The boy nodded, his face crimson as he looked down at the ground. "Yes, ma'am," he whispered, his voice trembling.

Silence fell as Alexandra looked off into the distance, her lips pursed. Eulalia was suddenly struck by the similarity between Alexandra's behavior and how Lee acted toward junior officers who had fallen short of expectations. The young woman had something of the same powerful aura of leadership that Lee possessed.

At first Eulalia had worried that Alexandra might thrash the boy; now it seemed to her that the young woman was humiliating Timmy in a way that was far more cruel than any thrashing. She started to protest, but Alexandra spoke first. "All right, go to your room, Timmy."

The boy gasped in relief and raced away. Alexandra turned to Janessa. "A kind word from his sister would be a great deal of comfort to him right now, don't you think?"

"I expect it would," Janessa agreed, smiling slightly.

"After you've spent a moment with him, you may go to Dr. Martin's house. I'm sure you have things to do."

As the girl left, Eulalia noted that Alexandra was also able to exert control over Janessa. It appeared that the young woman would be able to deal with both children, which was surprising, but the methods she used were still very much open to question.

Clayton Hemmings then informed Alexandra that he had been helping Jonah and wanted to learn to be a groom.

"My mom says it's all right for me to stay here when she leaves," Clayton said, nodding toward Clara. "I aim to quit school, and I'd like to work for you full-time and take care of your horses."

"I'm sure we can agree on some kind of arrangement,

Clayton," Alexandra replied, "but you must continue to go to school."

Clayton, a tall youth of fourteen, shook his head. "No, I've decided to quit, ma'am. I can read, write, and calculate good now—"

"And I've told you that you must continue," Alexandra said, her tone like a whip as she interrupted him. "The fact that you want to stop going to school is evidence that your education is incomplete, because you haven't yet learned the value of education. The matter isn't open to discussion, Clayton."

The youth flushed, then shrugged. "Well, if I have to, Miss Alexandra, I guess I'll keep going to school."

"For the present, you can work with Jonah after school, during vacations, and on weekends, and you'll be paid a good wage," Alexandra assured him. "I'll also begin teaching you to ride, if you have a talent for it."

Touching his forehead, Clayton grinned and thanked Alexandra as he left. The three women went into the parlor, which was in use as the kitchen, with furniture that had been salvaged and repaired.

"I can see that you have Clayton's best interests in mind, and I'm mighty grateful, Miss Alexandra," Clara said.

"It'll be a fair arrangement all around," Alexandra replied. "Jonah isn't a young man, and Clayton will be a help to him. I found some mint beside the creek. Will you all have a mint julep?"

Clara declined politely, saying she would have ice water. Eulalia, unsure of what a mint julep was, could smell the refreshing aroma from a cluster of mint on the kitchen cabinet. Thirsty after her drive on the warm day, she accepted.

After filling a glass with water and chips of ice from the icebox, Clara sat at the table with Eulalia. Alexandra took down two tall glasses from the cabinet.

Eulalia wanted to know what conclusions Alexandra had drawn from the broken chimney foundations, but there was no opening for her to mention the house. The conversation revolved around other things as Alexandra filled the glasses with chipped ice, spooned sugar into them, and crushed mint leaves between her palms.

"I bottled a keg of bourbon from the cellar, Mrs. Blake," Alexandra remarked. "I'll bring along a couple of quarts for the general's liquor cabinet when I return to the house."

Eulalia thanked her absently, wondering in alarm as Alexandra worked over the glasses if bourbon was an ingredient of a mint julep. Just as Eulalia started to turn and look, Alexandra stepped to the table with the glasses and placed one in front of Eulalia.

Alexandra took a deep drink from her glass, but Eulalia knew better than to do the same; the young woman could drink straight whiskey as if it were water. Eulalia took a cautious sip. It was absolutely delicious, freezing cold and with a sweet, lively flavor from the sugar and mint. There was a distinct alcoholic undertone, but Eulalia was sure there could be but little bourbon in it. Although she had never tasted hard liquor, she knew it was harsh and bitter, while the mint julep had a hint of flavor as smooth and mellow as a rich, aged wine.

Sipping the drink, Eulalia waited for an opportunity to mention the house, but Clara had asked when she might be able to proceed with her own wedding arrangements.

"I would certainly appreciate it if you could stay for a day or two after Toby leaves," Alexandra said.

"Why, of course!" Clara exclaimed, surprised. "I thought you might want me to stay until after the wedding."

"No, no," Alexandra said firmly. "I certainly won't disrupt your affairs for my convenience." She drank the last of her mint julep and put the glass down. "And you'll also have a nice bonus as a wedding present."

Eulalia drained her glass. Alexandra seemed the most sweet and obliging young woman in the world, so considerate of others that Eulalia wanted to hug and kiss her.

That surge of emotion was like a warning bell in the back of Eulalia's mind. She realized that the drink had contained a formidable amount of liquor, and its effect swept over her like a tidal wave. She felt numb and detached, and the other women's voices sounded very distant.

Alexandra, apparently impervious to liquor, tilted her glass up and drank a few drops from the bottom, then asked Eulalia if she would like another. Speaking carefully to avoid slurring her words, Eulalia declined and explained that it was time for her to go. She unobtrusively held the edge of the table to steady herself as she stood up.

Feeling as if she were walking on marbles, Eulalia took careful steps to the door. After making her farewells, she moved outside, where the effects of the liquor were even worse. The sunlight was suddenly so bright, she could hardly see, and the world tilted one way, then the other.

Concentrating on each step, she made it to her carriage without stumbling. The driver appeared to notice nothing unusual as he helped her into the carriage. Then she could finally relax in privacy. Each time she closed her eyes, however, the world spun wildly. She tried to fan her face with her handkerchief but kept hitting the end of her nose with her hand.

By the time she reached Portland, the effect of the liquor was beginning to fade, leaving in its wake a headache and nausea. Recalling that Lee needed tobacco, she called to the driver and told him to stop at the tobacconist. When the carriage drew up at the shop, she stepped out and went inside somewhat unsteadily.

After quickly choosing a package of tobacco, she went back out. When she relaxed on the carriage seat again and the vehicle turned toward the docks, Eulalia reflected that she had found out nothing about the house, but she had learned a valuable lesson. In the future, she would be extremely wary of anything Alexandra gave her to drink.

IV

As his coach, flanked by his guards, moved along the streets of Balikesir, Hermann Bluecher looked out the window in satisfaction. Although today the provincial capital was quiet because Bluecher had declared a holiday, the city was generally teeming with activity, particularly in the marketplace. Commerce moved regularly along the roads, and farmers had been able to work in their fields without danger of being attacked by bandits. Merchants were delighted to find that taxes were being assessed on the true value of goods, without the collectors demanding gratuities.

Shops were closed today, and other normal activities in Balikesir had ceased, for everyone had gathered at a field on the outskirts of the city to watch the public execution of the scores of bandits who had been sent in chains from the district capitals. Nearing the field, Bluecher could hear the murmur of the crowd. The murmur swelled to a tremendous ovation as his coach moved out into the field.

The vehicle drew up beside a large tent that had been set up for him and staffed by servants. As he stepped out of the coach, the applause rose to a deafening roar.

The captain of the guards quickly dismounted to assist Bluecher from the coach. "Your people fear you, Pasha, but they also love you," he announced over the uproar. He closed his right fist and struck it across his chest. "As do your guards, who stand ready to protect your life with theirs."

Nodding benignly, Bluecher sat on his cushioned chair and motioned to a maid. The woman opened an earthenware pot, selected a candied date, and popped it into Bluecher's mouth. He had been losing weight since his exile from Germany. The Turkish fare was less rich than that to which he was accustomed. The trimmer body was not a cause for alarm. In fact, in this sultry climate Bluecher felt more comfortable.

Chewing the date, Bluecher looked across the field, where five wooden blocks had been placed in a row. Beside each one stood a muscular guard, naked to the waist and holding his gleaming scimitar. Bluecher motioned to the captain. "Bring out the bandits," he ordered.

The captain shouted toward one side of the field. Another roar rose from the crowd, this time of revilement, as the shackled prisoners were escorted onto the field. The people in the crowd bellowed in rage and shook their fists, and a few men picked up rocks and threw them at the lines of men in their rattling chains.

Bluecher looked at the prisoners. He guessed that the garrisons had met their quotas by fleshing out the number of bandits they had sent with beggars, penniless wanderers, and others who would not be missed. Ridding the province of beggars and other unproductive rabble, Bluecher reflected, was worthwhile in itself. But many of the prisoners were obviously bandits, desperate-looking men who hurled defiant curses at the crowd.

He looked more closely at a man in one of the lines who weaved from side to side, keeping in line by holding onto the man in front of him. Bluecher beckoned the captain and pointed. "Is that man blind?" he asked.

The captain ran onto the field and stopped the prisoners, then examined the man and talked with him. A moment later, the captain ran back to Bluecher and sighed regretfully as he salaamed. "The man is blind, Pasha," he confirmed. "He was sent here by the garrison at Eskafed."

"Execute him quickly!" Bluecher snapped.

As the captain ran onto the field again, Bluecher fumed. Eskafed was the capital of the coastal district where the foreign archaeologists were working, and sending the blind man indicated indifference and a lack of discipline in the garrison. If the soldiers did anything to make the archaeologists complain to Constantinople, serious repercussions for Bluecher himself would result. He would, he decided, visit Eskafed again at the first opportunity and terrify the garrison commander, which would eliminate any potential problems.

Guards dragged the first five prisoners to the wooden blocks, and Bluecher dismissed the troublesome thought as scimitars flashed down and five heads rolled to the ground.

A roar of satisfaction rose from the crowd when the bodies were dragged to a nearby wagon and five more prisoners were unshackled. The crowd shouted again as the scimitars whipped down. As more prisoners were unchained, one twisted out of the grasp of the guards and ran toward Bluecher.

The captain drew his scimitar to cut the man down, and Bluecher flew out of his chair in case the captain missed. But the man fell prostrate in front of the awning, begging to be heard. Bluecher motioned to the captain. "Let him speak."

The man cringed from the scimitar poised over him, then drummed his head against the ground in gratitude to Bluecher. "I am wrongly accused, Pasha," he wailed, weeping. "I am a carpenter and was traveling in search of work when I was seized by soldiers and accused of being a bandit. I have never broken the law in my life, Pasha. I beg you to spare my life."

"I have never," Bluecher remarked conversationally to the captain, "seen a criminal who did not protest his innocence. This bandit has interrupted the proceedings in order to lie to me. For that, let him watch the other executions, then be the last executed."

The captain salaamed, then had guards drag the man as he wept and continued begging. The man's voice was drowned by cheers from the crowd as the executions resumed.

A few minutes later, a woman crept out of the crowd and moved around to the front of the awning. As the captain reached to stop her, she fell to her hands and knees, begging Bluecher to listen to her. He nodded, then motioned the captain away. The woman moved closer and knelt in front of Bluecher as she began speaking.

"My name is Salima, Pasha, and my brother is among

the prisoners. He is innocent of any crime. This I swear, Pasha. If you will allow me to explain? . . ."

Bluecher sighed and wearily agreed.

Salima edged even closer, relating a tale of how her brother had been at their mother's home when the crime was committed. Listening to her absently, Bluecher contemplated her punishment for bothering him. He thought about making her stand beside the wooden block while her brother was executed, then of having her hands bound to the scimitar hilt when it was wielded.

While the executions continued, Salima's eyes darted toward the wooden blocks nervously, and she talked more rapidly. Bluecher looked at her closely; she suddenly reminded him of someone else. A young, strikingly beautiful woman with olive skin, she was similar in many ways to Adela Ronsard, the most skilled courtesan Bluecher had ever enjoyed.

Finished with her plea, Salima kissed Bluecher's slippers and anxiously awaited his decision.

"If I spare your brother's life," he said quietly, "what will you do for me?"

Smiling radiantly, Salima lifted her head. "For as long as you want me, Pasha," she whispered, "I will make your nights eternities of pleasure. And after the first night, you will want me forever, because I will give you greater joy than you have ever known." She glanced back at the wooden blocks again. "But I beg you to act quickly, Pasha, because they are unchaining my brother."

"Stop the executions!" Bluecher ordered.

The captain shouted to the guards, who leaned on their scimitars and rested while the matter was being sorted out. Salima told the captain her brother's name, and he frowned skeptically as he peered at his list. Then he shook his head. "She is lying, Pasha. This man is a bandit, caught red-handed."

"Well, a mistake could have been made," Bluecher suggested evenly, "and it would be shameful to execute an innocent man. Hold him in the city prison while I review the case."

As the captain salaamed and shouted orders to the guards, Bluecher turned back to Salima. "Go to my residence. Tell the house steward that you are to have new robes, perfume, and anything else you need. You will attend me in my bath."

Smiling happily, Salima stood and moved away as she salaamed deeply. Then she disappeared into the crowd. The people muttered in disappointment that one of the prisoners was spared, but the mood quickly passed as the executions resumed.

Bluecher found the last part of the event to be the best. The guards were weary and could hardly hold the prisoners, who were wild with terror. Wrestling matches ensued, with the prisoners struggling up to the last second. It was more of a slaughter than an execution, which pleased Bluecher much more, and he laughed gleefully as he watched.

He waited with anticipation for the last one, the prisoner who had made a nuisance of himself. When the scimitar came down and the carpenter's protests finally ended, Bluecher's coach drew up at the awning. The crowd applauded again as he clambered into the coach. Bluecher reflected that it had been a very enjoyable day.

When he reached his home, he forgot all about Salima. A mail courier had arrived from Constantinople with a letter from one of Bluecher's informants in Germany. The letter concerned Josef Mueller, who had been one of Bluecher's most reliable agents in Germany. He was presently in prison, awaiting execution for his involvement in the same activities that had resulted in Bluecher's flight from his homeland.

Bluecher went into his luxurious study and sat at his desk. The letter had created a churning excitement within him. It stated that it might be possible to arrange Mueller's escape from prison by bribing guards, but it would be expensive. With millions in his Swiss bank accounts, the money meant nothing to Bluecher, but having Mueller back was of vital importance. It would allow him to proceed with his revenge against Henry Blake.

According to his latest information, Gisela von Kirchberg had gone to England. He knew she had an estate in England, where she spent vacations with her American husband. She would return to Germany, and Josef Mueller, a skilled assassin who could be sent to Germany, would kill the baroness.

Her death was the one thing that would make Henry Blake suffer.

Opening a drawer, Bluecher took out a bank draft and filled it out, then wrote a short letter to the informant, telling the man to write if he needed more money to arrange Mueller's escape. Then Bluecher rang a bell.

The steward rushed in. "Prepare a courier to go to Constantinople as quickly as possible," Bluecher ordered. "I have a letter that must go on the first ship leaving for Germany."

Captain Henry Blake stepped out of his cabin on the passenger steamer *Weymouth* and stopped in the passageway. The motion of the ship seemed more pronounced. He turned toward the door at the end of the passageway. At twenty-four, he was a muscular, wide-shouldered man, just over six feet tall. Wearing an immaculately neat uniform, he had tanned, handsome features. A pale scar ran down the left side of his face.

As he went out the door onto the side deck, Henry saw that the ship was headed toward a storm. Black clouds filled the horizon, and veils of rain trailed down to the whitecaps on the vast, tossing surface of the Atlantic. Gusts of damp wind swept along the deck as Henry frowned in concern, then went back into the passageway.

Several cabins were occupied by the retinue accompanying Baroness Gisela von Kirchberg. A stir of activity and murmur of voices came from clerks and accountants who were busy behind the doors. The affairs of her financial empire were uninterrupted even by a voyage to save her life.

One of her employees was leaving the baroness's cabin, and the man held the door open for Henry. When Gisela saw him stepping into the cabin, it appeared that she quickly tucked something under the business papers on the desk beside her chair. He dismissed it and smiled at her.

She was as beautiful as always, Henry thought, the only sign of her illness being a slight pallor. Her gleaming black hair accented the deep blue of her large eyes. Although her classically beautiful face had strong lines that revealed her ruthlessness as a businesswoman, her eyes were soft with her unqualified devotion as she smiled, her charisma reaching out to him like a physical touch.

Henry kissed her, then sat near her. Their conversations were always in her native language because he spoke perfect German, with the Prussian accent he had picked up from her, while her only other language was French. "How are you feeling now?" he asked.

Gisela shrugged. "The pain comes and goes, Heinrich. The ship seems to be tossing about more."

"Yes, we're heading straight into a fairly strong storm, so the captain will probably decrease the speed for the comfort of the passengers. If I see him during lunch, I'll ask if this will delay us."

"We will be there when we arrive, Heinrich," Gisela commented philosophically. "In any event, you said that the doctor probably won't arrive until two or three days after we do."

"Yes, but there are many variables. The important point is that you'll be much better off when we get to New York. Traveling takes a toll on your strength and can make your condition worse."

Gisela changed the subject, not wishing to belabor the point. Henry was worried about her attitude. While she seemed cheerful enough, he suspected that that was merely for his benefit and she actually considered this journey futile.

He was presently on leave, with orders to report to Fort Abercrombie in the Dakota Territory, after attending to his personal affairs. Gisela had expressed regret over their indefinite separation but not the dismay that would be her normal reaction. Henry wondered if that was because she had resigned herself to death. She had insisted on bringing a large, ornate coffin with the baggage.

Henry broached his concern. "I know it's difficult, but you must maintain an optimistic attitude. If you give up, all is lost."

"Have you ever known me to give up on anything?" she countered, smiling. "No, I am simply waiting to see what happens, Heinrich. It would be foolish not to allow for all possibilities, and you know yourself that Dr. MacAlister considers my prospects to be poor."

Henry smiled. The doctor, the household physician at Grevenhof, Gisela's palatial estate, was a dour, blunt Scot. "And *you* know that Dr. MacAlister is overcautious. There's no question that your condition is serious, but hope and the will to live are vital factors for anyone who is ill, and the doctor would be the first to agree with that."

Gisela sighed, weary of the subject. "I will never abandon hope," she said, pointing to the papers on the desk. "On the contrary, plans for future business ventures occupy me constantly when I am without the pleasure of your companionship."

Reflecting that she would be thinking about her business affairs with her last breath, Henry dropped the subject. He missed their baby, Peter, who had been left at Grevenhof in the care of his nurse. He mentioned the child, but Gisela, anything but a typical, loving mother, replied that she enjoyed being away from his crying. While he loved the beautiful, fascinating woman, Henry recognized her character faults, one being a strong dislike for children. He had omitted telling her that Janessa always accompanied Dr. Martin and assisted him, because he knew it would be an irritant to Gisela.

A subdued gong sounded in the passageway, the signal that lunch was being served. The doctor permitted Gisela to have only light, bland foods, which her maid brought to her cabin. Henry kissed her, then left to go to lunch. The ship was rolling and pitching even more than before.

The only officer Henry saw during lunch was the purser, who said that he was sure the vessel had slowed and told Henry that the captain was on the bridge. After lunch, Henry went up to the bridge to talk with the man.

He found the watch officer studying a chart and the helmsman gripping the large, polished wheel. Captain Wilcox, a heavyset, bearded man, was standing at the wide, rain-streaked windshield and gazing down at the bow as it plowed through the foaming waves. He turned as Henry entered. "How is the baroness today, Captain Blake?"

"About the same as before. Will the storm delay our arrival in New York?"

"No, no," the captain assured Henry. "The way the

waves are running, this storm doesn't have great depth, so we should be back to normal speed by this time tomorrow. Unless we run into several storms like this one, we'll make our schedule with time to spare. I hope that this heavy sea isn't causing the baroness any distress."

"No, she isn't at all inclined to seasickness. It appears that many passengers are, though, because the dining hall was almost empty at lunch."

The captain nodded, then brought up Henry's forthcoming assignment to Fort Abercrombie. The captain asked if there were Indian problems in the territory. "No serious problems," Henry replied. "Gold has been found in the Black Hills, on Indian lands, and the prospectors have created some unrest, but no Indians are on the warpath yet."

"Then the army just happened to need an officer at that fort, and your name came up to be assigned there?"

"There was more to it than that. A railroad company sold land to a large number of immigrants who came there as a group from the Crimea. They're German-speaking people, mostly Mennonites, who shun violence. The gold strikes brought in riffraff, as they always do, and they're making life miserable for the Mennonites. Part of the reason I'm being sent there is because I speak German and can help the Mennonites."

"I speak a bit of German myself," the captain commented, "but I've heard you talking with the baroness's employees, and it's like a native language for you."

Henry explained that he had been stationed in Germany for several years. He talked with Wilcox for a few more minutes, then went back down the companionways to the passenger-cabin deck.

Dr. Ian MacAlister was coming out of Gisela's cabin as Henry stepped toward it. A short, portly man with thick, gray sidewhiskers and an irascible disposition, he nodded when Henry asked if he had been examining Gisela. "She doesn't seem to be any worse than yesterday," he said, "but no better either, of course."

"If she can just hold her own until we get to New York, then she'll at least have the chance of a cure."

"I don't think it's much of a chance," the doctor said soberly. "But we'll know more when we talk with Dr. Martin."

Henry stepped into the cabin as the doctor walked away. This time he saw without a doubt that Gisela was hiding something under the papers on the desk. But she moved too hastily and knocked some papers on the floor. She froze.

Henry crossed the cabin and recognized what Gisela had been trying to hide: a framed daguerreotype of Cindy, one she had sent to him years before, when he had been stationed in France. As he gathered the papers from the floor and replaced them, Gisela looked uncharacteristically embarrassed.

"I took it out of your room at Grevenhof, Heinrich," she explained. "If you are angry, I apologize."

He smiled and kissed her. "No, I'm not angry, Gisela. I am surprised, though. Why did you take it?"

"I simply like to look at it," Gisela replied. "I often think about her, and I have a very fond regard for her. Do you consider that strange?"

"Somewhat, I suppose. I didn't realize that you thought about her at all."

"Ever since you and I met, I have frequently thought about her, always with goodwill. She is very beautiful."

"You are very beautiful."

"Do you still love her, Heinrich?"

"I love *you,* Gisela."

"I know, Heinrich, but I believe one's first love in life is too deep ever to fade completely. If I die, I would like for you to try to make amends with her."

"You're not going to die," Henry said firmly. "You're going to have medical treatment to cure your illness, then live for many years."

"No one can see into the future, loved one. I would be more at peace if I knew that you would—"

"Gisela, I don't want to discuss this," he interrupted brusquely. "Dwelling on morbid thoughts is harmful. Now let's talk about other things."

Gisela hesitated. "No, hear me out, Heinrich," she said. "You are life itself to me, and your happiness is my only concern. If I must leave you, please tell me that you will at least see her. Tell me that, and I will never mention this again."

Henry hesitated, then nodded. "Very well. I will, Gisela."

There was a knock on the door then, and the doctor came in, with Gisela's personal maid following him. "Into bed, Madam Baroness," the doctor ordered. "I'd like you to start resting for a few hours each afternoon."

"Sitting here in this chair," Gisela replied irately, "does not make me weary. I will rest tonight, and until then I will attend to my business affairs."

"Gisela, please do as the doctor asks," Henry said. "I'll come back and talk with you later."

Frowning resentfully, Gisela sighed but agreed. When the doctor left, the maid started to turn back the covers on the bed. Henry bent over Gisela and kissed her again. "That's my darling," he said. "I'll see you later."

As he stepped along the passageway, Henry heard the wind and rain outside. He stopped in his cabin for his raincoat before going out on the deck.

The storm raged around the ship. While the wind tugged at his raincoat and the drops of moisture pelted his face, Henry looked moodily out at the tossing waves.

With her characteristically keen insight, he reflected, Gisela had been right about his feelings for Cindy. That special, precious fascination of a first love still glowed deep within him, where it would never die. He often thought of her, and he wondered if, during quiet moments at the end of her busy days in Paris, she ever thought of him.

A long time had passed since Toby had been near the Portland Charity Hospital, and he was struck by how dilapidated it looked. Built with an emphasis on economy, it was now decades old, and makeshift repairs during those years had done little to improve either the appearance or the condition of the huge, barnlike wooden building.

Despite its condition, Toby noted it was kept clean. The entrance lobby floor sagged, but it was spotless. Toby crossed to an office and looked in. Janessa and Dr. Martin were thumbing through papers at the desk.

After the exchange of greetings, the doctor explained

that they were preparing notes on patients for Dr. Wizenuski, who was the director of the hospital. "When that's done, Janessa and I will be ready to leave tomorrow. Have you received any word from Washington?"

"No," Toby replied, "but I'm not surprised. A telegram can get across the country faster than it can move between adjacent desks in Washington. Several freighters are heading south within the next few days, and as soon as I find out what I need to know, I'll leave on one of them."

"Those freighters are faster than the packet," the doctor commented. "You'll probably be in Washington before we're in New York. Did you just drop by for a visit, Toby? You're not feeling bad, are you?"

"No, I'm fine, thank you. You know, it's a great privilege to serve my country, but I pay a high price, because I would like nothing better than to spend every day of my life with my children on the ranch. I don't want to interrupt anything important here, but I'd sure like to spend the rest of the day with my daughter."

Janessa flushed with pleasure.

"Of course, Toby," Dr. Martin said. "I can finish this. You go on with your dad, Janessa. Is your horse outside?"

"Yes, sir," Janessa replied, putting the papers aside and getting up from the desk. "I'll see you at the packet tomorrow, Dr. Martin."

Knowing it would please the girl, Toby asked her to show him around and explain what she did in the hospital. Janessa reacted with the satisfaction he expected and led him to the examination room.

They discussed other subjects as well. At thirteen, Janessa was like an adult in most respects, but the few exceptions could cause problems. He mentioned his close relationship with Henry Blake.

"I know that you and I don't have the same opinion of him," Toby said. "I wouldn't want that to cause any ill feelings between us, Janessa."

Janessa shook her head quickly. "It doesn't for me, Dad. I've known people who detested each other, while I've got along with both of them. That sort of thing happens. Here, I'll show you what we believe is wrong with that woman."

She took a medical text from the shelf and thumbed through it. She opened it at an illustration showing the internal organs of the body. "Well, this is a man," she said, "but the veriform appendix is the same." She pointed. "It's this little organ right here. It somehow becomes putrescent, then bursts and causes massive abdominal inflammation, killing the patient."

After Toby looked at the illustration, Janessa replaced the book, then talked about the danger of infection, explaining that it could sometimes be prevented by using phenol, a method pioneered by a man named Lister. To demonstrate she then led Toby upstairs to the children's ward.

She stopped beside a cot where a boy lay, his right leg covered with a bandage that reeked of the acrid, penetrating fumes of phenol. Explaining that a wagon had run over his leg, causing a compound fracture, Janessa removed the bandage.

The boy's thin leg was in splints, and it was obviously healing. In any similar instance that Toby had ever heard about, the leg had been amputated. Remembering when he had been in a hospital during the Civil War, with infection claiming more lives than the wounds themselves, it seemed a miracle to Toby.

After replacing the bandage, Janessa continued the tour. He became more and more interested in what she did. Other memories of when he had been hospitalized returned to him.

That was where he had met Janessa's mother, a beautiful Indian woman named Mary White Owl. Toby realized that he had spoken very little about his relationship with Mary, so as they passed through the corridors, he assured Janessa about how deeply he had cared for her mother. The girl's blue eyes sparkled as she listened.

When they left the hospital, Toby glanced back at it from horseback. "I didn't realize the building was in such poor condition. Something needs to be done about it."

Janessa agreed. "But like Dr. Martin says, everyone favors having a new charity hospital until the first hint about a tax levy to pay for it."

"That's how people are. When I get back, I'll talk to Mayor Edwards and ask him what he intends to do about it.

You and Dr. Martin are doing wonderful work there, Janessa. I'm very proud of you." One of her infrequent, wide smiles wreathed her pretty face.

"While I'm gone, there's something I'd like you to try for me. You know that your grandmother will be displeased by my decision to lift all restrictions pertaining to your work. But you're growing into a responsible young adult now, and I think you can handle adult situations."

"Thank you, sir. What do you want me to do?"

"For me—and your grandmother—I'd like you to give up your cigarettes. It was a peculiarity we accepted, not wanting to create too many problems while you settled in here and adjusted to your mother's death. But now that that period is long since over and you're turning into a fine young woman, it is, in my opinion, unseemly for you to smoke cigarettes."

Janessa frowned but said, "I guess I'll try, sir, for you and Grandmama."

"Thank you, Janessa." Satisfied, he tried to lighten the mood. "From things you've said, it appears that in addition to medical procedures, Dr. Martin is teaching you the wider issues of how to get along in life as a doctor."

Janessa nodded. "Yes, for example, he's told me that I mustn't ever accept a Christmas turkey as a present from an undertaker, because patients may lose confidence in me if they find out."

Toby laughed heartily. He and Janessa rode through the town and along the road toward the ranch, Toby keenly enjoying every moment of it. While the girl was never outgoing, he prided himself on the fact that she talked with him more freely than with anyone else.

After they reached the ranch and unsaddled their horses, Toby started toward the lawn beside the house with Janessa. But she pointed to the pastures, suggesting they go there, and he did as she wanted. He slung his arm around her shoulders as they walked across the rolling, grassy hills that lay back from the house and barns. They found a spot that provided a nice view of the countryside and sat, enjoying the sun. After a few minutes he asked what she thought of Alexandra.

Janessa smiled. "As far as I'm concerned, she's perfect."

"As far as *you're* concerned?" Toby repeated.

"Well, what *I* consider important isn't the same as what others do," Janessa explained. "I believe Grandmama would like it better if Alexandra were older and had a child or two of her own." She laughed. "And didn't wear trousers."

Toby laughed, too. "And how about Timmy?"

"What he would like wouldn't be what he needs," Janessa replied. "I think he's going to get what he needs." She paused. "Tell me more about my mother."

Toby smiled as he began reminiscing. "The first time I ever saw her was when I was taken into the hospital, because she helped put me on the cot. But what I'd call our actual meeting, when she really noticed me, was about a week later."

"What happened?" Janessa asked, smiling expectantly.

"A man on another cot used foul language in front of her. I tried to get up from my cot to deal with him, but I couldn't, and I was so mad that I was almost foaming at the mouth. Mary was touched by my concern for her." He shook his head. "There was still a lot of boy in me then, but I'd feel the same thing now. Mary was far too sweet and gentle for anyone to act offensively around her."

"What did you two talk about?"

"The war, mostly. She told me about where she had grown up, and I told her about Portland. We also talked about other things, but mostly it was about the war. It was all around us, people getting killed and our country about to be torn apart, so it was all we thought about."

Janessa took out a cigarette, then remembering her father's request, slid it back into her pocket. She was rewarded with a wink. "Do you regret what happened between you and my mother?" she asked quietly.

"Well, leaving your mother pregnant was by far the worst thing I've ever done," he replied. "Neither of us knew it, but that isn't an excuse. Also, what your mother and I did is something that only married couples should do." He put an arm around the girl. "But if you're asking if I regret what brought you into my life, I don't at all. What I regret are all the years we missed being together. I wish Mary had written to me about you. You know how much I love you."

Janessa moved closer to him. "I often come here. This is my favorite place on the ranch."

He suddenly realized where she had brought him. When he had met her for the first time, she had been withdrawn into a shell of hostility. This hill was where they had first sat and talked, where he had won her confidence.

She smiled in response to his smile, then sighed contentedly as she looked away.

In addition to enjoying her companionship, Toby had wanted to make certain that the bonds between them had not been weakened by his absences from home. He was gratified by the fact that they were still firmly intact.

When the steam packet left the next day, Toby was at the pier with Alexandra, Tonie Martin, Timmy, and several men from the ranch. They waved at Janessa and Dr. Martin, who stood at the rail, waving in return.

As the packet turned into the main channel, Alexandra said, "I'll take Mrs. Martin home, then return to the fort. Your mother is taking me to a meeting of officers' wives this afternoon."

Toby, thinking of the nice time he'd had with Janessa, said, "I thought I'd take Timmy fishing in the mountains—an overnight trip."

"That's a good idea," Alexandra said. "Don't you worry about me. Go and enjoy yourselves."

Toby called to Timmy, who was climbing into the wagon with Calvin. "How would you like to go fishing, Timmy? We'd come back tomorrow."

The boy's eyes became wide, a radiant smile spreading over his face. "Yes, sir! I'd like that, Dad!"

"But can you catch us some trout for supper?" Toby asked, chuckling. "I don't want to go up there and spend a hungry night."

"I'll catch all the trout you can eat!" Timmy shouted happily. "And I'll cook them for you!"

Toby laughed, enjoying his son's excitement. "All right, we need to get started if you're going to catch any trout

before dark. White Elk, please help him round up fishing and
camping gear, back at the ranch. I'm going to the telegraph
office."

As the Indian youth helped Timmy up behind his saddle,
Toby beckoned Stalking Horse closer. "Tell Clara to put us up a
bag of provisions," he said quietly. "Bacon and potatoes will
make a more substantial supper than Timmy's good intentions."

The foreman laughed and nodded in agreement as the
group rode away in a clatter of hoofbeats. Toby went in the
other direction.

At the telegraph office, Toby checked to see if a reply
had been received to his telegram to Washington, asking if
the President's reason for summoning him would prevent his
going to Oklahoma Territory.

The clerk in the telegraph office shook his head apologet-
ically to Toby's inquiry.

Back at the ranch Toby found Timmy ready to go, with
fresh horses saddled and the camping and fishing equipment
on a packhorse. Stalking Horse quietly pointed out a canvas
bag of food among the other things. Toby changed into old
clothes, then he and Timmy set out.

While Timmy was keenly intelligent and had a preco-
cious mechanical ability, he was still very much a child. He
was talkative and completely candid, his reactions displayed
openly on his bright, adorable face. In the boy's attitude
toward him, Toby detected a strong measure of the hero
worship he had always felt for his own father. Timmy listened
with rapt interest as Toby described New Mexico and talked
about some of the events that recently had taken place there.

The last of the scattered farms left behind, the road
turned into a trail leading into the mountains. Timmy talked
about Rufus Gooch, an inventor in Portland, and pointed out
small animals that fled as the horses approached.

When Toby asked him what he thought of Alexandra,
Timmy was silent for a moment, then shook his head. "Well,
I'm not supposed to say anything bad about people, so I'd
better not say anything."

"I asked you your opinion, Timmy," Toby told the boy.
"You can say what you think."

"All right, then," the boy said, shrugging. "She's friendly when she wants to be, but she's been really mean about what happened to the house."

Toby was speechless for a moment. "What do you expect, Timmy? You practically tore down the house she was expecting to live in. I don't like what you did either, and neither does your grandmother or anyone else."

"But you said what you thought," Timmy protested, "and so did Grandmama and everyone else. All Miss Alexandra has done is look at me about it. I thought Janessa could look mean, but her mean look is a grin compared to Miss Alexandra's."

"Well, that's just her way, Timmy," Toby said, concealing a smile. "I think when you get accustomed to her, you'll get along all right."

The boy agreed somewhat doubtfully, but Toby was satisfied. Timmy, accustomed to immediate and very vocal disapproval whenever he misbehaved, was finding Alexandra's silence a far more effective punishment.

Never one to dwell on unpleasantness, Timmy was soon cheerful. An hour later, Toby led the way to a creek in a valley where he had often camped and fished in his youth.

After camp was set up and the horses hobbled to graze, Toby and Timmy started fishing. By Toby's standards the fishing was poor, but it was perfect for Timmy. Trout too small to eat were biting furiously, keeping the boy whooping excitedly as he hauled them in and released them.

Toby was interested in finding out if Timmy had any problems he wanted to discuss. None came up, as Toby had expected, because the boy was surrounded by adults who gave him attention. In particular, Calvin Rogers was Timmy's constant companion.

"There are some things Calvin doesn't know much about," the boy said. "He thinks that storks bring babies from somewhere. But women hatch babies in their stomach, don't they?"

The sudden change in subject took Toby aback for a moment. "Yes, that's pretty close, Timmy," he said carefully. "I guess you talked to Stalking Horse or one of the men who knew more about it, did you?"

"None of the men know anything about it, Dad," the boy

said seriously. "So when I found out, I tried to explain it to them, but they kept talking about other things."

Toby smiled. "How did you find out, then, Timmy?"

"Mrs. Hemmings just turned red and hid her face," the boy replied, "so I asked Janessa. She told me about it and showed me a picture in a book of a baby all hatched out in a woman's stomach."

"What did you think about the picture, Timmy?"

"Well, I wondered how they got the top back on her stomach after they finished drawing the picture. How do you think they did it, Dad?"

Concealing his amusement, Toby gave an answer that satisfied the boy, then began concentrating on catching some large trout for dinner.

Dusk settled while Toby cooked dinner. The aroma of food cooking was even more appetizing as it blended with the wood smoke in the clear, fresh mountain air.

Later, when they were lying in their blankets beside the fire, Timmy asked Toby about the men he encountered during his travels, who were armed and dangerous. Toby explained that he always tried to settle every situation peacefully if possible. "Never look for trouble, and always give people the benefit of the doubt. If you'll follow those two rules, you'll be able to avoid a lot of problems with people."

Timmy repeated the words slowly. Then he nodded. "All right, I'll remember that, Dad." The boy dropped off to sleep a few minutes later, then Toby went to sleep.

The next morning was perfect. When they began fishing, Timmy hooked a trout that weighed upward of four pounds. Toby was as delighted as Timmy, since he knew that the outing was one that the boy would remember fondly in years to come.

Midafternoon they returned home. Timmy displayed his large trout to an admiring audience, while Toby rode to town, to the telegraph office. The clerk smiled as he handed him a telegram.

It was from James Honnold, President Grant's secretary, stating that Toby would be completely free to go on about his affairs after the meeting with the President. Toby estimated the travel time involved, then sent a telegram to Rob Martin, with the approximate date of his arrival in Oklahoma.

Although it was still summertime, school was in session to make up the weeks lost during planting season. So the following day, Timmy returned to school, where he had occasion to use the advice his father had given him about dealing with people. Alexandra had given him a note that explained his absence the previous day, and when he reached the schoolhouse, he went to exchange the note with the principal's secretary for a pass that would admit him to his classroom.

Two ragged, disheveled older boys were standing in the hall outside the office. Timmy knew they were brothers, Jake and Jim Fogarty, eleven and twelve years old, and the worst troublemakers in the school. Their father, Jeremiah, was a roustabout at the fairground, and everyone in town avoided him. Timmy stood in the doorway and waited for the secretary to look up. Jake suddenly shoved Timmy, who staggered sideways and banged against the doorjamb.

"Hey, you!" he barked angrily.

The secretary looked up. "You keep your voice down, young man!" she snapped sternly. "What do you want?"

The brothers snickered as Timmy, fuming with resentment, stepped into the office. His lips were sealed by the inviolable code that prohibited tattling. He silently handed the note to the secretary.

"You were absent to go fishing with your father?" she exclaimed in disapproval, then immediately changed her mind. "Well, you don't see your father very often, do you? Very well, wait outside, and I'll prepare a pass."

As he stepped back out into the hall, the two boys sneered. "He went fishing with his father," Jake said caustically. "They're so rich they probably hired men to carry them fishing."

"Probably," Jim agreed derisively. "And if they caught anything, they had to hire somebody to do that for them, too."

"We don't hire anybody to do anything!" Timmy retorted hotly. "And I caught a four-pound trout all by myself."

The two brothers laughed in scornful disbelief. "Liar,"

Jake said. "All the fish you've ever caught wouldn't weigh four pounds."

"You're the liar, Jake!" Timmy shot back. "I caught a four-pound trout, and—"

Jake seized Timmy's shirt and pulled him close. "No, you're the liar!" he snarled. "You wait until after school. I've been wanting to beat you up for a long time!"

"Yeah, me too," Jim growled. "You wait until after school, and we'll give it to you good."

Fear raced through Timmy. "I'm not looking for trouble, and I'm giving you the benefit of the doubt."

The two rules for dealing with people were lost on the brothers. As the secretary crossed toward the door, Jake released Timmy and pushed him away. "You just wait until after school," he repeated ominously.

The secretary handed Timmy a pass, and he went to his classroom, unable to think of anything for the rest of the day, except the threat that hung over him. Although the odds were against him, Timmy would not ask for help. While he might be beaten up, he preferred that many times over to being a coward.

When the school day ended, Timmy joined the stream of students flowing out the door. He did not see the Fogarty brothers. Reflecting that the principal might have sent the brothers home, Timmy sighed in relief. Calvin had told him to wait by the general store after school for his ride home, so Timmy set out along the sidewalk.

Less than a block from the schoolhouse, the two brothers, grinning in cruel glee, stepped from behind a tree straight in front of Timmy. "I'm going to beat you up good," Jake threatened.

"This is going to be a trouncing that you'll remember for a long time," Jim growled.

As the boys moved closer, Timmy fought the urge to flee. "Now wait a minute," he said, desperately trying his father's rules for dealing with people one more time. "I'm not looking for trouble, and I'm giving you the benefit of the doubt."

"Is that right?" Jake snarled. "Well, this is what I'm giving you!"

His fist shot out so suddenly that Timmy barely turned aside. It connected solidly with his right cheekbone, and he reeled sideways, then sprawled facedown in a flower bed.

Laughing gleefully, the boys pounced on Timmy, one raining blows on the smaller boy's back and sides as the other one savagely kicked him.

The attack suddenly stopped when a woman ran down the path. "Get out of my flower bed! Stop tearing up my flowers!"

Timmy lifted his head. The woman was swiping at the brothers with a broom, and while they were backing away, Jake tried to snatch the broom from the woman.

"I'll take that broom away from you and break it over your head, you old cow!"

"What did you say?" the woman stormed in outrage. "I know who you are!"

"What are you going to do about it?" Jake taunted. "Send your husband to make our dad do something about it?"

"Yeah, do that," Jim challenged her. "But you'd better follow him in a wagon to haul him back in, because he'll be in little pieces by the time our dad is finished with him."

The woman fell silent. Timmy, seeing the fear on her face, knew she would say nothing to her husband. The two brothers moved away, jeering at the woman, and Jake pointed a finger at Timmy. "We'll get you Monday in the schoolyard, where everybody can watch."

As the two boys left, the woman took Timmy's arm and helped him to his feet. "Did they hurt you?"

Fighting back tears of humiliation, Timmy shook his head. "No, ma'am. I'm sorry about your flowers."

"Oh, don't worry about those flowers," the woman said, solicitously dusting him off. She looked at where Jake had hit him. "You're going to have a black eye. A nice boy like you shouldn't have anything to do with trash like those Fogartys. You just stay completely away from them."

V

On Monday morning, Timmy's heart sank as he woke. It was the day when he would again have to face Jake and Jim Fogarty. He got out of bed and looked around, depressed by the utter confusion into which his life had been thrown. Clara Hemmings had left the day before, and she always had put out clean socks, underwear, and a shirt for him every night, then had gathered up the things he had taken off. Now Alexandra was in her place. The clothes he had worn the day before were still scattered around the floor, just where he had thrown them, and he had nothing clean to wear.

After dressing in the dirty clothes, Timmy washed and combed his hair. He avoided looking in the mirror, the bruise under his right eye a reminder of what faced him that day. When Calvin had asked about it, Timmy managed to avoid the question without lying. Leaving the bathroom, he went through the house toward the parlor, which was still being used as the kitchen.

Alexandra was talking with Calvin at the door. She was in riding trousers, white shirt, and stocking feet, while Juanita, sitting beside the fireplace, shined her mistress's boots, which already looked like shiny, black glass.

"Stalking Horse and White Elk are going to town this morning in the dray, aren't they?" Alexandra asked Calvin.

"Yes, ma'am," Calvin replied. "They're going for a load of posts and timbers to build the jumping course for your horses."

"Ask them to see me before they leave, please. There's something I need from town."

"Sure thing," Calvin said, then limped out on his cane. Alexandra sat down, and Juanita helped her put on her boots. Timmy took his place at the table and glanced around the room. Clara had always managed to make it look neat. Now it looked like the total confusion that his life had become: Dirty pots, pans, and dishes were stacked everywhere. The floor needed sweeping, the ashes needed to be cleaned out of the fireplace, and newspapers were scattered about. Coffee was perking on the fireplace hob, but there was no sign that breakfast was going to be prepared.

Clara had bustled about in her orderly, energetic way, attending to everyone and everything; Alexandra seemed concerned only with her appearance. She stood with her hands on her hips as the maid tied her cravat. Juanita untied and tied it again three times, getting the folds just right, while Alexandra patiently waited.

A way of deferring his torment for a day suddenly occurred to Timmy. "I don't feel too good today, ma'am. Maybe I'd better stay home from school."

"Where do you hurt, Timmy?" Alexandra asked.

"I sort of feel bad all over," he replied vaguely.

Alexandra smiled. "Yes, I do myself sometimes. When I do, I take a small dose of the tonic that I give my horses when they're off their feed. It tastes bad, but it perks me up. Would you like a spoonful?"

Neatly outwitted by the offer, Timmy shook his head. "No, ma'am. I guess I'll be all right." Another thought occurred. "But I can't go to school without breakfast."

"That's true," Alexandra agreed. "Do we have anything for breakfast, Juanita?"

"There are eggs, Doña Alexandra," the woman replied. "I will wash a pan and fry them."

"No, don't bother washing a pan. Boil them."

"The pots are dirty as well, Doña Alexandra."

"Then put the eggs in the coffeepot."

Watching the bizarre breakfast preparation, yet another thought occurred to Timmy. "I need something for lunch," he told Alexandra.

"Go to Mr. Biddle's general store at lunchtime," Alexandra suggested. "Ask him to give you a piece of cheese, some crackers, and a bottle of grape juice, and put it on the ranch account." She paused. "Why don't you want to go to school today? Does it have something to do with that bruise under your eye?"

Timmy felt his face turning red as he tried to look away, but as always with her, he was unable to avert his eyes. Finally he blurted out: "Jim and Jake Fogarty! They beat me up on Friday and said they'd do it again today!"

"Well, that sort of thing happens now and then," Alexandra commented philosophically. "Don't be overly concerned about it. Are those boys in your class?"

"No, ma'am," Timmy replied, upset with her complacent attitude. "They're eleven and twelve years old, and they're the meanest boys in school. Almost everyone is afraid of them."

"I see. Do you know anything about their family?"

"Yes, ma'am. Their father is Jeremiah Fogarty. He works at the fairground. Just about everybody is scared of him, too."

She nodded briskly. "Well, I'll take care of it, Timmy."

"What are you going to do?"

"That isn't important. The important thing is that you worried about this all weekend, and you should have told me about it Friday. If you had, I could have set your mind at rest then."

Timmy was skeptical. Alexandra thought she could merely tell the Fogartys to do something and they would obey. The troublesome family was far more likely to do the opposite, Timmy knew.

As he was trying to convince himself that Alexandra could indeed stop the boys from beating him up, he heard the wagon. He ran to the window. "There go Calvin and Clayton," he said in dismay. "They're supposed to take me to school."

"You can go with Stalking Horse and White Elk," Alexandra replied. "They're taking the dray to town. I asked Calvin to take care of something for me."

Timmy watched as the wagon turned onto the road to

town. He had intended to stay close to Clayton, a big boy never bothered by bullies, until he got inside the school-house. That protection now gone, Timmy returned to the table, hoping that the Fogarty boys would get to school late, as they often did.

As Juanita poured cups of coffee and fished the eggs out of the coffeepot with a spoon, Timmy thought wistfully of Clara. "Mrs. Hemmings always made biscuits and fried ham or bacon with eggs for breakfast," he said to Alexandra. "Will you do that sometimes?"

Alexandra smiled. "No, I can't cook, Timmy."

The reply stunned the boy. He had believed that girls were born knowing how to cook. "Who did the cooking at your house in Kentucky, ma'am?"

"A cook until we got on hard times," Alexandra replied, cracking an egg on the table. "Then Jonah did it. And my father cooked sometimes. Eat some eggs, but be careful—they're hot." He thought about the absence of clean clothes in his room that morning. "Have you ever done any washing and ironing?"

"Yes, but Juanita does it for me now."

"Will she do mine, too?" Timmy asked hopefully.

"No, doing mine and her own is a lot of work, and she also has many other things to do."

The answer threw him into even more confusion. He would apparently have to wash and iron his own clothes. If other boys found out, he would be subjected to unbearable ridicule.

There was a knock at the door, and Stalking Horse stepped in. Taking off his hat, he said, "Good morning, Miss Alexandra. Calvin said that you want me to fetch something from town for you."

"Yes, thank you, Stalking Horse," she replied. "Sit down and have a cup of coffee."

His brown, wrinkled face creased in a warm smile as the tall, spare Indian tweaked Timmy's ear affectionately. Alexandra told Stalking Horse what she needed.

Timmy listened to the conversation in surprise. Alexandra wanted Stalking Horse to stop at the hardware and get a cooking stove, which seemed absurd. "Get the best and largest they have," Alexandra requested.

"Yes, ma'am. Do you want a wood or a coal stove?"

"What is the difference between them?" Alexandra asked.

"The price, for one thing," Stalking Horse replied. "A coal stove costs more, because it's made of better metal. Coal burns at a higher temperature than wood."

"Well, get a coal stove. Even if we only use wood in it, it should last for a long time."

Alexandra then began asking him about the fairground. Timmy thought she was leading up to Jeremiah Fogarty, but for some reason she was interested in the fairground itself.

"It is rarely used except for the small county fair," Stalking Horse said. "Frank Copeland, the manager, does his best, but he doesn't have a lot of money to work with."

"Well," Alexandra commented, "the solution is to spend the money for a more lavish fair, which will draw a sufficiently large crowd to make a profit. Mr. Copeland could also set up off-season entertainment to produce profits."

Stalking Horse shook his head. "Never happen. The bank holds a mortgage on the fairground and finances the fairs. The bank manager, Hector Peabody, won't put out money at risk. For the most part, Frank keeps his permanent crew busy cutting firewood and selling it for a few dollars."

Alexandra and the foreman talked about other things for a few minutes, then he stood and patted Timmy's shoulder. "When you finish breakfast, get your books and come on out, Timmy. White Elk and I will be outside."

As depressed as ever, Timmy went to his room for his books.

When he stepped back into the parlor, Alexandra was reading a newspaper. She looked up from it and smiled at him. "Good-bye, Timmy," she said cheerfully.

"Good-bye, Miss Alexandra," he responded, glancing around. The table was now littered with eggshells. Oblivious to the disarray around her, Alexandra was sipping coffee while Juanita brushed her mistress's riding coat and hat. His life in an upheaval and a dire ordeal awaiting him, Timmy went out to face the day.

*　　*　　*

The sense of doom lasted only a short time longer. White Elk asked about Timmy's black eye.

"They did what?" the Indian exploded. "Those worthless Fogarty boys are twice your size!" He was fuming. "Don't worry, I'll take care of this."

Stalking Horse smiled at White Elk's outburst. "Don't get so mad you take on the whole family, White Elk," he advised. "You should carry a lunch with you if you intend to whip Jeremiah Fogarty, because it might take you a while."

"Jeremiah Fogarty could whip me," White Elk admitted. "But I don't expect any trouble out of him. He isn't stupid. He knows that if he starts trouble with the Holt ranch, he's asking to be tarred, feathered, and hauled out of town on a rail."

"That's true," Stalking Horse agreed, his smile fading as he lifted a finger in warning. "But you're not to hurt those boys. Cuff them around some and warn them, then let it go at that. Do you understand?"

"I understand, Grandfather," the Indian youth replied grimly. "I'll get out with Timmy at the schoolhouse, then I'll catch up with you at the hardware store."

The relief that Timmy felt was overwhelming. Unfortunately, however, his sense of well-being caused him to be talkative. "Miss Alexandra told me she would take care of it, but she didn't say what she was going to do."

Stalking Horse glanced at White Elk soberly, then shook his head. "Then it's Holt business," he said. "I'm sorry, Timmy, but that leaves White Elk and me out of it."

"What?" White Elk exclaimed in dismay. "Grandfather, she's not a Holt yet, and she's hardly more than a girl. She can't face up to either those boys or Fogarty."

"That's enough, White Elk!" Stalking Horse snapped sternly.

"I meant no disrespect to Miss Alexandra," the Indian youth said softly.

Silence fell, and Timmy was almost in tears.

Then White Elk spoke. "I never have given Timmy any pointers on fighting, and there wouldn't be anything wrong with it if I did. That wouldn't necessarily have anything to do with the Fogarty boys, would it?"

"No, it wouldn't," Stalking Horse agreed. "In fact, if you haven't given him any pointers on fighting, you certainly should." The foreman tugged on the reins. As the wagon stopped, White Elk jumped down. He looked around on the road, picked up something, and held it concealed in his hand as he climbed up to the seat. Stalking Horse smiled in understanding as he snapped the reins and the wagon moved along the road again.

"Timmy, hit your left hand with your right fist as hard as you can," White Elk said.

Mystified, the boy held up his left hand and smacked his right fist into it with all his strength. Nodding in satisfaction, White Elk took Timmy's right hand and placed in it a stone about the size of a finger, then closed the boy's hand around it.

"Now hit your left hand again," White Elk said.

Timmy smacked his fist into his palm again. "That really hurt!" he exclaimed, wincing.

White Elk laughed. "When you hold something hard in your fist, it turns that fist into a club."

"Now show him where to hit," Stalking Horse suggested.

White Elk placed a finger on Timmy's stomach just below where his ribs met. "You hit somebody right there in the gizzard, he'll know he's been hit. Hit when you're leaning forward, even if you have to take some punches to do it. Then put your whole body behind your fist, from your toes up."

As the wagon went through the outskirts of town, White Elk demonstrated how to break free of a clench and other useful techniques. It all seemed simple enough, and Timmy's self-confidence began to grow.

It disappeared entirely, however, when the wagon stopped at the school. His books under his left arm and the stone in his right fist, Timmy climbed down, trying to conceal his returning apprehension. White Elk and Stalking Horse spoke a final word of encouragement, but their voices were unconvincing, and they looked worried. Timmy trudged fearfully toward the school as the wagon moved away.

Jake Fogarty was in the schoolyard, and neither Clayton nor any other large boy who might be of help was in sight. A number of boys had gathered around Jake, who apparently had announced that there was going to be a fight.

Jim Fogarty was not there, which did little to ease Timmy's feelings, because he was so far outmatched by either one of them. The quaking fear that swelled within him made him want to turn and run, but while he might be beaten up again, he was determined not to be a coward.

Placing himself in Timmy's path, the larger boy laughed derisively. "Watch this now," he boasted to the other boys. "Watch me make him holler uncle, just like he did last Friday."

"I did not," Timmy retorted. "You're a liar, Jake! I didn't make a sound last Friday."

Jake frowned darkly. "You will now," he barked, rushing at Timmy. "I'll beat you up until you do!"

Dropping his books, Timmy charged forward. As White Elk had instructed him, he ran with an upright stance until the last instant, then ducked. The larger boy was swinging at Timmy's face, and his fist passed over Timmy's head. Timmy leaned forward, and clenching the stone in his hand so hard that it hurt, he swung his fist, putting all his weight behind it.

The effect of the blow surprised everyone, including Timmy. Jake was impelled backward and landed on the ground. His face turned red as he clutched his stomach and made hoarse, gasping sounds.

Timmy and the other boys looked in amazement at the boy on the ground. "Well, you sure hit him, Timmy," a boy commented.

"You sure did!" another boy said more enthusiastically. "You've got him right where you need him. Give him a good trouncing, Timmy."

After the beating on Friday and his torment of anxiety over the weekend, Timmy was tempted to follow the suggestion, but attacking someone who was helpless was as cowardly as running. There was also the very practical fact that Jim Fogarty could show up at any instant.

Acting as nonchalant as he could, Timmy picked up his books. As he walked toward the schoolhouse, the boys gazed at him in reactions ranging from astonishment to awe. It was only when he was a few yards away that he realized that he had actually bested Jake Fogarty. No one, he reflected, including his father, could have done it better.

His triumph was short-lived. Jim Fogarty's voice rang out as he reached the schoolhouse steps: "We'll get you for this! You just wait until recess!"

Timmy looked back. Jake had caught his breath, and his brother was helping him to his feet. Despondent, Timmy went into the schoolhouse. He had made things worse, he thought, because now the brothers would be seeking revenge. He was still clenching the stone tightly in his right hand, which was damp with sweat, and he slid it into his pocket as he walked along the crowded hall toward his classroom.

After filing through the door of the classroom with others, Timmy went to his desk. The room buzzed with whispers because word had quickly spread about what Timmy had done.

The boy on Timmy's left leaned toward him and whispered, "Did you see the picture of old hound's tooth? I wonder who did that?"

Timmy shook his head, then saw that the boy was referring to a comical chalk caricature of Elmer Hunstead, the principal, on the wall.

The whispers faded as the teacher came in. Irene MacDougall ruled her classroom with an easy but absolute authority. She greeted the class, and the students replied in unison.

The school day began, but the routine was interrupted when one of the older students stepped in and whispered something to the teacher.

Miss MacDougall nodded, then glanced around the room. "The principal is visiting the classrooms. Sit up straight. Center your books on your desks. Tom Stiles, button your collar. Alice Markham, tie your ribbon."

There was a stir, then the lesson resumed, but the atmosphere was tense. A few minutes later, the principal stepped in. "Stand," the teacher said quietly.

The boys and girls scrambled to their feet with a burst of noise that was followed by absolute silence in the presence of the august authority. Elmer Hunstead exchanged a nod with the teacher, then folded his hands behind him and gazed somberly over the classroom. "During the weekend," he intoned, "some miscreant trespassed upon school property and defaced a wall. As I am unable to identify the culprit, the innocent must suffer with the guilty. Today there will be no morning recess."

The room remained silent as the principal exchanged another nod with the teacher and went out. Then when the teacher told the boys and girls to sit down, there were murmurs of disappointment. Timmy, inwardly glowing with satisfaction, struggled to appear as disgruntled as the others.

But the reprieve seemed very brief. Timmy knew that the Fogarty boys would surely pounce upon him at lunchtime.

When lunchtime came, Timmy suddenly realized that he was saved by having been told to go to the general store for his lunch.

The other boys and girls trooped out into the schoolyard in a clatter of lunch pails and a babble of voices, while Timmy went out the door and darted quickly around the other side of the schoolhouse. A moment later, he was on the tree-lined street leading toward the center of town.

Timmy had a joyful sense of salvation as he skipped along.

At the general store, the proprietor gathered up the cheese, crackers, and bottle of grape juice that Alexandra had told Timmy to get for his lunch. Munching the cheese and crackers, he left the store and went behind it to the alley, where rats, opposums, and other interesting animals could occasionally be seen in the garbage. He ate and walked along the alley, kicking stones. He crossed a street and walked along an alley behind houses, where he finished his lunch.

When the schoolhouse came into view, the bell was ringing, and the students were filing back inside. The Fogartys were nowhere in sight as Timmy ran and caught up with the last of those going in. He hurried to his desk and stood behind it.

The boy at Timmy's left leaned toward him. "Jake and

Jim said they were going to beat you up during lunch today,"
he whispered. "They said you hid somewhere."

"They're lying," Timmy replied. "The woman taking care
of me can't cook, and I had to go to the general store for
something to eat."

"They said they're going to get you really good during
afternoon recess. What are you going to do?"

Timmy shrugged. "I'll have to beat them up before they
beat me up." Then he noticed more whispering than usual.
"Is something going on?"

"Tom Stiles snuck a snake in the drawer where the
teacher keeps her books!" the boy whispered.

Timmy gasped as he glanced at Tom, who was gazing
nonchalantly into the distance and basking in the admiration
of the other boys. Timmy eagerly awaited the pandemonium.
Irene MacDougall came in, and the whispers faded as she
went to her desk. She looked around the class, glanced down,
examining her chair, then sat. "Seats," she said quietly.

Everyone sat, and the teacher studied the class as silence settled. Moving her chair closer to her desk, she opened
the drawer where her books were kept. "For the geography
lesson today, you were to memorize. . . ." Her voice faded as
she put her hand into the drawer. Then she stood up, holding
the snake with a thumb and forefinger behind its head. "The
names of the states and their capitals," she continued imper-
turbably, stepping toward the window with the snake.

A girl in the front row squealed. Another shrieked. "Don't
be silly!" Miss MacDougall snapped, turning on the girls.
"It's only a garden snake!" Having crushed the uproar before
it began, she went to the window and dropped the snake
outside.

Turning back, she dusted her hands together. "Some
would say that I should wash my hands quickly because
touching a garden snake causes ringworm," she said, glancing
around. "But that's only a superstition," she finished, pointing at the boy who was peering at his hands. "Tom Stiles, you
will memorize the names of the presidents tonight and recite
them tomorrow as punishment for disturbing the class and
tormenting one of God's creatures. That poor snake was
undoubtedly terrified."

His face crimson, Tom looked miserable. Timmy felt even worse, having been lifted to the heights by the hope that afternoon recess would be canceled, then plunged back into despair. When the bell rang for recess, icy apprehension gripped him. He put his books inside his desk, then sat up straight, waiting for the teacher to speak. But instead of dismissing the class, she picked up a sheet of paper from her desk.

"For the arithmetic lesson," she said, "I need to have a set of multiplication problems written on the chalkboard. I have other things to do during recess, so I'll have to ask someone to stay in and write them." She glanced around. "Would you do that for me, Timmy Holt?" With an extreme effort, Timmy concealed his joy and nodded woodenly. "Yes, Miss MacDougall," he replied glumly.

The teacher dismissed the rest of the class, and as they filed out, Timmy pulled a chair to the chalkboard and began writing the problems on the board.

After a few minutes, Miss MacDougall said, "Timmy, is something bothering you?"

"No, ma'am," he replied.

"I understand your father's fiancée is looking after you," she remarked casually. "Does she thrash you, Timmy?"

"No, ma'am," he replied.

"I notice that you have a bruise on your face. Have any of the larger boys—" Changing her mind, she rephrased the question. "Have you been involved in any sort of trouble with other boys that you'd like to tell me about?"

Timmy knew the teacher had reworded the question so he could avoid lying. But no matter what, he would not whine to a teacher. He shook his head. "No, ma'am."

"Very well, Timmy." The teacher turned back to her papers, and Timmy drew another set of numbers on the chalkboard. Just as he finished and was checking the numbers to make certain they were all correct, recess finished and the class filed back in.

In many ways, that final wait of the day was the worst for Timmy. He wished Janessa were in Portland instead of going to New York, so she could attend to his wounds.

The bell signaling the end of the school day sounded like

a death knell to Timmy. He was going to his doom. As he
went out, he saw boys gathering near the edge of the schoolyard, and those near Timmy raced to see what was happening. Timmy continued trudging forward at the same leaden
pace because he knew what was happening: The Fogarty
brothers were gathering a crowd to watch while they beat
him up. He took the stone out of his pocket and clenched it
in his right fist, determined to get in at least one good punch.

As he approached the crowd, Timmy saw the two boys,
all right, but instead of waiting for him, they were trembling
as their father berated them. A heavyset, unshaven man in
grimy clothes, Jeremiah Fogarty was a terrifying sight. Timmy
craned his neck to look over boys in front of him.

"Do you think I send you here to make trouble for me?"
Fogarty barked, cuffing both boys on the head. "I send you
here to get book-learning, not to make trouble!"

"We didn't mean to make no trouble for you, Pa," Jake
wailed tearfully.

"Well, you did!" Fogarty roared, slapping the boys again.
"And what's more, that Holt boy ain't half the size of either of
you! Am I raising a couple of cowards?"

"We didn't really beat him up, Pa," Jim sniveled, dodging the blows. "We just pushed him around a little."

"Don't you lie to me!" Fogarty thundered, slapping the
boys harder.

Watching the completely unexpected development,
Timmy wondered what had caused this miracle. Then he
thought of Alexandra. It now appeared entirely possible that
she had done just what she had said she was going to do.

Timmy left the crowd and went toward where Calvin
Rogers was waiting in the wagon. The man smiled as Timmy
settled himself on the seat. On the ride home the boy related
what had happened, then asked Calvin if he thought Alexandra had been responsible.

"Yes, she took care of it. I heard some talk about her
seeing Fogarty today."

"But he's about the meanest man in town."

"It's easy to underestimate Miss Alexandra," Calvin said,
smiling, "but she has a way of finding the key to a situation,
then quietly turning it."

Timmy nodded. "Where's Clayton?"

"He went to pick up some saddle soap sent up from San Francisco," Calvin replied. "It's a special kind that Miss Alexandra likes for her tack. He'll be home later."

"She sure has people running for a lot of things," Timmy commented. "What did she want you to get this morning?"

Calvin shrugged. "Oh, just some things," he said vaguely.

With the major crisis in his life now resolved, Timmy's mind moved on to other things. Foremost among those was his most precious possession, his road locomotive. It needed an entirely new steering assembly, and the steam lines were broken. It had been towed to the barn and dumped there. Timmy had been afraid to mention it to his father, fearing that would only be a reminder to dispose of it. He brought up the subject to Calvin. The man replied that what happened to the road locomotive was up to Alexandra. Timmy glumly dropped the subject.

Calvin stopped the wagon in front of the house, and Timmy hopped out. As he went inside, he heard a man and woman talking in the makeshift kitchen. The man was Jonah Venable, and Timmy listened closely, identifying the woman's voice. She was Amy Givens, who lived on a farm near the ranch. She and her sister, Abby, were dull and plain, and Timmy had overheard quiet comments that their father, Horace, had resigned himself to having two unmarried daughters.

Timmy went in, then stopped and looked around in surprise. The room was fully as spick-and-span as Clara had kept it, and Amy was hovering over pans at the fireplace while Jonah stirred a bowl on the table.

"Hello, Timmy," Amy said ebulliently. "I'm the cook now, and Mr. Venable is learning me how to do Kentucky fried chicken."

"I will if you'll keep your mind on what you're doing," Jonah grumbled. "This batter is about ready, and I want that frying grease to be good and hot. But don't let it burn, because that'll make the chicken taste bitter."

The boy grinned as he went out. Fried chicken was one of his favorite meals. The problem of having cooked meals had been resolved, and as he passed the wreckage of the kitchen, he saw that Abby Givens was working at washtubs behind the house, washing all the clothes.

As radiantly happy as her sister, the young woman greeted Timmy. "I'm the housemaid here now. Me and Amy have real wages. Our ma and pa are really proud of us."

"Well, I'm glad you're here," Timmy remarked earnestly.

"You couldn't be as glad as we are to be here," Abby chortled, scrubbing a shirt on the washboard. "Miss Alexandra is somebody real important! The manager of the fairground and the mayor was here today to see her!"

"I know she's somebody really important," Timmy affirmed stoutly. "My dad wouldn't marry anybody who wasn't."

"That's true, Timmy," Abby agreed. "She's at the lawn table, talking to some foreign fellow. You'd better let her know that you're home."

"I will," Timmy said, ducking to go under the clotheslines. As usual, Alexandra was in her immaculately neat riding clothes. The small, dark-haired man with her was poring over notes on sheets of paper as they talked.

After greeting Timmy warmly, Alexandra introduced him to the man, whose name was Fossi. Speaking with an Italian accent, the man acknowledged the introduction and commented on the physical resemblance between Timmy and his father.

"All Holts look alike," Alexandra said. "Timmy, your dad and I met Mr. Fossi on the steam packet. He's a construction engineer, and he's going to repair the house."

"Will you be able to fix it, sir?" Timmy asked worriedly.

"Yes, indeed," the man replied, laughing. "I've repaired houses that were damaged in earthquakes, so I will be able to repair it." He turned back to Alexandra. "I can have the kitchen ready for your stove within the week."

"Excellent," Alexandra said, standing. "While you're taking the measurements, I'll go show Timmy something, then I'll rejoin you."

The man took out a tape measure as Alexandra walked toward the barns with Timmy. The boy asked her about her talk with Fogarty, but she only repeated her admonishment from breakfast.

"That isn't important, Timmy. The only important thing

is that you worried about it all weekend. When something is bothering you, you should tell me about it."

"I—" Timmy started to speak, then suddenly froze, looking toward the barn. Stalking Horse and White Elk had opened the doors of the barn where the steam locomotive was kept and were grinning at Timmy as Calvin drove the machine out of the barn, smoke belching from its stack and its engine chugging loudly under a full head of steam.

It looked better than ever. It had been painted, and the front wheel turned smoothly as Calvin pushed on the steering lever. "You sent Calvin to get parts to fix it, didn't you?" Timmy asked in astonishment and delight.

"That's right," Alexandra replied. She pointed to the pasture behind the barns, where a large area had been marked off with pegs. "You're to drive it only inside those pegs, Timmy. You're not to start it up by yourself, and Calvin must be with you when you drive."

"Yes, ma'am!" the boy agreed, eagerly hurrying away to catch up with the machine.

"Timmy, come back here."

Her soft, steely voice stopped him in his tracks. He turned. "Timmy," she said quietly, "it's only natural for you to see how far you can push things with me. I expect that, but don't do it with anything that's important to you. If you disobey me concerning that road locomotive, I'll have it barged out onto the river and dropped overboard. There'll be no excuses, explanations, or discussion. Do you understand?"

As her eyes bored into his, it occurred to Timmy that the same level glare might have been the reason Fogarty had been at the schoolyard to chastise his sons. He swallowed. "Yes, ma'am."

"Very well," she said, turning back toward the house. "Go ahead and drive your road locomotive."

He started to run toward it, then hesitated. That morning, everything around him had seemed a shambles. Now everything had been reversed, all the problems eliminated, and there were reasons for happiness everywhere he looked. And in one way or another, all of it could be traced to the young woman walking away from him. "I'm really glad that you're here and looking after me, ma'am," he called after her.

Alexandra turned. "I'm glad that I'm here, too, Timmy. And you and Janessa are a large part of the reason I'm so glad."

They exchanged a smile, then Timmy ran to catch up with the road locomotive as Alexandra walked toward the house.

VI

Sitting in an anteroom outside the cabinet room in the White House, Toby noted that the carpet, draperies, and other furnishings were in good taste but far short of lavish. The same could be found in any moderately wealthy household, but the atmosphere throughout this building was one that could be found in no other structure in the nation. He had a sense of being at the center of events, where decisions were made that influenced daily lives at the distant reaches of the nation.

The building was quiet, but he knew there was constant activity, as staffs assembled the data that was discussed in the cabinet room. Aides passed through the anteroom and into the cabinet room, then out again.

One aide now stood beside the door. "Mr. Holt, would you go in now, please?"

Toby was wearing a new, dark-wool suit with black velvet lapels and a black muslin tie around the starched collar of a new shirt. He straightened his coat as he stood and stepped toward the cabinet room.

Inside, cigar smoke eddied up from a long table where the secretaries and undersecretaries of the governmental departments sat, with the President at the head of the table. Toby had met him several times, most recently in Connecticut, where Toby had thwarted an assassination attempt. A charismatic man with a military air, President Ulysses Grant was wearing his usual immaculately neat, dark suit, and his beard was trimmed short.

The President stood and came to meet Toby. "Mr. Holt, it's a great pleasure to see you again."

"It's a pleasure as well as a privilege to see you again, Mr. President," Toby said, shaking hands.

The President took Toby's arm and led him toward the table. "Everyone here either knows you or has heard about you at length, but let me introduce you, and then we'll get down to business, Mr. Holt."

Grant led Toby around the table, and the men stood to shake hands as they were introduced. Through the various tasks he had performed for the government over the years, Toby did have a passing acquaintance with several of the men.

The last official was a big-boned, clean-shaven man named Vincent Caldwell, secretary of the interior. While they had never met, Toby had gone to the New Mexico Territory several months before to deal with the comancheros at Caldwell's urgent request, for his department was responsible for the administration of organized territories. The man thanked Toby for what he had done.

"I had plenty of help," Toby modestly said. "The local authorities did far more than merely cooperate, and an army lieutenant named Walter Stafford put his life at risk many times while we were working together."

The aide who had escorted Toby into the room moved a chair for him to the table at the right side of the President, then placed a folder of papers in front of the President and left. Toby sat as Grant, puffing on a cigar, settled himself comfortably, then opened the folder. The others at the table sat back, waiting as the President glanced over the papers.

He began relating problems encountered in coordinating actions in the West. While the Department of the Interior was responsible for organized territories, the War Department, Bureau of Indian Affairs, and other agencies were also involved. The territorial governors were directly responsible to the President, adding to jurisdictional conflicts, and the mixture of states and territories in the West, with their different systems of administration, complicated the situation further.

"In the West we have this tangle of all three branches of

government with responsibilities overlapping in some instances
and other areas in which no one is clearly responsible," Grant
explained. "Also, while we have telegraph communications, it
is so far from Washington that we often lose touch. Do you
see a solution, Mr. Holt?"

"Yes, sir," Toby replied promptly. "A central point of
authority for matters relating to the West, located west of the
Mississippi."

"Precisely," the President agreed, glancing around the table
in satisfaction. "It doesn't take Mr. Holt long to find the
keystone of a situation, does it?"

The men murmured in agreement.

"The specific type of authority that we agreed upon is a
regional commissioner of the West," Grant said. "Is that what
you have in mind, Mr. Holt?"

Toby pondered for a moment, then nodded. "Yes, sir. A
commissioner with designated areas of authority, as well as a
coordinating and advisory role, could pull all loose ends together. The office of a commissioner would supplement rather
than replace any existing agency with responsibilities in the
West, so it should work well. It should also be economical,
because a commissioner wouldn't need a large staff."

"Economy above all," the President commented dryly.
"We think along the same lines, Mr. Holt, and I must say
that I'm very pleased by that. I trust you won't disagree with
me when I say that you're the best men for the job. I'd like
you to be the initial appointee to the office of regional commissioner to the West."

Toby was completely taken aback by the offer of the new
position, one of the highest appointed offices in the land. He
collected himself quickly. "I'm honored by your confidence in
me, Mr. President, and it will be a great privilege to serve in
that office. I accept, of course."

"Good, good," the President said in satisfaction, thumbing through the papers in the folder. "I have your commission here, Mr. Holt, along with a charter for the position,
which outlines your authority and responsibilities. You'll see
that in some areas your authority will take precedence over
that of territorial governors, but at the same time, I believe

we've worked it out so the commission won't be unduly burdensome."

"I'll be more than happy to do whatever is needed, because my nation comes before everything else with me."

"I know that, Mr. Holt," the President said. "I'll appoint a deputy who can keep you informed and see to routine matters. The name of your stepfather, Major General Leland Blake at Fort Vancouver, has been mentioned. Would you concur in his appointment as your deputy?"

Toby grinned. "In addition to being on the best of terms with my stepfather, I have every confidence in him. I'm also sure he'll be glad to accept."

"Good, we'll make that appointment, then," President Grant said, nodding to the secretary of war. "General Blake has a full administrative staff, of course, to see to routine matters. Please keep the general notified of your whereabouts so he can pass information along to you by telegram."

"That will work out well for me, sir, because there's some trouble in the Oklahoma Territory that I'd like to look into."

"Yes, by all means do," the President said. "Feel free to contact me through my secretary at any time. For routine matters, I suggest you work with the secretary of the interior." He handed the folder to Toby, then looked at his watch as he stood. "Those papers will explain everything in detail, Mr. Holt, and for now I suggest that we all adjourn for lunch. I'm very grateful that you've accepted this position."

"It's a pleasure and an honor, sir," Toby replied, standing with the others. "I'll do my best to deserve your confidence."

"Yes, I'm sure of that." President Grant smiled. "For the record, I had intended to give you lunch whether or not you accepted the position."

The meeting ended in laughter. Toby tucked the folder under his arm as he and the President went to the door. Conscious of the heavy responsibility he had accepted, he was also deeply gratified that he had been singled out for that honor.

*   *   *

As she helped the aged Dr. Martin down the steps from the train at the huge, teeming station in New York, Janessa saw Henry Blake up the platform, looking around. Seeing the doctor and Janessa, he walked toward them, followed by a portly older man.

When she had first met Henry years before, the girl had been at a total loss over what Cindy had seen in him. Now thirteen years old and more adult, she understood. Tall and muscular in his neat, tailored uniform, he was singularly handsome with a powerful aura of authority. Even so, Janessa thought that his eyes looked cold and secretive, and she detested him.

He shook hands with the old doctor, thanking him for making the long journey, then turned to Janessa as he greeted her. Receiving only a silent glare in reply, he bowed and then introduced his companion, Dr. Ian MacAlister.

"We have a carriage waiting outside, Dr. Martin," Henry said. "We'll all get your baggage, then go to the country home where—"

"No, Mr. Blake," Janessa cut in crisply, taking out the baggage stubs. "*You* get the baggage, and I'll take the doctor to the carriage. He needs to rest as much as possible after such a long, hard trip."

"Yes, of course," Henry agreed quickly, gravely apologetic as he took the baggage stubs. "You're absolutely right, Janessa. That was extremely inconsiderate of me. Dr. Mac-Alister, if you'll show Dr. Martin and Janessa to the carriage, I'll find some porters and fetch the baggage."

Janessa guided the doctor through the milling crush of people, then emerged onto a wide street no less congested.

When they were seated in the carriage, Janessa took out the flask she carried for the doctor and filled one of the small silver cups nested on top. She looked at him with concern. His faded blue eyes were rheumy, his wrinkled face pale, his hands trembling. He took a sip, then glanced at Janessa and nodded toward the other man. She filled a cup for him.

"Och, now!" MacAlister exclaimed after he downed the drink. "That nectar is so smooth, it could wean me from scotch."

"It's bourbon aged thirty years in wood, sir," Janessa

replied, noting with satisfaction that a tinge of color had returned to Dr. Martin's face.

As the doctors began discussing the baroness's condition, Henry led the porters over and had the baggage put on top of the carriage.

The vehicle rumbled away. When the outskirts of the city finally fell behind and the carriage was moving along a wide road beside Long Island Sound, Henry said, "The phenol and other items you listed in your telegram are ready at hand, Dr. Martin. Will you perform the surgery today?"

"I'll decide that when I see the patient," the doctor replied. "If it appears too dangerous to delay, we'll do it today."

Henry continued talking with the doctor, and Janessa listened. She had hated the tall man ever since he broke his engagement with her beloved aunt, but now she was intensely gratified that he had. He talked about the baroness in a way that seemed very impersonal, Janessa thought, with less feeling than most people would have expressed for a favorite dog that was ill. He was perfectly courteous but without warmth. All in all, he appeared to be the most cold-hearted man Janessa had ever met.

At long last they turned onto a tree-lined drive, which led back to a large mansion set in acres of well-kept grounds. The carriage drew up at the house and was met by a swarm of servants. Dr. MacAlister led Janessa and the old doctor upstairs, while Henry remained behind.

The baroness was in a huge, lavishly furnished bedroom, the French windows open to let in the breeze. Janessa reluctantly had to admit that she had never before seen such perfect beauty—but it was the beauty of a statue, as cold and lifeless as stone. She was the most arrogant-looking person Janessa had ever met, with a haughty uplift to her chin. When she and MacAlister conversed briefly in German, Janessa knew her presence in the room was being questioned.

The baroness stared at Janessa in annoyance. The girl glared back, refusing to be intimidated. After a moment, the woman gave Janessa a slight, enigmatic smile.

Dr. Martin examined the patient as the girl took her temperature. The woman's face revealed nothing, but Janessa saw her fingers clench a fold of the sheet. She had to be in extreme discomfort, Janessa knew, although she showed little sign of it. "Four degrees of fever, sir," Janessa said, replacing the thermometer in the bag.

"We'd better do it now," he said. "We're extremely fortunate that the acute stage has held off this long."

"A surgery is set up down the hall, Dr. Martin," MacAlister replied.

MacAlister spoke to the baroness in German. She nodded indifferently, then reached for a sheaf of papers and pince-nez on the nightstand. Henry was at the staircase, and when MacAlister told him what had been decided, he nodded in the same way. Janessa reflected that they were a good match, the most cold-blooded pair she had ever seen.

A few minutes later, everything was prepared: instruments soaking in diluted phenol, a bright lamp hanging over the operating table, a maid working the handle on an atomizer for spraying a mist of the watered-down solution. Janessa and Dr. Martin rinsed their hands in diluted phenol.

Two menservants carefully carried the baroness into the room, placed her on the table, and filed back out. She wrinkled her nose at the penetrating odor of the antiseptic as she settled herself on the table, while MacAlister blinked away tears from the strong fumes. He placed a gauze cone over the woman's mouth and nose and began dripping chloroform onto the cone. A moment later, he thumbed back one of her eyelids. "She's unconscious."

As Janessa opened the baroness's nightgown and used a swab dripping with diluted phenol to disinfect the surgical area, she noticed faint striations on the woman's stomach, evidence that she had given birth to a child a year or two before. After tossing the swab into a bucket, Janessa handed a scalpel to the doctor. Her eyes were stinging from the phenol fumes, and she could see that the disinfectant was bothering him even more. When he seemed uncertain, she placed a forefinger on the patient's stomach and drew an imaginary line four inches long over the veriform appendix. The doctor nodded, then applied the scalpel.

Blood welled up. As he cut into the layers of muscle tissue with a larger blade, blood flowed more copiously.

When the scalpel passed through small arteries and veins, Janessa fastened clamps over the ends of the severed blood vessels and swabbed up the blood.

"It looks like your assistant has four hands," MacAlister commended.

"Janessa has a rare talent," Dr. Martin replied. "One day she'll be one of the most skilled doctors the world has seen."

The incision was made through the stomach muscles, and the peritoneum gleamed in the lamplight, then the scalpel sliced through the thin membrane and exposed the viscera.

"I can't see a thing in there, Janessa," Dr. Martin said. "Is the veriform appendix the problem?"

"Yes, sir," she replied. "It's inflamed."

"Good, good!" the doctor exclaimed. "Go ahead and ligature it, then remove it, Janessa. Be careful—we don't want any of that purulence escaping."

The doctors fell silent, contemplating the peril that now threatened the baroness. After she had tied the ligature tightly around the base of the veriform appendix, Janessa reached in with a scalpel and severed the organ at the base, then lifted it out. She put it in a basin, and the doctors moved closer to examine it as Janessa began stitching up the incision. A few minutes later, she put a bandage over it. MacAlister went out and returned with the two servants, who gently carried the baroness to her bedroom. Maids began cleaning the room as Janessa and Dr. Martin went to wash up.

MacAlister followed them, looking at his watch. "The baroness will wake in an hour, so there's time for a light repast. I asked the cook to put out a selection of cold foods. I'll see you in the dining room after I tell Captain Blake that the operation is over."

Janessa felt tired and hungry, and she could see that the old doctor felt the same. They walked slowly downstairs.

The light repast that the Scot had mentioned was actually a wide variety of delicacies. Having plain tastes, Janessa took a slice of ham, bread, and an apple. When Dr. MacAlister joined them he explained that Henry was not hungry and then heaped his plate, while Dr. Martin took the same as Janessa. When she finished eating, the girl went outside.

Stepping out into the cool, fresh evening air, she stood

on a path leading through the flower gardens, taking a deep breath. Smelling cigar smoke, she looked around and saw Henry standing a few feet away, smoking. "How do you view Gisela's prospects?"

"I'm surprised that you thought to ask," Janessa snapped. "From your attitude, you appeared to have forgotten all about her!"

"You don't understand, Janessa," he said quietly.

"I understand all too well! I've attended women in labor whose husbands showed their concern by carousing with friends! And at noon or so the next day, the husband might think to ask whether he had a son, a daughter, or a dead wife!"

The tip of Henry's cigar glowed as he puffed on it. "Dr. MacAlister told me the surgery was successful," he said in the same calm tone. "But you have treated this disease before, and he hasn't. How do *you* view Gisela's prospects?"

"Impossible to predict," Janessa replied irately. "Infection may develop, or it may not. But if you were worried about her, you would be at her bedside!"

Disgusted, she went inside. At the table Dr. Martin commented that the woman should be waking soon. Janessa and the men went upstairs.

The baroness was just beginning to recover consciousness. She was pale and drawn, but Dr. Martin nodded in satisfaction as he checked her pulse. MacAlister put a cool, damp cloth on her forehead, then she woke.

The Scot leaned close as she whispered weakly. "She wants her maid to come in and fix her up a bit," he translated. "Then she wants to see Captain Blake."

"She can see the captain for a moment," the doctor replied, "but she can do without the maid. I don't want people running in and out of here. Her health is more important than her appearance."

The baroness nodded in resignation as MacAlister translated, then she whispered again and pointed. The Scot brought a small case she had asked for, then opened it on the bed beside her. After taking a mirror and brush out of the case, the woman began trying to brush her hair, but her hands trembled violently.

Janessa suddenly felt pity for her. The baroness desperately wanted to make herself as presentable as possible before Henry saw her, even though he seemed to be very cold toward her. Janessa took the brush and helped the woman. She applied rouge to her lips and cheeks, dusted powder over her nose and forehead, then handed her the mirror. The baroness looked at herself, then smiled and nodded in thanks.

Having felt the icy, intimidating blast of the woman's displeasure, Janessa now experienced the powerful, compelling tug of her warmth. The girl wanted to remain impersonal, but despite herself, she felt a responsive glow.

MacAlister brought Henry in from the hall. Janessa saw that he had been right—she had failed to understand his feelings. What she had interpreted as indifference had been calm, stoic courage. He knew the baroness wanted to look her best when he saw her, and he had humored her by staying away until she was ready for him.

It was the first time Janessa had seen them together, and their deep, devoted love was evident. The tall, commanding man looked boyish as he crossed the room with eager steps. The woman's eyes sparkled, her beautiful face wreathed in a glowing smile. As Henry sat down beside the bed and held Gisela's hand, Janessa left the room.

Wanting to be alone, the girl walked out a door onto a balcony at the end of the hall. For years, Henry had been an object of contempt, and the baroness had been a formless person with decadent morals. Now, against her will, she was beginning to understand them, which created a violent conflict with her loyalty toward Cindy.

The next morning, Janessa was up and about at sunrise. Intending to check on Dr. Martin, she opened another door by mistake and was confronted by a large, ornate casket in front of the window. Pondering the meaning of the casket's presence, she quietly closed the door.

The doctor was snoring soundly as she opened his bedroom door, so she went to Gisela's room. The maid who had sat beside the bed through the night stood and curtsied as Janessa entered. The girl nodded to her, then looked at Gisela, resting quietly. Janessa left to go downstairs. She started to enter the dining room but froze in the doorway, seeing Henry at the head of the table. He stood, then pulled a chair back from the table for her. "Good morning, Janessa. Please join me."

"No, thank you. I'll have breakfast in the kitchen."

"As you wish. But the servants are having breakfast, and it would make them uncomfortable if you joined them."

Having no other choice, Janessa sat down, trying to keep Henry from helping her with her chair. He stepped to the buffet. "Cocoa? Coffee?"

"Just coffee. I can get it myself."

"No trouble," he said, pouring the coffee. "Would you like to read part of the newspaper?"

"No, thank you."

Henry folded the newspaper and put it aside as he sat back down. "Good. I'd much rather find out what's been happening in Portland. What is Toby doing?"

"He was going to a meeting in Washington, then on to the Oklahoma Territory."

Against her will she was drawn into conversation. Also against her will, her feelings for the tall, handsome man were growing more favorable. He was charming, with an amiable, respectful attitude, and his deep affection for Toby was obvious.

Servants moved silently in and out of the room. Then a servant set a covered dish in front of Henry. "Will you have part of this omelet?" he asked, lifting the cover. "This is far more than I can eat."

"I'd rather have a bowl of porridge, with bread."

The captain gave instructions to the servant, who soon returned with Janessa's breakfast. The conversation had moved on to Alexandra, another subject that made Janessa more talkative than usual.

"It's obvious that you like her very much, Janessa."

"Next to Cindy, I've never liked anyone more."

The reference to Cindy slipped out, but Henry took it in stride.

After thoughtlessly mentioning Henry's ex-fiancée, Janessa felt much less like talking with the man. But the conversation continued.

A few minutes later, Dr. Martin came in, still looking

very weary. Henry beckoned a servant and arranged for the doctor's breakfast.

"Sir," Janessa said firmly, "there are comfortable chairs in the garden. After we've checked the patient, please go out there and rest. I'll watch the patient."

"I'd better do as she says," the old doctor commented wryly to Henry. "Otherwise, she might put laudanum in my coffee."

Dr. MacAlister came in and took a seat, then ordered his usual hearty breakfast. "The baroness pays me a good wage," he said in satisfaction, "but as good as my wages are, I get paid half again as much at her table."

The remark brought a laugh from everyone except Janessa, who smiled politely. The portly Scot dug into his breakfast with his normal ravenous appetite, and as he finished, a servant announced that Gisela was ready for the doctor to see her. Everyone went upstairs.

After examining Gisela, Dr. Martin commented favorably on her vital signs and lower temperature. Henry translated for Gisela, then they left her to rest.

In the hall Henry said to Dr. Martin, "I have permission to remain on leave until I finish attending to my personal affairs, then I'm to report to Fort Abercrombie in the Dakota Territory. As soon as I find out when I can leave here, I'm to inform Washington."

"We should know within the next day or two if infection will develop. It will take some weeks for her to recover totally— this *was* major surgery after all—but she'll be getting around after a week."

"Very well. I'll plan on leaving a week from today, then. I'll send a telegram to Washington."

"Informing Washington will be easy compared to informing her," the doctor commented, nodding toward the bedroom door. "If I were you, I'd get that over with first."

Two hours later, Janessa went to check on the baroness. As she entered into the room, smoking a cigarette, she saw she had interrupted a quiet conversation between Gisela and Henry, who was sitting beside the bed. They had obviously been discussing his departure. Gisela's face was as pale as the night before, and she was struggling to hold back her tears.

She looked at Janessa's cigarette, her eyes opening wide in surprise, then she burst into laughter. Gasping with pain and holding her side, she tried but was unable to stop laughing. Humorless as always, Janessa saw nothing amusing. "Don't they have cigarettes in Germany, then?" she asked, puffing on the cigarette.

"Yes, indeed," Henry replied, chuckling. "But like here, it's unusual to see a young lady of thirteen smoking one."

"Well, I'm trying to stop smoking," Janessa said, putting out her cigarette in the ashtray Henry had been using for his cigar. "Dad asked me to stop, but I'm having a hard time doing it."

As she finally stopped laughing, Gisela smiled at the girl, creating the same warm satisfaction within Janessa that she had experienced the night before. She started to smile in return until the woman said something to Henry. Janessa heard Cindy's name in the sentence.

"Gisela says that you look very much like a photograph that she has seen of Cindy," Henry translated. "She's absolutely right, of course."

"I'd rather not discuss Cindy, if you don't mind," Janessa replied curtly, putting the bag on the edge of the bed and opening it.

"Very well," Henry said amiably. "Gisela and I both understand your strong loyalties, which are entirely to your credit." He abruptly changed the subject. "I told Gisela about your training in medicine. She said you are a very interesting young lady."

"Yes, well, she's very interesting herself."

The woman pointed to her side and asked something. Henry translated. "Gisela wonders if she may have loosened the stitches in her incision by laughing so hard."

Janessa shook her head confidently, as she took the stethoscope from the bag. "No, I put those sutures in. You see, the orderlies at the charity hospital in Portland are volunteers. They do their best, but they're untrained, and some are pretty old. Every now and then they drop a patient, and I've made it a habit to allow for that. When I suture patients, they can fall off a roof without loosening a stitch."

Henry smiled and translated as Janessa leaned over Gisela, listening to her heartbeat. The woman suddenly burst into laughter again, then held her side in pain as she struggled to stop laughing. Her face flushed as she choked back the laughter, she reached up and pinched Janessa's cheek affectionately. Janessa smiled.

The girl checked Gisela's heartbeat, pulse, and temperature, then nodded in satisfaction as she put the instruments into the bag. "Her temperature has fallen a little more, and that's very good."

"Yes, it is," Henry agreed. He and Gisela exchanged several comments in German. "Gisela wants to buy something for you, Janessa. Is there anything you would like? Bear in mind that cost is not a consideration. I know you're well provided for, but perhaps you'd like to do something for the people of Portland."

Janessa hesitated, then shrugged. "Well, if the baroness wants to, she could make a contribution to the charity hospital. We're always short of everything there, particularly money."

Henry turned to Gisela and spoke at length. Then he nodded and turned back to Janessa. "Gisela said she will have a new hospital built and endow it for operating expenses."

Janessa was speechless for a moment. "That would cost hundreds and hundreds—"

"More like tens of thousands," Henry corrected her, chuckling. "By endowing it, I mean that money will be invested, and the interest will pay staff salaries and other expenses."

"This is wonderful!" Janessa exclaimed, her normal reserve dissolving. "I don't know what to say. This is very generous, and the people of Portland will be very grateful."

Henry laughed wryly. "Gisela isn't inclined toward philanthropy, Janessa. The hospital is for you. She wants to remain anonymous, and the hospital is to be named for you. A business assistant who speaks English will leave for Portland to make the arrangements. He'll need the name of someone there to contact who can give him advice on the local area."

"If the baroness wants to keep her name out of it, I think her business assistant should contact Alexandra. She's discreet, and I've never known anyone who can deal with anything as quickly and quietly as she can. And I really wouldn't want a hospital named for me. I think it would be much better to name it for Reed Kerr."

Henry turned to Gisela and translated what the girl had said. Then silence fell for a moment, and the baroness again smiled fondly at Janessa.

Janessa leaned over and kissed the woman on the cheek, then picked up the doctor's bag and hurried out. She ran downstairs, along the hall, and out the back door. The doctor was dozing on a chair in the garden, but as Janessa trotted down the path toward him, she knew he would be more than glad to be awakened to hear what she had to tell him.

VII

As she approached her destination, Cindy Holt Kerr was even more fascinated by the exotic scenery than she had expected. The deck of the small coastal steamer was crowded with swarthy people in burnooses, turbans, and fezzes, surrounded by bundles of belongings, crates of fowl, and goats and sheep with bound legs. Amid the babel of conversation and bleating of the animals, two passengers were playing a twanging stringed instrument and a flute, while the wheezing and thumping of the old vessel's rickety engine made a steady background to the other noises. .

Ahead, under bright sunshine beaming down on the Aegean, was the small port of Karahisar, at the western end of the Dardanelles. The shoreline was dotted with crumbled ruins of Hittite, Byzantine, Greek, and Roman construction, which had been plundered for materials to make walls for crop fields and clusters of tiny dwellings. The successive waves of conquest had swept along the coast and subsided, leaving in their wake a remote backwater peopled by peasants with allegiance only to their land.

The passengers bustled about and gathered up their belongings as the steamer moved toward the Karahisar piers. Among the people on the waterfront, Cindy saw a couple in European clothes, whom she recognized as her employer for the next few months and his young wife. In his early fifties, Heinrich Schliemann was a slender, immaculately neat man of medium height, with close-cropped hair and handsome

118

Teutonic features. His wife, Sophia, was a strikingly beautiful Greek woman in her twenties.

As soon as the gangplank was in place, Schliemann stepped aboard with his wife to greet Cindy in English with barely a trace of a German accent. He had lived in California for years and was a citizen of the United States. "I'm very grateful that you came so soon. When Jules had to leave, we were without an artist to document our excavations."

"I'll do my best to provide whatever artwork you need," Cindy replied.

Schliemann smiled. "We are to be considered your friends as well as co-workers."

Sophia, who also spoke English, talked enthusiastically as she led Cindy down the gangplank to a buggy at the end of the pier. Cindy found out that the happy, companionable marriage between the Schliemanns was based on intense dedication to the same goals. A scholar of ancient Greek history and literature, Sophia was an archaeologist in her own right and was in charge of the work site when her husband was absent.

A short time later, the buggy rolled out of the town and past fig and olive groves, tobacco and vegetable fields, and vineyards on the higher elevations. As she looked at the farmers patiently toiling with their primitive implements, Cindy thought the scene appeared very peaceful.

When she expressed that, Schliemann opened his coat to reveal a pistol in a shoulder holster. "This area is much safer than it was just a short time ago, but there are still bandits about."

"And the soldiers are little better than bandits," Sophia added. "We have our own guards at the site and can cause trouble for the soldiers in Constantinople. Even so, it is wise to be cautious. I never leave the site by myself, Cindy, and you must not, either."

Much controversy surrounded the work at the site. Most established archaeologists considered Troy a myth; Schliemann and Sophia, however, firmly believed that the city had existed and that accounts of the ancient Trojan War were based on fact.

"Then there really *could* have been a Trojan horse," Cindy said.

Schliemann smiled. "One of my pet theories is that Greek warships could have been disguised as merchant vessels, with soldiers hiding aboard. The important point is that Troy was a historical city, and the ruler of Troy, King Priam, existed. We have analyzed all the references to Troy and compared the descriptions. Only one place fits what was written about it, and that is a hill now called Hissarlik."

A few minutes later the hill came into view, rising almost two hundred feet from a level plain. Beside it were wooden barracks for the scores of workers, while on the shoreward side of the hill, shaded by trees, was the comfortable Schliemann villa.

The hill, the Schliemanns explained, was the accumulated debris of some thirty centuries of human habitation. Somewhere in those levels, the Schliemanns assured Cindy, were the ruins of Troy.

Now on the site, Cindy was in awe at the scope of the undertaking. Countless tons of debris had been removed by hand. In one place, workers were dismantling a stone wall and dragging it away a huge slab at a time. Elsewhere, lines of workers were carrying away dirt in baskets on their shoulders.

"In order to dig deeper," Cindy ventured, "you must destroy the ruins above. I see why you need to document them. They may be of value to archaeologists in future years."

At the bottom of the hill, the Schliemanns took Cindy into a guarded warehouse where artifacts were catalogued and stored. Recently unearthed and intact treasures filled several shelves. The one that drew Cindy's attention looked like a small, flat pitcher with a slender, graceful handle and tiny spout. She carefully took it down from the shelf.

Sophia smiled. "That one is my favorite."

"What is it?" Cindy asked.

"An oil lamp," Sophia replied, pointing to the spout. "Oil is poured in here, then a wick is placed in it. The last time it was used was many centuries ago."

Cindy reluctantly replaced it, then followed the Schliemanns into the villa, where Sophia showed her to a large, well-furnished bedroom with a pleasant view, then left her to get settled.

Cindy later joined the Schliemanns to study sketches that Jules Choubrac had made. Cindy was confident that hers would be at least as good. Sophia disappeared for a few minutes while Schliemann showed Cindy a map of the excavation and pointed out where he wanted her to start working the next morning. Presently Sophia returned and rejoined the conversation through dinner and until bedtime.

When Cindy went to her room, she realized where Sophia had gone. On the nightstand beside her bed was the small, beautiful lamp, filled with oil and illuminating the room with a soft light.

The day started early at the site. Cindy took her sketch pad and pencils to one of the places that Schliemann had pointed out and set to work. The morning passed quickly. She met Sophia and Heinrich on the way down the hill at noon. They were pleased with the sketches that Cindy had done and commented that she worked faster than Choubrac.

Over lunch, Schliemann shared his concern that bandits might be drawn to the site. "I've told the foreman to watch for any sign of trouble. But please be very cautious."

After lunch, Cindy returned to her work, finding a comfortable spot in the shade and drawing in the details of a row of broken columns that had once helped to support a temple roof. As she glanced up from her sketch pad, she saw a man, clad in a grimy, ragged burnoose and worn sandals, standing less than ten yards from her. He stared at her fixedly.

Cindy was suddenly aware that she was in an isolated part of the excavation. It seemed an eternity that she sat unmoving, looking at the man, who stared back at her. Then he bowed and stepped past her. Two others followed him out of a passage in the ruins. As each salaamed, Cindy nodded to them, her heart pounding and her hand trembling. Obviously they were workmen, and she tried to put the momentary fright out of her mind. But she was unable to, because it seemed too much like a warning. The excavation was a mass of crumbling walls and broken passages, with blind turns on every side. An army of bandits could hide in it without being detected.

As their buggy moved along a rural road in the countryside east of Chandannagar, Edward Blackstone and Ramedha Cochrane enjoyed a lively conversation. Cool breezes from the northeast made it a sunny, pleasant afternoon.

Ramedha asked Edward if he had found out anything concerning the whereabouts of his friend, Edgar Dooley, and Edward shook his head.

"Edgar is given to bouts of tippling," Edward replied. "He's probably off on a binge and will show up in his own good time. The East India Company officials at Calcutta seem to share my opinion, but they're more angry than worried."

Ramedha laughed, her golden eyes glinting with something more than humor. Her flirting had made him slightly uneasy; he had not been a widower for long and certainly was not ready for a romance. But Ramedha was a charming, vivacious girl, a delightful companion. She was also intriguing. Most of the time, she wore simple muslin dresses and seemed like an exceptionally pretty young girl. But occasionally she lounged about the house in a diaphanous sari, and then she appeared both older and ageless, a sensual, exotic creature of the mysterious Orient.

Changing the subject, Ramedha began talking about the man they were on their way to visit. "I believe you will find it entertaining to meet and talk with Mr. Witherspoon."

Edward nodded, privately hoping to find it more than entertaining. The previous evening, Ramedha had mentioned the man, a friend of hers and a naturalist. Edward had to avoid revealing his purpose for being in India, but through indirect questions, he might be able to resolve the crucial point of whether Brahman and European cattle would produce a viable crossbreed or a hybrid. "Yes, I'm sure I will. You say he attended Oxford?"

"Yes, he took a first in biology at Oxford, and he also studied with Charles Darwin for a time. Turn right at the next fork ahead, Edward."

He looked at the side road, a narrow path that disappeared into dense trees. "That road appears to lead off into a wilderness," he commented. "Are you certain you know where the man lives?"

"Yes, indeed, Edward," she replied firmly.

Her confident tone and attitude failed to convince him completely, but he turned the buggy, and dense foliage closed in on both sides.

Towering trees festooned with vines blotted out the sunlight. In their midst were the ruins of a temple, its crumbling walls covered with ornate carvings. Immense statues flanked the ruins, gazing down on the passing buggy with benign indifference.

Then the silence was shattered as a band of screeching monkeys, hurling stones and clumps of dirt, erupted from the broken walls. Ramedha laughed, ducking and covering her face while Edward held the reins tightly to control the frightened horse.

A last stone struck the rear of the buggy as the trees opened out as suddenly as they had closed in. Ahead was a checkerboard of small crop fields around a lavishly large, shaded bungalow. A tall, thin Englishman wearing a straw hat and dusty work clothes was standing in a field with a dozen Indian laborers. Ramedha called to him, and he waved to her happily as he hurried toward the buggy.

The girl introduced Edward to Cecil Witherspoon.

As they talked, Witherspoon switched abruptly from one subject to another and occasionally broke off in the middle of a sentence to ponder, his blue eyes going vacant. Returning Ramedha's friendship in full measure, he directed the conversation more toward her, but when she mentioned that Edward lived in the United States, Witherspoon was electrified.

"Have you seen the scuppernongs?" he demanded.

"Scuppernongs?" Edward echoed, totally mystified.

"Yes, yes! In North Carolina!"

"I've never been to North Carolina, but I do know something about the place. I believe you have the wrong term. A few Cherokee live there, along with Tuscarora, Catawba and—"

"Scuppernong grapes!" Witherspoon cut in. "They are a native North American wild grape but bear fruit larger than *Vitis vinifera*! They are fascinating!"

"Yes, well, I'm sure they are."

Silence fell, and Witherspoon seemed stricken with disappointment.

"Perhaps Edward can arrange to have a few scuppernongs sent to you," Ramedha suggested placatingly. "That would be better than drawings, wouldn't it?"

"This is the wrong climate for them," Witherspoon replied, gazing reproachfully at Edward. He sighed heavily, then turned toward the house. "Well, let's go and have tea, shall we?"

As they walked toward the house, Edward listened and looked at the various types of rice, melons, and vegetables growing in the fields. Regardless of the man's eccentric personality, Edward saw that Witherspoon's work was eminently practical. It was also apparent that much of Ramedha's friendship for the older man was founded on sympathy, for he could have but few friends.

Edward contributed a remark now and then, hoping to recover from the disgrace of having never seen scuppernongs, as well as for a conversational opening to bring up the crossbreeding of Brahmans with European cattle. He felt sure that the devoted naturalist would be able to provide valuable information—if he could be kept on the subject long enough.

After an hour Ramedha indirectly introduced the subject, although Edward had never told her the specific reason for his trip to India. "Edward asked if you do any work with animals," she said. "Do you?"

"Yes, some selective breeding," Witherspoon replied. "Would you like to see?"

Edward nodded quickly when Ramedha glanced at him, then she agreed. Witherspoon led them along a path behind the bungalow to several large wire enclosures for fowl, with stock pens and small barns farther back.

Waiting for an opportunity to bring up cattle, Edward heard a movement behind him. He turned to see a cow stepping out of a barn and into a pen. His excitement swelled as a calf followed the cow outside.

The cow had the short horns, spotted color, and head shape characteristic of a Holstein, but it was enormously large compared to any of that breed and had the Brahman hump over its shoulders. The calf, a smaller version with the same characteristics, nuzzled at the cow's udders. Concealing his excitement, Edward asked Witherspoon about them.

"A crossbreed between Brahman and Holstein," he replied. "European cattle don't do well here. But the crossbreed has the hardy characteristics of the Brahman and produces milk like a Holstein."

"But it's been my understanding that crossing different species usually results in a sterile hybrid," Edward commented.

Witherspoon pursed his lips. "Crossing some species will produce a sterile hybrid, while others will not. This was an interesting experiment, but I did it mostly for my workers' children, to provide milk for them. Brahmans can't be used as milk cows."

Edward nodded and basked in deep satisfaction as he followed Witherspoon and Ramedha back toward the buggy. His theory had been proven to be correct.

When Edward and Ramedha were in the buggy, Witherspoon asked them to visit again. They both agreed, and then Edward snapped the reins. He urged the horse into a trot to get past the monkeys, then put an arm around Ramedha to protect her. She happily cuddled against him, as a couple of rocks bounced off the buggy.

When they arrived at the Cochrane home, Edward saw that his uncle was home early. The reason soon was revealed: The major was being transferred. During the past months, he explained, dacoits in the Assam Province had become increasingly bold and troublesome. A few days before, a steamer on the Brahmaputra River had been attacked, with loss of life, and a small army outpost on the river had been overrun.

"They're Gurlungs, a hill tribe and a thoroughly bad lot. I've been ordered to take my battalion to Barapani, a hill station in Assam, and either disperse the dacoits or wipe them out."

"And we're going with you," Mathilda chimed in.

"Now that's absolutely senseless, Matty," Cochrane said in exasperation. "There's no point in disrupting your life and the children's. When my task is done, I'll be back."

"Which could be years from now," Mathilda countered firmly. "Once your battalion is in garrison at Barapani, you'll remain there until you're relieved or Assam is completely pacified. Your family is a soldier's family, Winslow, and it will be with you."

"But Barapani is at the end of the earth!" Cochrane protested. "I'm not going there to have tea, you know. It won't be safe."

"Hill stations are very pleasant, with an agreeable climate," Mathilda persisted. "If a rifles battalion couldn't provide us with sufficient protection, I don't know what could."

"It's out of the question," Cochrane grumbled. "I've been ordered to leave immediately, and it will take weeks to pack up the household, even with Ramedha helping you. That means you and the children would end up traveling without an escort, which I simply won't allow."

"Then leave a rifles company here as an escort," Mathilda suggested. "Closing up the household will entail a great deal of work, but I'm sure Edward will want to help."

"I was hoping he would come with me," Cochrane replied. "But I suppose I could leave a company here to escort you—as long as Edward was available to look after you and the children. Would you be willing to do that, Edward?"

Concealing his reluctance, Edward nodded. The last thing he wanted to do was go wandering off to a remote hill station, for that would delay his finding Edgar. He was in no position, however, to refuse. "Of course, sir. I'll be glad to help."

"Very well, then." The major sighed. "I do hope I'll have better success against the Gurlungs than I did against my own family."

The discussion ended, with everyone having different reactions over its outcome. Edward regretted the delay in his plans, while the major was grimly resigned to the situation. Mathilda glowed with satisfaction. Ramedha was ecstatically happy, her golden eyes shining with delight and her fingers touching Edward's as she handed him a glass of gin and tonic.

From the first moment Toby Holt rode into Folsom in the Oklahoma Territory, he could feel the tension. Folsom was quiet, but it was the steely, gripping stillness that preceded the violent fury of a thunderstorm. The town was a typical center of commerce in cattle country: It consisted of a single wide, dirt street of wooden buildings, most with false fronts for second floors. Three were saloons, one a newspaper office, and the rest included general stores, hardwares, and other businesses to serve the ranches.

Atypically, few women and no children moved about. The men on the street wore pistols that were too much in evidence.

As he reined up his dusty, weary horse in front of the marshal's office, Toby noticed a land dealer's office and shook his head in disgust. In the same way that buzzards trailed after death, land dealers flocked to trouble, buying up land for a pittance from those fleeing the conflict, then selling it at inflated prices when order was reestablished.

The marshal's door was standing open on the sultry afternoon, and a large, bearded man was behind the desk. He looked up warily as Toby came inside. "What can I do for you, mister?"

"Thought I'd drop in to talk with you, Marshal," Toby replied. "The name is Toby Holt."

The man smiled in delight as he jumped up and hurried around the desk. "I'm Josh Hubbard, and it's a mighty great pleasure to meet you. I've heard so much about you, I feel like I already know you. Sit down, Mr. Holt." He hesitated. "Have you been sent here because of the trouble we're having?"

"I came to help out at the M Bar B, which is owned by friends of mine. Naturally, if I can help settle the trouble here, I will. Do you know how it started?"

The marshal explained that another man had been the law officer when the trouble had begun, but there had been a gradual buildup of increasingly serious clashes rather than one specific incident. The opposing interests of homesteaders, small ranchers, and large ranchers in the area would always cause conflict unless there was give and take on all sides.

"Usually the ranchers will gang up on the homesteaders or vice versa. Here, everybody is at each other's throat. Ranchers have as much trouble among themselves as with homesteaders."

"What kind of trouble?" Toby asked.

"Rustling each other's cattle, ruining waterholes, and

bushwhacking. The homesteaders are just as bad, burning each other's haystacks, trampling crops, and so forth. On top of that, everybody who can afford it has hired gunslingers."

Toby frowned but did not comment.

"The newspaper here is owned by a man named Percival Sloat, and he seems to be deliberately making things worse by printing accusations. He keeps things stirred up to a boil."

"Have you tried getting the different factions together to air their problems and work them out?"

"Can't be done," Hubbard replied firmly. "When you get them together, you've got a fight on your hands."

"Sounds like a real mess, Marshal," Toby said. "When I get settled, I'll talk to the people around here and try to calm them down."

"If anyone can do it, you can," the marshal said, stepping to the door with Toby. "Your name is well-known, and people will listen to you and trust you. If there's anything I can do, just let me know."

"Thank you. I understand the M Bar B is about five miles from town."

"Right. It's on the road north of town, backing onto the Indian reservations."

"I didn't know that," Toby said, "but I'm glad my friends have good neighbors on one side. There's never been any trouble to speak of with the Indians here."

"That's true"—the marshal sighed—"and I hope it stays that way. If the conflict we're having here spills over onto the Indian lands, we're liable to have trouble that'll make this look like nothing. I hope that doesn't happen."

Toby shook hands with the marshal again and left on a somber note. Thirsty from his long ride and about to begin another, he rode back to the first of the saloons, tethered his horse, and went inside.

A long bar filled one wall, with cuspidors spaced along the brass foot rail. There were a dozen or so tables and chairs on the sawdust-covered floor. Two women wearing thick cosmetics and bright satin dresses were circulating among the men. But the place was too quiet for the number of customers, and many of the men sat with their backs to the walls.

Several men eyed Toby warily. One ruddy-faced man,

wearing a suit instead of Western clothes, was at the bar. He had a smug, pompous manner, and as he fingered a large gold watch fob hanging from a vest pocket, diamond rings glittered on his fingers.

The bartender brought a beer to Toby and picked up his coin. Then a woman approached. "Hello, cowboy," she said. "My name's Pearlie. Want to buy me a drink?"

Startled, Toby looked at her. Despite her heavy makeup, Toby realized she was very young. "I won't buy you a drink," he replied, "but if you want to go back to your family, I'll buy you a stage ticket."

Her wide, false smile faded. "You want to rescue me, is that it? Well, mister, I like it here a lot better than where I was before."

"A few years from now, I believe you'll see things differently. I'm not trying to rescue you—I'm simply offering help, like I would to anyone who needs it."

"I don't need your help," the girl retorted.

"If you change your mind, my name is Toby Holt, and I'll be at the M Bar B."

The man in the suit, who had been listening to the conversation, beckoned the girl. "I'll buy you a drink, Pearlie. Step on over here."

The girl was less than enthusiastic, but she forced a smile and moved toward the man. "Hello, Mr. Rossiter."

"Call me Charlie, honey." The man chuckled expansively as he pulled her over and ran a hand down her hip. "I'd like us to be friends. You should have come to me first for a drink, because I know how to treat a lady."

Toby looked at the man, remembering that Rossiter and Steed had been the names on the sign at the land dealer's office. "Are you saying that I don't know how to treat a lady?"

The man turned to Toby and stared deliberately for a second before he spoke. "I wasn't talking to you."

"I know who you were talking to. I asked you a question, and now I want an answer."

Silence fell in the saloon as men at the tables turned to look. Rossiter's self-assurance faded, and he glanced at the bartender to see if he was going to interfere. The stolid bartender, however, busied himself with polishing glasses.

Pearlie was having trouble concealing her glee over Rossiter's discomfiture.

"I don't get involved in brawls," Rossiter blustered. "I'm a respectable businessman, and it's below me to—"

"You're scum who grubs money from the misery of others," Toby cut in. "And if you don't give me an answer pretty soon, you're going to be in a brawl, whether you want to be or not."

The man cleared his throat, his face crimson with resentment. "I didn't mean anything by what I said," he grumbled.

Toby went back to his beer, and Rossiter threw money on the bar, then stamped out. After darting a smile at Toby, Pearlie moved away. As the soft mutter of conversation in the saloon resumed, Toby finished his beer and left.

Riding north, Toby reflected that he had never seen better land for ranchers or homesteaders. The rolling, fertile hills were covered with lush grass and groves of trees, and ample water was available from creeks and shallow wells. The land had the boundless, expansive feel that was characteristic of the West. It was a place where people should be expending their energies on building their lives, not warring with each other.

Evidence of unrest was all around, however. At intervals were wagon roads leading back into ranches, with no-trespassing signs—the first Toby had ever seen in the West. Where the road crossed a rise, he saw a man working in a field. Seeing Toby, the man stopped working, picked up a shotgun, and watched suspiciously as Toby rode past. Behind the barns set back from the farmhouse was a large, charred circle where a haystack had been burned—a good reason for the man to be wary.

It was late afternoon when Toby reached a wagon road with the M Bar B brand on the signpost beside it—but without a no-trespassing sign, which pleased him. The wagon road led for miles back into the rolling hills, and Toby saw longhorns grazing here and there. The heat of the day was fading when the large, comfortable-looking ranch house and outbuildings came into view.

A young woman was taking down wash from a clothesline beside the house, and even from a distance, Toby saw that she was not Rob's wife. The moment she saw Toby, she ran to the front porch and began ringing a bell. The bell clattered furiously, and then the woman darted into the house and slammed the door.

The echoes of the bell rippled over the hills. Then a rider, also a stranger, came galloping into view, holding a rifle at the ready. Stalwart and determined-looking, he reined up in front of Toby. In his late teens, he was thin and angular, his patched, threadbare work clothes, floppy hat, and heavy boots those of a homesteader. The woman, who was really more of a girl, was prepared to help. She held a pistol in one hand as she peered out the window. From inside, Toby could hear a baby crying.

When Toby waited quietly, the youth became less suspicious. "Are you by any chance Mr. Toby Holt?" he asked.

"That's who I am," Toby replied, laughing, "but not by chance. I'm here by invitation."

The youth grinned and quickly replaced the rifle in the scabbard on his saddle. "It's all right, Sally!" he called, then turned back to Toby. "I'm Billy Collier. My wife and I work for Mr. Martin."

"Is Rob about?"

Just then, Rob rode around the house at a gallop. He and Toby dismounted and greeted each other warmly. Toby brushed aside Rob's thanks for coming to help him and asked about his family.

"Kale finally agreed to take Cathy to New Orleans when she knew you were coming," Rob replied, "which was a big relief for me."

"I'm sure," Toby remarked. "They're much better off in New Orleans than here."

"Let's go inside," Rob said briskly. "I'll give you a hand with your things. Billy, will you see to the horses? We may as well call it a day."

The house reflected the preferences of Edward Blackstone, who wanted comfortable, attractive surroundings when possible. Rob showed Toby to a large, well-furnished bedroom that was more evocative of New Orleans than Oklahoma.

Toby washed up, then took a bottle of bourbon from his bags and joined Rob on the front porch. The redheaded man exclaimed in pleasure over his first sip of the bourbon, and Toby told him about Alexandra.

Then Rob and Toby looked around the barns and calf pens. Most of the thoroughbreds had died of tick fever, Rob explained, and at present, he was simply holding on in the hope that Edward's trip to India would yield results.

"It hasn't been easy," Rob confided. "I've tried to mind my own affairs and avoid problems with others, but that's getting more difficult."

Toby thought about the possibility that the conflict was being deliberately created and explained his reasoning to Rob.

"I usually wouldn't put it past land dealers," Rob replied, "but the trouble started before they were in the area. It became really bad after Percival Sloat arrived, and that's because people are foolish enough to believe what he prints in his newspaper."

Toby wondered how Sloat could profit from the trouble but came up with no reason. He went on to another subject. "Anyone who wants to stay on good terms with neighbors needs to have property lines clearly marked. I ordered ten tons of barbed wire for you from Chicago to fence your ranch. It'll be freighted to Folsom, so that'll give us plenty to do while we're trying to settle this trouble."

"Ten tons?" Rob exclaimed. "Toby, I'd like nothing better than to fence the ranch, but Edward and I can't afford it."

"Yes, you can," Toby replied firmly. "My factory manufactures it. If things improve for you, you can pay for it at cost; otherwise, we'll forget it. You and Edward need a fence around your land."

Rob expressed his deep gratitude as they walked into the house, where Sally was busy preparing dinner. Billy carried in firewood, then went to the kitchen garden to gather vegetables.

Toby commented that he had never seen a more hardworking young couple. Rob emphatically agreed, then explained that they were working for him because the buildings on their homestead had been burned. A few minutes later Sally called Rob and Toby to dinner.

The dining room was spacious and comfortable. A chandelier made of lamps mounted on a wagon wheel hung over the table. The food was plain but delicious: fried steaks with potatoes, fresh vegetables, and pie. The windows were open to catch the evening breeze as darkness fell, and Toby enjoyed the meal and the atmosphere.

Sally proved she was spirited—she sat in silence until Billy's clash with the owner of the Circle S was mentioned. Then she animatedly joined the conversation.

Toby thought about the story that Billy had related. "I wonder who killed that steer and hung it in those trees."

"It must have been Elmo Lummas," Sally chimed in. "He just wanted an excuse to burn us out. But we'll make another start."

"Has Lummas been watering his cattle in your creek?"

"No, sir," Billy replied. "No one has been near it."

Toby exchanged a glance of understanding with Rob. Billy and Sally were, of course, resentful over what had happened, but their allegations made no sense: The only reason a rancher would have for driving them off their land would be to use it for his own cattle. If the owner of the Circle S had been malicious, he would have hanged Billy. On the face of it, if Lummas had been convinced that Billy had rustled a Circle S steer, the man had reacted with measures any rancher would call moderate.

After dinner, Toby and Rob returned to the front porch and discussed the situation.

"Have you had any trouble with the Circle S?" Toby asked.

Rob puffed on his cigar. "No, I haven't had direct trouble with anyone, including Lummas. He won't go far out of his way to avoid trouble, but he's kept his gunslingers in hand recently."

"What happened to Billy is a real puzzle, isn't it?"

Rob agreed, and the two men discussed the incident at length but came to no conclusions.

The next morning, after a hearty breakfast, Toby rode across the ranch with Rob and Billy. It consisted of thousands of acres of some of the best ranch land Toby had ever seen. While they were crossing a rise, Toby thought he glimpsed a rider in the distance, disappearing among trees. He reined up and told Rob and Billy.

"If it was somebody skulking around to bushwhack us," Billy said, "he'd have to get a lot closer than that. Those trees are a mile away."

Toby agreed, and they rode on. A short time later, the boundary with the Indian lands came into view. They stopped on a hill, and Rob pointed out the property-line markers. While they were talking, Toby scanned the countryside, unable to shake off an uneasy feeling. A mile off to one side, he distinctly saw a movement in the trees, then the gleam of sunlight on metal. He shouted a warning as he reached out with a foot, jabbed Billy's horse with a spur, and jerked his reins toward the other side, bumping his horse into Rob's.

As the horses pranced apart, Rob and Billy looked around for what had alarmed Toby. Toby saw a puff of smoke in the trees, followed an instant later by the deadly whisper of a bullet flicking past his head. The bullet slammed into a tree behind him, ripping out a chunk of bark and wood the size of his fist. Then a second later the thunderous report of a powerful rifle reached the top of the hill.

"That's a Big Fifty!" Rob shouted. "Somebody is shooting at us with a buffalo gun!"

Toby recognized the characteristic report—it was a Sharps .50-90, popularly called a Big Fifty, a favorite among buffalo hunters because it was accurate up to a mile. Toby spurred his horse at a headlong run to get within Winchester range of the man, as Rob and Billy followed.

The man fired again when Toby was a thousand yards from the trees, and a three-inch sapling twenty feet in front of him erupted as the heavy bullet ripped through its trunk. Toby rode into a prairie dog village, his young, agile horse dodging the holes while at a dead run.

The man fired once more, and the bullet clipped the right edge of Toby's hat brim just as his horse veered to the left. Now on the other side of the honeycomb of holes, Toby was five hundred yards from the trees. He took out his Winchester and began firing.

The tree limbs thrashed as bullets ripped through them.

A moment later, Toby glimpsed a rider, a tall thin man on a roan, carrying the long, heavy Sharps.

Toby crashed through the trees, ducking branches and being thrashed by limbs, with Rob and Billy right behind. As they rode out of the trees, the man was lashing his horse and galloping up a hill ahead. Rob, Billy and Toby rode after the man.

The Sharps was much too cumbersome to shoot from horseback, so the assailant began wildly firing a pistol. Then he disappeared over the hill. When Toby and the other two reached the hilltop, the man had reached the next valley, in the Indian lands.

Toby reined up hard. "Let him go. The last thing we want to do is take our problems onto the reservation."

"But if we run into some Indians, we can explain what happened," Billy protested. "They'd understand, wouldn't they?"

"It isn't worth taking a chance," Toby said, and Rob agreed. "They don't want our problems on their land any more than we want their problems on our land."

The youth reluctantly turned his horse back. "I'll bet that was somebody from the Circle S," he grumbled.

"I don't think so, Billy," Rob said. "We've been over at our boundary with the Circle S any number of times, with their hands just on the other side of the property line, and they haven't offered us any trouble. Also, he wasn't shooting at us; he was shooting at Toby. Do you have any idea of who he is or why he was shooting at you?"

Toby shook his head. The only enemy he had made thus far was Rossiter. It was conceivable that Rossiter had hired a gunslinger, but that seemed too extreme for what had happened in the saloon.

The attack was puzzling, and, Toby reflected, it was definitely an indication of future trouble.

VIII

Eulalia Blake stood next to her husband at the rail of the ferry. "It makes no sense whatsoever," she said in annoyance as the vessel moved toward Portland. "Just when the repairs to the ranch house are being completed, Alexandra is going to have another house built, then the ranch house torn down. A waste of money! Where is her logic?"

"Well, she and the children will have a comfortable house while the new one is being built," Lee suggested. "Are you absolutely sure of your facts, Eulalia? You haven't been to the ranch to see for yourself, you know."

"No, I haven't," Eulalia admitted. "But yesterday I talked with Wilma Givens, and her daughters are working for Alexandra as the maid and cook, and they said that the same man who repaired the house is about to build a new one."

"That's third-hand information, Eulalia," Lee pointed out.

She nodded but still believed what she had heard. Wilma had relayed the information that huge stacks of building materials were being assembled, and *that*, Eulalia thought, was a fact impossible to misinterpret.

Eulalia was reluctant to go to the ranch. While she acknowledged Alexandra's right to do as she wished, Eulalia shrank from seeing that house torn down. It would be unbearably painful, for the house meant too much to her.

Eulalia thought about something else Wilma had told her: Alexandra was allowing Timmy to drive his new road locomotive. In addition to being an obvious danger to the boy, it seemed completely irrational, considering what had happened before. It appeared, just as Eulalia had feared, that Alexandra was attending to her own affairs while permitting Timmy to run riot.

A few minutes later, the ferry docked, and while she was waiting for the driver to bring the carriage from the livestock deck, Eulalia realized she was being unfair to Lee. She had no right to spoil their Sunday afternoon outing and resolutely became at least outwardly cheerful.

For the past two weeks, the regimental band at Fort Vancouver had been hired to perform at the Portland fairground on Sunday afternoon. From all accounts, it had been an unqualified success. The bandsmen were glad to earn the extra pay, and the people of Portland flocked in delight to enjoy the concerts. Having a free Sunday afternoon, Eulalia and Lee had decided to attend a concert themselves.

"In the past," Lee said as the carriage moved along the streets, "the fairground manager hasn't been overly imaginative. But now Mr. Copeland seems to have come up with a very good idea."

"Well, in all fairness," Eulalia reminded her husband, "financing must be his first consideration."

"I'm sure he isn't overspending," Lee said. "Mr. Peabody at the bank keeps a close eye on expenses, and I've heard that the refreshment stands at the fairground seem to be doing well."

A few minutes later, the carriage arrived at their destination. In addition to stands selling lemonade and other drinks, others were doing a brisk business selling candies, sandwiches, and other food.

No longer having to act cheerful, Eulalia looked around. The people of Portland, starved for entertainment, had found an escape from the boredom of sitting home on Sunday afternoons. The atmosphere at the crowded fairground was festive and relaxed.

Couples were dancing in front of the colorful marquee where the band was performing, while others sat on benches and listened to the music. Families were gathered around picnic baskets on the grassy expanse; horseshoe tossing and other games were in progress; and courting couples were sharing glasses of lemonade.

As they walked toward the benches, Eulalia forgot everything else when she saw her grandson, a radiant smile on his face as he waved. Timmy rushed to Lee and Eulalia, and Calvin Rogers followed.

Eulalia and Lee hugged the boy affectionately, then listened as Timmy said he had been tossing horseshoes. This pleased Eulalia; it was a safe, normal activity for the boy, while his road locomotive was just the opposite.

"Would you like some lemonade, dear?" she asked.

The boy nodded quickly, and Eulalia and Timmy walked toward the lemonade stand, where a man inside was squeezing lemons while two boys hurried back and forth, attending to the long lines of customers. Eulalia started to stand in a line, but Timmy waved and drew the attention of one of the boys. He nodded, and Timmy led Eulalia around behind the stand.

A small door in the rear of the stand opened, and the boy handed out two glasses of lemonade. Timmy gave him a dime as they exchanged amiable remarks.

"Is he a friend of yours?" Eulalia asked as she and Timmy walked away.

"Sort of," Timmy replied. "That's Jim Fogarty. He and Jake used to pick on me at school, but then Alexandra went to see their dad about it. They stopped, but Alexandra said I have to be friendly toward them. So I guess we're friends."

Eulalia was somewhat skeptical about Timmy's story. "Alexandra is absolutely right. Once trouble with someone is over, you must be ready to begin anew. But she undoubtedly sent Stalking Horse or one of the other men to see that man."

"I believe she went herself, Grandmama."

"I'm sure you're wrong," Eulalia replied lightly, patting the boy's head. "Alexandra wouldn't do that. I understand that a new house is going to be built at the ranch."

"Yes, ma'am. I heard Mr. Fossi say that he's going to start on it pretty soon."

Her fears confirmed, Eulalia resolutely put the subject aside. "I see. How are you doing in school, dear?"

As the boy replied, Eulalia listened in satisfaction, because he appeared to be applying himself. She wondered why he didn't seem that interested in his road locomotive, but she hoped it would be permanent. When she and Timmy rejoined Leland and Calvin, who had been sitting on the bench in front of the marquee, she brought up the subject.

"He still drives it occasionally," Calvin answered, "but just driving it back and forth doesn't hold his interest like working on it. Miss Alexandra told me that would happen, and she was right. She's talked about finding other things that will be as interesting and educational for Timmy as the road locomotive was at first."

For the first time Eulalia wondered if Alexandra's youth might actually be an asset in dealing with the children.

"What time is it, Calvin?" Timmy suddenly asked in concern. "Alexandra told me to be home at four o'clock."

"We still have a few minutes," Calvin replied, looking at his watch.

The boy gulped his lemonade. "If it's near time to go, we'd better leave. I don't want to be late."

Calvin smiled. Timmy had always been anything but punctual, and Eulalia was pleased that he was becoming more responsible. As she made her farewells with her grandson, she reflected that Alexandra was a good influence in at least some areas.

Lee expressed the same thought after Calvin and Timmy left. While they were talking, Lee noticed Frank Copeland, the fairground manager, near his small office building. Deciding to congratulate him on the Sunday entertainment, Lee and Eulalia strolled toward the man.

Copeland greeted them warmly. "I wish this had been my idea," he said wistfully at their thanks, "but it was Miss Alexandra's."

"Alexandra?" Eulalia exclaimed in surprise.

"I work for her now," Copeland explained. "She bought the mortgage on the fairground. I never thought I'd live to see the day, but that mortgage has turned out to be a good investment. We're making money hand over fist."

"My word," Lee murmured, while Eulalia remained speechless in astonishment. "This is the first we've heard about that."

"I'm not surprised, sir," Copeland said. "She stays in the background and runs things through me. But in addition to the fairground, she seems to be taking a hand in quite a few things around town. She and Mayor Edwards are on very good terms."

Lee continued discussing the subject with Copeland as Eulalia listened. Alexandra seemed to have a great deal of concern for her new community.

Lee and Eulalia went back to the band marquee. They danced for a while, then sat and listened to the music. By the time the sun set, Eulalia knew she would fondly remember that afternoon for the rest of her life.

Some people, reluctant to bring the day to an end, remained at the fairground until darkness fell. Eulalia and Lee did the same, leaving just in time to catch the last ferry back. As she stood at the rail with Lee, his arm around her, Eulalia felt happy despite the cares that lingered in the back of her mind: Even though she knew that some things that were precious to an older generation were often discarded by a new, the forthcoming destruction of her first home in Oregon made her sad. She hoped she would be able to come to terms with it and to keep it from affecting her relationship with Alexandra. She did want to feel close to the young woman. She decided to steel herself sufficiently, then talk with Alexandra about the destruction of her house. Eulalia had been listening to Lee absently until something he said caught her full attention. "What was that?"

"Calvin said that Alexandra has been corresponding with a dealer in San Francisco about the prices of passenger balloons."

Eulalia's eyes grew wide. Then she shrugged off the thought as entirely too preposterous. Although Alexandra wanted to find things that would be interesting and educational for Timmy, Eulalia fervently hoped that Alexandra would never get the boy anything as dangerous as a passenger balloon.

The entry hall of the Roosevelt estate was crowded but silent, with Janessa, Dr. Martin, Dr. MacAlister, the servants, and the business employees waiting for Henry Blake to make his farewells with Gisela. Then the tall man finally came down the stairs in his neat uniform.

He spoke to each servant and business employee, and to Dr. MacAlister. Then he turned to Dr. Martin. "Words can't express my gratitude for what you did. I'm indebted to you for life."

"I'm just pleased that everything turned out well, Hank," the doctor replied. "Take care of yourself out there in the Dakota Territory."

As Henry turned to Janessa, she was prepared to shake hands with him. Instead, he put his arms around her and kissed her cheek. "Gisela is in very poor spirits. I'd be very grateful if you would go and sit with her."

"I had intended to, Mr. Blake. Good-bye."

Henry paused and looked at her, and Janessa knew he was remembering Cindy in bygone years. He touched her face and turned away. "Good-bye, Janessa."

The others followed Henry outside to watch and wave as the carriage moved away. Janessa went up the stairs. The house felt empty without Henry there.

Gisela, her face pale and drawn, lay in bed. Seeing Janessa, she beckoned, and the girl stepped toward the bed. Gisela suddenly began weeping, and reaching out, she clutched Janessa and pulled her close. Janessa held Gisela as she sobbed and talked brokenly. Comprehending none of the German, the girl still understood the woman's emotions perfectly.

Janessa passed the afternoon with Gisela, providing companionship. The baroness remained grief-stricken that evening, refusing dinner and wanting Janessa to stay with her, but she started pulling herself together the next morning.

Janessa helped her out of bed, and Gisela leaned heavily on the girl as they made their way to the French windows. In the flower garden below, the servants carried the casket to the end of the path and chopped at it with axes and hatchets until it was a pile of costly fabric, hardwood, and brass fittings. Gisela watched, then Janessa helped her back to the bed, and the woman began summoning her business employees.

The next day, a messenger brought telegrams from the city, and the employees, frequently pale from scathing reprimands, scuttled up and down the stairs with sheaves of papers. With a constitution that matched her personality, Gisela rapidly recovered her strength and began working part-time at a desk in her room.

Whenever Janessa went into the room, Gisela's impatient glare changed to a radiant smile. Janessa smiled, returning the beautiful, complex woman's deep affection. After the thermometer and stethoscope were put away, Gisela took Janessa's hand and pulled her to a chair, where the girl remained for hours, in communication more profound than words with the woman.

One evening, many days later, when Janessa was visiting Gisela, Dr. MacAlister and Dr. Martin entered the room.

"Janessa," the Scot said, "the baroness would like you to go to Germany and stay there with her."

Janessa smiled as she shook her head. "I'd like very much to go with her," she said, tugging the thread with the tweezers. "But I must return to Portland."

The doctor translated and Gisela replied. Then he spoke to Janessa again. "You would have your own house, servants, and everything else. You could study medicine in any university in Europe, including Edinburgh, the foremost medical university in the world. Such an opportunity can't be dismissed lightly, Janessa."

"No, it can't, sir," Janessa agreed. "But I have to return to Portland. I would truly like to stay with the baroness, but I can't."

Dr. Martin chuckled. "Whatever trouble Hank Blake might find in Dakota would be nothing compared with what I'd have to face in Portland if I showed up without Janessa—so I don't intend to risk it."

The Scot laughed, translating what Janessa and Dr. Martin had said. Gisela smiled and nodded in wistful resignation.

The next morning, two maids packed Janessa's bag, although the girl would much rather have done it herself. Dr. Martin went to see Gisela for a last time, then talked with Dr. MacAlister at the front door as servants carried his and Janessa's bags out to the carriage. Janessa went to make her farewells with Gisela.

They hugged and kissed each other, and then Gisela

took a heavy velvet purse from the nightstand and put it into the girl's pocket. Janessa started to return it, but Gisela shook her head, her eyes pleading. The woman then took a large ring off her finger and pushed it into Janessa's pocket with the purse. The girl kissed Gisela again and hurried out of the room, tears stinging her eyes.

A few minutes later, Janessa was in the carriage with Dr. Martin as it moved down the drive. She looked back at the house, thinking about her complete change in attitude toward Gisela and, to a lesser extent, Henry.

"Well, Janessa," the doctor said, "now we've cured two patients who had perityphlitic abscess. I'm looking forward to getting back to Portland and resting for a while."

"I'm looking forward just to getting to the train station," Janessa replied, "so I can order some steak and potatoes. I don't like to be rude, but the baroness's cook certainly devotes a lot of time and trouble to ruining food."

The doctor laughed, then put on his spectacles and took out a purse. "I asked for fifty dollars and expenses," he said in satisfaction, counting the money in the purse. "But I was paid a thousand and expenses."

Thinking of the purse Gisela had put in her pocket, Janessa took it out and opened it. The doctor peered over his spectacles and smiled as the girl poured gold coins into her palm. "It looks like you got paid more than I did, my dear."

The girl nodded disinterestedly as she replaced the money in the purse. Born into abject poverty but into an immense wealth of purpose in life, money was meaningless to her. She took out the ring and looked at it. The doctor leaned closer and examined it, then whistled softly. "I'm not a jeweler," he said, "but I'd guess that's worth several times the amount of money you have there, Janessa."

She smiled. The ring was of far more value to her than the money. The heavy gold ring had several large diamonds set in a circle around the Kirchberg crest, which was reproduced in bright, colorful cloisonné. Exquisitely beautiful, it reminded her of Gisela. She sat back in the seat, looking at the ring and admiring it.

*   *   *

Hermann Bluecher was relaxing after an inspection trip around the province on the afternoon that Josef Mueller arrived. A servant led Mueller into the huge, marble bathroom in the villa, where Bluecher was lying naked on a soft pallet as Salima put steaming, scented towels on him and massaged him with perfumed oil.

Bluecher had grown accustomed to the deep Turkish salaams, so Mueller's European bow seemed much less respectful. Mueller was discomfited by the setting. A vaguely embarrassed expression on his face, he looked away from Bluecher and Salima.

Mueller was a physical wreck, a thin, haggard shadow of the man he had once been. He had one shoulder bandaged and was dressed in rags. "You look terrible, Mueller," Bluecher said.

Mueller frowned resentfully, knowing he looked halfdead. Bluecher, on the other hand, had never looked better. He thought for a moment, then replied, "Well, the food in prison was poor, sir," he explained. He pointed to his shoulder. "Something went wrong during the escape, and a guard shot me. But I'm very grateful to you for arranging my escape, sir."

Bluecher grunted, having wondered when Mueller would get around to expressing gratitude. "I suffered hardships myself, Mueller," he commented philosophically. "The journey here was grueling."

Mueller glanced around the lavish bathroom. "Yes, sir."

Salima pushed Bluecher, rolling him onto his left side, and he sighed in satisfaction as she put fresh hot towels on him and resumed massaging him. "We are now exiles Mueller, driven from our native land. In addition, we are exiled from our homeland because of a foreigner."

"Ah, the American," Mueller said, nodding in understanding. "Yes, and he caused us great difficulties more than once didn't he, sir?"

"Great difficulties indeed," Bluecher agreed. "When I first heard of him, I should have dedicated myself to eliminating him. But I failed to realize how dangerous he was, so the action I took was inadequate." He sighed, dismissing it. "Would you like to get revenge on Blake, Mueller?"

"Yes, sir," the man replied, then shook his head doubt-fully. "But it would be difficult, if not impossible. As you say, he is a dangerous man. I have never seen another man as dangerous."

"But he has a weakness," Bluecher pointed out. "His wife, Baroness Gisela von Kirchberg. If she is killed, he will suffer as we have suffered. He will be grief-stricken and enraged, and an angry man is a careless one. First we kill the baroness, then we kill Heinrich Blake."

Mueller pursed his lips, then nodded. "It could be done, sir. Killing the woman will be easy. Killing the American will be much more difficult, but several agents should be able to do it."

"Very well," Bluecher said happily. "I knew I could depend upon you. The woman is gone from Germany at present, but she may be back by the time you get there and arrange an ambush. I will give you forged papers, money, and everything else you need. After you kill the woman, return here. We will discuss killing the American."

"Could I rest for a few days before leaving, sir?" Mueller asked. "My imprisonment was hard on me, and the accom-modations and food on the ship—"

"You can rest during the journey," Bluecher snapped. "During the journey, you will have nothing to do but rest. And you can rest now for a time. Leave me, and we will talk again later."

Mueller bowed and left.

Watching him leave, Bluecher decided that the man was no longer a match for the American. He would undoubtedly fail. He could kill the woman, though, which was, Bluecher reflected, just as well. The baroness's death would create an uproar in Germany, and it would be disastrous for evidence to lead to an official of the Ottoman Empire. When Mueller returned, a guard with a length of piano wire could quietly eliminate him. Then, with Mueller out of the way, plans could be made to deal with the American.

The entire situation thought through and his mind made up, Bluecher dismissed it. Salima began spraying scented menthol mist on his body and wafting him with an ostrich feather fan, and he sighed blissfully as he relaxed.

"Pasha," she said in a sultry whisper, "after you have rested, I will dance for you, then I will do whatever you wish."

Anticipation stirred within Bluecher. In addition to being as skilled in lovemaking as Adela Ronsard, Salima was a superb belly dancer.

"Pasha," she murmured, "will you decide my brother's case soon?"

Bluecher grunted in annoyance. "I told you I would decide in good time and not to bother me about it again."

"A thousand pardons, Pasha."

Thinking about Salima's brother, Bluecher smiled. The case had been decided days before—the man had been garroted. In time, Bluecher knew, he would think of some story to tell Salima to keep her quiet and happy.

On the road leading into the Circle S ranch, Toby slowed his horse as he approached three hired gunmen on horses, blocking the road. The one in the center spoke as Toby stopped. "There's a no-trespassing sign back there. Can't you read?"

"Everything that I want to read," Toby replied mildly. "I have business with Elmo Lummas."

"What kind of business?"

"I'll discuss that with him."

"You discuss it with me first!" the man barked. "And if you give me any trouble, you'll talk to my gun."

"Go ahead, draw."

The man's face flushed with anger, and he reached for his pistol. As his hand touched it, he froze in astonishment, for he was looking down the wrong end of Toby's pistol, held at arm's length, the hammer cocked. The other two gunslingers, who had started to reach for their pistols, also froze.

"Now turn your horses around and ride ahead of me," Toby commanded quietly, "and don't make any sudden moves. It's a hot day, and I don't feel like digging three holes."

The three men sullenly reined their horses around while Toby eased down the hammer on his pistol. A few minutes later, the ranch house came into view. It was little more than a cabin, but the barns set back from it were large and spacious. The contrast between the makeshift house and large barns told Toby what kind of man Lummas was.

A half-dozen men were culling calves around the corrals beside the barns, and Toby followed the gunslingers around the house toward the pens. The men stopped working and turned to look. Toby recognized Lummas from Billy Collier's description. A tall, burly man, his rugged face revealed honesty and a sense of justice, not maliciousness, as Billy had said. He was a type Toby had met many times before in cattle country—basically a good man who was difficult but not impossible to deal with.

Glowering in resentment, the three gunslingers reined up at one side. Lummas and his ranch hands looked at the gunmen and Toby for a moment, then Lummas laughed. "Well, if you're looking for a job, mister, I'll talk business."

"I'm not a gunslinger, Mr. Lummas. My name's Toby Holt."

The man nodded. "I've heard of you, Mr. Holt. What can I do for you?"

"First I'd like to shake hands, then I'd like to talk."

"Be glad to. Get down from your horse and give it a rest," the man invited, stepping toward Toby.

The ranch hands resumed working as Toby and Lummas talked and walked. The gunslingers returned to the ranch's entrance. After about fifteen minutes, Toby got down to business.

"So from what I've seen of Billy Collier, he seems a good, honest boy. I don't think he rustled your steer," he summarized.

"It was on his property!" Lummas barked. "Somebody had been butchering it and eating it. How do you explain that?"

"I can't, no more than Billy could. But if you had hanged him, I believe it would have been murder."

"If I had," Lummas growled angrily, "it might keep others from rustling my stock. Other ranchers have been slapping their brands on my calves!"

"How do you know?"

The man beckoned for Toby to follow him to a corral. In it was a longhorn cow with a Circle S brand, while its calf had a Lazy H brand. A longhorn cow would drive away any calf not its own but would never be separated from its own. Mistakes were impossible, because the first problem in branding a calf on the range was fighting off the cow.

"I read in the newspapers that John Hendricks said he had plenty of calves," Lummas grumbled angrily. "When my hands brought in this cow and calf, I rode over to the Lazy H to see him. I told him that I'd read about all his calves and accused him of getting them from my ranch. Then he called me a liar."

"What did you expect? You went over to call him a rustler."

"What do you call that?" Lummas shouted, stabbing a finger at the cow and calf. "What would you do?"

"I'd go see the owner of the Lazy H," Toby replied coldly, "but I wouldn't start out by calling him a rustler. That makes about as much sense as it does for you to stand here shouting. You don't have to bellow like a bull caught in a briar thicket to get a point across, Mr. Lummas."

Lummas shrugged. "Well, Hendricks does his share of calling names. He came over here accusing me of filling in one of his watering holes. Me and my hands have more to do than go around filling in watering holes, and if he'd dig some wells over there, he wouldn't have to worry about water."

"We have a lot of accusations and no discussions," Toby remarked. "If you have trouble with anyone else, I'd appreciate it if you'd just let me know about it, Mr. Lummas. I'd like to be the one to broach the subject with them, or at least go with you." He lifted a hand as Lummas started to object. "I'm not suggesting that you can't deal with trouble. But if we don't have less heat between people here, we're going to have a range war. None of us wants that."

"All right," Lummas replied gruffly. "I'll do it if you can convince the others to do the same."

"Very well, I'll go to the Lazy H today, then to other places soon. In the meantime, I'd like to be able to come and see you without fighting my way on to your ranch."

"I'll let my men know you can come and go as you please."

Lummas started to turn toward the corrals. He hesitated

and turned back, reluctantly shook hands with Toby, then stamped away. Toby mounted his horse and rode back past the house toward the road.

An hour later, he reached the Lazy H ranch. John Hendricks and several of his hands were near the road, driving cattle back toward the pastures at the center of the ranch. As Toby talked with the owner, four gunslingers sat on their horses and watched.

In personality, Hendricks was much like Lummas but quieter, reserved and watchful, with steely blue eyes. Having heard of Toby, he was friendly enough in his aloof fashion.

"There's no reason for things to be this way, Mr. Hendricks," Toby said. "The only ones profiting from this situation are gunslingers and land dealers."

"The land dealers won't profit from me," Hendricks said firmly, "because I'm not going to leave. If it takes hiring more gunslingers, then I'll do that."

"The solution, Mr. Hendricks," Toby said patiently, "is for people to work out their problems, not to hire gunslingers. All people need to do is to stop arguing and start talking."

Hendricks's eyes were cold. "You can't talk to Lummas. I read in the newspaper that he was bragging about how much water he has on his spread. Lummas does have plenty of water, and I'd have more if he hadn't ruined one of my best watering holes. The tracks from it led straight to the Circle S."

"Why would he do that?"

"Because," Hendricks replied angrily, "if we have a dry year, which we do now and again, I'll either have to buy watering rights from him or pay to have wells dug. That watering hole was one of the few I have that never dry up. It was in the newspaper that Lummas is about the only one who can sell water during a dry year."

"From what I've heard, that newspaper makes more trouble than sense. Did you tell Sloat that you have plenty of calves?"

Hendricks hesitated. "He asked me about my calves. I believe I said that I'm having a pretty good increase in my herd this year, so maybe he stretched it a little. I suppose

Lummas told you he had a cow turn up with a calf that has my brand on it, didn't he?"

"He did more than that, Mr. Hendricks. He showed me the calf."

"Well, he probably put that brand on it himself. Lummas would have more calves if he would cull his stock instead of spending time causing trouble."

Toby knew the conversation was leading nowhere. But he was getting a closer feel for the attitudes in the area, and Hendricks was airing his grievances to a neutral party, which also served a purpose. Toby suggested that he be contacted if Hendricks had problems in the future.

"If others will, then I will, Mr. Holt. But it appears to me that you're taking on a passel of trouble for yourself."

"It would be more trouble for me and everyone else if a range war got started here, Mr. Hendricks, or if trouble spreads onto the Indian lands. I'd also like to be able to visit you without having trouble with your gunmen."

"I'll tell them that you can come and go at will."

The rancher rejoined his men as Toby turned back toward the road. A short distance along the road in the direction of the M Bar B, Toby noticed a large homestead set back in a shallow valley beside the creek. Toby turned off the road toward the homestead.

The near end of the farm had been planted in corn— some two hundred acres that had evidently been the cash crop—the produce to be sold to obtain seed, supplies, and other necessities. But fire had swept through it, leaving only blackened furrows and a few charred stumps. Off to one side of the barns behind a small, neat house was a large, black circle where a haystack had burned.

Toby saw a curtain in a front window of the house move. A moment later, a stocky, bearded man stepped from behind a tree in front of the house, his shotgun leveled at Toby. "Far enough, mister. What do you want?"

"I'd like to talk with you," Toby replied, reining up. "I'd also appreciate some water for my horse."

"I don't have anything to say to you!" the man barked. "And that horse can make it to the next creek! Now turn around and get off my land!"

A woman suddenly stepped out of the house. She had a strong, careworn face. "If we ever get to the point where we can't give somebody who passes a drink of water for his horse," she said acidly to the man, "then I'll be ready to sell out and leave! Bring your horse over here, mister."

As she spoke, she went to the well and drew a bucket of water. Toby tried to lighten the situation. "I'd rather let my horse go dry than get into the middle of an argument between a wife and husband."

The man waved him on. "Go ahead and give the horse a drink, then."

Toby dismounted and led his horse to the well, and the man tucked his shotgun under his arm as he followed. The horse drank thirstily from the bucket as Toby introduced himself. The man, somewhat less hostile, did the same. He and his wife were Asa and Sarah Buell, and they had two small children, who peeked out the door.

The man began talking about the burned cornfields. He was convinced that another homesteader had done it. "Somebody else who's growing corn for cash must have done it," he said. "The newspaper said that the less there is of a crop on the market, the more money it'll bring. That makes sense."

Toby had expected to hear something about the newspaper. "Was that haystack burned at the same time?"

"No, it was a week or two before then," Buell replied unhappily. "I can probably scrape up enough hay to get my horses through the winter, but I don't know what I'll do about my wife's four milk cows."

"Milk cows?" Toby exclaimed in surprise. "They must be longhorns, or they'd be dead from tick fever. But this is the first time I've ever heard of anyone taming a longhorn and making a milk cow out of it."

"If it's a cow, my Sarah can milk it," Buell said proudly.

"I intended to start selling milk and butter," Sarah added dejectedly. "But now we're going to be short of hay, and we may have to butcher my cows. I don't see how we can get them through the winter."

"The pastures at the M Bar B will get the herd through the winter with plenty of grass left over," Toby said. "You can come there and cut hay for those cows."

The offer took the couple by surprise. "We certainly do appreciate that, Mr. Holt," Sarah said gratefully. "That's mighty good of you."

"It certainly is," Buell agreed. "You're the first one around here who's given us anything except trouble. Like that rancher to the north of us: He drives his cattle back and forth across the end of my land, and one of these days I intend to go up there with my shotgun and put a stop to it."

"That must be the Rocking T," Toby said. "I'm going to see the owner there within the next few days, Mr. Buell, and I'd appreciate it if you'd let me talk to him about that."

"I can protect my own, Mr. Holt," Buell said, frowning.

"There are several hired guards at the Rocking T, and the way tempers are around here, you'll probably get into a fight. I'm a neutral party, and I can reason with him if he'll listen."

"What will you say?"

"First I'll find out why he's doing it. If there's something about the lay of the land that makes it handy for him to drive stock across your property, he's supposed to ask your permission. If he does it often, it's customary for him to give you a calf now and then. So instead of confronting him, I'll find out the facts and remind him of his obligations."

"I'll think about it and let you know what I decide," Buell said.

"Think long and hard, Mr. Buell. When you come over to the M Bar B to cut hay, bring your wife and children. Sally Collier would enjoy the company."

The woman added her thanks as her husband replied. Toby made his farewells, then rode back the way he had come. Hours had passed, and it was late afternoon. Wanting to reach the M Bar B before nightfall, Toby urged his horse into a canter.

He absently noticed a flock of birds rise from the edge of trees at the top of a long, gentle slope at one side of the road. He frowned. They were quail, which would normally be settled for the night by sunset—unless something disturbed them. Toby pulled his reins back sharply, stopping his horse abruptly, to take a closer look at the trees. The memory of the unknown bushwhacker was unpleasantly clear.

As the horse slid to a stop, a geyser of dirt and rocks exploded from the road under its nose. The horse reared up and then bucked and whinnied in fright as the thunderous, rippling boom of a Big Fifty carried down the hill. Controlling the horse, Toby wheeled it around toward a copse of trees that led up the hill. The horse raced toward the trees as Toby leaned over the saddle horn.

Over the noise the horse made as it pounded up the hill toward the trees, Toby thought he heard the sound of distant hoofbeats. When he reached the top of the hill, he saw that the gunman was taking no chances on being caught within Winchester range. He was fleeing.

It was the same tall, thin man on a roan. Too far away to continue pursuit, Toby turned his horse toward the road, angrily wondering who the gunman was. It was a frustrating, dangerous situation, with a range war on the verge of exploding and every shadow a potential place of ambush.

IX

Sitting close to a broken stone pillar that sheltered her from the cool night breeze, Cindy Kerr peered closely at her sketchbook in the dim light as she rapidly roughed in the major features of the scene before her. It was a market plaza from ancient times, which the workmen had finished excavating and cleaning off a couple of days before. The bright, full moon above illuminated it with a soft light.

The sketch was for her private collection, as were numerous others she had made at Hissarlik. Many had been made on clear, moonlit nights, when the workmen were gone and the Schliemanns were asleep. In the stillness and the moonlight, the ruins were profoundly mysterious to Cindy, seeming to come alive with the shadowy ghosts of the ancient people who once lived there.

The Schliemanns had examined the architectural style, shards of pottery found in the debris, and other details that indicated the date of the plaza. Cindy was more interested in the plaza itself, the paving stones that had been worn smooth by sandals and the crumbled stone walls of tiny shops. To her, it was a place where human beings once lived, not merely an abstract archaeological find.

As she was drawing in details, Cindy thought she heard the distant sound of horses. She listened closely, but detecting nothing but the whisper of the wind, she dismissed the sound. A few minutes later, rocks clattered and fell somewhere on the other side of the plaza, but so deep was her concentration that she barely noticed; small rock and dirt slides occurred almost constantly in all parts of the excavation.

Then she saw a movement on the other side of the plaza, a little over a hundred feet away. At first she thought it was her imagination, that the dark shadows in the moonlight were making her eyes play tricks on her, but as she watched, a man emerged from the shadows of the walls, followed by two more.

Icy fear gripped her as Cindy immediately thought of bandits. The three men began crossing the plaza toward her. Although she was in the deep shadow beside the broken pillar, her dress was a light color. More importantly, her open sketchbook was a patch of white the men were sure to notice.

Cindy slowly closed the book as the men continued across the plaza. If she remained where she was, they might notice her. If she made a sound while moving, the men would hear it. If she was going to move, she had to do it soon.

Slowly and soundlessly, she lifted to a low crouch to creep behind the broken pillar. She took cautious steps, watching the men and feeling with her feet for loose stones. But when she was almost hidden, she brushed against a broken edge of the pillar, and a large chunk fell off and tumbled to the rocks below with a loud clatter.

For an instant, the men froze and looked toward Cindy. Stifling the impulse to scream, she darted into the warren of crumbled walls that had once been small shops at the side of the plaza. The men raced after her, scrambling over the low walls as she zigzagged through them.

The men seemed very clumsy, for they dislodged showers of stones, and Cindy could hear them bellow oaths when they occasionally fell. For a moment she thought she was going to be able to reach a straight, wide street, where she might be able to get close enough to the house or the workmen's barracks to scream for help. But she was handicapped by her skirt, and soon the men bore down on her.

One man exclaimed gleefully as he grabbed Cindy roughly. The other two men joined him and held her arms. The three sweaty, unshaven men reeked of cheap wine, and she gasped in surprise as she got her first close look at them.

"You're soldiers!" she exclaimed, seeing their uniforms. "You're not supposed to be sneaking around here!"

She might as well have remained silent. The slight relief that she had felt immediately faded. "Look," she said, trying again, "just turn me loose and leave, and I won't say a word to your officer."

Her voice was choked off by a grimy hand clapped over her mouth. Two men tied her hands and feet with their belts while the third gagged her with a grubby rag. Cindy struggled frantically, managing to get in a well-placed kick that brought a howl as one of the three bent and held his crotch. Then a heavy fist struck the side of her head. She felt a searing pain, her legs went weak, and the world spun.

One man carried her sketchbook, and the other two carried Cindy as they made their way through the ruins to mount their horses. One soldier dragged Cindy up in front of him on the saddle.

Still dizzy from the brutal blow on her head, Cindy was scarcely aware of what was happening for a time. The three men lashed their horses mercilessly, riding at a furious pace. Then Cindy's head cleared, and she realized the horses were heading west, toward Eskafed.

The district capital came into view from the top of a hill. Only a few lights were burning in the late night. A few minutes later, the soldiers reined up at a low, sprawling building on the near edge of the city, which served as the garrison guardhouse and the city prison. The men pulled Cindy off the horse. Two carried her, and the other brought her sketchbook inside.

In the grimy, dimly lighted office, a fourth soldier was dozing drunkenly at a desk. He woke as the three men, shouting and laughing, came in with Cindy. The other man blinked, peering stupidly, then he leaped from his chair with a whoop of glee and joined the other three as they untied her and removed the gag. Silence fell, and Cindy shivered in terror as the four gazed at her in lewd anticipation.

One of the men poked at her, saying something and moving his feet. As she looked back in confusion, he repeated the same motion, this time speaking more imperatively. Cindy realized they wanted her to dance for them. Outrage overcame her fear, and she spit in the man's face. Wiping his face, he reeled back in astonishment. Then, as the other three laughed at him, he lifted his fist.

The door opened, and a fifth soldier came in, carrying two large jugs of wine. He was a larger man, more filthy than the other four. He looked at her in surprise, but as the three who had captured her began explaining, a wide grin spread over his ugly, unshaven face.

He pulled the cork from one of the jugs. Wine trickled down his chin as he upended the jug and drank deeply. Then he belched and made a comment, his beady eyes moving lecherously over Cindy. The others laughed raucously and nodded in agreement as they passed the other jug and took drinks.

A moment later the men began arguing, loudly and heatedly. Terror stricken, Cindy realized they were debating who would be first with her. She looked around, searching for some means of escape, but there were none. The men were between her and the door.

One of the men shushed the others, pointing and saying something in a warning tone. The other four quickly lowered their voices, then quietly continued their dispute. Weighing that, Cindy knew that there must be an officer nearby, whom the five feared.

She drew in a deep breath to scream, but one of the men leaped at her and put a hand over her mouth. After replacing the gag, another man smacked her solidly on the side of the head and snarled something. Cindy reeled to one side, knocking her head against the wall, and slumped to the floor in a semiconscious daze.

One of the men stepped to a broom leaning against the wall and plucked five straws from it, then offered them as a means of settling the argument. The tall, burly man who had come in last snatched one of the straws and crushed it in a fist that he shook at the other four. The four conceded, then drew straws among themselves. He would be first.

The large man lifted Cindy from the floor and dragged her through the cell-block door. The other four began passing around a jug of wine and taking drinks as they awaited their turns. The muffled sounds of a struggle came through the open cell-block door; then the struggle stopped.

The man who was next took a drink from the jug and passed it on as he held up his straw and laughed in gleeful anticipation. The other three offered to buy it, but the man firmly refused. As the minutes passed, all three men offered more and more money.

The front door suddenly flew open, and the garrison commander stepped into the office. The bedlam abruptly faded into silence. The tall man was just coming back through the cell-block doorway, fastening his belt. He froze, and all five soldiers stared at the officer.

The officer looked at the open sketchbook on the desk, then glanced around at the men, his initial anger changing to suspicion. He shoved past the man in the cell-block doorway, stepped into the cell block, and stopped at the cell where Cindy lay curled and weeping on the floor.

She looked up with reddened eyes, and when she saw the soldier with an officer's insignia on his epaulettes, she felt hopeful.

Sitting up and straightening her clothes, she started to speak in French, hoping the man could understand. "My name is Cindy Kerr," she said, "and I work with Dr. Schliemann at Hissarlik. I was abducted by those men, and I want to be taken back to Hissarlik at once."

Beads of sweat stood out on the man's face. "You are from Hissarlik," he said in broken, heavily accented French. "Foreigner from Hissarlik."

"Yes, and I want to return there at once. I want those men out there to be punished, but most of all I simply want to go home."

The man suddenly closed and locked her cell door, then stepped out of the cell block and slammed that door. Cindy was stunned; she had expected apologies and assurances that the men would be punished. Instead, she was being held prisoner.

Outside, she heard the officer thundering orders and waking the entire garrison. A few minutes later, she heard a rider leaving at a dead run. Cindy sat on the edge of the cot in the cell, confused. Then an explanation occurred to her.

Fear gripped her as she decided that the scenario was entirely logical. Soldiers often mistreated villagers, but a foreigner could cause trouble. Schliemann would be enraged and complain bitterly to Istanbul, resulting in official wrath descending upon the province.

That could be avoided by killing her, burying her in an unmarked grave, and blaming her disappearance on bandits. A rider had been sent to the provincial capital to ask for instructions. In all likelihood, he would return with her death warrant.

The first light of dawn was coming through the window in the cell when Cindy heard a coach accompanied by a number of riders. The cavalcade drew up outside the guardhouse, and orders rang out. A moment later, Cindy heard voices in the office.

The officer did most of the talking, his tone fearful and apologetic. A few minutes later, he came into the cell block, his face pale and stiff. He unlocked the door and motioned to Cindy to follow. In a state of shock from her ordeal, she numbly stepped out of the cell and walked toward the office.

The men who had abducted and tormented her had been chained and were lined up against the wall. Their eyes were glassy with terror. The reason for their fear was a European man with piercing blue eyes wearing the robes and fez of a pasha. He had Cindy's sketchbook on his lap and was looking through it. As he put it on the desk, he began talking, his voice high and soft. Speaking in German, he asked if she spoke that language.

Cindy spoke in French, replying that she did not. Then she changed to English, telling the man who she was. He responded in English with a German accent. "I am Bluecher Pasha, lieutenant governor of Serabatan Province. You have been the victim of an unfortunate misunderstanding. The men mistook you for a village woman."

The statement was absurd, but Cindy immediately understood that dire trouble for him would unquestionably result if Schliemann complained to the authorities in Istanbul.

Collecting herself and trying to appear convincing, knowing that her life depended on it, Cindy nodded. "The misunderstanding was unfortunate. But if I can be returned to Hissarlik, we can forget the entire matter, and nothing more will be said about it."

"Your attitude is commendable," Bluecher commented, his cold, hard eyes examining hers for lies. "But I'm certain you can understand my need for some assurance that you won't later decide that this incident was more than a mere misunderstanding."

Almost at the breaking point, Cindy cleared her throat to keep her voice from quavering. "I can, but you must also understand that the only assurance I can give is my word. I must ask you to believe me when I tell you that you will never hear of this again."

The pasha pondered. "Your employer at Hissarlik and his wife," he said. "Will they question you about where you have been?"

"No," Cindy replied. "I often rise before daybreak to sketch the ruins in the early morning light. If I return in the forenoon on the road from the west, which cannot be seen from the house or the ruins now under excavation, they will not know I have been gone."

Bluecher fell silent again, studying her. Her palms damp and her mouth dry, Cindy kept herself from trembling by force of will, knowing that her life hung in the balance. Finally he nodded. "Very well," he said, his eyes conveying a savage warning. "I will take you back to Hissarlik in my coach. But let me caution you about changing your mind about what happened here. I have agents throughout the district."

"I said I would not talk," Cindy replied, her voice almost breaking, "so I will not." Her lips trembling, she stabbed a finger at the five men. "But I want those men punished!"

"They will be," Bluecher said, his lips twitching in a slight smile. He turned to a guard standing nearby and spoke rapidly in Turkish, then turned back to Cindy. "There is a woman named Salima in my coach. She will take you to the inn across the street and assist you in putting your appearance in order so you won't be questioned about it. We will set out for Hissarlik as soon as I have attended to certain details here."

Not trusting herself to speak again, Cindy silently followed the guard out into the fresh air and early morning sunlight. He went to the coach and rapped on the door. The door opened, and a dark, strikingly beautiful young woman pulling a cloak around her looked out. Speaking in Turkish, the guard pointed to Cindy.

Salima frowned in concern, and her large, dark eyes conveyed sympathy as she pushed the guard aside and stepped down from the carriage. She held out her arms, speaking in Turkish as she rushed to Cindy, but the compassion in her eyes reached across the language barrier. After the torment of the night before and the tension of talking with Bluecher, Salima's warm, openhearted sympathy brought Cindy to tears. She struggled to control her sobbing as Salima led her to the inn.

The proprietor bowed rapidly as Salima snapped orders, pointing to a tear in Cindy's dress and then motioning. He beckoned a woman, who showed Salima and Cindy to an upstairs room, then others came in with needles and thread, basins of water and towels, and brushes and combs.

When they were alone in the room, Salima murmured in a consoling tone as she helped Cindy wash. Then Cindy sat on the edge of the bed as Salima brushed her hair. Cindy buried her face in her hands and cried as if her heart were breaking. Salima dropped the brush and sat on the bed beside Cindy, holding her and rocking her as she comforted her softly in Turkish.

Soon, hearing something, Salima sat up and spoke in a louder tone. She stepped to the window and threw it open. In the courtyard behind the guardhouse, a tall wall around it blocking the view from the window, there was a babble of voices. Cindy could hear the five men wailing and begging.

Salima smiled in grim satisfaction as she made a gesture that eliminated the language barrier. She held up five fingers, indicating the men, then swiftly drew a forefinger across her throat.

*   *   *

Edward Blackstone had seen many awe-inspiring views during his travels, but none had impressed him more profoundly than his first glimpse of the Ganges River. When the riverboat passed the junction of the Hoogly River with its vast parent stream, Edward and Ramedha were standing at the bow and talking. They fell silent as they looked out at the Ganges.

The riverboat and the barge trailing behind it, both the size of oceangoing vessels, seemed insignificant in the wide river. On one shore, countless lifetimes of grueling labor by multitudes of artisans had transformed a towering stone cliff into a huge, ornate temple, but it appeared minute in the distance.

Even though the river was enormous, the absorbing impression that it made on Edward came from more than its size alone. It had the same ageless, enduring atmosphere that pervaded its setting—a land where the present existed side by side with past centuries. "This river seems very unique," Edward mused, searching for words to express his feelings.

"The Ganges is much more than a river," Ramedha said quietly. "It is a source of life, as well as death. Its floods make the soil fertile at the same time that they devastate the land and drown thousands. A baby's first bath must be in its water to assure long life and prosperity, and the aged and infirm journey to the Ganges to die so their ashes will be cast into it and assure their progress to nirvana. Since the dawn of time, the Ganges has been the center of life and death in India."

Edward looked at her as she talked. Although she was wearing a colorful gingham dress and a sun hat, when she spoke of India, her mood seemed more to fit the times when she was wrapped in the silky folds of a sari. She was alluring, an exotically mysterious young woman, stirring a reaction within him that tugged compellingly. He shrugged off the feeling, smiling at her. "It will be many years before you'll have to worry about having your ashes cast into the Ganges."

"My ashes cast into the Ganges?" she echoed in astonishment, her large, golden eyes glittering merrily as she turned to him. "I should hope that when I die, this mortal body will be given a proper burial instead of being dumped into a river. I'm just as good an Anglican as you are, Edward Blackstone!"

"Very well," he conceded, laughing. "But sometimes I wonder if even you yourself know what you are. Not that I object to your double life; others are very dull in comparison with you."

"In that event," Ramedha replied with a coy smile, "I'll do my best to be as confused as possible about myself." She sighed. "But meanwhile, I must go and help my aunt organize dinner. We are a soldier's family, and we must endure the hardships of military life. I'll call you when dinner is ready, Edward."

Edward watched her walk away. Like the small fleet that had transported the major and the bulk of his battalion, the riverboat and the barge it was towing had been provided by a grateful East India Company, which wanted its tea plantations protected from the dacoits.

Primarily a cargo vessel, the ship provided few conveniences for passengers. There were only three passenger cabins, which had been turned over to Mathilda, her family, and female servants. Her male household employees were billeted with the soldiers on the afterdeck, where Edward shared a tent with the officers, and the remaining deck space was stacked high with equipment and supplies. Edward walked carefully around the crates as he went to the afterdeck.

The barge was even more congested than the riverboat because the rifles company consisted of some one hundred sepoys and three officers who were accompanied into the field by almost twice that number of bearers, sweepers, and cooks. Most of them and their belongings were in the barge, along with saddle horses, grooms, baggage elephants, and their keepers, known as mahouts.

The afterdeck was crowded but orderly. The company commander, Subadar Ved Birbal, had set up his temporary headquarters under an awning at the rear of the superstructure. A stocky, briskly military man in his forties, he was using a crate for a desk and poring over a stack of papers with one of his officers, Jemadar Om Kamsing.

They looked up as Edward approached, and the subadar pointed to another stool. "Join us, Mr. Blackstone."

"Am I interrupting?" Edward asked.

"No, no." Birbal pushed the papers aside. "We were only going over one of our endless lists of supplies. Jemadar Kamsing, see if any of the men have made tea, if you would."

The younger officer left as Edward talked with the subadar. Chosen by the major as the one to protect his family, Birbal was one of the most experienced company commanders in the battalion, with a row of medals on his tunic. He was extremely interested in the American army and weaponry.

As the jemadar returned with tin cups of tea, the subject centered on the Winchester in Edward's baggage, a far superior weapon to the single-shot Snider that was standard equipment for the army in India. Edward liked the two men and enjoyed the conversation.

Near sunset, Ramedha came to tell Edward that dinner was ready, and he went with her to the cabins. With no oven available, light crisp chapitis took the place of bread, but otherwise, it was a full, delicious meal: boned chicken marinated in spices and stewed in a savory curry sauce, fried fresh vegetables, and steamed rice flavored with a hearty, fiery chutney.

During dinner, Mathilda expressed concern that her household belongings would be damaged. Edward reassured her, but Subadar Birbal had expressed concern that the large amount of baggage might be so tempting that a force of dacoits would challenge even a full rifle company to gain possession of it.

The subadar had also mentioned that Gurlung dacoits had been known to take women and children captives for ransom. That concerned Edward far more than the baggage.

When dinner was finished, Mathilda shook her head as Ramedha started to help her organize the maids to clear the table. "No, I'll attend to this, Ramedha," she said. "You and Edward go for a stroll on the deck."

The girl smiled happily, and Edward suppressed a sigh. Mathilda openly encouraged Ramedha's flirting with him, making the situation even more difficult. Ramedha put her arm through his and held it firmly as they went out on deck.

Darkness was settling, and the cool breeze stirred Ramedha's long, thick hair and caused the scent of her perfume to waft around Edward. Although he had carefully avoided revealing his purpose in coming to India, Ramedha, with her quick mind, was uncomfortably close to figuring it out. They talked about many things as they stood at the rail, and then Ramedha asked, "Exactly why did you decide to visit India, Edward?"

"Why, to meet you, of course," he teased, hoping to get her off the subject.

"I'll accept that reply," she came back quickly, "because I like it better than any other answer you could give. Well, it's getting late, so I must go in." She lifted her cheek. "You may kiss me good night, Edward."

Smiling, Edward bent over to kiss her cheek. She turned quickly and planted a firm kiss on his lips, then walked away. "Good night, Edward dear," she called cheerfully over her shoulder.

Edward shook his head. Although he regretted this pursuit by the headstrong girl, he didn't mind it nearly as much as he thought he should.

The riverboat made good speed, and at daybreak it was at the mouth of the Brahmaputra River, where the huge engine began laboring against a powerful current.

After breakfast, Edward saw that a rowboat, tied to the riverboat, had been put over the side. Soldiers were climbing down into it as others put gatling guns and ammunition into the boat, Subadar Birbal looking on.

"I'm going to send some heavy weapons and ammunition back to the barge so the men there can set up defenses for the barge and the riverboat, Mr. Blackstone," he explained. "We're now in dacoit territory, and until we reach the garrison at Barapani, we'll be vulnerable to attack at any time."

Edward nodded, then went to his tent, where he took out his Winchester and Colt. After loading the weapons, he placed them and his sword where he would be able to get to them quickly.

The soldiers remained on the alert, but the following days passed without incident. Fewer boats were on the river as it wound through steep hills covered by dense masses of tropical foliage. The ornate peaks of isolated temples jutted up here and there, and villages surrounded by crop fields were tucked into the narrow valleys.

After the riverboat passed through a winding gorge that stretched for several miles, the region became a virtual wilderness. It was even more remote than Edward had expected.

On the sixth day of forging up the river, an outpost of civilization came into view. A large village named Pandu Ghat was located on the south bank of the river, adjacent to an immense, sprawling East India Company complex of large warehouses, workers' barracks, and other buildings. Piers reached out into the river, and for as far as the eye could see, the surrounding hills were covered with straight, neat rows of tea bushes.

When the riverboat came into sight, a swarm of workers and villagers raced to the piers, waving and shouting happily. Edward saw the plantation's factor push his way through the crowd, grinning at the prospect of visitors from outside. His young wife seemed even more excited, for she straightened her hat and dress nervously.

As soon as the gangplank was in place, the factor and his wife hurried up it to Edward and the women to introduce themselves—they were Larry and Catherine Atwater—and to invite them to visit. Subadar Birbal agreed to send horses to the factor's house when the company was ready to move out, so Edward and the Cochranes disembarked and went with the young couple to their large, comfortable bungalow.

They sat on the veranda, drinking tea as Catherine chatted happily with Mathilda and Ramedha. The women speculated about being able to visit occasionally if an escort of soldiers could be provided from Barapani.

"I don't want to dash your hopes," Larry said, "but from what I hear, the soldiers are fully occupied with dacoits."

"Have there been any major battles?" Edward asked.

"No, only minor clashes," Larry replied. "The Gurlungs always avoid pitched battles unless the rewards are well worth the risk. Major Cochrane hasn't been able to locate their village, but he's driven them away from the plantations."

Edward found an opportunity during the conversation to ask about Edgar Dooley.

Larry shrugged. "The day after he finished going through

the accounts, he suddenly disappeared. But he had some bolabang, so I had workmen search the area in the event he had become ill and wandered off. When they found no sign of him, I concluded he had gone back to Calcutta."

"Bolabang?" Edward asked.

"It's a liquor the workers make from tea leaves and mangoes," Larry explained. "Its effects are very strange, as well as unpredictable."

"It's a horrid, poisonous liquor," Catherine chimed in emphatically. "Last week, Larry had to lock four workmen in a shed because they were drunk on bolabang and kept trying to throw themselves into the river."

"Yes, those men thought cobras were crawling on them," Larry continued. "It is my opinion that Edgar has ended up in some city downriver and will eventually show up in Calcutta once he sobers up and finds some means of transportation."

A short time later, Jemadar Kamsing rode up to the bungalow, leading horses for Edward and the Cochranes. After making their farewells, they mounted and caught up with the company in the tea groves. The riverboat and barge had been unloaded; the remainder of the journey would be accomplished by land.

With a squad deployed a hundred yards ahead, the officers rode at the front of the main body of foot soldiers. Behind them, a platoon flanked the spare horses and the baggage train, which consisted of a dozen plodding elephants. The horde of bearers, sweepers, and other servants brought up the rear. Edward left the Cochranes in the center of the soldiers, then took his place with the officers.

The road became a narrow track winding through rugged, verdant hills. The chanting of the servants was almost drowned by the incessant screeching of birds and chatter of monkeys. Knowing that the company was now extremely vulnerable to attack by dacoits, Edward and the officers rode in tense silence, watching the trees.

A few hours after setting out, the company passed what remained of a mountain village that dacoits had ravaged. The jungle was already beginning to reclaim the trampled crop fields, while weeds were sprouting in the streets between the crumbling, fire-blackened walls of the houses. A steely silence hung over the scene of death and destruction.

The next day, when the company passed an inhabited village, the residents lined the road in a jostling crowd, cheering wildly. Sincerely grateful to the soldiers for the protection they might afford, some villagers tossed garlands of flowers on the officers, while others trotted alongside the column with water jugs and food, passing them among the men.

During midmorning of the third day after the company left Pandu Ghat, a volley of rifle fire rang out in the trees on the right flank of the elephants. The dacoits had struck, and pandemonium erupted. The elephants trumpeted shrilly, and the servants at the rear screamed in panic.

The soldiers on the right flank immediately returned the fire, supported by those on the left flank. Subadar Birbal roared orders. "Jemadar Kamsing, get the baggage train back into the trees and have the mahouts kneel the elephants! Mrs. Cochrane, please take your family into the trees! All platoons, follow me and fire at will!"

As Edward pulled his Winchester from the saddle scabbard, he glanced back at Ramedha and Mathilda. They were running into the trees with the children. Edward worked the lever on his rifle and ran toward the trees with the subadar, the soldiers following them and firing at the puffs of smoke in the trees.

The momentary confusion changed into a rapid, orderly withdrawal off the road. As the gunfire from the trees continued, Edward recognized the characteristic report of muzzle-loaded rifles. A soldier beside him jerked and pitched forward, wounded, and he saw another soldier fall. "More dacoits must be joining those who fired the first volley," he said to the subadar.

"More are," the officer confirmed over the roar of the gunfire. "They expected the first volley to make the elephants flee in panic, and most of the dacoits were waiting to chase them down and snatch the baggage."

The first and second platoons ran across the road to take up positions, dragging and carrying those who were wounded. Farther back in the forest, the elephants were huddled together on the ground, protesting with piercing shrieks. Jemadar Kamsing had organized the bearers and sweepers to build hastily a breastwork of logs and limbs to protect them and the elephants. The subadar shouted orders, and the soldiers moved back through the trees toward the makeshift stockade.

Bullets thudded into the logs as Edward leaped over them, looking around for the Cochranes. Ramedha and Mathilda were attending to wounded soldiers, while the children's nurse was sitting with the boys behind a large tree. Seventeen soldiers had been wounded, none seriously, and two of the elephants were shrieking in fright and pain as their mahouts dug bullets out of their thick, wrinkled hides.

Listening to the gunfire from the other side of the road, the officers estimated there were fifty to sixty dacoits.

"What do you think they'll do next?" Edward asked.

"Until darkness, probably nothing," Birbal replied, peering through a crack in the logs at the enemy position. "Then they may close in and send a number of men around to the other side of us."

"Perhaps we should have the bearers and sweepers cut down trees to build a stockade all around our position," Kamsing suggested. "The protection of the major's family and the baggage train is our primary consideration now, and we can deal with dacoits at another time."

The other officers fell silent, considering the suggestion, but Edward spoke. "If we set up a fully defensible position," he pointed out, "they may withdraw, but they'll probably attack us again farther along the road. I believe we should deal with them here and now."

Birbal agreed. "One should never relinquish the initiative to the enemy." He turned to Kamsing. "Take the first platoon around behind them, and I'll send another platoon to cover their flanks. I will lead the remainder of the men in a frontal assault and blow my whistle as the signal to cease fire, close in, and use bayonets."

As the jemadar turned away, Edward told Birbal that he would accompany Kamsing. "Please be careful, Mr. Blackstone," Birbal warned. "That will be an extremely dangerous position when we close in."

Edward checked his weapons as he moved away. Ramedha

frowned worriedly when she saw Edward leaving with the soldiers. He smiled reassuringly and winked at her, and she forced a wan smile.

When Edward, the jemadar, and the soldiers were deep in the forest, they turned to the left in a wide circle that would take them to the rear of the dacoits. Some two hundred yards from where the company had been attacked, the jemadar lifted a hand for absolute silence as the gunfire became louder through the trees ahead. A few minutes later, Edward glimpsed the ragged, bearded dacoits kneeling in clusters in the foliage, firing and reloading. Kamsing motioned the men into a line, pointing out trees for them to shelter behind. When they were in position, Edward took aim with his Winchester.

He squeezed the trigger, and a dacoit lurched and sprawled to one side. Other dacoits fell, as the jemadar and the soldiers and Edward fired with deadly effect. When the ragged men scrambled for cover, Edward aimed and fired rapidly at the moving forms.

Bullets thudded into the trees around Edward and the soldiers as the dacoits spread farther apart and fired back. As soldiers moved in on the dacoits' flanks, gunfire broke out on both sides of the enemy. Stray bullets clipped branches from the trees around Edward and the soldiers.

Kamsing drew his sword and shouted over the gunfire, "Fix bayonets! Fix bayonets!"

The soldiers unsheathed their long, gleaming bayonets and fitted them over their rifle muzzles, and Edward loosened his sword. The gunfire became a steady, battering roar, and the dacoits darted about in panic. The dense gunpowder smoke made them seem like shadowy wraiths. With dozens of bodies strewn around, the remainder of the dacoits crowded into a dense stand of trees.

A whistle shrilled over the uproar, and Jemadar Kamsing lifted his sword and shouted at the top of his voice, "Cease fire! Cease fire! Charge! Charge!"

Drawing his sword, Edward leaped up and ran forward beside the officer, the line of soldiers racing through the trees on each side of them. A roar of whoops rang out as the main body of the company burst through the trees toward the enemy.

The swords and bayonets were a bristling mass of deadly, gleaming steel. As they charged into the dacoits, the disorganized, confused enemy reeled out of the trees, trying to flee in all directions.

Some thirty bandits ran toward Edward and the soldiers on each side of them, the other soldiers hot on their heels. The thin line of the first platoon stood between them and escape. Edward and the soldiers began swinging their swords as they clashed with the ragged, grimy mob.

The first platoon was forced back, then it stood fast, battling furiously. Edward saw one dacoit raise his rifle and point it at the jemadar. Edward shouted in warning, but the rifle fired and Kamsing fell, shot through the heart. Enraged, Edward leaped forward and slashed his sword across the dacoit's neck, decapitating him.

The melee lasted for several minutes, with soldiers and dacoits struggling around Edward as he dodged rifle butts. Then it was suddenly over. The ground was a mass of bodies, and the soldiers looked around numbly as blood dripped from their bayonets.

A moment later, the officers organized the soldiers to carry their dead and wounded to the road. After wiping and sheathing his sword, Edward waved aside two soldiers who were picking up Kamsing's body, and he gathered it up in his arms. As he went toward the road, Ramedha came dashing through the trees, glancing around in fright. Her smile of relief upon seeing Edward faded as she looked at Kamsing's body. Edward put the young officer's body down beside others. Birbal stepped over, one sleeve of his tunic bloody from a wound on his shoulder.

"Jemadar Kamsing was a good soldier and a good officer," he commented sadly, looking at the body. "We will all miss him very much." He sighed. "When we find out where the dacoits have their base of operations, we will put an end to them once and for all."

"I want to be there when that happens," Edward said quietly.

Birbal nodded in understanding. "I'm sure that Major

Cochrane will be more than pleased to have you there, Mr. Blackstone. Although you wear civilian clothes, you are an excellent soldier."

The subadar walked away, calling out orders to soldiers, and Edward looked down at the young officer's body once more. Edward had been enraged when he first saw the death and destruction the dacoits had wreaked among the villages. Now, with Kamsing's death, the dacoits were his personal enemy. He put aside all thoughts of leaving India until the reign of terror was ended.

X

Their spurs jangled against the floor as Toby Holt and Rob Martin stepped into the dim, cluttered hardware store in Folsom, with Billy Collier following. The portly, amiable proprietor looked up from a newspaper on the counter and peered at them over his spectacles. "Howdy, gents," he greeted, smiling affably. "Your barbed wire got here yesterday, Mr. Holt. It's in my storage shed, out behind the store."

"I'm much obliged to you for receiving it from the shipper, Mr. Sands. How much do I owe you for your trouble?"

"No charge, Mr. Holt," Sands replied firmly. "I'm glad to do something for you, considering that you're risking life and limb trying to settle this trouble we're having here."

"No, I must pay you for handling the wire," Toby insisted. "This is just the first of several shipments I'm expecting, and I wouldn't feel right unless I pay you for your time and trouble."

Taking off his spectacles, the man said, "We'll call it five dollars, then, Mr. Holt." He pointed to the newspaper. "I was just reading the interview you had with Percival Sloat. Have you read it yet?"

"Yes," Toby replied, taking out his wallet. "One of the reasons I came to town was to have a talk with Sloat. I didn't know I was being interviewed when I stopped by his office, and I certainly didn't say some of the things he attributes to me."

"I didn't think it sounded like you," Sands commented.

"For instance, when he quotes you as saying that you'll kill anyone who offers you trouble, I figured Sloat was exaggerating." He accepted five dollars from Toby. "I hope that interview doesn't cause you trouble with hotheads and gunslingers."

"I plan on it causing some trouble for Sloat," Toby observed. "You sell ammunition?"

"A little," the man replied. "The general store next door has a much better stock."

"Yes, I've talked to the owner there. I'm looking for Big Fifty ammunition."

Sands blinked, then laughed. "There aren't any buffalo to speak of in Oklahoma. But it's funny you should ask, because I used to have a box of Big Fifty ammunition. I sold it a while back."

"Who bought it?" Toby asked.

"Why, it was Percival Sloat," Sands replied.

Toby exchanged a glance with Rob. The man with the long-range rifle was definitely not the newspaper owner, but he could have been hired by Sloat. Why would Sloat want him killed? Toby wondered.

He asked Rob to take the wire to the ranch. "I want to talk with the marshal and with Sloat. I'll be here for a while, but I'll give you a hand unloading that when I get back."

"Billy and I will see to it," Rob replied firmly. "But you be careful, Toby, particularly at open spaces on the road. Whoever is gunning for you is still around."

With Billy emphatically echoing the warning, Toby nodded, turned away, and walked toward the newspaper office. The violent atmosphere was pointed up by a man coming along the boardwalk toward Toby. He was a tall, rangy man with saturnine features and the blank, lifeless eyes of an experienced killer. When he was a few yards away, he hesitated for an instant, looking as though he was going to challenge Toby. Toby moved his hand closer to his six-shooter, and the man apparently changed his mind, for he resumed walking and brushed past. Toby relaxed as he continued making his way along the boardwalk to the newspaper office.

Percival Sloat, a lanky man of forty with sharp features and an air of superiority, stood behind his desk as Toby came into the office. "Well, well, it's Mr. Toby Holt—" he chuckled

"—the hero who's going to end the trouble and protect everybody. What may I do for you today?"

"You can explain these lies," Toby replied, slapping his newspaper on the counter.

"Lies?" Sloat echoed in innocence. "I printed what I understood you to say."

"Most of what you printed isn't true," Toby retorted angrily. "We both know that, so there's no point in pretending otherwise. I want to know why you did it."

"If you think I've libeled you, by all means hire a lawyer," Sloat urged as he started to turn away from the counter.

Toby reached across the counter and seized the front of the man's shirt. He dragged Sloat up onto the counter and glared into his eyes. "If you print another word about me in that rag you call a newspaper, I'll beat you to a pulp. Do you understand?"

Stark fear rippled across his face. "Turn me loose!" he demanded, tugging at Toby's hands. "You've got no right to come into my office and—"

"And you have no right to operate this newspaper just to serve your own interests. I asked you if you understand me, Sloat! Now answer me."

"Yes! Yes!" Sloat shouted. "I understand."

Toby shoved Sloat across the counter, where he lost his footing and slammed against his desk.

"I hear that you have a Big Fifty, Sloat. Where is it?" Toby demanded.

The man, straightening his shirt and tucking it back into his trousers, suddenly became wary. "I sold it. To a man I never saw before or since. Now that's all I have to say about it."

Sloat was clearly lying. For a moment Toby stared at the other man, then turned and left the office. Crossing the street, he went to the marshal's office.

Joshua Hubbard greeted Toby coolly.

"What in tarnation did you tell Sloat?" Hubbard asked angrily. "Threatening to kill people won't make my job any easier."

"I never said that, Marshal," Toby assured him. "I just came from setting him straight."

"Glad to hear it," Hubbard said, shaking Toby's hand and pulling out a chair. "Take a load off."

Toby told Hubbard about his limited success, that a number of ranchers and homesteaders had agreed to let him deal with the friction among them. The marshal considered that remarkable, but Toby was less than satisfied.

"I still have no idea of who's behind the trouble here," he complained. "And his motive is a complete mystery to me."

He told the marshal about the heavy rifle Sloat had owned. "He isn't the one shooting at me, and I don't know why he might want to hire someone to kill me."

"I don't either," Hubbard mused. "But maybe he was telling the truth. And there could be more than one Big Fifty around here."

"Maybe," Toby said, then left to attend to other errands. Crossing the street, he entered the saloon where he had first met the girl who called herself Pearlie. Sensing that the life of a saloon girl was not for her, he had talked with her several times since then, hoping to encourage her to return home. Her real name was Rachel Gibbs, and she had run away from home, in Kansas, to escape her father's wrath after he caught her in an indiscretion with a boy from a neighboring farm. Toby guessed that her father now regretted his anger and wanted her back, but he had been unable to convince Pearlie of that.

As he entered the saloon, Toby saw that Pearlie was caught in one of the innumerable degrading situations that he had warned her about. A drunken young cowboy was holding her on his lap at a table and fondling her, while Pearlie protested and tried to escape his tight grip. Some patrons ignored it; others watched in amusement. A few disliked what was happening, but none wanted to confront the muscular young cowboy.

Stepping up to the table, Toby grasped the cowboy's wrists and pulled his hands away from Pearlie. "Turn the lady loose, son," he said.

Flashing Toby a grateful smile, Pearlie wriggled away and fled toward the bar as the cowboy leaped to his feet, his face flushed with anger. "I'm not your son!"

"No, you're not," Toby agreed, laughing. "If you were, I'd take my belt to your butt. Now sit down and drink your—"

He broke off when the cowboy reached for his pistol. As the six-gun cleared the holster, Toby gripped it, placing his thumb over the hammer to prevent it from firing. With a quick twist, he jerked the weapon out of the young man's hand, then rapped him on the forehead with the grip. The cowboy slumped to the floor, knocking over his chair with a clatter.

"Does this lad have any friends in here?" Toby asked, glancing around.

"He works at the ranch where I do," an older man at a nearby table replied. "He's a good kid but can be hard to handle when he has a skinful of popskull."

"I've noticed," Toby commented, handing the pistol to the man. "It might be a good idea to get him out of town before he gets himself into serious trouble."

The man pulled the cowboy to his feet and helped him toward the door, and Toby stepped to the bar, where Pearlie thanked him.

"I was glad to do it, Pearlie," Toby said as the bartender put his usual glass of beer in front of him. "But you know that worse is going to happen, and no one will be around to help you. Write to your dad and go home."

Pearlie shook her head emphatically. "After what he said to me, I never want to see him again."

"You did wrong, Pearlie," Toby said firmly, "and now it's up to you to apologize. Nothing hurts a parent more than being disappointed by their child. If you offer to make peace, I'm sure your father will apologize for what he said and take you back. That's where you belong, not here."

The girl looked down at the floor. She didn't disagree but was obviously feeling reluctant. Toby liked her proud, independent spirit, but that same nature was keeping her from doing what was right.

Their conversation was interrupted by a loud voice at the rear of the saloon. "You've shown that you can deal with boys, Holt, but can you deal with a man? I'm saying that you can't."

As Toby turned, he stared death in the face. The man standing across the saloon was the one Toby had noticed while going to see Sloat. He realized that the man had indeed been on the point of challenging him but decided that the time and place were wrong. Now the man had been quietly waiting to see if Toby would drink enough to slow his reflexes.

This man had the look of an experienced, professional killer: His pistol was in a well-oiled cutaway holster, devoid of boastful notches, and he was thirty feet away, a skilled professional's distance. Accuracy at thirty feet required cool determination and a steady hand.

"I'm not looking for trouble," Toby said.

"I'm calling you a coward, Holt," the man challenged coldly, flexing the fingers of his right hand over his pistol. "I'm saying that you can't deal with a man, and I'm going to prove it."

His hand poised over his pistol. Toby faced the killer squarely. "Go ahead and make your move," he said quietly.

There was a sudden scramble as men dived out of the path between Toby and the gunslinger. Then absolute silence settled for some seconds.

As the man's hand darted down, Toby reached for his own pistol, knowing that he had to shoot to kill: The gunslinger would continue firing if only wounded. Ignoring the deadly gleam of the man's six-gun flashing up toward him, Toby pulled the hammer back as he lifted his pistol at arm's length.

Aiming for the man's heart, Toby pulled the trigger. He shot a bare instant sooner than the other man, and the report of his pistol faded into the boom of the enemy's six-gun. Toby's bullet had ripped into the other man's heart, throwing him backward and spoiling his aim, and the bullet brushed Toby's left ear.

The saloon was a mass of sudden movement as men crowded around to look at the corpse on the floor. Toby remained poised for action, in case the man had any friends who were going to take up the challenge. Seeing none, he crossed the saloon toward the dead man.

"I read in the newspaper where you said that you'd kill anyone who offered to give you any trouble," a man commented.

"You saw what happened here," Toby replied angrily, "but what Sloat printed in his newspaper was a lie."

No one wanted to argue with Toby. He was grimly resigned to the fact that the newspaper article would inevitably cause trouble, which was the last thing he needed.

The marshal rushed in, drawn by the sound of gunfire. When he saw that Toby had been involved, he relaxed, dismissing the matter. He looked at the body of the dead man. "Does anybody here know who he was?"

The bartender spoke up. "He's been hanging around here for a few days, broke and looking for a job. He's been sleeping in the stable and filling up on my free lunch counter."

The marshal bent over the body. "Let's see if he has any identification." After taking a wallet from the dead man's pocket, Hubbard straightened up and poured money into his hand. "He's broke, you say?" he asked the bartender.

Along with small change, five gold double eagles sat in the marshal's palm. The bartender shrugged, but Toby knew where the man had got the coins: Someone had paid the gunslinger to kill him.

At sunset on the fifth day after leaving the railhead, Henry Blake was a few miles from Fort Abercrombie. His saddle horse and the two packhorses loaded down with his baggage were dusty and streaked with sweat, and Henry was grimy from the long, hard ride. Instead of continuing on to the fort, he made camp in a cottonwood thicket beside the Red River, hobbling the horses to graze in nearby lush, thick grass.

By midmorning the next day, Henry had finished breakfast, groomed the horses until they gleamed in the autumn sunlight, and cleaned up his tack, polishing each piece of brass until it glittered. Then he shaved, took out a clean, new cavalry uniform, and shined his knee boots. When he finally rode out of the trees, he was as immaculately neat as he had ever been for parades at West Point.

The region was one of beautiful, rolling hills set back on each side of the river—rich farmland but mostly unsettled. The crops had been gathered at the neat, isolated farms, where people were preparing for a tranquil winter, but Henry's first glimpse of Fort Abercrombie was discouraging.

He had known all along that it was a small, backwater post where a single company of cavalry and a few other personnel were stationed. Some twenty miles south of Fargo, it had been established as a staging point for cavalry deployed to quell Indian unrest of years before. It had been maintained as an active fort by the recent discovery of gold in the Black Hills, but it revealed years of neglect.

Its palisade walls were crumbling, and through the open gate, Henry saw that the quadrangle was covered with weeds. The soldiers assigned to a wood-gathering detail on a nearby hill were lying about on the grass, while the two sentries at the gate were laughing and talking together.

The sentries fell silent, appearing to view Henry as an apparition from a magazine illustration of a cavalry officer, when he rode up the road to the fort. One suddenly snapped to attention; the other followed. Henry reined up at the gate, and the sentries presented arms.

He touched a gloved hand to his hat brim. Eyeing their unbuttoned tunics, he ordered, "Button your uniforms." As they hastily fastened their buttons, he said, "If I ever see either of you talking on guard post again, you'll spend a week in confinement on bread and water. And you should be on each side of the gate, not standing together."

One of the men quickly stepped to the other side of the gate, and both stood rigidly at attention as Henry rode into the fort. The buildings around the quadrangle were in the same poor condition as the walls. Men peered at Henry from the barracks windows as he crossed the quadrangle and reined up in front of the headquarters building.

A clerk at the desk in the outer office, wearing a sweater instead of a uniform tunic, gazed at Henry in shock for a full second, then leaped up and stood at attention, his chair falling over. "Tell the first sergeant to report to me," Henry ordered.

The man snatched up a hat and dashed out the door. Then the inner office door opened, and a second lieutenant stepped out, wearing a civilian jacket with his insignia on it and a nonregulation white shirt and cravat. He looked at Henry in surprise, then smiled and offered his hand.

"I'm Harv Watson, sir," he said, "and you certainly don't look like you've just arrived after a long trip. I'm very glad you're here, because I've been serving as interim commander, and it's been more than I . . ." Seeing Henry's cold glare, the man's voice and smile faded.

"I can't hear you when you're out of uniform, mister," Henry said in a soft, icy voice. "The reason the clerk is out of uniform is because you are. Now go to your quarters and get into uniform."

The man flushed. "Well, after all, sir," he stammered, "this is a frontier post, and surely some latitude in—"

"I said I can't hear you when you're out of uniform," Henry cut in. "And it's just as well that I can't because if I ever get the idea that you're arguing with an order, the drill masters at West Point will seem like Sunday school teachers when I'm through with you."

His face and neck crimson, Watson took his hat and hurried out. Henry stepped around the desk and set the chair upright, then glanced over the papers on the desk. He heard footsteps on the porch, and then a master sergeant entered the office. He stopped, stiffly at attention, and saluted.

"Sergeant Olsen reporting as ordered, sir!" he barked.

Returning the salute, Henry looked the man over. He was a small, wiry man in his late forties, and his lips and drooping mustache were stained with tobacco juice. He was wearing a faded but neat, clean uniform. "How long have you been here, Sergeant Olsen?"

"About a month now, sir."

"This fort doesn't look like it would withstand a hard rain, much less an attack. What have you been doing?"

"As best I could, sir," Olsen replied woodenly. "Mostly I've been hoping that the officer who comes here to take command of the fort will be a soldier." His eyes moved up and down Henry, then gazed into the distance again. "And I guess he is," he finished.

Henry laughed as he nodded. "Yes, I am. Stand at ease and give me your opinion of the men, Sergeant."

The man folded his hands behind his back. "Most are

recruits or castoffs from other outfits, sir. Maybe they could be soldiers, but they sure ain't now. Two are in jail in town for being drunk, and the sheriff wants ten dollars a head to turn them loose. The men gripe about everything, but they have a right to complain about the food. What they're being fed ain't fit for a hog to eat."

Henry stepped toward the door. "All right, let's begin with the mess hall, Sergeant Olsen."

The sergeant followed Henry across the quadrangle to the mess hall, a long, low building beside the barracks. The cook, a private who was flushed and sweaty from the heat of his stove, was starting to prepare salt pork and hardtack for the next meal. The meat was rancid, and the hardtack was infested with weevils.

"It's what the commissary issued to me, sir," the cook explained defensively, "and he issued me this batch just this morning."

"Very well. Put it all into the original containers to turn back in to the commissary."

The cook began gathering the food as Henry and the sergeant left to go to the commissary building. Olsen told Henry that a civilian named Scanlan was in charge of provisioning the fort. Inside the commissary was a small, hand-lettered sign on the door advertising whiskey at ten cents a shot.

Henry plucked the sign off the door as he went inside, then handed it to the big-boned, craggy-faced man behind the counter. "I'm Captain Blake, the new commander here, Mr. Scanlan. Until further notice, there'll be no more whiskey sales at this fort."

"But what's wrong with selling a little whiskey?" the man demanded hotly. "I make a few dollars from it, and the soldiers—"

"Don't question my orders, Mr. Scanlan," Henry advised quietly. "If I want a discussion, I'll ask for it. When I give an order, I expect compliance. Do you understand?"

The man's belligerence suddenly faded under the compelling force of Henry's calm, authoritative attitude. "Well, now, I didn't mean to question your orders, Captain Blake. No, sir, I sure didn't mean to do that."

"Very well. Open a can of your hardtack."

The man started to ask why but changed his mind and stepped into another room. He returned with a large can of hardtack, which he placed on the counter and opened. Henry reached into it and picked up a piece with a weevil wriggling on it, then regarded Scanlan in silence.

The man cleared his throat. "Well, now, that can might be a little old," he muttered, "but it's what I was issued when I went to my depot at Fort Selby."

Henry dropped the hardtack back into the can. "Then I want you to take all of your stock back to the depot and draw a fresh issue."

"I might have a problem doing that, sir. I have to follow my depot officer's orders too, you know."

"Yes, I know," Henry replied. "When you go there, tell him that I can arrange for the senior officers in the commissary department to have dinner in Washington." He tapped the can. "And this is what they'll be served. Ask your depot officer to pass that on up the line. I think he'll find some good rations for you."

"Probably," Scanlan agreed quickly. "Well, I'll haul my stock back down there, sir, but I'll need some help loading everything up. It usually takes me three days to make a round trip, and the fort will be without provisions during that time."

"I'll see to the provisions during those three days, and to the help you'll need, Mr. Scanlan."

Then Henry left, with the sergeant following. Lieutenant Watson, waiting outside in regulation uniform, stood stiffly at attention and saluted as Henry stepped out. Henry returned the salute and took off a glove, introducing himself as he offered his hand. Watson responded likewise, and then he and the sergeant followed as Henry returned to the headquarters building.

Henry told Watson and Olsen to assemble the men in the quadrangle. "After I talk to them," he said, taking twenty dollars from his wallet and handing it to the sergeant, "give that to the cook and send him and two men to buy a couple of large hogs and fresh vegetables from the nearest farm. That should be enough food for three days."

"Yes, sir," the sergeant said, brightening, "more than enough. You want me to send some men to help the commissary load up his stock, sir?"

"Yes, and have three horses saddled for me. I'll ride to Fargo and get those two men out of jail. Divide the men who aren't on details into squads and have them foot drill on the quadrangle."

"Yes, sir. How long do you want them to drill, sir?"

"Until dark, then for ten hours each day until those weeds are worn down. After that, we'll begin on mounted drill, small-arms training, and rebuilding the fort. Lieutenant Watson, have you met the Mennonites who have farms in the area?"

"Yes, sir," Watson replied. "All of their farms are a few miles north of Fargo, and I rode up there one day. The only one who can speak English is a man named Klaus Lukenbill, who isn't a Mennonite. He acts as their go-between for dealing with merchants and so forth, because they never go to town. In my opinion, Lukenbill is an opportunist who's cheating those people."

"After I get the men out of jail, I'll ride up there and see what I can do to help them. Assemble the men."

The lieutenant and the sergeant saluted, then marched out. A moment later, Henry heard the bugler sounding assembly. He waited for a few more minutes.

The men were in four long ranks, with Olsen and Watson standing at attention in front of them. The lieutenant saluted as Henry came out of the headquarters building. "All present or accounted for, sir."

Henry returned the salute, then surveyed the men. He reflected that Olsen's description had been accurate. A high proportion of them were very young, and several were slovenly, older privates. Three were deliberately slouching. Henry stared at them in turn until each straightened up. Then he began speaking.

"I am a soldier," he said, "as you will be. You have various reasons for dissatisfaction, which I intend to correct. You have no self-respect, but once you are soldiers, you will be proud of yourselves. A bad attitude makes the process of becoming a soldier very unpleasant, but with a good attitude you will accept it in stride. Until further notice all personnel, with the exception of special details, will be restricted to the immediate area of the fort."

A mutter passed through the ranks, then faded as Henry glanced over the men. After exchanging another salute with the lieutenant, Henry turned away, leaving Olsen to call out the men for the work details. Henry led his horses to his quarters, in the building adjacent to the headquarters, and carried in his baggage. Matching the rest of the fort, his quarters consisted of two small, drab rooms provided with a few sticks of old, battered furniture.

After stacking his baggage in the bedroom to sort out later, Henry opened a case. He took out his pictures of Gisela and their son, Peter, and put them on the table in the sitting room, then went back outside. A soldier had brought three saddled horses, and as the foot drill began in the quadrangle, Henry mounted and rode through the gate, leading the two extra horses.

The pleasant countryside made Fargo seem even more squalid to Henry. A sprawling shantytown larger than the town itself lined the river. Drunks and ragged loiterers wandered along the main street, where saloons were doing a booming business. The hotels were, in fact, brothels, and women leaned out the windows, exchanging ribald remarks with men on the street.

The general stores and similar businesses were on the quieter side streets. The sheriff's office was at the end of the main street, and Henry dismounted there, tied up the horses, and went inside. He took an immediate dislike to the sheriff. He was a large, muscular man who had become paunchy. His coarse features were splotched with broken veins, and he had an overbearing attitude.

"I'm Sheriff Slattery," he said after Henry introduced himself. "I guess you want them two soldiers out of jail, do you?"

"That's right."

"Well, it's going to cost you ten dollars each," he growled belligerently, "and they won't leave here until the money is paid." He sat back, watching as Henry silently took out his wallet and put the money on the desk. "Ain't you got no questions about their fine or anything?" he asked.

"No, I haven't," Henry told him evenly. "If drunkenness were an offense here, you could fill this jail to overflowing without reaching the end of the block. So it's perfectly obvious that you're using those soldiers to put twenty dollars in your pocket."

The man guffawed appreciatively as he stood and scooped up the money. After pocketing it, he took out a key and went through the cell-block door. He led the soldiers out a moment later.

Both well built and in their late teens, they looked to be among the more promising of the men at the fort. They stood stiffly at attention, embarrassed and apprehensive as they muttered apologies. Henry nodded. "Take the roan and the bay that are outside, and go back to the fort," he said. "Tell Sergeant Olsen that you're volunteering for a week on stable detail."

The two men agreed eagerly, saluted, then hurried out. Pulling on his gloves, Henry turned to follow them. Slattery sat down behind his desk, tilting his chair back against the wall as he chuckled. "You're quite the little soldier boy, ain't you?" he commented.

In three long, quick steps, Henry was behind the desk. Hooking a toe under a leg of the chair, he jerked it out from under Slattery. The man squealed in surprise as he landed heavily on the floor.

"I'm not any sort of boy, Slattery," Henry said softly, standing with his booted foot in the center of the sheriff's chest. "I'm an officer in the United States Army, and I am a man."

His eyes sliding away from Henry's glare, Slattery tried to smile. "I didn't mean nothing by that," he stammered. "I was just making a passing remark, and I don't want no trouble with you."

"No, you don't," Henry agreed quietly. "The last thing in the world you want is trouble with me."

Henry turned and left the office. He dismissed his anger as he rode out of Fargo to the north, toward the Mennonite farms.

The farms were virtually identical: The houses were built in the same neat and comfortable if austere pattern, with outbuildings that were also similar. These were wheat farmers, and each house was surrounded by hundreds of acres of stubble where the grain had been reaped.

Henry knew that the Mennonites refused to use modern mechanical devices. As expected, the stubble in the fields was slightly uneven, having been cut by hand with a scythe. At the edge of one field he found a stalk of wheat still standing. The grain had a reddish tinge, and it was huge in comparison to any he had ever seen.

Henry stopped at two farms but found no one at home; then he saw a crowd at another farm where a barn was being raised. As he rode toward them, he saw that their clothing was as similar as their farms. The women wore dark, plain dresses and bonnets that completely covered their hair, while the men were dressed in black trousers and wide, flat-brimmed hats. Henry noticed a number of black, old-fashioned frock coats laying on a trestle table.

One man was conspicuously different from the others, both in his clothing and in what he was doing. Wearing a checkered wool suit, he was sitting at a trestle table and eating food the women were putting out while the other men labored. Recalling what Watson had said, Henry concluded that the man was Klaus Lukenbill.

The people stopped working as Henry rode up. He touched his hat and nodded to the women, then turned to the men. "I am Captain Heinrich Blake," he said in German. "Are any of the elders of the congregation present?"

A white-haired but brawny, active man of about sixty stepped forward. He eyed Henry suspiciously. "I am Ludwig Zimmerman, the senior elder. Why have you come here?"

"To see if I or my men can be of assistance," Henry replied. "I am the commander of Fort Abercrombie."

The man at the table stood and also stepped forward. He had small, alert eyes and a patronizing smile as he spoke in English. "You need to talk to me, Henry. I'm Klaus Lukenbill, these people's agent. I take care of their business affairs."

"Please address me as Captain Blake, Mr. Lukenbill," Henry said in German, "and speak in German so everyone

can understand what we say. Why should I talk to you in
order to offer assistance to them?"

The man's smile changed to an annoyed frown. "As I told
you, I am these people's business agent, and I attend to all
matters between them and others."

"If they wish to have you as their business agent," Henry
said, "that is their concern. And if they wish to have my help
or advice on any matter, including business, that is also their
concern." He turned back to Zimmerman. "My men and I
stand ready to help you in any way we can."

The old man shook his head brusquely. "We need no
help from Prussian military officers."

"I learned to speak German among Prussians, but as you
can see from my uniform, I am an American military officer.
If your people would like a military escort when they go to
Fargo, I will provide it. Also, I can serve as translator for
your people to talk with the tradesmen in the town."

Many of the people exchanged glances. Lukenbill looked
alarmed, but he relaxed as Zimmerman shook his head once
again. "We rarely go to the town," he said, "and when we do,
Mr. Lukenbill speaks for us. And," he insisted stubbornly,
"you act like a Prussian military officer as well as sounding
like one."

Lukenbill laughed. "You see, *Captain* Blake? Like I
said, you should have talked to me."

It occurred to Henry that Lukenbill might have fabri-
cated stories to influence the Mennonites against accepting
help from anyone. "Very well," he said, glancing around at all
of the people as he turned his horse away. "If anyone wishes
to talk to me, I will be at Fort Abercrombie."

It was midafternoon when Henry returned to the fort.
The men were still marching about the quadrangle. Henry
busied himself going through the recent fort correspondence,
all routine, then began cleaning up his quarters and putting
away his belongings as the men continued marching until
dinner. After dinner, they resumed marching until nightfall.

When his quarters were clean, Henry wrote a long letter
to Gisela. At midnight he put on his hat and tunic and walked
to the headquarters building, where the duty sergeant was
dozing behind the clerk's desk. As the man leaped to his feet

Henry said, "Tell the sentries to light the carbide lamps at the gate and turn them toward the quadrangle. Have the bugler blow assembly."

The sergeant saluted and dashed out. A moment later, the bright glare of the carbide lamps shone through the door, then the blare of the bugle shattered the stillness. An outburst of sleepy oaths erupted from the barracks, while Henry glanced at his watch and lighted a cigar. When the footsteps of men running out of the barracks stopped, Henry stepped out onto the porch. The men were half-dressed and sagging on their feet after marching most of the day, and Watson was rumpled and sleepy. "All present or accounted for, sir," he reported, saluting.

Henry returned the salute, then looked at his watch. "It took the men almost seventeen minutes to assemble, Lieutenant Watson," he mused. "They would require thirty minutes or longer for Boots and Saddles. That's far too long. Please instruct the men on how to place their uniforms and equipment so they can dress and be out of the barracks more rapidly."

"Yes, sir."

After exchanging another salute with the lieutenant, Henry went to his quarters. He hung up his hat and tunic, then sat down and smoked his cigar, listening as Watson lectured the men. Presently, the lieutenant dismissed the men, and the carbide lamps were extinguished.

Henry put out his cigar, went to his bedroom, and took off his boots. Looking at his watch in the dim light, he decided to sleep for about three hours before ordering the men to assemble again.

A week after arriving at the fort, Henry was returning to his quarters during the early evening when he saw a soldier lurking in the darkness at the corner of the building. He had been expecting something of the sort, because the men who would be led were falling into line, while those who had to be driven were near the breaking point.

Swinging a heavy piece of wood at Henry's head, the soldier leaped out of the darkness. Dodging the club, Henry gripped the man's arm and pulled him off balance, then drove a fist into his stomach. The man dropped the club and doubled over. Henry shoved him back against the building, gripped his hair, then knocked the back of his head soundly against the thick logs.

As the man sagged, Henry pushed him upright against the building. Watson's door opened, and the lieutenant, in stocking feet and long underwear, looked out. "Is everything all right, sir?" He peered at the man beside Henry.

"Yes," Henry replied. "I'm just talking with"—he struck a match and looked at the man in its light—"Private Innes."

The lieutenant nodded, then closed the door. The brawny private groaned in pain and breathed rapidly.

"You know," Henry remarked conversationally, tossing the match away, "it's frightening to think that I might have to depend upon someone like you to fight if we ever have trouble with Indians here. You couldn't whip a sick papoose, Innes."

"I can fight," the man grumbled, then added, "sir."

"After the demonstration we just had," Henry said dryly, "I'll rest my case." He took out a cigar and lit it, then thoughtfully studied its glowing tip. "Well, for assaulting an officer, I can put you in a military prison for ten years at hard labor. But if you would stop sulking and set your mind to becoming a soldier, we could forget this ever happened."

"I'll be a soldier, sir," Innes mumbled.

"All right. Dismissed."

The man saluted and hurried away. Henry was pleased that the incident had happened. Innes was a ringleader of the malcontents, and if he changed, the others would.

As Henry went to his quarters, he paused at Watson's door. While their first meeting had been unfavorable, he had since found the lieutenant to be a dedicated, efficient officer. Henry knocked on the door and invited Watson to his quarters for a drink. The lieutenant accepted eagerly. After pulling on his clothing and boots, he followed Henry to his quarters.

A wagon had arrived two days before, loaded down with cases of wine and liquor, delicacies, and furnishings that Gisela had sent. With Persian rugs on the floor, paintings on the walls, and ornate hardwood furniture, Henry's quarters had been transformed. Watson gaped and commented in wonder as he seated himself in a soft leather chair.

Henry poured brandy and gave Watson a cigar from a box, then sat as they discussed the affairs of the fort. The weeds of the quadrangle were now ground into dust, and the men had been practicing horseback maneuvers. Henry planned to begin small-arms training the next day.

For the most part, the men had accepted being restricted to the fort in better spirit than Henry had expected. Watson explained that the soldiers had been a favorite mark for the riffraff in town to beat and rob. "And for the sheriff to arrest," he added. "I don't know which is worse, the bums or the sheriff."

"The sheriff, I believe," Henry mused. "If he were an effective lawman, he would clean up the town. But that's a civil matter."

The lieutenant agreed, and the conversation moved on to other subjects. Having graduated from West Point only a few months before, Watson made a remark that startled Henry. "I heard quite a lot about you at the Point, sir. You're something of a living legend there."

Henry laughed heartily. "Don't be absurd, Watson."

"That isn't overstating it, sir," Watson insisted. "Everyone knows you were promoted to captain in an extraordinarily short time. It's said you know many officials in Washington and you've performed numerous important missions for them. It's also said you know many heads of state in Europe." He pointed to Gisela's picture, at which he had been glancing frequently. "And everyone knows about the baroness, of course. She's even more beautiful than I expected."

"Well, as usual," Henry commented in amusement, "the stories have apparently been improved upon with each retelling." Looking at the picture, he sobered. "But it would be impossible to exaggerate about Gisela."

A few minutes later, Watson finished his drink and left, expressing his thanks. As he prepared to go to bed, Henry thought again about what Watson had said and shook his head in amusement.

The next morning, a sergeant took one platoon of the soldiers to the rifle range with their Spencers while the rest of the company practiced cavalry maneuvers. Henry rode to the range and listened to the sergeant's lecture on the techniques of good marksmanship.

The sergeant opened a case of ammunition, then hesitated and turned to Henry. "Is there anything you want to add to what I said, sir?"

"No, you covered everything well," Henry replied. "Carry on with what you're doing, Sergeant."

As the sergeant began passing out the ammunition, someone among the men crowding together muttered a rejoinder to the exchange between Henry and the sergeant. "He probably ain't got nothing to say because he don't know which end of a rifle the bullet comes out."

The remark was followed by snickers. The sergeant started to bellow, but Henry shook his head to silence the sergeant, then pulled his Winchester out of the saddle scabbard as he dismounted. "Out of the way, men," he ordered. "Sergeant, find three small stones and throw them up into the air at the same time."

The men exchanged puzzled glances as the sergeant gathered up three stones. Henry loaded the firing chamber and nodded to the sergeant. The man heaved the stones into the air. Henry shouldered the Winchester.

As the stones reached the peak of their flight, he squeezed the trigger. The first disappeared in a puff of dust, and Henry worked the lever and followed a second stone in the sight. He squeezed the trigger again, and the stone exploded, then reloaded the firing chamber and shot the third one before it hit the ground.

The men gaped in awe as Henry replaced the rifle in the scabbard. "I don't expect you to shoot like that," he said, mounting his horse, "because over the years, I've probably put a ton of lead into the air while practicing. Also, I'm using a Winchester 1873, one of the finest rifles ever made. But I do expect you to be able to hit those targets, and the best marksman in each platoon will receive a quart of whiskey. Carry on, Sergeant."

The men exclaimed in delight. The sergeant grinned as he saluted. Henry returned the salute and rode toward the course where the men were practicing cavalry maneuvers.

Watson was sitting his horse, watching them. Henry informed the lieutenant that he was going to Fargo.

While in town at other times during the past week, Henry had spoken with the proprietors of several businesses and found out, as he expected, that Lukenbill had been cheating the Mennonites. The drayage company that had hauled the farmers' wheat to the railhead charged ten dollars a ton, but Lukenbill had demanded a bill from the company that showed twelve dollars a ton. At businesses where he made purchases for the Mennonites, Lukenbill had done the same thing.

Lukenbill was crafty, buying only in bulk, which obscured unit prices so the individual Mennonites would fail to notice the difference during their infrequent trips to town to make small purchases. A number of the merchants in Fargo, however, had refused to be a party to the scheme.

One was the owner of the fabric and notions store. "I could certainly use the business," she said, unfolding curtains Henry had ordered made for his quarters, "but I won't help that man cheat those good, honest farmers. The sooner they find out what he's doing, the happier I'm going to be."

"That won't be very long," Henry promised her. "As soon as I get all the facts together, I intend to talk to them." He looked at the curtains and smiled. "These are very nice."

"They are, even if I do say so myself," the woman agreed. "I put extra effort into them. It's a pleasure to do something for a man who cares about his surroundings. I'll wrap these so they won't get dusty on the ride back to the fort." She pulled a length of paper off a roll, then glanced at the front door and frowned. Although the store was on a street away from the saloons, a half-dozen drunks were staggering past, cursing and singing. "This town is getting worse every day," she complained bitterly. "The owners of the saloons and brothels pay Sheriff Slattery to let them operate unhindered, and it's getting to the point where decent people can't live here."

"Then the established citizens of the town should vote him out of office and elect a better sheriff."

"But we can't do that, Captain Blake," the woman explained sadly as she wrapped the curtains. "You see, the rabble that came here after gold was found vote for Sheriff Slattery, and there are more of them than us." She forced a smile. "Perhaps things will change in time."

"I'm sure they will," Henry said. He paid the woman, picked up the package, and left. After tying it behind his saddle, he rode south, looking at the drunks and grubby loiterers on each side of the street. He wanted a decent place for his men to go for relaxation after he ended their restriction to the fort.

When he was several miles out of Fargo, Henry heard a faint, distant commotion from the direction of the town. Reining up in front of a rise in the road, he listened closely. Along with the pounding of horses running toward him and the rattling of a wagon, several men were shouting. Then, hearing a woman scream, Henry wheeled his horse and touched his spurs to its flanks.

At the top of the rise, Henry used his spurs again, urging his horse into a headlong run. A Mennonite family was in the wagon, being chased by riffraff from the town. The woman, her clothing rumpled and torn, was driving the wagon, while the man lay in the back, where two children crouched in terror. The loiterers were having a hard time catching the wagon because a dozen of them were riding only four horses.

Henry guided his horse at a dead run between the horses behind the wagon. Then he drew his saber. Using the flat of the blade, he swung it toward the men on the horse to his right. The heavy blade struck the first man with a thud, peeling him and the others off the horse as though they had run into an invisible wall. With a backhand stroke to the left, Henry swept the men off a horse on that side.

Seeing the blade bearing down on them, the men on the other two horses tried to rein up. Henry whipped his saber to the right and left again. Men tumbled from the horses in a mass of bodies and flailing limbs. With the ragged, bearded men sprawling all over the road and the weary horses milling to one side, Henry wheeled his mount and spurred it toward two men who were drawing pistols.

As the men scrambled out of the path of the pounding hooves, Henry leaned to the right and slashed with measured force. The razor-sharp edge of the blade scored a deep cut on one man's right forearm, and he dropped his pistol. Leaning to the left toward the other man, Henry jabbed and drove the keen tip of the saber into the man's right shoulder. Howls of pain mixed with the chorus of oaths and angry bellows as Henry rode on through the men, then turned his horse and reined up.

"This ain't none of your business!" one of them roared furiously. "Your business is at that fort!"

"When a family is being chased by worthless scum, it's my business!" Henry retorted. "Now get back to town before I turn you into buzzard feed." He pointed his saber toward a man who was moving toward the horses. "Those horses have done enough for one day. You'll walk back to town."

"I ain't walking nowhere!" another man yelled angrily. "I ain't one of your soldiers, and you ain't going to tell me what to do."

Touching his spurs to his horse's flanks so it leaped forward, Henry leaned down and beat the man with the flat of his saber. The man bellowed in pain as he tried to escape the stinging blows. Henry then turned his attention to the others. All the men began running along the road, cursing viciously as they ducked the gleaming blade.

After sheathing his saber, Henry turned toward the wagon, which had stopped a short distance away. The woman was tending to her husband and calming her children. She began thanking Henry tearfully in German as he rode up to the wagon, but he dismissed her thanks, his gaze on the man. Battered and bloody from a severe beating, he was unconscious.

"We were at a store in the town," the woman explained, "and several men attacked us. I pulled Ernst into the wagon and drove away, but those with horses began chasing us. I drove out of town toward the fort, remembering what you said about helping us—" The woman cried in earnest now.

"It's finished," Henry said, patting her shoulder. "Follow me, and I'll have the medic examine your husband."

"But how can we get home?" the woman wailed. "Our farm is on the other side of the town."

"I'll see that you get home safely," Henry assured her. "Leave everything to me."

The woman nodded and climbed to the wagon seat.

Henry rode at a slow pace toward the fort, the wagon rattling along behind him.

By the time they reached the fort, the man had recovered consciousness. At the gate, Henry sent a sentry to get the lieutenant and the first sergeant, then led the wagon across the quadrangle to the dispensary. As the medic helped the injured man into the building, Watson and Olsen galloped up.

The two men flushed angrily as Henry described the incident. "That mustn't happen again, sir," Watson said. "Casual regard for law and order is one thing, but for a family to be attacked in a town in broad daylight is something else entirely."

Henry agreed. "Civil affairs are out of our hands, but we can provide escorts for the Mennonites, and this incident might change their senior elder's mind about accepting our help. Sergeant Olsen, pick a squad of our best men and have them saddle up."

The sergeant saluted and left, while Henry and Watson discussed the details. A few minutes later, Olsen returned with the men, all in neat, clean uniforms and mounted on groomed horses. The medic led the injured man, his head bandaged, out of the dispensary and helped him into the wagon as Henry and Watson assisted the woman and children. After mounting his horse, Henry led the men and the wagon out of the fort.

Henry knew that what happened on the road could cause animosity toward the fort among the shantytown rabble of Fargo. When he reached the town, ne'er-do-wells lined the street and glared resentfully at the squad. Obviously those he had driven back toward the town with his saber had spread the story. The loiterers did no more than glare, however, because instead of the rumpled soldiers who had straggled into town before, the squad was an organized, well-armed force, riding in neat files on each side of the wagon.

The squad also caused a stir of curiosity among others. Men stepped out of saloons to watch, and people looked out of windows. Down the street Henry saw the sheriff come out of his office and stand on the porch. Henry reined up there, lifting a hand to stop the squad and wagon.

"Sheriff," Henry said, "the family in the wagon was assaulted and chased out of town."

"That so?" the sheriff replied indifferently. "Well, I can't be everywhere at once. And when people won't fight even to protect theirselves, they've got to expect a little shoving around now and then."

"Their beliefs are their affair, and they have a right to come and go as they please. Do you want a description of the men who were trying to catch them?"

The sheriff smiled sardonically. "It wouldn't do no good. People arrive and leave here every day, and I wouldn't be able to find them." He laughed. "And I have more to do with my time than worry about people who won't fight to protect theirselves."

Barely controlling his anger, Henry turned his horse and rode on. The squad and wagon followed him, and the loiterers who had listened to the conversation laughed.

When they were on the road north of town, the woman in the wagon pointed out the way to Ludwig Zimmerman's farm. As they turned onto the lane leading to the house, Henry saw Lukenbill riding along a creek at the rear of the property. When he saw Henry, he quickly turned his horse toward the barns, obviously intending to defend his interests.

The white-haired man was working on a fence, and Lukenbill reined up near him at the same time that Henry stopped with the wagon and soldiers.

Henry explained to Zimmerman what had happened to his people, but the elder was already climbing into the wagon. Tears of sorrow and sympathy in his eyes, he embraced the man and woman in turn, then gathered the children in his arms and hugged them. The woman added her comments when Henry finished, crediting him with a much more heroic role than he had wanted to claim.

The old man expressed deep gratitude, which Henry shrugged off as he began explaining Lukenbill's scheme. His eyes wide with alarm, the agent tried to interrupt, but Zimmerman angrily motioned him into silence.

When Henry had finished speaking, Lukenbill exclaimed, "That is not true! I have been—"

"Do not call me a liar, Lukenbill!" Henry cut in. "If you do, you'll regret that you ever saw me."

Zimmerman glanced between Henry and Lukenbill. "I know when a man speaks the truth and when he lies." Glaring at Lukenbill, he stabbed a finger toward the road. "Get off my land!"

Fuming, Lukenbill rode away as Zimmerman began apologizing to Henry for refusing his help before. Henry smiled. "We understand each other now, and nothing else is important," he assured the man. "When you and your people want to go to town, let me know a day in advance. Send a rider around the town to the fort to tell me, and the escort will be here."

The old man agreed. Henry touched his hat as he turned his horse, and the squad followed. As he rode back down the lane, he reflected that the problems at the fort were working themselves out. But the problem with the town, a civil matter, still remained.

XI

Pulling his coat closer against the chill, Edward Blackstone listened to his uncle conferring with the company commanders a few yards away. Silhouetted by the first light of dawn, the soaring, majestic peaks of the eastern Himalayas filled the horizon to the north and east. Directly ahead, still shrouded in darkness, was a steep mountain with a fortified village on its upper slopes—the home of the Gurlung dacoits.

After the battle a few days before, scouts had trailed fleeing dacoits and finally located their base of operations. The entire battalion had been assembled for a long trek into the mountains, climaxed by a forced night march, which set the stage for a final, decisive battle with the dacoits.

The conference finished, the company commanders moved away to join their men as Major Cochrane stepped over to Edward. Only his white mustache was clearly visible in the dim light as he rubbed his hands together briskly. "Well, Edward, it won't be long now," he said. "As soon as we get word that the gatling guns are in position on the other side of the village, we can have it out with them."

Edward nodded, his satisfaction matching his uncle's. "Perhaps I should have gone with the gatling guns."

"No, no, you're better off here," the major replied. "Nothing will happen over there unless the dacoits try to escape that way. Then it will merely be a grisly slaughter. The battle will be on this side." Hearing a murmur of voices, he peered into the darkness. "Is someone looking for me? Over here!"

A soldier emerged from the shadows and saluted. "The guns are in position, sir," he reported.

"Very well. Tell your jemadar that we're moving up the mountain," the major said. Turning to one side, he called to the artillery officer, "Subadar Chatterji, cease firing when we're a hundred yards from the village!"

The officer replied, and Cochrane blew a whistle. Other whistles shrilled on both sides as Edward started up the mountain with his uncle, the early morning darkness alive with companies of soldiers tramping up the steep slope, which seemed small in comparison to the towering Himalayas. The rising sun touched the tall, formidable stone walls surrounding the village, although darkness still lingered on the slope.

"No one seems to be moving about up there," Edward commented to the major. "Are you certain they're there?"

"Oh, yes," Cochrane replied confidently. "Our scouts have kept a close watch on this place, and all the dacoits are there. They'll be unpleasantly surprised very soon."

The shattering roar of a cannon came from behind, followed by five more in quick succession. The ground trembled as the shells screamed past overhead. The first round fell a few yards short of the wall, then the next five were direct hits. The explosions echoed across the slope, the shells slamming into the wall and ripping loose huge stones.

Tiny figures darted back and forth on the walls in the distance as answering explosions rippled down the slope. Then the corner of the wall suddenly collapsed into an avalanche of boulders.

A roar of approval rose from the companies as the wall was breached. The cannon fell silent for a moment, then began blasting again, pounding into a long section of the wall. Then the shriek of artillery shells arcing overhead was joined by the whoosh of rockets with flaming tails.

The rockets ignited fires in the village, and thick smoke billowed up in the pall of dust being raised by the cannon shells as full daylight spread over the slope. Scattered rifle fire began coming from the village.

A bullet pinged on a rock in front of Cochrane, then ripped his sleeve, but missed his arm. "Well, there goes a good tunic," he shouted philosophically to Edward. "Those old fusils have excellent range—although their rate of fire is pitifully slow."

An infantry advance in the open was a new experience for Edward, so his attitude was less academic. "If the dacoits start firing in volleys, we'll wish that some of the men had fusils instead of Sniders."

"They won't," the major replied. "Subadar Chatterji will soon begin lobbing in rounds of canister, to make them keep their heads down. Then we'll soon be close enough to use our Sniders."

Another rousing cheer swelled among the soldiers as a wide section of the wall collapsed into rubble. Shells hit the top of the wall with loud thuds instead of shattering roars. The canister rounds, exploding into masses of flying shrapnel, raised immense clouds of dust. The rifle fire from the village ceased, then the cannon shells slammed into another corner of the wall and sent huge rocks flying into the air.

At five hundred yards from the village, the maximum range for the soldiers' rifles, Edward cocked his Winchester and waited for the command to open fire. A group of women and children suddenly rushed out the first gap the cannon had opened in the wall. The major commented that they were undoubtedly captives.

"A rocket must have hit the place the dacoits were holding them, allowing them to escape," he continued. "We'll probably find others." He frowned as the captives began dodging behind rocks. "Those dacoit swine are shooting at the women and children! We'll put a stop to that!" He blew two short blasts on his whistle.

The company commanders repeated the signal with their whistles, and the soldiers fired at the top of the wall. Edward snapped off shots at figures he glimpsed on the wall. Cochrane blew his whistle three times, and the company commanders blew theirs. The rifle fire from the companies diminished as the soldiers fixed their bayonets, then resumed.

At two hundred yards, smoke and dust from the village swirled around Edward. The dacoits were firing again, and

bullets were slapping into the ground. Rockets rained down
on the village, their explosions blending with the deafening
roars of cannon shells slamming into the wall in an attempt to
open another breach before the assault.

The major drew his sword and pointed it at the village as
he began running and blowing his whistle. Suddenly soldiers
were all around. The companies closed together and rushed
toward the breaches in the wall.

Another section of wall collapsed, rolling down the slope,
and a company broke ranks to avoid the huge rocks. Suddenly
the artillery barrage ceased.

Shrouded in dust and smoke, the stone wall rose menac-
ingly on each side of the breach. Edward fired at dim figures
on the wall, and dacoits toppled down and thudded on the
ground. Then he and the major were pressed tightly together
in a crush of soldiers clambering over the rubble in the
breach.

Inside the village was a nightmarish scene. Burning buildings cast a ruddy glow through dense smoke and dust, and
there was pandemonium in the narrow streets, which were
crowded with friend and foe on every side. Edward shot a
dacoit in the face at point-blank range, then raised his sword
as another dacoit slashed at him with a kukri, a short, heavy
sword.

The keen, thick blade of the kukri clanged against Edward's sword as he parried, fenced, then searched for an
opening. It came a moment later, when the dacoit swung,
leaving his chest unprotected. Edward lunged and sank his
sword into the man's chest.

The bedlam began breaking up. Dacoits fled down streets,
with soldiers chasing them; Edward and the major fired at
dacoits darting between doorways and along roofs; and the
gatling guns took their toll on those trying to flee from the
other side of the village.

Edward had just exchanged his Winchester for his Colt
when he saw a dacoit standing on the edge of a roof above the
major, poised to leap on him with a knife. Shouting, Edward
fired his pistol, and the bullet hit the man in the head. As the
major turned to look around, the dead dacoit fell on him.

The major was knocked to the ground, his sword and

pistol flying from his hands as another dacoit rushed forward
with a kukri. Lifting his sword, Edward ran to meet him. The
dacoit gripped the kukri in both hands, his bearded face
twisted in rage as he chopped at Edward.

Off-balance but unable to give ground while protecting
his uncle, Edward could only partially parry the powerful
blow with the heavy blade. It slashed across his left thigh.
The dacoit stumbled, and Edward quickly ran his sword
through the man's chest. Then he dropped his sword and
gripped his thigh.

As Cochrane scrambled to his feet, he looked in alarm at
the blood welling up between Edward's fingers. "That's a
nasty cut, Edward," he said anxiously.

"It'll be all right, sir," Edward replied, wincing with
pain and taking out his handkerchief. "You'd best catch up
with your men."

"You just saved my life, Edward, and my men are doing
very well on their own. No, I'll see to you."

Edward shook his head as he held the handkerchief
tightly to his thigh. "I'll be all right here," he insisted. "I'll go
into one of these buildings and sit down."

"Well, you certainly should get off that leg," the major
agreed. He stepped to a doorway and peered in. "Very well,
you go in there and wait, my boy. As soon as the battle is
finished, I'll bring the doctor to you."

Edward picked up his sword and limped toward the
building as his uncle hurried away. It was a tiny one-room
dwelling with a dirt floor. There was a cot against the far wall,
and Edward lay down on the grimy bedclothes.

The sounds of the battle were moving on to other streets.
Keenly aware that dacoits could be lurking nearby, Edward
kept his eyes on the door, his rifle on one side, his sword on
the other, and his pistol ready to fire.

The clamor of the battle moved farther away, but Edward, hair prickling on the back of his neck, heard someone
moving under the cot. He cocked his pistol and leaned over.
The barrel was an inch from the nose of a grimy, unshaven
man, who was sliding from under the cot.

Edward gaped in astonishment at the man, who looked
up at him in equal shock. The cocked pistol still almost

touching his nose, the man gulped and spoke in a rich brogue. "After living through torment at the hands of the most fiendish devils who ever inhabited the face of the earth, am I to have my brains blown out by my good friend Edward Blackstone?"

"Edgar Dooley!" Edward laughed. Lifting the pistol, he eased the hammer down.

Dooley, very much the worse for wear, pushed himself to a sitting position as he joined in the laugh. "How did you even come to be in India? Wounded in battle, no less, and not even in the army."

"I'm visiting with my uncle, Major Winslow Cochrane. He's the commander of the battalion that attacked the dacoits."

"I knew you were well connected. I'm forced to say that your uncle could have been less generous with his rockets and saved the queen's treasury a few quid. Three hit the place where captives were being held, while one would have more than sufficed to free us. But I'm not one to complain about a good turn, even when its abundance is almost the end of me."

"It would take more than a rocket to kill you," Edward said, laughing. "How did you get captured by the dacoits?"

The cheerfully unrepentant old reprobate related a rambling story of misfortune. It boiled down to the fact that he had wandered away from Pandu Ghat while drunk on bolabang and had run into a roving band of dacoits. "Some of them drank the last of my bolabang, then got the idea I had tried to poison them."

"From what I've heard," Edward commented, "they had reason to think that."

"Nonsense," Dooley said firmly. "Bolabang reminds me of poteen, the Irish potato whiskey." He looked closely at Edward. "I believe I know why you're visiting your uncle. I recall a conversation we had about Brahman cattle."

"Not a word about that to anyone, Edgar. It could be very embarrassing for my uncle."

Dooley assured Edward that he would mention it to no one. A few minutes later, Cochrane rushed in, followed by the medical officer.

Worried about his nephew's wound, the major shook

hands with Dooley absently, then watched the doctor bandage Edward's thigh.

"The muscles in that leg must be allowed to heal," the doctor told Edward. "If you don't stay off your feet for at least two weeks, you could be permanently crippled. I'll get some men to carry you on a litter."

Edward reflected that fate was against his ever getting cattle out of India; now that he had just found the one man who could advise him on what to do, the wound would keep him bedridden for weeks.

Two soldiers carried Edward down the mountain, and Dooley walked beside the litter. Camp was being set up and arrangements made to return the captive women and children to their homes. Settled comfortably beside a fire, Dooley happily sipped a bottle of Edward's brandy and discussed the cattle.

"I'll look into the matter while your leg is healing at Barapani," Dooley suggested.

"But after your long absence, your work with the East India Company will be piled up and waiting for you," Edward pointed out.

Dooley fell silent for a moment. "I've been in and out of plenty of scrapes, but this one took something out of me. I've often thought about your ranch, and I'd like to spend the rest of my years in peace and quiet. So if you'll let me go there, I'm ready to chuck it in here and help you."

"But you'd be trading security for a very uncertain proposition," Edward replied. "Rob and I are anything but well-fixed financially. If we could get some Brahman cattle there, we'd probably make a success of our ranch. But that's our only chance, and you know that getting the cattle there safely is only a remote possibility."

"Even so," Edgar insisted, "I'm willing to take my chances. I qualify for a modest retirement annuity, which I can fall back on if the ranch fails. If it doesn't, all I ask is bed, board, and an occasional bottle." He put out his hand. "And I'm ready to seal the bargain."

Edward hesitated, then shook hands with Dooley. If cattle could be spirited out of India, Dooley was the man who could do it.

*   *   *

It was late afternoon when Eulalia Blake set off for the ranch from Portland, where she had been shopping. Having found out about something that simply had to be dealt with immediately, she had sent a note to Lee and instructions to the cook about his dinner, then hurriedly summoned her carriage.

When the driver brought her carriage to her, she stepped into it and uncharacteristically snapped at him to hurry to the ranch.

Eulalia grimly contemplated the situation that was making her so upset. During the past weeks, her reluctance to see the house that had replaced her own first home in Portland had kept her from visiting the ranch. But she had heard from numerous sources what Alexandra was doing, and the news was alarming.

An enormous new charity hospital that had to be costing an immense amount of money was being built on the outskirts of town. Enrico Fossi, who was building the house at the ranch, was also hired to build the hospital, with Alexandra in overall charge of the project. Apparently she was also paying for it with Toby's bank account, because Eulalia had been unable to think of any other conceivable source of money. Eulalia speculated that Alexandra was doing it to please Janessa.

Furthermore, Eulalia had recently heard from several sources that the girl was now helping Dr. Martin treat male patients. That was a violation of the doctor's agreement with Toby, which Alexandra apparently had seen fit to overrule.

The influence that Alexandra was having over Janessa's attitudes also concerned Eulalia. When her granddaughter had come to Fort Vancouver to visit briefly after her return from New York, Eulalia had the impression that the girl's attitude toward Henry Blake's baroness had changed. Eulalia wondered if being around Alexandra had caused Janessa to be less critical of immorality and less loyal to Cindy.

Satisfied that she had done her best to warn Toby, Eulalia had seen no reason to interfere directly and had been waiting for Toby to see for himself the penalties of leaving his family and affairs in the care of an inexperienced young woman. But a short time before, she had heard something that caused her spontaneous trip to the ranch.

Eulalia had bumped into Wilma Givens, the mother of Alexandra's cook and maid. Wilma had said that Timmy and Calvin Rogers had gone to San Francisco to buy a passenger balloon for Alexandra, then wondered aloud if they intended to fly it to Portland.

Eulalia had rejected the idea as being ridiculous, then began having second thoughts. Why the young woman was spending Toby's hard-earned money for a passenger balloon was an annoying question. Worse, she knew that Timmy would press Calvin to set out from San Francisco in the balloon. Calvin was pleasant, but his many accidents with balloons indicated a lack of judgment. Her anxiety increasing with every moment, Eulalia had summoned her carriage to take her to the ranch.

As the carriage moved along the road, two wagons coming from the ranch passed. Fossi and some fifteen workmen were in them, apparently having finished for the day. They lifted their hats as they passed, and Eulalia nodded coolly in response.

The carriage approached the ranch, and Eulalia sat dreading the sight of the house that had replaced the home in which Toby and Cindy had grown up. At her first view of the structure, Eulalia's heart sank in despair. Her first home in Portland had been replaced by an enormous house. Three stories tall, it dwarfed the comfortable, familiar home that had stood there for decades.

The carriage drew up in front of the huge structure, and Eulalia stepped out. She was so heartbroken and resentful over her house, she was reluctant to go inside the mansion. As she started to walk around it to look for Alexandra, the young woman suddenly came around the front corner.

Wearing her usual riding trousers, white shirt, and boots, Alexandra smiled radiantly. "Why, Mrs. Blake! I thought I heard a carriage. It's such a delightful surprise to see you." Her smile faded as she looked at Eulalia more closely. "Is something wrong, Mrs. Blake?"

Overwrought, Eulalia had to control an impulse to shout the multitude of things that were wrong.

"Alexandra," she said in a quiet, restrained voice, "I have tried never to interfere in my children's lives. When Toby decided to leave you in charge of his family and affairs, the only comment I made about it was for the purpose of ensuring he had considered it thoroughly. But where my grandchildren are concerned, I feel that I have not only the right but a duty to make certain their welfare is not jeopardized."

"Of course you do," Alexandra agreed in concern, "but don't limit your opinions to the children. If you consider anything at all amiss, you have every right to—"

"Please don't change the subject, Alexandra," Eulalia cut in firmly. "My grandchildren are my main concern, and that is why I am here. Is it true that you sent Timmy and Calvin Rogers to San Francisco to get a passenger balloon for you?"

"Yes, that's right," Alexandra replied. "Miss MacDougall and I agreed that Timmy has been doing so well in school that he deserves a reward. He'll miss only a few days."

"Has it occurred to you that they may try to fly that balloon back from San Francisco?" Eulalia demanded.

Alexandra was speechless with amazement for a moment, then shook her head. "No, they wouldn't attempt to do that, Mrs. Blake."

"Did you specifically tell them not to, Alexandra?" Eulalia insisted heatedly.

"Of course not," the young woman retorted. "But neither did I tell them not to try to swim back here with the balloon strapped to their backs. Calvin isn't insane, Mrs. Blake. Balloons go wherever the wind takes them, and it could go out over the Pacific as easily as it could head north. Calvin knows that far better than I do."

"Well," Eulalia said defensively, "why on earth do you want a passenger balloon, Alexandra?"

"It's for the county fair."

"The county fair?" Eulalia echoed, puzzled.

Alexandra explained that the gondola would hold twelve people, and rides on the balloon at the end of a cable should be a popular attraction, drawing additional people and making the fair more successful. "Also," she added, "at fifty cents for each person in the gondola, the balloon should begin producing a profit within three days. Now do you wish to talk about Janessa?"

Momentarily distracted by the ingenuity of Alexandra's plans, Eulalia collected her thoughts. "Yes, in fact I do," she replied, becoming more cordial. "I presume it's with your permission that she is working with all patients in the hospital now. Perhaps you don't know that Toby and Robert Martin agreed for Janessa to work only with women and children patients."

"Yes, I know about the agreement," Alexandra said, "but I didn't give her permission to work with all patients. Toby did that."

"He did?" Eulalia exclaimed, frowning. "I wonder why he didn't tell me about it."

"I'm sure he simply overlooked it," Alexandra suggested. "He didn't tell me either, but he was attending to so many things just before he left. When I found out, I spoke with Dr. Martin. Toby asked him to use judgment with regard to Janessa's involvement, and he's doing that."

Alexandra talked about other things Janessa and the doctor were doing and mentioned the new charity hospital. The subject having been raised, Eulalia pursued it. "Alexandra, have you written to Toby about the new hospital?"

"No, I decided to wait until he gets home and let it be a surprise for him."

"It may be a very unpleasant surprise," Eulalia warned. "There can be no question that it's an extremely worthwhile purpose, but it may be costing more than Toby can afford."

Alexandra laughed. "I'm not paying for that with Toby's money, Mrs. Blake. An enormous sum is involved. The hospital is being endowed to pay staff salaries and operating expenses. Beyond that, the building itself is costing thousands."

Eulalia gasped. "Who is paying for all that?" she asked.

"A donor who wishes to remain anonymous. I know you'll be discreet, so I'll tell you it is the Baroness von Kirchberg. One of her employees set up a bank account here through which all financial arrangements are made."

The very mention of the name aroused Eulalia's temper, but at least she now better understood the change in Janessa's attitude toward the woman.

Each of the issues she had been worrying about had been resolved by Alexandra's simple explanations. Eulalia felt somewhat foolish.

Alexandra smiled warmly. "It's been far too long since we've talked, Mrs. Blake. We mustn't let this happen again."

Eulalia agreed. Nothing less than her deep feelings about the house could have kept her away, because she always enjoyed the beautiful young woman's charming companionship. While they had been talking, Eulalia forced herself to turn and look at the house, actually seeing it for the first time.

Like pictures she had seen of large homes built during the past few years, it was eclectic Victorian. The upper floors had a Tuscan overhang above a horizontal band at the top of the first floor, while there was a hint of Gothic in the decorative edging on the gables and dormers. It had bay windows in front, and a round tower on the left was balanced by a widening of the porch on the right corner into a pavilion. Eulalia was forced to admit that the house had an air of dignity and graceful beauty.

The fact remained, however, that the familiar ranch house was gone. Searching for something polite to say, Eulalia commented on the fact that the trees she had planted as saplings around the ranch house were still standing.

"Of course they are," Alexandra replied. "You don't think I'd let anyone touch one of those lovely trees, do you?" She took Eulalia's arm. "Come, you must see the inside."

"No, thank you, Alexandra," Eulalia demurred. "I must get back home. But first I want to apologize for allowing myself to get carried away."

"Please, Mrs. Blake, no apology is necessary. I understand completely how you felt. But I would appreciate it if you would come inside. I'd like very much to show it to you."

Knowing that she would have to go into the house sooner or later, Eulalia nodded in resignation and forced a smile. She and Alexandra then went up the sweep of steps and across the wide front porch to tall double front doors surmounted by an ornate fanlight.

The first thing Eulalia noticed was that the entry hall looked very familiar. Then she realized that what had been

the parlor of her house had been opened up to make an entry
hall with a high ceiling. Instead of her house having been
torn down, the new house had been built around it.

For a long moment she was speechless, then she expressed her astonishment about what had been done. "I
wouldn't even have contemplated having the original house
torn down," Alexandra replied. "Enrico said it was one of the
most solid buildings he'd ever seen, and these paneled walls
are priceless."

Eulalia felt tears of relief and happiness burning in her
eyes. Although her house had been swallowed by the Victorian
mansion, it was still there.

The young woman broke off, suddenly remembering
something. "When I heard your carriage, I was at my still,
and I left it unlocked. Would you mind going with me while I
lock it?"

Eulalia followed Alexandra down a hall. In a huge kitchen
that was still under construction, Abby and Amy Givens were
cooking and ironing. Behind that were a scullery and then a
back porch. Eulalia and Alexandra finally reached the backyard.

They crossed to the still, and Alexandra locked the door.
Eulalia decided to clear the air about that, too. "Do you think
that it's proper for a young lady to make whiskey?"

"No, Mrs. Blake," Alexandra replied. "But making good
bourbon is a family tradition that goes back some sixty years.
Since my father didn't have a son, it was up to me to continue
the tradition."

For a moment Eulalia was dumbfounded. Tradition was
something she respected. "Then by all means, you should do
so."

"As you know," Alexandra said sadly, "I'm not making
any this year."

"A matter of circumstances, my dear. I'm sure your
father and grandfather would understand."

"They would be disappointed in me. They made their
whiskey during war, famine, and flood. Blight struck their
corn, locusts infested it, and sometimes they were so ill that
they had to drag themselves out of the house. But somehow
or another, they made the mash and their whiskey." She
smiled sadly at Eulalia.

Deeply touched by the young woman's remorse, Eulalia had an idea. "Alexandra, all you need is some corn."

"Special corn, and two hundred bushels of it, Mrs. Blake."

"The man who sells corn to the fort grows the best corn in Oregon. I've heard any number of people remark on how excellent it is. He has only a select number of customers, but I'm sure he would sell some to you. Lee and I will go talk to the man. Either he'll sell it to you, or he'll never sell another ear of corn to the fort."

Smiling happily, Alexandra thanked Eulalia as they went back into the house. It was not until they were in the parlor that Eulalia realized she had somehow managed to involve herself in making whiskey. She put the thought aside; it was past sunset, time for her to return home. But Janessa came in, smiling at Eulalia.

"I thought that was your carriage, Grandmama," she said.

Deciding to stay for a few minutes longer after all, Eulalia sat. Janessa said that she had gone past the new charity hospital to see how construction was proceeding.

Eulalia felt compelled to comment on the change in Janessa's attitude toward the baroness. "Donating the money for a hospital was commendable, but one would expect her to make some gesture, considering that her life was saved. Under the circumstances, however, I can understand why you feel more kindly toward her than before, Janessa."

The girl turned to Alexandra with a pleading look.

"Janessa and I have discussed this, Mrs. Blake," Alexandra said. "Her very warm affection for the woman conflicts with her love and loyalty for Cindy."

"Affection?" Eulalia exclaimed. "For that despicable creature? She has the morals of an alley cat."

Janessa looked down at her hands. "In some ways she's meaner than I thought anyone could be, and in others she's the opposite. I tried to ignore it when she liked me, but it was like trying to ignore the sun shining in my eyes. She has something inside her like the President and other important people probably have."

It was a long speech for Janessa; Eulalia felt sorry for the girl. "Well, don't let it upset you, my dear, but don't be

misled as to what is between Henry Blake and that woman.
What keeps them together can't be anything approaching a
wholesome emotion."

"They love each other," Janessa corrected. "I've heard
that having a child makes a man and woman closer, so that
could be part of it."

Eulalia was stupified by the revelation. She had another
grandchild, a child with the same claim on her love as Janessa
and Timmy, yet she detested the baby's parents. She simultaneously wanted to know every minute detail and earnestly
wished she had never heard any mention of the child.

Alexandra began questioning Janessa about it. It took
several questions before Alexandra learned that Janessa had
never seen the child, which had presumably remained behind in Germany. Several more extracted the information
that Janessa had found out only through seeing striations on
the baroness's stomach, which indicated the child was about a
year old. Alexandra then began probing for whether it was a
boy or a girl.

"I don't know," Janessa said. "They spoke in German all
the time."

Eulalia felt both relieved and regretful when the subject
was dropped.

Alexandra mentioned the distress that Janessa was expe-
riencing. "She wants to explain her feelings to Cindy, but it's
so complicated that I've advised her to wait until she sees
Cindy, rather than to write to her about it."

Eulalia nodded. "My advice is the same. And I also
advise you not to worry about it, my dear. Cindy will
understand."

The girl flashed a rare, wide smile, but Alexandra's grateful smile was even more radiant.

As dusk settled, Eulalia made her farewells. "You must
visit again soon," Alexandra insisted. "Please come earlier so
you can stay longer."

"I'll come next Sunday, and Lee will come with me. He
always enjoys looking at your horses."

"For lunch, then. I'll have Amy prepare something
special."

"We'd like that," Eulalia said, then exchanged a hug and

kiss with Alexandra and Janessa. As she stepped into her carriage, she felt satisfied by the results of her visit. In the back of her mind, however, was a nagging torment about the grandchild she would probably never see, a feeling of remorse that would always haunt her. She was relieved about Timmy, though. He was perfectly safe.

Timmy and Calvin were standing in a storage yard behind a wholesale equipment warehouse on the outskirts of San Francisco. The proprietor, Mickey Ellis, eagerly tried to convince Calvin that the balloon was an excellent bargain, while Calvin responded with studied caution and persistent questions.

"I ordered it for a circus that went bankrupt," Ellis explained. "I was stuck with it, so I quoted Miss Woodling a fair price, then she whittled me down some. The upshot is, you'll never find another one like this at that price."

"How long has it been in storage?" Calvin asked.

Timmy was uninterested in the men's conversation. His attention was focused on three wooden crates that two workmen had taken out of a shed. He moved closer, keeping out of the way as the workmen picked up crowbars and removed the top from the smallest, heaviest crate. Peering into it, he saw the balloon's winch and cable. Calvin and Ellis moved closer to examine it.

"Not a spot of rust," Ellis pointed out. "It's been in good, dry storage."

"I don't see any rust," Calvin allowed, "but it's covered with grease. There could be rust under the grease."

Ellis snapped his fingers at one of the workmen. "Hand me that rag over there and then get the tops off those other crates." Taking the cloth, he rubbed at the grease on the winch. "See? Not a speck of rust, Mr. Rogers."

Wary, Calvin took the rag and wiped away more grease as he and Ellis continued talking. The second crate the men opened contained the wicker gondola. Watching the men take that and other things out of the crate, Timmy noted that the balloon was equipped for free flight as well as ascents on the cable.

Working busily, the men unloaded sandbags, which were

used for ballast, and hung them on hooks around the lip of the gondola. Also included was a four-pointed grapnel hook attached to a large coil of rope, to keep the balloon envelope and gondola from being dragged along the ground by the wind when landing.

The third crate contained the huge gas envelope, its fabric panels in alternating colors of red, white, and blue. Timmy gasped in delight while Calvin, leaning on his cane and stepping to the crate, examined the rubberized fabric.

He frowned warily. "Storing a balloon envelope can be bad for it, particularly if it's folded up like this. Cracks can develop along the folds, and leaks in a gas balloon are much more critical than in a hot-air balloon."

"It hasn't been stored all that long," Ellis remarked. "But we can pump it up and see if there are any leaks."

Urgently wanting to see the balloon inflated, Timmy watched Calvin glance around and look at the sky. San Francisco sprawled over a cluster of steep hills. It was a cool, overcast autumn day, with light, variable winds.

"It isn't too windy to inflate it," Calvin decided, "but I'd rather not use the winch."

Ellis pointed to a short, thick post set in the ground a few yards away. "We use that as an anchor for a block and tackle to drag things back and forth out here. It should be able to hold this balloon."

The post was almost a foot in diameter, with a large steel eye set in one side. Calvin nodded. "Yes, that'll hold it."

Ellis turned to his men. "Let's get to work, then."

The men bustled about, and a few minutes later, the huge, colorful envelope was stretched at full length. Timmy helped Calvin fasten the ropes around its sides to the steel eyes around the edge of the gondola while Ellis tied a rope between the base of the gondola and the eye in the thick post. His men unrolled a hose to fill the envelope with gas from a hookup to the city gasworks.

When gas began hissing into a large valve at the envelope's top, Calvin carefully checked the valve to make certain it opened and closed smoothly. The envelope swelled, and its creases and wrinkles smoothed out.

After several minutes, the envelope slowly lifted off the

ground and expanded into its inverted pear shape. Timmy
watched in ecstatic awe. The balloon towered over the storage yard, its brilliant colors making the dull day come alive.
Lifting the gondola against the rope tied to the post, it
seemed to possess a life of its own.

Looking up at the colorful mountain of fabric, Calvin
limped around the gondola, then turned to Ellis. "It appears
we have a good balloon here," he announced. "I don't see
any point in wasting any more gas."

"That's up to you, Mr. Rogers," Ellis replied cheerfully.
"I want you to be satisfied."

The gondola was tethered close to the thick post by only
a few inches at the end of a long coil of rope on the ground
beside the post. Timmy surveyed the coils thoughtfully, then
plucked at Calvin's sleeve. "Could we go up in the balloon to
the end of that rope?" he asked.

"No, Timmy," Calvin replied, smiling fondly. "We came
to San Francisco to buy a balloon, not go up in one. And we
mustn't take up any more of Mr. Ellis's time than necessary."

"My time this afternoon is yours, Mr. Rogers," Ellis
remarked affably. "If this young fellow wants to go up, my
men and I can snub that rope around the post and pay it out
through the eye. There's a hundred feet of rope in that coil,
and it would sure give you a look at San Francisco from the
air."

"That's true," Calvin said, hesitating. "But the only safe
way to hold a balloon is with a cable and winch."

"I think it would be plenty safe," Ellis told him. "With a
turn on that rope around the post, my men and I wouldn't
have any trouble with it, and you could always let out the
gas, couldn't you?"

"Let's do it, Calvin!" Timmy pleaded excitedly. "Just a
few minutes."

Torn with indecision, Calvin smiled at Timmy affectionately. "I suppose I knew all the time this would happen," he
commented. He tossed his cane into the gondola and gripped
the edge to climb in. "All right, let's go, Timmy."

The boy whooped with delight. Ellis laughed heartily as
he lifted the boy and helped him in, then told one of the men

to turn off the gas. The gondola's edge was even with Timmy's shoulders. He peered over it as Calvin uncoupled the hose.

One workman helped Ellis untie the knot in the steel eye set into the post. Then, after taking a turn of the rope around the post, the three men stood in line with their feet braced, slowly paying out the rope. The balloon rose.

San Francisco and its surrounding area quickly came into view. The streets on the steep hills were lined with houses that were elevated on stilts at one side and below ground level on the other. Little more than a mile away, the vast bay was dotted with ships.

The balloon suddenly stopped rising when it was some forty feet in the air. "Is something wrong, Mr. Ellis?" Calvin called.

"No, Mr. Rogers," the man called back. "This rope has a thick spot in it—a splice that's about the same size as the eye. We're having a little trouble getting it through the eye."

Calvin frowned in concern. "That splice is good and strong, isn't it?"

"Oh, yes," Ellis assured him. "Stronger than the rest of the rope. One of my men used to be a sailor, and when he splices a rope, that rope will stay in one piece."

Satisfied, Calvin looked back out over the view as the workmen took a second turn of the rope around the post and braced themselves to keep it from slipping out of control as Ellis prepared to jerk the splice through the eye. He placed a foot against the post, gripped the rope tightly in both hands, then jerked on it.

The splice remained stuck tightly in the eye. Ellis jerked on it again. When the splice failed to budge, Ellis frowned irately. Taking a turn of the rope around one wrist, he muttered an order to his men. The workmen leaned back against their end of the rope, and Ellis gathered himself and heaved his weight back. The rope snapped, and all three men fell flat.

When the balloon jerked and drifted sideways, Calvin dropped his cane in a frantic lunge for the grapnel and rope. He began unrolling the coil of rope, which was stiff from being stored in the crate.

Timmy looked down as the balloon started to pass some

twenty feet over the roof of the warehouse. Calvin worked at
the rope, getting a few yards of it unwound, and tossed the
grapnel over the edge of the gondola. It thumped down onto
the roof of the warehouse and slid, none of the flukes catching, then fell off. The wind veered and began pushing the
balloon away from the hill.

The buildings below were immediately far out of reach of
the rope, even at its full length. Timmy looked back at the
storage yard, where the three men had climbed to their feet.
Ellis cupped his hands around his mouth and shouted, "Let
out the gas, Mr. Rogers!"

Timmy turned to Calvin, who was silently shaking his
head as he pulled at the knots. "Can't you let out gas,
Calvin?" he asked.

"Not now, Timmy," Calvin replied, smiling wryly. "This
balloon would drop like a rock if I did that, and now we're
about eighty feet up. And I couldn't open the valve over the
storage yard because the gondola would have hit that warehouse like a wrecking ball."

"The gas is explosive too, isn't it?" Timmy asked. "If we
went down over a chimney stack, that would be bad."

"Yes," Calvin agreed. "You have to keep your head
about you while ballooning, and it's still risky when everything goes right." He smiled reassuringly. "We'll be all right,
Timmy. Don't worry."

"I'm not worried." After searching for something to say
to prove that, he continued, "You know that man who splices
Mr. Ellis's ropes and used to be a sailor? I sure wouldn't want
to go to sleep on a boat that he had tied to a dock."

Calvin laughed too heartily, which made Timmy feel
uneasy. Earnestly hoping that Alexandra would never find
out what happened, he looked down. A few people on the
streets were waving, and Timmy waved in return.

As the balloon drifted toward higher ground, Calvin
coiled the rope loosely in readiness to cast the grapnel. "If at
some point I tell you to jump, Timmy, jump immediately,"
he ordered. "It may be a little higher than we'd like, but
jump anyway. Do you understand?"

"Yes, all right, Calvin."

The balloon drifted straight toward a house. At an altitude of some sixty feet, Calvin heaved the grapnel, and the rope snaked out behind it. Timmy watched as the grapnel arced down toward the rear of the house, where the eaves, porch railings, and other features offered a range of edges for the hooks to catch.

It struck a line filled with clothes in the backyard, and the line immediately started to bow upward as the balloon tugged it.

A woman darted out the back door. "What are you doing?" she shouted angrily.

"Trying to anchor this balloon, lady," Calvin shouted back, trying to dislodge the grapnel from the clothesline.

The ends of the line broke, and clothes and line were dragged after the rope. "You're flying around to steal people's clothes! Bring my clothes back here!"

Calvin snapped the rope again, and the clothesline finally fell loose and dropped onto the dirt street by the house. "There you are, lady," Calvin called. "I'm very sorry that happened."

The woman looked at her clothes scattered in the dirt, then shook her fist. "Look what you did to my clothes!" she wailed. "I'll make you sorry, you . . ."

Her tirade faded in the distance. Pulling in the rope, Calvin sighed, then looked ahead for another opportunity to anchor the balloon.

The wind suddenly changed and freshened, carrying the balloon more rapidly. It veered toward the bay. As the balloon moved over the water, it lost altitude, gradually leveling off some fifty feet above the bay.

Timmy and Calvin waved and shouted to people on boats and ships, and the people waved back. Timmy shook his head in disgust. "I guess they all think we're just having a good time," he grumbled.

"Here comes one that is going to pass right under us," Calvin said, reaching for the grapnel.

Looking ahead, Timmy smiled in relief. The vessel was a tug, with two crewmen on the foredeck. As it steamed toward the piers, Calvin dangled the grapnel a few feet above the water in the path of the tug.

A third man suddenly stepped out of the wheelhouse,

motioning to the two men, who then picked up boathooks and stood ready to fend off the grapnel as the tug passed under the balloon.

"We're in trouble!" Calvin shouted. "We need to get back to the shore!"

"Turn around and fly back!" the man beside the wheel-house replied.

"We can't! We go where the wind takes us!"

"Then get a steamer instead of a windjammer!"

Calvin started to shout again, but the tug was already past and continuing on its way. He pulled in the rope. A stronger wind pushed the balloon toward the mouth of the bay.

Timmy noticed a fishing vessel tacking sharply across the wind and working its way up the bay, on a course that would intersect the path of the balloon. He pointed it out to Calvin.

The man nodded and picked up the grapnel. "Ahoy, the boat!" he shouted. "We need help!"

A lone man working over a net snapped bolt upright in shock, startled by the sudden voice seemingly coming from nowhere. The lowered grapnel skimmed past the sail and cabin of the boat, then slammed into the rail at the stern of the boat. One of the flukes hooked it solidly.

The man on the boat was thrown off his feet, and his vessel came to an abrupt standstill. The balloon also stopped, tilting with the wind.

As the wind pushed against the huge mass of the enve-lope, the balloon pulled the stern of the boat around and began towing it backward in the water. The fisherman sat up, his head moving rapidly as he looked in panic at the water, his sails, and the tiller. Finally noticing the grapnel on the stern rail, he looked up at the balloon. His mouth fell open in astonishment.

"We need help!" Calvin called. "We're about to drift out to sea!"

The man sprang to his feet, snatched up a net hook, and levered the grapnel loose from the rail. "Well, you ain't taking me with you!" he bellowed as the grapnel splashed into the water.

The balloon drifted away from the boat, and once again

Calvin hauled in the rope. He looked at the nearest shoreline. "You're an excellent swimmer, aren't you, Timmy?"

Timmy shook his head. "I heard you tell Mr. Venable that you can't swim, so I'm not going to swim."

"Now, Timmy," Calvin said in a voice that encouraged no dissension, "you remember what I told you about jumping? If I tell you to jump, you must go ahead and—"

"I'm not going to swim, Calvin," Timmy cut in. "I know I'm supposed to do what you tell me, but I'm not going to do that."

Calvin smiled in resignation. "You are your father's son."

Calvin continued talking, but Timmy knew the man was only trying to cheer him. The light was fading into sunset, and the mouth of the bay was opening out as the balloon drifted toward the banks of fog on the edge of the vast Pacific. The fog edged inward at sunset, and then there was nothing but gray mist all around. Calvin dropped a few ballast bags into the sea, talking about the gas cooling and giving less lift, then he and Timmy sat together. Sitting close to the man provided very little warmth against the night and the clammy fog. The balloon bobbed slowly, making Timmy keenly aware of the immense reaches of water in the darkness below. Presently he thought of a ray of hope. "Aren't the Sandwich Islands out here somewhere?"

"Yes, well, a considerable way out, Timmy. But we're headed in the right direction, no doubt about that."

"Maybe a typhoon will come up and push us over there."

"Yes, that's certainly a thought."

Calvin pointed out that the variable winds could be pushing the balloon back toward land. Timmy, cold, tired, and hungry, pretended he had fallen asleep so Calvin would feel no pressure to talk.

Presently the boy did doze off. When he woke, daylight was penetrating the dense fog. Shivering with cold, he was curled on his side near Calvin, who was asleep. He climbed to his feet and looked out at the fog. The silence was absolute, but he knew that seabirds were usually quiet on foggy mornings. Then he heard a dog barking below and to one side.

"Calvin!" he shouted. "A dog!"

The man woke suddenly and snatched up his cane. Blinking the sleep from his eyes, he limped to Timmy's side and listened. Then he beamed in relief. "I hear it too, Timmy, and I also smell woodsmoke."

Timmy sniffed, then nodded happily. "Unless that dog is on a steamer that's burning wood, we must be over land."

Calvin laughed heartily. "I think we can safely say we're over land."

The sound of barking faded, then a vague, dark shadow became visible below and ahead. It was the top of a tree. Timmy and Calvin pointed to it and whooped gleefully as it slowly passed under the gondola. A few minutes later, the fog thinned and broke up ahead of the balloon. A hillside planted with crops came into view.

At the top of the hill, the dim outlines of a house and barns became visible. Calvin quickly readied the grapnel, holding it in one hand and grasping the rope connected to the gas valve in his other hand. The balloon slowly drifted closer to the house, then Calvin heaved the grapnel as the roof passed under the balloon.

The grapnel slammed down on the wooden shingles, plowing up a line of them as it dragged toward the ridge of the roof. A hook on the grapnel caught on the ridge, jerking the gondola to a stop. Just as Calvin started to pull the rope and open the gas valve, the ridge pole on the house snapped with a loud crack.

Calvin and Timmy groaned as the grapnel slid down the rear slope of the roof in an avalanche of shingles. The grapnel fell to the ground and dragged across the barnyard behind the house, passing through a flock of chickens, which exploded into a squawking mass of fluttering wings, then headed toward a rail fence.

Geese fled ahead of the grapnel, adding their alarmed honking to the cackling of the chickens and quacking of nearby ducks. As the grapnel bounced along the ground toward the fence, Calvin watched it intently. The hook caught the fence solidly, the gondola halted abruptly once more, and the balloon tilted as he pulled the gas-valve rope.

Calvin pulled the valve wide open to ground the balloon immediately. Gas rushed from the envelope with a roaring hiss, and the gondola plummeted. As it slammed down on its side next to the fence, Calvin cried out in pain. The envelope settled in the barnyard, which was in pandemonium. Hogs in a pen squalled shrilly and raced about; mules in a corral beside the barn brayed and kicked; and a half-dozen sheep fled in terror.

Half-stunned from the hard landing, Timmy lay in the overturned gondola, Calvin beside him. Then the boy sat up and looked at him. Calvin was grimacing and clutching his left leg, the one that had been broken several times in balloon accidents. "Are you all right?" Timmy asked worriedly.

"I'm not sure, Timmy," the man admitted. "This fool leg may be broken again. How about you?"

"I'm fine." He climbed to his feet and bent over the man. "Let's get you out of here and see about your leg."

The last of the gas escaped from the balloon, and it collapsed in a mass of fabric as Timmy hauled Calvin out of the gondola. The man sat beside the gondola and gingerly felt his leg.

"It doesn't feel like it's broken," Calvin said cautiously. "It may only be bruised."

"Stay off it for now," Timmy ordered. "I'll see if anyone is in the house."

"Someone is there, all right," Calvin said, looking up. "But I don't think he'll be of much help."

Timmy turned and looked. A broad-shouldered, bearded man had come out, a shotgun under his arm. He was looking at the destruction and muttering to himself.

"I'm very sorry for the damage to your house," Calvin called out quickly as the man stomped toward him and Timmy.

"You're *sorry*?" he barked in a menacing tone. "I've just finished fixing that roof for the winter, and now look what you've done to it! Being sorry ain't enough, mister!"

"I'll be more than glad to pay for the damages, cash in hand," Calvin added quickly, looking up at the stranger.

The man shook his head. "I don't want no cash," he growled, "but you'll pay all right. I'm going to fill you full of buckshot. That's how you're going to pay."

As the man lifted the shotgun, Calvin rapidly repeated his offer to pay for the damages. Timmy, his heart thudding, looked at the bearded man, hoping that his threat was only bluster. He studied the man closely: His eyes were irrational.

Icy fear raced through Timmy as he realized the man was a dangerous mental incompetent. He and Calvin had landed in a far more perilous situation than floating over the ocean.

Calvin's continued efforts to pacify the bearded man were futile. "Wait! Wait!" Timmy babbled as the man brought the shotgun to Calvin's temple. "If you shoot that gun, you'll blow up this whole farm. There's hydrogen gas all over the place."

"That's right," Calvin verified, following Timmy's lead. Perspiration had popped out on his forehead and upper lip. "The gas from the balloon is explosive. The muzzle flash from your gun would ignite it."

The bearded man looked skeptical. "I don't see nothing. You're lying." He put pressure on the trigger.

"We're not," Timmy squealed. "You can't see or smell hydrogen gas, but it's here. Ask someone else if you don't believe us. Does anyone else live here?"

"Yeah, my brother Sherm," the man replied, easing off the trigger. "Sherm went to get the cows from the pasture, and he'll be back."

"Then ask him," Timmy urged. "Anyway, he'd be mad at you if you shot us."

The remark hit the right note. "Do you really think Sherm would be mad at me?" The man looked worried.

Both Timmy and Calvin hastily assured him that his brother would be furious. The bearded man was not entirely convinced and continued to finger the shotgun. While he and Calvin tried to pacify the man, Timmy wondered if the brother might be even harder to deal with.

That point was resolved a few minutes later when another man raced around the barn to see what had created the commotion. He was smaller and older than the bearded man, but he was completely rational. He looked in alarm at the shotgun his brother was wielding.

Everyone began talking at once. Sherm eased the shotgun away from his brother. "There's no reason to shoot anybody, Clem."

"But look at what they done to the roof, Sherm," Clem muttered.

"That's still no reason to shoot anybody," Sherm said in a placating voice. "Now just settle down and go to the house, and I'll attend to this here."

While the two brothers were talking, Timmy retrieved Calvin's cane from the gondola and helped him to his feet. His leg was only bruised, and Calvin sighed in relief. As Clem shuffled toward the house, Sherman Lewis, Timmy, and Calvin introduced themselves and shook hands.

The short, stocky man was as amiable as his brother was unpredictable. "I ain't never had anything to do with balloons, and I sure wouldn't want to go floating out over the ocean at night. We ain't very far from San Francisco here, and if you like, I'll hitch a team to the wagon and haul you, the boy, and your balloon back there."

Calvin quickly accepted the offer and offered to pay for the damages.

"Oh, it ain't damaged all that much," Lewis said, glancing at the house. "Me and Clem can fix that roof back up easy enough. The fact is, I'm glad you landed here. With the way Clem is, I don't get many visitors, and I like company."

Calvin replied cautiously. "Well, needless to say, I'm very grateful for your understanding as well as for your help."

"Any time," Lewis said cheerfully. "If you come here again, though, it would be better if you landed in the pasture. That way, Clem wouldn't get all riled up."

"There's no danger of our ever doing that again," Calvin replied firmly. "If there's ever been anything of which I'm entirely certain, it's that Timmy and I will never repeat what we did with that balloon."

XII

Ever since her kidnapping, Cindy had had nightmares. So when she was abruptly wakened one night, she cried out in alarm. Then she realized Sophia Schliemann was bending over her in the dim lamplight and shaking her shoulder. "I didn't mean to alarm you, Cindy. But, please, be very quiet," Sophia whispered.

Blinking the sleep out of her eyes, Cindy sat up in bed. "What's wrong?"

"We have found it!" Sophia whispered excitedly, sitting on the edge of the bed and squeezing Cindy's arm.

Cindy pushed her hair back. "Found what, Sophia?"

"Troy! We have found Troy!"

Now wide awake, Cindy suddenly remembered that Heinrich Schliemann had been absent from the table at dinner the previous evening. He had been removing rubble from the mouth of a tunnel that the laborers had uncovered just before the end of the workday. As the full implications struck her, Cindy had to put a hand over her mouth to keep from crying out. "Are you certain?"

"Absolutely positive, Cindy."

"Then we should be climbing on the roof and shouting this to the world, Sophia!"

Smiling, Sophia explained. Her husband had worked through the night in the tunnel, finding that it led to a small chamber under the thick, stone floor of a temple. He was still there, removing rubble and dust that had fallen onto the artifacts in the chamber.

"Some of the artifacts are gold," Sophia continued, "and others are electrum, which is an alloy of one-part silver to three-parts gold. Heinrich wishes to have them sketched *in situ* and removed to safety before the men begin work."

Immediately understanding the danger if word about the treasure spread, Cindy nodded and climbed out of bed, dressed hastily, and gathered her leather portfolio. She tucked it under her arm and followed Sophia into the thick darkness.

Fearing that a light would draw attention, Sophia led Cindy without a lantern. They moved through the ruins, feeling their way in the darkness, until a light glowed ahead—a lantern that Sophia had left in the mouth of the tunnel. Cindy ducked her head to follow Sophia into the low, narrow tunnel.

It led to a lower level. The women's skirts stirred up thick dust from the floor that swirled in the light of the lantern. The tunnel opened out into a small, stone chamber that was flooded with the light of several lanterns. Heinrich Schliemann, wary and dusty but radiantly happy, was sitting on a stone bench and savoring his moment of triumph as he waited.

He grinned broadly. "Well, what do you think of our find, Cindy?"

A moment of silence passed as Cindy looked around, trying to take in everything at once. Artifacts filled stone shelves, with overflow stacked on the floor. There were stone and pottery artifacts, as well as the gold and electrum treasures that Sophia had mentioned. "It's absolutely marvelous," Cindy finally managed. "What is this place? Some sort of storeroom?"

"Yes, a treasure repository for the temple above," Schliemann confirmed. "The door in the temple floor is blocked by a fallen column, and the tunnel we found must have been a secret entrance. The level above is covered with ashes, which means that when Troy was conquered, the temple and the rest of the city were burned. The priests must have been either killed or enslaved, so all information about this chamber was lost."

"But how can you be sure it's a Trojan temple?" Cindy asked.

Schliemann pointed to a small electrum statue, then to identical ones of gold and marble. "These are statues of Ilium Athena, the guardian goddess of Troy. Even those who have been ridiculing our work will be convinced. You see, in addition to Homer, numerous Greek and Roman classical historians refer to Ilium Athena as Troy's guardian goddess."

"Look at this, Cindy," Sophia said, pointing to a small pottery figurine of a hippopotamus. "This is Egyptian, evidence of a trade link between the Nile and Troy. There is also a carving that appears to depict ships paying tribute to Troy."

"It strongly suggests that Sophia's theory is correct," Schliemann added. "The Trojan War could very well have been waged by those wanting to sail merchant fleets through the Dardanelles without paying tribute to Troy."

"Well, I'm not an archaeologist," Cindy stated, "but I've spent many hours reading the *Iliad*, and I simply can't accept that the Trojan War was fought by people grubbing for money. It was fought because Menelaus wanted to retrieve his beautiful Helen, and as far as I'm concerned that's the end of it."

Both of the Schliemanns burst into hearty laughter. "I have known all along that Cindy is a pure romantic, Heinrich," Sophia said.

Schliemann sobered. "We must put your talent to work, Cindy. Everything here is precisely how I found it and how it must be sketched. When can you have the sketches finished?"

"About four or five hours," Cindy estimated.

"Could you make rough sketches and finish them later?" Schliemann asked, frowning. "I must have the electrum and gold out of here before the workmen see it. I intend to lock it in the cabinet in my study, then request armed guards to escort it to a museum for safekeeping."

"I was talking about rough sketches," Cindy told him. "There's so much detail here, it will take four or five hours to block all of it in, then several days to finish off the sketches."

The Schliemanns looked worried. "We could give the men a day off," Sophia suggested.

Schliemann shook his head. "Without a good reason,

they would become suspicious." He looked around the chamber again. "The arrangement of the artifacts may be of the utmost importance when we begin studying them individually. Priceless information will be lost by moving them without having a record of their arrangement."

"Tell the men that it's your birthday, and you're giving them a day off so you can take the day off," Cindy ventured.

Schliemann agreed eagerly, but then his smile faded. "But when Sophia and I carry the valuable artifacts away under our coats, the men will know we haven't taken the day off."

"The men are accustomed to my coming to the ruins at daybreak to catch the light just right," Cindy said, "then to my returning to the house for a late breakfast. I'll act as if I've done that." She pointed to her large leather portfolio. "And I'll hide the gold and electrum artifacts in that."

The Schliemanns immediately accepted Cindy's plan. They left as she opened her portfolio to get to work on the sketches.

For a few minutes, Cindy's mind was occupied with technical matters as she moved the lanterns to illuminate fully all the artifacts and selected the positions from which to make sketches. When she began sketching, her pencil moved almost automatically over the paper. Her mind was free to conjure up images of the past in the tiny subterranean chamber, where the ponderous silence of centuries had settled.

On the nights when she was in the ruins sketching by moonlight, it had often seemed that she could detect some lingering presence of those who had been there when the ruins had been buildings. In the small room that had escaped the ravages of time, she felt an even closer contact with those who had revered the artifacts as holy objects.

As she was visualizing robed priests filing down the stone steps to take figurines up to the main temple for a ceremony, Cindy heard a soft voice at her elbow. A chill racing up her spine, she leaped to her feet and looked around in alarm. Then she realized that the tunnel's acoustic quality had carried the voice of a workman into the chamber. Someone shouted to him, apparently informing him of the day off, because he whooped in delight.

As soon as all was silent, Cindy resumed working. Time passed unnoticed. When she finished rough sketches of each side of the room, she stored them in her portfolio, which she had opened on the floor. Acutely aware that the artifacts had been untouched since centuries before the first beginnings of the Roman Empire, Cindy carefully gathered them up.

She arranged the gold and electrum artifacts, all of which were small, in rows on the flattened portfolio to avoid making bulges. When they were placed to her satisfaction, she folded the other side of the portfolio over and fastened it. Then, picking it up, she encountered a problem: The portfolio was now extremely heavy.

After extinguishing the lanterns, she lugged the burden up the tunnel, gripping the handles with both hands. Emerging into a windy, overcast midmorning, she continued through the ruins. At the path leading down to the house, Cindy saw dozens of workmen enjoying their free day.

Drawing in a deep breath, Cindy held her portfolio in her right hand and tried not to lean against its weight as she started down the path. The Schliemanns were walking about in front of the house and chatting, while Heinrich smoked his pipe. Within earshot of numerous workmen, they called out a cheery good morning to Cindy.

It became increasingly hard for Cindy to avoid struggling with the portfolio. Fortunately the Schliemanns strolled up, Heinrich announced that it was his birthday, and Cindy expressed surprise, then wished him a happy birthday.

"When you weren't at breakfast," Sophia added, "Heinrich and I concluded that you must be working early."

"Yes, that's right."

"The cook is keeping your breakfast warm for you," Schliemann said. "Here, let me carry the portfolio for you."

"Why, thank you, Heinrich."

The three started down the path, continuing their light conversation for the benefit of workmen within earshot.

"Is anyone suspicious?" Cindy whispered to Sophia.

"No one thus far," Sophia replied softly.

Schliemann carried the portfolio to his study. Sophia and Cindy stood at the door as he opened the case on the floor in front of a cabinet, placed the artifacts on the shelves, locked the cabinet, and put the key in his pocket.

"After that," Cindy commented emphatically, "I'm more than ready for breakfast, with plenty of hot coffee."

"I'll join you," Heinrich said, looking mischievous. "It is early in the day, but I feel like having a brandy."

Sophia smiled. "Then I'll join you. I also need a brandy."

Laughing heartily, they filed out of the study toward the dining room, and Sophia called to the maid.

During the remainder of the day, Cindy worked on the sketches from memory, filling in some of the details. After dinner she took out a few of the gold artifacts and drew in their details on the sketches. The following day, when the workmen brought the stone and pottery artifacts from the chamber and placed them on shelves in the warehouse, Cindy sat in the warehouse, completing the sketches.

By the end of the third day, the sketches were ready to be used as masters to make plates for etchings. In the meantime, Schliemann had requested armed guards to escort the priceless artifacts to a museum. In order to avoid arousing suspicion, the request had been sent by routine means, so it would be several days before the guards arrived.

After dinner on the fourth day, Cindy was sitting with the Schliemanns in the parlor, discussing some of her sketches. The sound of a carriage drawing up outside interrupted the conversation. Then a small, thin man stepped into the parlor.

"Jules!" Heinrich exclaimed. Sophia echoed his astonishment. "We weren't expecting you for several more months! Why didn't you let us know you were returning?"

"I decided I could get here as quickly as a letter," the man replied, then patted his chest. "The doctor said I am completely cured." He turned to Cindy, smiled, and bowed. "And you must be Madame Kirovna's friend, Cindy Kerr. I am Jules Choubrac."

Cindy politely greeted the man, but his sudden, unexpected arrival meant that she would now have to return to Paris. The time she had spent at Hissarlik was one of the most enjoyable periods of her life, and she had been anticipating many more months of the same pleasure.

As he sat talking with the Schliemanns, Choubrac looked

at Cindy's sketches and lavishly complimented her on her skill, which made her feel no better at all about the situation. Sophia glanced at her. The woman's large, dark eyes reflected remorse as deep as Cindy's.

After the servants carried in Choubrac's baggage, the conversation ended. Before the gathering broke up, Choubrac handed her two letters from Paris: One was from her mother, the other was from Pierre Charcot, whose ardent pursuit of her would undoubtedly resume as soon as she returned.

When she was in her room, Cindy sat on the edge of her bed and opened the letter from Pierre. To her surprise, it was relatively short, and she smiled in relief. She had always regretted that his feelings for her had prevented a simple, uncomplicated friendship. But now that possibility was on the horizon.

His mother had contrived his betrothal to the daughter of old friends, a commitment he felt obligated to fulfill. There seemed to be subtleties and responsibilities that Cindy failed to understand, but while the letter hinted that his feelings for her would remain unchanged, her problem with him was ended.

An immediate return to Paris began to appear more favorable to Cindy. Smiling in satisfaction, she opened the letter from her mother.

As she read the first sentence, she gasped in delight. Toby and Alexandra Woodling were to be married. Cindy's friend Marjorie White had met Alexandra and considered the young woman a perfect match for Toby. Reading her mother's comments, Cindy shook her head in amusement. There were glowing sentences about Alexandra's beauty and charm but a glaring absence of mention of other qualities.

Confident that everything would work out, Cindy put the letter back into the envelope, wondering if she could make the trip to Portland to attend the wedding. She dismissed the idea immediately; her abrupt arrival after her long absence would take some of the attention and excitement of the wedding activities and the wedding day away from Alexandra, which Cindy considered unfair.

There was a tap on the door, and then Sophia stepped in. Sitting on the edge of the bed beside Cindy, she gave her a hug. "I will miss you. Our friendship is very precious to me."

"And to me," Cindy replied. "I will miss you also, but when you and Heinrich come to Paris, we can visit."

"I look forward to our next trip to Paris," Sophia said. She and Cindy agreed to write often, then Sophia pointed to the ancient Greek oil lamp she had put in the room the first night Cindy arrived. "When we pack your baggage, we will wrap that carefully so it won't get broken."

"I can't take that, Sophia," Cindy protested. "It's a valuable archaeological artifact."

"It has no unique archaeological value," Sophia stated firmly. "We have others identical to it. But that one has a special meaning to you, so you must take it with you."

Cindy hesitated, then said, "Yes, it is special to me. Thank you, Sophia."

The woman stepped toward the door. "It will remind you of the time you spent at the scene of the Trojan War," she said. "Which," she added, her eyes dancing, "was fought because Menelaus wanted to rescue his beloved Helen."

Cindy laughed as Sophia went out. Then she looked at the oil lamp, delighted that the beautiful ornament was hers, and prepared for bed.

As on the first night after she had arrived, she lay and looked out the window at the bay where Agamemnon's warships had anchored. Then, before she fell asleep, she thought again about Toby and Alexandra's wedding. If only she could find a way to attend the festivities without taking away anything from Alexandra!

With his injured leg resting on another chair, Edward Blackstone sat in the walled flower garden behind the spacious, comfortable Cochrane bungalow in Barapani. Leafing through a weeks-old copy of the London *Times*, he fumed over his enforced idleness.

Edward heard the sound of a horse clopping toward the stables behind the garden. A few minutes later the rider appeared. It was Edgar Dooley.

The cheerful man grinned at Edward's surprise. "I told

you it doesn't take me long to get about when I'm in a hurry."

"Where did you get the horse?" Edward asked.

"I borrowed it from Larry Atwater at Pandu Ghat," Dooley replied. He took the chair Edward indicated. "It got me here and will get me back to the river, even though my backside fits a bar stool much better." He pointed to Edward's injured leg. "How's it coming?"

"I'll be able to get about well enough on a cane within the next week or two." Edward saw that the Irishman was brimming with excitement. "Do you have news?"

Dooley's eyes sparkled as he glanced around. "Are we alone?"

"Completely."

Dooley began by telling Edward that he had found a perfect arrangement. In Calcutta, he said, he had met the captain of a ship who sailed from port to port, finding cargoes wherever he could. His ship was being unloaded in Calcutta, after which he would go to Bombay to load cargo destined for Rio de Janeiro.

"Bombay is the best place in India for us," Dooley continued. "South of the city are mud flats, and the land beyond is too poor for farming. We can drive the cows there, then bring them out to the ship on a raft. No one lives within miles of that place."

"That does sound very good. What sort of ship is this you're talking about?"

"I was going to ask the captain of a luxury steamer to haul Brahman cows out of India for me," Dooley teased. "It's a windjammer, Edward, but it floats."

Edward knew that only a captain feeling hard pressed for cargoes would agree to such an undertaking. "I wouldn't want those cows hauled as deck cargo. It'll soon be winter north of the equator, and we could run into some bad storms."

"The captain said he could find room in a hold for twenty-five head."

A momentary silence fell. "How much money does the captain want?" he asked, dreading the answer.

"Six hundred quid," Edgar replied, then lifted a hand as Edward winced. "It's a fair bargain—the man could be barred from every port in the British Empire if he's caught. Also, he'll load the cows at Bombay, then sail straight to Galveston Bay in Texas to unload us and the cows before going on to Rio de Janeiro."

"That is certainly fair," Edward remarked morosely, "but it's a very large sum, Edgar, much larger than I had anticipated. We'll have other expenses, won't we?"

"Yes," Dooley confirmed. "I'll have to hire men in Bombay to gather up the cows. There'll be other expenses as well, so I believe we should have an even one thousand quid on hand to take care of everything."

Calculating the exchange rate, Edward came up with the figure of five thousand dollars. The amount was almost totally unexpected, and the problem of where to get the money was one he would immediately have to face, but at the moment, he had no idea of where to turn. There certainly had not been enough money in the ranch's bank account when he had left Oklahoma.

"I'll have to think it over," Edward said. "I'll have someone prepare you a room in the bungalow."

"Edward, I don't need a room!" Dooley exclaimed. "I'm ready to set out for Pandu Ghat immediately. If it will help, I can find a hundred quid or so."

"I don't want you to put any money into this," Edward replied. "It's too risky. Won't you even stay for dinner?"

Dooley shook his head. "I can get something in the village and eat it on the road. But," he added quickly, "I wouldn't say no to a drink."

Laughing, Edward rang a small bell on the table beside his chair. Ramedha, who was tutoring the boys, stepped out the back door a moment later. She hesitated in surprise as she saw Dooley. "Why, good day to you, Mr. Dooley!"

Dooley jumped from his chair and bowed. "Top of the day to you, Miss Cochrane. It's a pleasure to see you again."

"As it is to see you, Mr. Dooley. Did you ring, Edward?"

"Would you have a servant bring Edgar a gin and tonic, please?" Ramedha nodded and went back inside. Edward turned to Dooley. "Do you have any idea of how long it would take a telegram to reach the United States?"

"Depends on whether or not the telegraph lines along

the Suez Canal are in working order," Edgar replied. "When they are, no more than a few days."

"I think I'll send a telegram to my partner, along with the name of my bank in Calcutta in case he can raise the money. Do you have pencil and paper on you?"

Dooley took out a notebook and pencil. "I'll send the telegram, then wait in Calcutta for a reply."

Reflecting that the telegram would probably be a sheer waste of money, Edward began writing. A servant came along the path, carrying a tray with a glass of gin and tonic.

Finished writing, Edward opened his wallet and counted out money on the table. "That should be enough for the telegram. Do you need any money for traveling expenses?"

After taking a deep swallow from the glass, Dooley pulled out his purse and peered into it. "I can travel more or less for free," he remarked. "I have some money here, but I could use an extra florin to buy a couple of bottles of bolabang."

Edward added another two shillings to the money on the table. "Very well, but be careful with that bolabang. I don't want you to end up in Benares when you're supposed to be going to Calcutta."

Dooley shook his head as he drained the glass. "Don't worry about me, Edward. You just worry about healing up that leg so you can get about."

Edward shook hands with Dooley. Then the man picked up the notebook and money, hurried to his horse, and rode away. After Dooley left, Edward's smile faded. The possibility that Rob could obtain five thousand dollars seemed very remote, and he could visualize his friend's wry amusement when he received the telegram and read it.

A few minutes later, Ramedha came out and glanced around. "Where is Mr. Dooley?" she asked.

"He left," Edward replied.

"Left?" Ramedha exclaimed in surprise, then laughed. "That was a short visit indeed!" She adjusted Edward's collar, then sat beside him, her hand placed possessively on his arm and her large, golden eyes gazing at him warmly. "Is Mr. Dooley making progress on the arrangements to get Brahman cows for you?"

Edward sat up, speechless with shock for a moment. "What do you mean?" he temporized.

"Edward," Ramedha said, affectionately patient, "I have read about tick fever. You were very interested in Mr. Witherspoon's cows, and Brahman cattle are resistant to disease. It is evident that you want some as breeding stock, and Mr. Dooley is looking into it for you."

Edward nodded. "Yes, but you must not say a word about this to anyone."

"Do you think I would betray you?" she exclaimed, angry and hurt.

"No, no," he assured her quickly. "I mean that if you mention this to the major, it would put him in an embarrassing position."

Mollified, she moved closer. "Well, I'm sure Uncle doesn't think you came to India for the lack of elsewhere to go. He may even suspect the real reason. If so, I'm sure he's more concerned with your safety than embarrassment to himself."

"Perhaps so, but please don't mention it to him."

"Very well, Edward. In any event, I'm sure he would be gratified that someone could find some use for a few of these cows that are simply standing about. However," she added quickly, "they are holy animals, so you must make certain that they come to no harm. You will do that, won't you?"

Although Edward had become accustomed to Ramedha's abrupt veering between Christian and Hindu points of view, he was still fascinated by it. She was more intriguing than anyone he had ever met. He smiled. "They are to be used for breeding stock."

"When will you return to India?"

"This proposition about the cows is far from being settled," he replied uncomfortably, "but if it does work out, I don't know that I'll ever return to India, Ramedha. I'm quite a lot older than you, my dear. You're very attractive, and in time you'll become interested in a man more your own age."

She shook her head. "No, but perhaps it would be best if we were separated for a time. It would allow me to draw closer to you in age."

"What do you mean?"

Ramedha patted his arm. "If a woman has a child when

she is twenty, the child will be ten when she is thirty, or one third her age. When she is forty, the child will have become a full one half of her age at twenty. Obviously, those who are younger draw closer in age to those who are older, Edward."

Laughing heartily, Edward shook his head as he started to point out the flaw in her logic; then his laughter faded. "Well, perhaps so," he admitted reluctantly.

"Of course it is so," she said cheerfully. "If this proposition does work out for you, you must be very careful. The government would take an extremely stern view of what you are doing."

"I intend to be as careful as possible. I don't want to end up in jail."

"I don't believe you would be jailed, but it would prevent you from ever taking a position with the East India Company or a commission in the army here. One must always protect one's options for the future, mustn't one? And," she added, "you must be careful at your ranch. From what I've read, that part of the world can be violent."

"Not Oklahoma," Edward corrected. "All the time I was there, it was very peaceful."

In the edge of dense trees that crowned a long ridge, Toby Holt tied his horse to a sapling and took off his spurs, then hung them on his saddle horn. Constantly watchful of places where the bushwhacker could take a shot at him with the Big Fifty, he had seen the sun glint on metal in the edge of the trees on the ridge. Immediately turning off the road, he had approached the ridge from the side.

The vantage point looked much like other places the gunman had waited in ambush. Below the edge of the trees, the slope overlooking the road was a grassy meadow, giving a clear shot at anyone on the road. On the opposite side of the ridge, the terrain consisted of rugged, wooded hills, good for an easy getaway.

Toby moved quietly through the trees, his Winchester under his arm. Seeing fresh hoofprints in the leaves and soft dirt under the trees, he stopped, slowly and silently working the lever on his rifle to load the firing chamber. Then he loosened his pistol in the holster as he crept forward.

The hoofprints led through the trees to a point halfway along the ridge, and Toby glimpsed a horse through the foliage ahead. Tethered to a tree, it was the roan he had seen before. Knowing it would neigh in alarm if it heard or scented him, Toby worked his way down toward the edge of the trees.

A few minutes later, he saw the man—the same tall, thin man he had glimpsed before, sitting under a tree with the Big Fifty across his lap as he watched the road. Toby crept slowly around a clump of underbrush, positioning himself so the man would be in clear view.

When he was on the other side of the underbrush, Toby called out, "Drop the rifle and put up your hands!" The man jumped in surprise, his eyes wide as his head snapped around; then he began lifting the rifle. "Don't try it!" Toby warned.

The man swung the long, heavy rifle around to bring it to bear on Toby. Intending to wound, not kill, the man, Toby drew a bead on his enemy's shoulder. But the man tried to dodge and get off a shot, and the bullet passed through his heart.

As the rifle kicked against Toby's shoulder, its loud report ringing out, he saw a hole appear in the man's coat over his heart. The impact of the bullet sent the man flying, and he was dead by the time he hit the ground.

Toby slammed his fist against a tree in frustration, then stepped toward the body. Looking at the face closely, he knew he had never seen the man before. Nothing in the pockets revealed his identity or whereabouts, but a small leather pouch contained a substantial amount of money. Toby led the roan down to the edge of the trees and put the body across the saddle, then led it toward his own horse.

After an hour of backtracking the hoofprints from the ridge, Toby found a temporary camp that the man had made in a remote valley a few miles away. Bags hanging in a tree beside the bedroll and the ashes of the fire contained ample supplies, but again Toby found no personal papers or anything else that hinted at the man's identity. He put the belongings on the horse with the body, then set out for Folsom.

The horse with a body across the saddle created a stir of

interest in the town. People stared curiously, and men stepped off the boardwalks to follow the horses and peer at the body. Someone went for the marshal.

Joshua Hubbard nodded when Toby told him what had happened, then sent a bystander to get Percival Sloat. While they were waiting for Sloat, the marshal asked the other men standing about if they had ever seen or talked with the dead man. They shook their heads.

"I think I've seen him in town," one man commented, "but I've never talked to him."

Another said the same thing. "But no one heard him say his name or saw him with anyone else who might know anything about him?" the marshal persisted.

The men shook their heads; no one knew anything about the dead man.

Sloat heard the man being questioned as he strode across the street. "Maybe he's somebody that Holt has been pushing around," he suggested.

Hubbard ignored the remark. He pointed to the long, heavy rifle tied to the saddle. "Is this the rifle you sold, and is he the man who bought it?"

The newspaperman grunted. "Yes, but I never saw him before then, and I haven't seen him since."

While the marshal was talking with Sloat, the crowd around the horses grew, and other passersby paused to find out what had happened. The land speculators, Rossiter and Steed, were among them. Toby watched them carefully as they passed, to see if they made eye contact with Sloat; but they didn't give any sign of even knowing the man, let alone being in cahoots with him. Pearlie hurried across the street to make certain that Toby was unharmed, and several townspeople commended him for his actions.

But no one admitted to knowing anything about the man, and the reason why he had been trying to kill Toby remained a mystery. As the marshal led the horse away, the body across the saddle, Toby rode back out of town, toward the M Bar B.

At the ranch Rob took an optimistic view of what had happened. "For the first time since you came here," the tall redhead pointed out, "you don't have to worry whether or not a bullet is going to come flying at you."

"Well, at least a Big Fifty bullet," Toby qualified.

"You came here to stop the trouble in the area, and to a large extent you have," Rob continued. "You've eliminated a lot of jobs for gunslingers. The man could have been one of them, Toby."

Toby agreed that it was a possibility. His efforts had produced positive results: There was much less friction now between and among ranchers and homesteaders.

Later, over dinner, Rob reported that the last of the thoroughbred Herefords had died of tick fever, and he was anxiously waiting to hear from Edward in India. In the meantime, he and Billy had been working hard at fencing the ranch. Toby offered to help them when he was free.

After dinner, Toby and Rob sat in the parlor over cigars and drinks while Sally washed dishes and Billy chopped wood outside the kitchen door. Gunfire suddenly rang out, and a parlor window shattered as a bullet slammed into the wall.

Toby reacted immediately. He jumped up and blew out the lamp on the table. "Put out the light in the kitchen, Sally!" he called. Then he and Rob moved, crouching, to the gun rack beside the front door for their weapons.

Two more shots were fired, the bullets thumping into the east wall of the house as Toby and Rob hastily buckled on their pistol belts. Billy ran in, slamming into Toby in the darkness. "It sounds like they're in those trees east of the house," he said, fumbling for his rifle.

Toby agreed. "Their horses will be nearby, so they'll be gone just as soon as we try to pin them down. Go to the corral and saddle three horses. Bring them around there. Rob and I will go after them."

Billy raced off the porch in the direction of the corral. Rob followed Toby in the other direction, circling around to the east side of the house. The copse of trees was a thicker shadow in the moonlight, and the red muzzle flashes were clearly visible as the rifles were fired again.

Crouching low as they trotted toward the trees, Toby and Rob held their fire. When they were a hundred yards from the copse, Toby lifted his Winchester. He fired rapidly at the muzzle flashes, while Rob did the same. The gunfire from the trees stopped, then there was the pounding of hoofbeats.

Just then, Billy galloped up on a horse, leading two more. Toby and Rob flung themselves onto the horses' backs, and the three set out after the gunmen. Toby had little hope of catching them, and he was proven right. While the gunmen rode at a dead run, Toby, Rob, and Billy had to rein up occasionally to listen for hoofbeats. The gunmen's hoofbeats grew more faint each time Toby and his friends stopped to listen. When they reined up at the ridge overlooking Indian territory, the hoofbeats were far away, then suddenly drowned in the rumble of a cattle herd breaking into a stampede as the outlaws rode through a herd of Indian cattle, which had been bedded down for the night.

Toby, Rob, and Billy rode back to the ranch, discussing the unprovoked attack. The evening's events would certainly have repercussions because some understandably angry Indians were now faced with rounding up a stampeded herd.

The results of that came the next day when Marshal Hubbard appeared at the ranch. Three chiefs from the Indian reservation had come to town and complained.

"This is what we've been afraid of all along, isn't it?" the marshal said. "And it's coming just when you're getting things settled down."

"But I still don't know what's at the bottom of this trouble," Toby said. "Someone is obviously stirring it up, but why?" He looked away, deep in thought, then said, "I've been thinking about getting everyone together to talk things over."

Hubbard stroked his beard, then nodded. "Maybe that would be a good idea. It would have been impossible before, but the way you've got things settled down, maybe people can talk peaceably to each other. We'll have to do something, though, because time is running out on us. We can't let things spread to the reservation."

Toby agreed grimly.

The following day, in his continuing rounds of the ranches and homesteads, Toby talked with the owners about the prospects for a meeting of everyone in the area. As he anticipated, all the owners agreed that such a meeting would be a good idea, but none wanted to attend.

Undaunted by the initial reaction, Toby gave the people time to think about the idea. When he made his rounds a second time, the same owners grudgingly agreed to attend a meeting if everyone else did. Toby knew that it might take a few weeks to talk everyone into it, but at least the meeting would be held.

On the fourth day after the marshal visited the M Bar B, Toby met Rob and Billy on the road from Folsom. Billy was driving the wagon, and Rob was riding beside it. At first, the conversation puzzled Toby. Billy was excited about something, but Rob clearly was holding back. At last Billy blurted out, "Mr. Martin got a telegram that came all the way from India!"

"From Edward?" Toby asked, turning to Rob. "Why didn't you tell me?"

Annoyed with Billy for bringing up the subject, Rob shrugged. "We've run into a snag on that business with Brahman cows, Toby. It isn't going to work out."

Weighing the reply and knowing his friend well, Toby had a strong suspicion that the telegram was a request for money. "Let me see the telegram, Rob."

"No, it's a dead subject," Rob replied. "There's no point in talking about it."

"Rob," Toby insisted, "I want to read that telegram. Now hand it over."

Glaring at Billy, Rob reluctantly took out the telegram and gave it to Toby. After reading it quickly, Toby said, "If all he needs is five thousand dollars, that can be taken care of in very short order."

"We're not going to take the money from you, Toby," Rob stated emphatically. "Five thousand dollars for twenty-five head of cattle would make them the most expensive cattle in history."

"If they're a means of solving the problem with tick fever," Toby pointed out, "they'll also be some of the most valuable cattle in history, and worth far more than five thousand dollars."

"Perhaps, but we can't take the money from you. It's

more than enough that you've come here to help, and I don't know how we're going to pay you for all that barbed wire."

"We can call it a loan—" Toby began, then lifted a hand as Rob started to interrupt. "No, hear me out, Rob. The finances are beside the point. This country needs a breed of large beef cattle that's immune to tick fever. If we can provide that, then it's our duty to do so. That's what's important."

"That's true," Rob admitted reluctantly. "We can talk about it when things are settled here. The way they are right now, you don't have time to think about this."

"I don't intend to think about it," Toby replied. "I'll send a telegram to my business manager in Chicago and ask him to attend to it. Dieter can have the money transferred to India."

"You're the best friend a man could have, Toby," Rob said, as he put out his hand, "and I'm really grateful for this, along with everything else you've done."

Toby shook hands with Rob and turned his horse toward Folsom as Rob and Billy continued toward the ranch. Having a breed of large cattle that was immune to tick fever was a gratifying prospect, but he knew that if the area's trouble spread onto Indian lands, nothing else would matter.

XIII

The smell of new wood and fresh paint was strong as Alexandra, still in her nightgown, climbed the steps to the small room at the top of the tower on the left flank of the nearly completed house at the Holt ranch. She looked out the window at the dawn sky. In order to complete all the preparations, she had delayed the county fair for almost a month, perilously close to winter. But the opening day was going to be crisp and sunny.

Smiling in relief and satisfaction, Alexandra went down the stairs to her room on the second floor, where Juanita had put out the usual clean riding trousers and shirt with a pair of boots.

"I'd like to wear my green dress and hat, instead," Alexandra told the maid, "with a cape, because it will be cool. And only one petticoat, please. I'm going in the buggy, which has a small seat."

"You'll be escorted, won't you, Doña Alexandra?" Juanita asked. "Crowds at public events can be unruly."

"Yes, Clayton Hemmings will drive the buggy."

As Juanita put away the riding clothes, she said, "But you should go in riding costume on one of your horses in the parade and take credit for what you did."

"No, I like to stay in the background," Alexandra replied. "Also, the ranch hands will be competing in the rodeo. If they do as well as I hope and I was at the forefront of things, people might suspect the contest was rigged."

The maid nodded. Opening the clothes closet, she took out the green dress and helped Alexandra get ready. Then Alexandra went down to the dining room.

Janessa, sitting at the table with coffee, smiled as Alexandra sat down. "You look beautiful," she said sincerely.

"Thank you, Janessa," Alexandra said, pleased at the compliment.

A moment later, a buoyantly cheerful Timmy thundered down the stairs and bounded in, wearing his Sunday suit and ready to leave for the fair. He had told Alexandra about the incident with the balloon in San Francisco, which she immediately dismissed as an accident. He took his place at the table as Abby Givens served breakfast.

Alexandra told Timmy what she expected of him, covering each point in detail and making certain he understood. "Most of all," she continued, "you're to do precisely as Calvin tells you. You're not to offer him any advice or try to talk him into anything."

"Yes, ma'am," the boy promised.

"Are you sure you don't want to go, Janessa?" Alexandra asked. "You might enjoy it."

Janessa shook her head. "Most of the hospital volunteers will be at the fair, so Dr. Martin won't have much help. I'd better stay at the hospital with him."

When breakfast was over, Alexandra and the children went outside, where the ranch seethed with excitement. The men were gathered in front of the bunkhouse, listening to Stalking Horse. The foreman was warning them about drinking too much and was giving the younger men a pep talk on upholding the honor of the ranch in the rodeo—the first one in Portland.

Calvin had been up for hours and was just returning from filling the balloon envelope with gas at the fairground. He assured Alexandra that it was a perfect day. "There's very little wind, and it's cool. That will make the balloon easy to control."

"That's good to hear," Alexandra replied. "Safety is our first concern. If you have any doubts at all about safety, then please stop everything." She turned to Timmy. "Have a good time, but remember what I said."

The boy grinned, then leaped into the wagon with Calvin. As they drove away, Alexandra walked toward the men. "Will someone have time to take Juanita, Amy, and Abby to the fairground?"

"I will, Miss Alexandra," Jonah Venable volunteered. "And I'll bring them home tonight. They can stay with me if they want an escort."

Alexandra thanked him, then went to her room to finish getting ready. A short time later, she came downstairs wearing the hat and cape that matched her dress. The new buggy, gleaming with polish, was waiting at the front steps. Clayton helped Alexandra in, then turned the buggy toward town.

A few minutes later, Alexandra saw the results of the broadsides advertising the fair that had been plastered on trees for miles in all directions during the past weeks. Farm wagons and tents belonging to families from the outlying areas had been parked and set up beside the road.

"Everyone within miles must be here," Clayton said.

"It certainly does look promising," Alexandra remarked, her casual tone belying her feelings. Hoping to draw and hold a crowd, she had scheduled the rodeo for the first day, the main circus events the second, and the judging of livestock, produce, and homecrafts on the third, with sideshows and other attractions every day. The results were important to her because she had invested heavily in the fair.

Clayton parked the buggy on a side street, then he and Alexandra went to the back door of the bank. The bank manager opened the door at Clayton's knock and led them upstairs to an office. The mayor, several city councilmen, and other notables who were at the windows bowed to her as she stepped in.

"You've worked wonders, Miss Alexandra," the mayor said. "This looks more like the Chicago fair than other fairs we've had in Portland."

"Thank you," she replied, "but so many people have been involved that I certainly can't take all the credit." She stepped to a window as the men moved to make room for her. The fronts of the buildings on Main Street were decorated with red, white, and blue banners and streamers. A solid, teeming mass of people lined the street, their voices raised in excitement as they watched a parade, led by the circus calliope, moving slowly toward the fairground. The calliope's cheerful music was almost overwhelmed in the bedlam. It was followed by Leland Blake on horseback, the grand marshal of the parade. Behind him were the jugglers, clowns, trapeze artists, and other circus acts, then the elephants, camels, and more circus animals.

The cheering crowd streamed toward the fairground in the wake of the parade, leaving a deserted street behind. As Alexandra and the men left the bank, a city councilman named Burke ventured, "If you're interested in selling shares of that mortgage you hold on the fairground, Miss Alexandra, I'll buy any amount and pay you a hundred percent premium on what you paid."

"I'll make that a hundred and fifty percent," another man chimed in.

The offers were in a joking tone, for the men knew that Alexandra had no intention of selling any part of the mortgage, but they were a vote of confidence. She laughed and said, "Sorry, gentlemen," as they went to their carriages.

Clayton brought her to the fairground headquarters, where Alexandra entered her small office, adjacent to the manager's. Through her window she had a good view of the balloon and the rodeo arena.

The sideshows and other attractions were doing a booming business and people were waiting in a long line for rides on the balloon. Timmy acted as the conductor in the gondola as it rose and came back on its cable. The elimination events at the rodeo arena were held, and the Holt ranch was well represented among the contestants for the final events. Throughout the day, Frank Copeland, the fairground manager, rushed in and out of his office, overseeing everything.

During the afternoon, a serious problem arose when the beverage vendors ran short of ice. "The icehouse is delivering plenty," Copeland explained, "but it's as soft as mush when it gets here. By this time of year, the ice stored up during winter is almost a year old, and it's so soft that it melts quickly."

Alexandra asked Copeland to have the stewards look for the mayor or a city councilman among the crowd. A short time later, the manager returned with Charles Burke. He listened as she explained the problem.

"An inventor named Rufus Gooch lives down beside the river," he said. "Gooch has a machine that makes large blocks of ice from water. I'll go talk with him, but I have little hope of success. Most likely he'll simply order me off his property."

"Yes, I know that Mr. Gooch can be difficult, Mr. Burke. But we'll gladly pay a reasonable price. He knows who you are, and I can think of many reasons why he would be amenable. For example, a hint that the city might exercise its right of eminent domain over riverfront property and set it aside for future wharfage would tend to make him agreeable, wouldn't it?"

Copeland smothered a laugh and turned away. Burke gazed at Alexandra in solemn silence for a moment. Then, his lips twitching in a smile, he left. He was back within an hour, telling Copeland to make arrangements to send a wagon for the ice that Gooch had agreed to provide for the duration of the fair.

At the rodeo arena, men from the Holt ranch were among the top three winners as each event took place. White Elk was the leader among them, and he and a young man from a neighboring town were in a seesaw contest for overall first place. During late afternoon, Alexandra stood at the window and watched the last event, bronco busting, in which the man from out of town was thrown from his horse and White Elk rode his to a standstill. Then the rodeo ended amid a roar of applause and cheers. Leland Blake handed out prizes and presented White Elk with a silver belt buckle for being best all-around cowboy.

When the evening shift took over at the sideshow, refreshment stands, and other attractions, the cash returns for the day started to come in. The expenses would be virtually paid off by the receipts from the first day, so the following days would produce profits. Copeland and the stewards were elated at the prospect of the first bonus they had ever received.

While Alexandra was looking over the columns of receipts, there was a knock on the door, and Charles Burke stepped in. "Would you consider a two hundred premium over what you paid, Miss Alexandra?"

"No-o-o-o, I don't think so."

"I was just checking," Burke said. They were both laughing as Burke went back outside.

Henry Blake stepped out of his office to greet Howard McKinnon, Fargo's mayor. It was an unsalaried position; the man was a store owner with a strong sense of duty to the community. He was a portly, sober man in his forties whom Henry liked.

McKinnon spoke above the noise of axes and hammers resounding all over the fort. "Seems like you're rebuilding everything from the ground up. This place looks like an army fort now. Your soldiers are really putting themselves into the work. You've done wonders with this place and with the men, Captain Blake."

"They're glad to be doing something besides drills for a change," Henry replied with a laugh. "Come in and sit down, Mayor McKinnon. For the most part, they were basically good men. What I did was help them to find some pride in themselves."

Puffing on the cigar Henry had offered him, McKinnon got to the point of his visit. "I talked with Sheriff Slattery this morning and told him that I'd stop his salary if he didn't clean up Fargo and drive the riffraff out of town. The man laughed in my face, Captain."

"I've heard talk that the owners of the saloons and brothels are paying him to let them do as they wish. They must be paying him more than his salary."

McKinnon sighed heavily. "That must be it. In the meantime, Fargo has become so unruly that decent people can't walk down the street. Your men who escort the Mennonites to Fargo are being harassed by the rabble. Furthermore, it's a disgrace that the Mennonites need an army patrol to protect them. We must have law and order." He paused. "You could take your soldiers to town and clean the place up."

"I'll be more than glad to do it, Mayor. First, though, you'll have to get the territorial governor to declare martial law in Fargo."

McKinnon shook his head. "We can't do that, Captain. That would be a black mark against this territory when it comes up for statehood. Also, martial law would be a big setback to getting settlers established here."

"I've heard that Governor Curran will be leaving soon," Henry said, "but the new man will be faced with the same problems that keep Governor Curran from declaring martial law."

"Unfortunately, that's true," McKinnon agreed. "The only solution I see is for you to take matters in hand. I can assure you of the wholehearted support of every decent citizen in Fargo." He lifted a hand as Henry started to speak. "Please, Captain Blake, just give it serious consideration. Then I'll leave it up to you to do whatever you think best."

After the meeting, Henry accompanied the mayor to the hitching rail. It was a cold, bleak day, and McKinnon buttoned his coat against the gusty wind as he said good-bye to Henry. The dark clouds swirling across the sky matched Henry's mood as he went back into the office.

The settlers in the region were making a substantial contribution to the economic welfare of the nation. The Mennonites had brought with them the seeds to plant the Turkish red wheat they had grown in the Crimea, a hardy, drought-resistant grain that yielded a much larger harvest than other wheat grown in the country. But because of a corrupt lawman, they were unable to go about their daily affairs.

By nature, Henry was more inclined to take control and correct a problem than to waste time on legalities. The situation in Fargo was infringing upon people's rights, and it would present a serious problem for the fort in the near future. The soldiers, now a well-trained, disciplined force, were still restricted to the immediate area of the fort during their off-duty hours. The restriction would have to be lifted soon, and the only place they had to go was Fargo.

Henry was working on a plan when Lieutenant Watson reported in from escorting a group of Mennonites with a platoon of soldiers. Pale and trembling with anger, he had a cut on his face, and his uniform was spattered with dirt.

"What happened?" Henry asked, returning the lieutenant's salute.

"The crowd from the shantytown threw rocks and clods of dirt at the escort, sir," Watson replied stiffly.

"What did the men do?"

"I ordered them to hold their positions and remain between the crowd and the Mennonites, which they did." He nodded in satisfaction. "We have some good soldiers here, sir."

"Yes, we do, and you're one of them. Very well, carry on."

The lieutenant saluted again and went out, leaving Henry in a boiling rage. He believed that Klaus Lukenbill had instigated the attacks, in the hope that the Mennonites would lose their army escorts and be forced to welcome him back as their liaison with the Fargo stores.

Henry refused to allow his men to suffer such abuse again. He sent the clerk to saddle his horse, then rode to town through the gathering twilight. As usual, the saloons and brothels along the main street were doing a booming business, and he guided his horse around drunks who were passed out or fighting.

The sheriff was in his office with a crony. Slattery smirked as Henry stepped into the office. "Well, look who's here," he remarked.

Henry got straight to the point. "Slattery, when my men escorted a party of Mennonites to town, some of the mob you harbor here threw stones at them. That had better not happen again."

Both men burst into whoops of scornful laughter. The one sitting beside the desk stood and moved toward Henry. "Somebody threw stones? Did it hurt their feelings and make them cry?"

His mocking grin disappeared as Henry's fist slammed into his gut. He doubled over, clutching his stomach, and stumbled backward. Henry followed him, swinging his right fist toward the man's face. Blood exploded from the man's nose and mouth, and he snapped upright, then fell back toward the desk. He skidded across it, scattering papers, then sprawled on Slattery's lap. The sheriff's chair collapsed under them, depositing both men on the floor.

Stepping around the desk, Henry gripped Slattery's shirt and hauled him to his feet, then slammed him against the wall. "Now clean up this town, Slattery!" Henry ordered. "Or it'll be done for you!"

"I'll put you in jail for this!"

Henry pulled Slattery away from the wall and slammed him against it again. "Shut up and listen! This town is going to be cleaned up. You're the law officer. Now do your job!"

"This town ain't your business!" Slattery replied. "If you don't like it, stay at that fort and keep your men there!"

Henry realized with disgust that he was wasting his time. Releasing the man, he turned and went back out into the riotous night in the town. He rode toward the fort, knowing what he had to do.

During the night, the wind whipped into a northerly gale, bringing winter to Fargo and the north surrounding plains. The next morning was frigidly cold, with small, dry snowflakes in the wind. If the shantytown was destroyed in such weather, those who lived there would be forced to leave.

After breakfast Henry stood on the porch in front of headquarters with his overcoat collar pulled up against the cold, smoking a cigar as the snow skimmed across the quadrangle ahead of the wind. Watson strode up, saluting and wishing the captain a good morning. "Winter is here, sir."

"Yes, Harvey. Send the clerk to saddle my horse, if you would, and have the bugler sound Boots and Saddles."

The lieutenant hesitated in surprise, almost asking why, then saluted again and hurried away. Moments later, the notes of the bugle rang out, and the stir of morning routine activity changed into pandemonium. Soldiers bolted past each other as they raced to the barracks for their equipment, then buckled on pistol belts while dashing to the stable to saddle horses.

The company formed in two ranks. Sergeant Olsen and the lieutenant took their positions while the clerk led Henry's horse to the front of the headquarters building. Henry tossed away his cigar and mounted, then walked the horse to the front of the formation. When he announced what he intended to do, a murmur of satisfaction passed through the men.

"I'll have none of that!" he snapped, firmly silencing

them. "We're not going to town to punish anyone or to exact revenge. The situation in town is out of control, and we're simply going there to correct it. Minimal force will be used, and any man who loses control and acts like one of that mob instead of a member of a military organization will be court-martialed. Squad leaders, form a rank in front of the company."

As the sergeants moved forward, Henry explained in detail what was to be done. Knowing the men well now, he chose the most level-headed of the sergeants to lead squads where serious trouble was likely to develop, then singled out those squads that would be on the main street. "Have your men get the axes and crowbars being used to repair the fort," he said to the leaders. "The rest of you, resume your places."

The men moved about smartly, and several of the squad leaders summoned their men out of ranks, then led them away. A few minutes later, the men were back in ranks, axes and crowbars tied to their saddles. Henry led the company out of the fort, with Watson at his side and the guidon snapping in the wind. There was a loud thunder of hoofbeats and clatter of sabers from the long double file of cavalry following him.

The road was deserted on the raw, wintry morning, and the town itself was quiet. Only a scattered few shantytown inhabitants on the main street stopped to glare at the company. Henry reined up on the main street, then dispatched the squads.

Two squads remained in reserve behind him, along with the lieutenant and the first sergeant. Two others headed toward the upwind side of the shantytown, while others spread out along the street. They dismounted in front of saloons and brothels. One man remained behind to hold the horses as the others ran inside with axes and crowbars.

The quiet hanging over the town disappeared. The soldiers broke windows and destroyed furniture, then set to tearing down doors and walls. They hurled employees, prostitutes, and customers into the street, the half-dressed people shivering and looking around in shock. A burly bouncer clutching a shotgun reeled out of a saloon as a soldier grappled with him. Then the shotgun fired harmlessly into the ground as the soldier clubbed the bouncer with his service revolver.

Faro wheels and other gaming equipment flew into the street, along with beds and other furniture, which were thrown through upper windows. Bureau drawers rained gauzy, brightly colored garments. As more people reeled out into the street, a saloon owner, furiously angry, ran up to Henry.

"Have you gone crazy?" he demanded. "Your men are wrecking my place!"

"Leave town," Henry advised the man.

Spitting an oath, the man ran to the sheriff's office and went inside. A moment later, a disheveled and hung-over Slattery lumbered out and looked around in shock. Then, bellowing in rage, he bounded heavily up the street to Henry. "What's going on here?"

"What I told you would happen," Henry replied calmly, "and what you should have been doing during the past months."

"This town ain't none of your business!" Slattery bellowed.

"You let this town turn into a cesspool so you could line your pockets. That's finished now."

The man, speechless with rage, started to draw his pistol. Then he froze as Henry whipped out his saber. Slattery felt the keen tip pricking his throat. "Don't give me a reason to take your head off," Henry warned quietly. "Go back to your office and keep out of the way."

"The territorial governor is going to hear about this!" Slattery threatened. "And everybody else right on up to Washington!"

"I've no doubt about that," Henry replied, amused. "Now get back to your office, or I'll have you locked in the jail."

The man stomped away, waving his arms and yelling oaths at no one in particular. The bedlam on the street was matched by a similar uproar at the shantytown. Smoke was billowing from the shacks, which the soldiers were torching. Among those streaming out of a bordello, Henry saw Lukenbill hurry out into the street, pulling on his clothes as he ran.

Beckoning the first sergeant closer, Henry pointed out Lukenbill. "I'd like to talk with him, Sergeant Olsen. Bring him here."

The sergeant saluted, mounted his horse, then rode down the street. Charging into the people milling about, he leaned down and gripped Lukenbill's shirt, then wheeled his horse and rode back, dragging the man up the street and releasing him in front of Henry. Lukenbill glared at the captain.

"It's about nine o'clock, Lukenbill," Henry said. "If I see you in town after ten, I'll have you arrested."

"Arrested?" Lukenbill echoed in outrage. "You don't have the authority to arrest me, and what would you charge me with?"

"I'll assume the authority and lock you in the stockade at Fort Abercrombie until I think of a charge," Henry told him.

The man stiffened, his eyes glazed with fury. "All right, I'll go!" he hissed. "But I'll get even with you! You're going to be sorry that you ever stuck your nose into my business. What happened here will be nothing compared to what I'll do! Blood will flow, and it's going to be on your hands!"

As the man stalked away, Henry felt no personal fear, but he knew that in the months ahead, Lukenbill might cause trouble for the people in town.

Henry's attention was drawn away to Mayor McKinnon, who was hurrying along the boardwalk, followed by a score of merchants and other responsible citizens of the town. They were all carrying axes and wrecking bars, and they ran to help the soldiers. Watching them, Henry smiled in satisfaction.

A few minutes later, ruffians from the shantytown began gathering in the main street, mixing with those driven out of saloons and brothels. It was a volatile situation. Henry turned to Watson. "Deploy the reserve squads in a flanking line," he ordered, "and disperse that crowd."

The lieutenant saluted, then turned to the men on horseback and relayed the orders. The soldiers drew their sabers, formed into a line, and charged down the street. A roar of oaths and protests rose as the soldiers rode into the crowd, beating at the bums and outlaws with the flats of their sabers. The crowd quickly disintegrated.

Many of the inhabitants of shantytown, having been chased out of numerous other places, had accepted the situation and were leaving. It quickly became a mass exodus as others gave up and joined them. Wagons and horses loaded down with ragged, bearded men streamed out of Fargo. A short time later it was all over. The saloons and brothels had been put out of business, and the shantytown was a wall of flames.

As Henry led the company back toward the fort, he speculated about the reaction of the military and civil authorities to what he had done. While he was satisfied that he had taken the only action open to him, he was certain his superiors would disagree.

Three days later, the first reaction to what had happened in Fargo appeared in an unexpected form. After the clerk stepped into his office in a rush of breathlessly excited words, Henry put on his campaign hat and went out to meet two officers arriving at the fort. The senior officer wore a buckskin coat, a wide-brim hat cocked at a jaunty angle, and sported a long mustache. Henry immediately knew who he must be, having heard of George Armstrong Custer many times.

The man had once held the brevet rank of major general, so it was a conventional courtesy to address him by that rank. "Good day, General," Henry said, saluting. "I'm Captain Blake, the commander, and it's a pleasure to have you visit Fort Abercrombie."

"It's a pleasure for me as well, Captain Blake," Custer replied, snapping a salute in return as he dismounted. He glanced around, laughing. "It is also something of a surprise. The last time I was here, it looked more like a hideout for outlaws. Now it's put me in a frame of mind to take a close look at Fort Lincoln when I get back there. This is Major Reno, battalion commander in my regiment."

After exchanging a salute with the major, Henry invited the officers into his office. "I'll have lunch brought in, if you wish."

"This is an informal visit," Custer replied. "I want to have a quiet word with you about what happened at Fargo the other day, so your quarters would be better. I won't say no to lunch, though, because we've had a long ride in miserably cold weather."

After seating the officers in comfortable chairs in his sitting room, Henry opened a cabinet and took out a small cheese, jars of paté and caviar, and other selections from the delicacies that Gisela supplied in quantities. He put them on the table, then set out glasses and opened a bottle of good red wine.

The two officers were impressed by the lavish lunch and ate with good appetite. Custer glanced around the sitting room. "You certainly know how to live, Captain Blake."

"I like to be comfortable when I can, sir," Henry replied, spreading paté on a round of bread, "but I'm perfectly content to eat hardtack and sleep on the ground when my duties require it."

Custer eyed Henry reflectively. "Yes, I'm sure you are. I've heard that it isn't wise to underestimate you, and I can see that I heard the truth." He looked at Gisela's picture and smiled. "And I've heard about the baroness as well."

Henry waited for some mention of what he had done in Fargo, but Custer began talking about his own duties. The acting commander of the Seventh Cavalry Regiment, he had widespread responsibilities in the region. One was maintaining peace with the Indians.

"The prospecting in the Black Hills," Custer said, "has got the Sioux boiling mad. If Sitting Bull leads the Sioux off the reservation, other tribes will join them. Right now, we could have the makings of one of the biggest Indian uprisings we've ever had."

"If that's the case, it'll be more than one cavalry regiment can deal with," Henry remarked. "The Sioux by themselves can field several thousand warriors."

"That's right," Custer agreed. "I'm spending a lot of time training troops and reassigning them, which I don't mind doing, but I'd hate to be caught with too many recruits if the Sioux go on the warpath. Anyway, I've notified Washington of the situation."

"What are they doing?" Henry asked.

"All they can, I suppose," Custer replied. "General Alfred Terry is being sent here with a large force of infantry, but I don't know how much good that will do. If the Sioux move west into the Montana Territory, the infantry will wear out their boots without ever seeing an Indian."

Henry drank the last of his wine as he visualized the countless square miles of unsettled plains and mountains in the Montana Territory. "Yes, a million Indians could hide there without ever being seen and strike out at towns in complete surprise. That certainly isn't a place to send infantry, because just trying to resupply them would be a nightmare."

Custer stroked his mustache. "Well, we'll simply have to wait and see what happens," he said briskly. "In regard to what took place in Fargo a few days ago, Captain Blake, the army command here is turning a blind eye and a deaf ear to the incident."

"That's good to hear, sir," Henry replied, smiling wryly.

"I myself was pleased when I heard about it," Custer assured Henry, "and now that I've met you, I'm more pleased than ever. If the army reprimanded an officer of your caliber, it would be a very serious mistake. Well, Major Reno, we'd better be on our way."

Outside, Custer looked around. "I'm truly impressed with what you've done here, Captain Blake. If we do have trouble with the Indians, I could certainly use an officer like you in the Seventh Cavalry to shape up the men. What would you think about that?"

"I'd be more than pleased to serve in the Seventh, sir."

"We'll have to see what can be done about a transfer, then," Custer said, smiling. "Good-bye, Captain Blake."

Henry shook hands and exchanged salutes with the two men. As they rode out of the fort, he turned to his office with mixed feelings. The threat of trouble with Indians overshadowed his satisfaction concerning the attitude of the local army command toward what he had done in Fargo. In addition, the reaction of the civil authorities still remained in question.

That question was answered two days later, when a carriage rumbled into the fort and Henry went out to meet the territorial governor. Henry had met others of the same type as Governor Arthur Curran, a dedicated, ambitious public servant and a skilled executive who could get the most out of his resources.

A well-dressed man with a decisive manner, he revealed no hint of his feelings. "I thought I'd drop in to see you on my way back from Fargo—or what is left of Fargo."

When they went into Henry's office, Curran said, "People in authority often find themselves saddled with intractable problems. Sometimes, someone is about who doesn't wait for orders but simply deals with the problem. I happened to be that fortunate, and I'm very grateful, Captain Blake."

"I'm pleased that I was able to resolve the problem, sir."

"It's very refreshing to meet a man who pursues a course of action without waiting to be told what to do."

"That works both ways, Governor," Henry pointed out. "Those in authority aren't always as understanding as you are."

Curran smiled. "It's the attitude I'd have had to take in any event, because you have heavy artillery on your side, Captain Blake. Mr. Toby Holt, the commissioner of the West, heard about the incident and sent me a telegram supporting your action. In fact, he expressed great confidence in your judgment. I presume you know him?"

"You might say that," Henry replied, laughing. "Toby and I are from the same family. I heard that he had been appointed commissioner of the West, but I didn't realize he would follow events that closely. He's inclined to be impatient with paperwork."

"That fits what I've heard about him," Curran agreed. "Perhaps your name being involved is what drew his attention. When I get to Washington, you can be sure that I'll express my appreciation to the War Department for what you did."

"I'll be very grateful for that, sir."

After an hour of pleasant conversation, the governor left, and Henry was satisfied that he had heard the last of what had happened in Fargo.

There was, however, another result of the incident. The next day Henry was called to the fort gate, to see the mayor and a tall, clean-shaven man with a sheriff's badge on his coat. Behind them was a long line of wagons crowded with people—Mennonites, other settlers, and townspeople—who were peering through the gate expectantly.

The mayor greeted Henry jovially. "We had a special election, and Fred Holman here is our new sheriff now."

A businesslike, dependable-looking man, Holman smiled as he nodded to Henry. "I've heard quite a lot about you. I'm mighty pleased to meet you, Captain Blake."

"I'm very pleased to meet you, Sheriff," Henry replied,

then turned back to the mayor. "Why are all these people here, Mayor?"

"One group and then another got to talking about what they could do to thank you and your soldiers," McKinnon explained. "Finally we all decided to bring the fixings for a big feast for you and your men." He pulled up his coat collar and laughed. "And we're freezing out here, waiting for an invitation to come in out of the wind."

"Then come on in," Henry replied, beckoning and laughing. "Make yourselves at home."

A cheer rose from the wagons as the mayor and the sheriff rode into the fort, following Henry. He called to Watson and the first sergeant, telling them why the people had come and declaring the remainder of the day a holiday. Wagons rumbled inside, and the passengers climbed down with baskets of food. The lieutenant and Olsen assembled the men and put them to work preparing for the feast.

A short time later, the wide doors of the fort's warehouse were opened and the supplies moved back to make room for all the people inside the building. Fires blazed in front of the door and warmed the warehouse, while pans of vegetables simmered beside the fires and smoked hams and large joints of beef roasted on spits over them.

Trestle tables were hastily set up for the cakes, pies, jars of preserves, pickles, and other food that the women took out of baskets. Several musicians among the visitors put together a makeshift stage at one side of the warehouse with crates, then struck up a lively tune. Couples began dancing, and the fort rang with cheers and clapping as the quiet, routine day turned into a festive occasion.

For a time, a hand was extended to shake Henry's every way he turned. The people were profoundly grateful to him. After he made the rounds of the visitors, he stood at one side with Holman, who was committed to completing the clean-up in Fargo.

"I'd like to see your men allowed into town during their off-duty hours. What happened there to soldiers in the past certainly won't happen now."

"I've been wanting to lift the restriction," Henry replied,

"so I will next week. Naturally, if they get out of hand in town, I don't expect any special treatment for them."

"Well, a lot of them are young," Holman allowed, "and young men can get feisty. If they start acting up, I'll just stick them in the lockup and turn them over to whoever you send to get them."

Henry thought the arrangement was fair, and he thanked the sheriff as the women began dishing up the food, piling plates high with thick slices of ham and juicy beef, well-seasoned vegetables, and all the trimmings. Everyone came back for second servings, then for large pieces of pie and cake.

As the festivities continued, Henry talked with Ludwig Zimmerman. The aged leader of the Mennonites described how happy his people were, then mentioned Klaus Lukenbill.

"A dangerous man," Zimmerman said. "He deceived me completely."

Henry remembered the insane glare in Lukenbill's eyes as he had made his threats and hoped that the man had merely been venting his rage, but something told him that there was more to it.

It was well after dark when the gathering finally broke up. The visitors left amid a chorus of farewells and exchanges of thanks. When the fort settled for the night, Henry went to his quarters.

With a log blazing cheerfully in his sitting-room fireplace, he reread his last letter from Gisela. Like all her letters, it was long, the pages filled with her small, even lines of backward-slanted German script. But it still seemed short to Henry.

As he replaced the letter in the embossed envelope, he looked at her picture. It occurred to him that if he were transferred to the Seventh Cavalry Regiment, he might have an opportunity to take leave. Gisela would surely rush to meet him so they could spend a few days together.

Any chance of their being together was worth making tentative plans. He began writing to Gisela about it, pausing to form the ponderous German grammatical constructions in his mind. Occasionally he glanced at her picture, yearning for the sound of her voice, the scent of her perfume, and the touch of her soft hand on his.

Some three weeks later, during a wintry predawn in Germany, Gisela was rereading Henry's letter. Two days before, a courier from Grevenhof, her palatial mansion, had brought it to her in Berlin, where she had gone on a business trip.

Now in her private rail car returning home, she was waiting on a sidetrack in the Frankfort railyard for an early morning train. Without steam from the locomotive for its radiators, the car was cold. Gisela wore her long, thick sable coat as she sat reading by the light of an overhead lamp. Her hands were cold because she had taken off her gloves, wanting to touch again the pages her loved one had touched.

As she read and turned the pages, there was a soft murmur of conversation in the car. When it had been uncoupled from the express that shuttled between Berlin and Frankfort, her senior business staff had joined her for the last leg of the journey. The three men were seated on soft, ornate chairs and a couch at the end of the car, along with Weydrich, the butler who accompanied her on trips to attend to travel details and to act as a servant in the private car.

One of the three was Hans Guenther, her general manager and private secretary on trips. The second was Helmut Brunner, her senior business adviser. The third, her senior legal adviser, was Emil Koehler. He was also Gisela's father.

The men, bundled in heavy overcoats and scarves, thumbed through papers as they talked. Koehler suddenly drew in a deep breath and sneezed into his handkerchief. Gisela looked at him over her pince-nez. "Are you ill, Herr Koehler?"

"No, no, Madam Baroness," he assured her. "I am quite well, thank you."

"Good. Weydrich, please inquire if the train will arrive on time. If it will be late, tell the station manager to have a spare locomotive brought onto the siding and coupled to the car to heat it."

The butler bowed and went out. As the three men resumed talking, Gisela looked again at the letter. Having reached the end, she turned back to the first page and began rereading it. Like all the letters she had received from her husband, she had committed large portions of it to memory. She still enjoyed reading even those passages over and over, savoring the contact with him across the miles that separated them.

From time to time, she also looked through her past letters from him, which she kept in a special place. Among them was the first note he had ever sent to her, years before in France. It had been written in a rounded, schoolboyish hand. Now his letters were written with bold and manly strokes, reflecting his sophistication and maturity. To an extent, she had molded the forceful, cosmopolitan man who had emerged from the immature youngster, but he had also changed her. In making him less idealistic, she had become pragmatic instead of cynical. While teaching him to vanquish rather than merely defeat enemies, she had learned that not everyone was her enemy.

He had also taught her to enjoy life, to become more tolerant toward others and less driven for perfection. Her love for him had turned each day into a rich, colorful experience. Her employees, less frightened of her than before, were more efficient now because of their affection and deep loyalty.

Weydrich returned, his face flushed from the icy chill as he closed the door behind him. "The train is on time, Madam Baroness, and will be here within a few minutes." He hesitated, then continued. "The station manager here received a message from the stationmaster at Grevenburg. A man there was making inquiries as to when your private car would arrive."

The three men at the end of the car fell silent. They had suggested to Gisela on numerous occasions that she hire bodyguards, which she adamantly refused to do. The butler's statement having indirectly raised that subject again, Gisela looked at him woodenly over her pince-nez.

"The stationmaster at Grevenburg apparently considered the inquiry to be suspicious, Madam Baroness," Weydrich added.

"Then he should have asked the man why he wished to know," Gisela said crisply.

"The inquiry was made to a porter, Madam Baroness," Weydrich explained. "When the stationmaster undertook to find out why the man had made the inquiry, the man could not be found."

Koehler exchanged a glance with Guenther and Brunner, then spoke. "Weydrich, did the porter tell the man when the car would arrive?"

"Yes, sir," the butler replied.

"This does seem something to be concerned about," Koehler said to Gisela. "Your most recent business ventures have created dangerous enemies, and it is more advisable than ever that you—"

"Yes, yes, I know," Gisela cut in impatiently. She drew in a deep breath, controlling her temper. "The man was probably a journalist who will plague me until my driver attends to him. Please, let us devote ourselves to matters worthy of our attention."

The still-concerned men reluctantly agreed and resumed talking. Gisela, however, completely dismissed the matter. Physical courage came easily to her because the great fear in her life came from within her: In the same way that others avoided pain and danger, from childhood she had lived in abject fear of failure. Life had turned into an unrelenting battle against unwise decisions, moments of inattention, or misfortune. It was a battle that could never be won.

Over the sound of trains shunting about in the railyard, the noise from one became louder as it backed onto the siding where the private car was parked. It chuffed closer, brakes squealing, and then the baroness's car jerked as the train bumped against it, coupling it. A moment later, the radiators began clicking from hot steam rushing through them, and the car lurched forward, following the train off the siding onto the main tracks. The car swayed, and its wheels clattered against the rails as the train picked up speed.

The business trip to Berlin had been singularly successful, and now they were on the last leg of the trip home. It was an excellent time to recap what had transpired. During the trip Gisela had gained a controlling interest in one of the largest of the steel mills in the Ruhr Valley.

"All of the mill owners will be watching to see what you do," Brunner commented. "You can easily afford to operate the mill at a loss, sell below their costs, and force them out of business."

"Yes, they will want to meet with me soon," Gisela agreed. "I must first have complete information on production levels and profit margins of each mill. In the meantime, have our manager hire more workers so it will appear that we intend to increase production."

Brunner smiled. "That will make the mill owners uncertain of your intentions."

"Too dangerous," Koehler objected. "The owners of some of the smaller mills are inclined toward violence. They may not wait to see what your intentions are."

Gisela saw where the conversation was leading. "Herr Koehler, please don't bring up the subject of protection for me again."

"I won't," he replied, reaching in his coat and taking out a pistol. He defiantly placed it on the table. "You will have protection, whether or not you desire it. I have also taken the liberty of arming your driver. In addition to being my employer, you are still my daughter, a fact of which I am extremely proud."

Silence fell as the men awaited Gisela's reaction. At first she was angry, then suddenly overcome by a surge of affection for her father. They had never been close, he a stern parent during her childhood and she equally demanding as an employer in later years, but recently their relationship had been better than ever before.

"Proud?" she echoed, laughing. "Even though I am not the good hausfrau you intended me to be?"

"Perhaps you have been somewhat more successful on the path that you chose for yourself," he responded dryly, putting the pistol away. "You have at least achieved some modest financial success."

Everyone laughed, and the conversation moved to other things. Weydrich opened the draperies and extinguished the lamps so the gray dawn light could come through the windows.

Snow blanketed the terraced vineyards and farmsteads on the rolling slopes of the Main River Valley, but the sky was clear, promising a bright winter day.

Gisela informed the men that she might leave Germany on short notice for the United States and be absent for a time.

"I will make up a list of the staff to accompany you and review the procedure for transacting affairs during your absence," Guenther offered.

"Yes, let's do that," Gisela agreed. "We should also obtain the latest information on shipping schedules to the United States."

Guenther nodded, then asked whether or not Gisela would take her son along.

"Yes, of course," she quickly replied. "The captain loves his son and will certainly want to see him."

"But the captain knows that it is dangerous for small children to travel during winter," Koehler remarked.

"The boy will go with us," Gisela insisted. "He is strong and healthy and will come to no harm." She realized that in the past, she would have seized upon any excuse to leave the child behind. Since her return from the United States, however, her affection for little Peter had grown. The child had stopped crying so much, which she had detested, and looked more and more like his father. But the greatest factor was simply that, abeit belatedly, she had discovered maternal love within herself. During recent weeks, Gisela had spent time every day with the child, instead of leaving him with his nurse. He had come to know her better and enjoyed playing with her.

The conversation ended as the train entered the Grevenburg terminal. The three men gathered their papers and put on their coats while the butler helped Gisela with hers.

"We will go outside and look around before you leave the car," Koehler said.

Sighing patiently, Gisela agreed. As they went out, she glanced through the window to see her large, luxurious carriage parked at the edge of the road on the other side of the train-station yard. Gisela smiled, seeing that little Peter was in the carriage with his nurse.

While Koehler and the other two men glanced around the station, the aged stationmaster came out of the building and joined them. Satisfied, the three men walked toward the railroad car to escort the baroness.

Gisela went to the door, and the butler helped her down the stairs. She walked toward the carriage, with Weydrich, Koehler, and the other two men following.

The driver opened the carriage door, and the nurse, Adela Ronsard, stepped out with Peter in her arms. A wide smile wreathed the small face inside his fur hood as he strained against Adela and called to Gisela. She waved and hurried forward.

Then, what seemed to be some immense, invisible force struck Gisela on her left side, knocking her off her feet. The loud penetrating report of a rifle rang in her ears as she fell to the snow-covered ground.

Dazed by the heavy fall, Gisela was confused by the sudden pandemonium around her. Koehler, running forward with his pistol in his hand, roared orders. He shouted at Adela to get the child back into the carriage, then at Weydrich to take Gisela to it. Next he called to the driver and pointed at smoke in the vineyard overlooking the village and the station.

Weydrich slid his hands under Gisela to gather her up in his arms, but he cried out as he, too, was shot. He reeled away from her with a gaping hole in his neck. Clutching at his throat, he pitched to the ground as the thunderous roar of the rifle rang out again.

Koehler and the driver fired their pistols at the vineyard as Guenther and Brunner protected Gisela with their bodies and dragged her along the ground toward the carriage. She tried to help but was unable to move her legs. A bullet knocked Guenther away from her, then Brunner fell with a bullet through his heart.

Standing between Gisela and the vineyard, Koehler and the driver repeatedly fired their pistols. The aged stationmaster dashed up and joined them, wielding an old-fashioned muzzle loader. He fired once, then as he began reloading, a bullet struck him. The driver was next. He staggered and fell as a bullet ripped through his chest.

Gisela managed to call out, "It is hopeless, Father! Save yourself!"

For the first time in decades, she had addressed him as her father. A brief smile lit his face as he glanced quickly at her. Then he aimed his pistol and fired again. An instant later, he reeled back as a bullet slammed into his chest. He collapsed and fell across Gisela's legs, dying.

The battering roar of the gunfire ceased. Silence fell except for the terrified, muffled wailing of the child in the carriage. Adela lay protectively on top of him on the floor of the vehicle. Gisela saw the man in the vineyard, some two hundred yards away, stand and reload his rifle.

The numbness in her side changed into searing pain. She endured it, knowing it would soon end. Sickened by the carnage, she wished the man had killed her without slaughtering everyone around her.

She felt an agony of remorse as she longed to hold and kiss her child once more. The bliss she had known with Henry was over. If she could have held his hand while meeting death, as she had thought would happen during her illness, it would have been easier. Without a last kiss from him, she was departing life in sorrow but not in fear.

As the man in the vineyard methodically reloaded his rifle, Gisela idly wondered who he was and why he was killing her. Then she dismissed it, reflecting that he was already marked for death, along with whoever else might be involved. She knew her beloved husband would relentlessly track down everyone involved and be savage in his vengeance.

The sun rose over the valley, its rays reflected by sparkling facets in the snow. The man shouldered his weapon; his bullet struck her chest. Her consciousness faded rapidly, and the sound of the rifle was faint by the time it reached her. Gisela committed her soul to God.

At that moment, it was shortly after midnight in Dakota. Henry Blake woke suddenly and reached out into the thick darkness for his pistol on the chair beside his bed.

While he had survived gun battles, attacks by assassins, and other perils, never before had he experienced anything like the oppressive sense of doom gripping him now. The pistol belt fell to the floor as he snatched the pistol out of the holster and pulled the hammer back.

The room was silent except for the keening of the wind outside. His heart pounding, Henry turned his head, listening, convinced that someone was in the room, poised to kill him.

A moment passed. Nothing moved in the darkness. Henry quietly slipped out of bed, sweat bathing his body, and felt on the nightstand for a match. He struck it, his pistol at arm's length and ready to fire.

Henry gazed around in shocked disbelief in the dim, flickering light. No one else was in the room. The match burned down to his fingers. He dropped it and quickly struck another, then lit the candle on the nightstand and carried the candlestick to his sitting room.

As he went through the doorway, he snapped up the pistol to fire at a movement. A split second before the hammer fell, he stopped himself from firing at his dim reflection in a mirror.

His conviction that someone else was near faded, but the ominous feeling that had gripped him since waking remained. He tried in vain to shake off the sensation. He downed a glass of whiskey, then went to his bedroom and dressed.

When he returned to the sitting room, his gaze fell on Gisela's picture on the table. He looked away, then quickly back at it as a dread possibility occurred to him.

He recoiled from it. Trying to shake the dark, somber depression he felt, he poured another whiskey and drained the glass in a single swallow, then refilled it and sat in a chair, staring sullenly at the glowing embers in the fireplace.

XIV

"I appreciate your offering the use of your church, Reverend Lyons," Toby said. "I don't know of another building in Folsom that would be large enough—except one or two of the saloons, and I don't think it would be wise to have liquor at hand."

The minister agreed. An intensely earnest, boyish-looking man in his twenties, he was trying to grow a mustache and beard—apparently an attempt to make him look older—but the result thus far was only a scraggly growth. "My offer of the church for the meeting was the least I could do, Mr. Holt. It's a very small token of assistance compared to what you've done here."

They stood in front of the church, which was located on the outskirts of Folsom. In the early dusk a cold wind blasted the two men.

Toby shrugged. "I'm not sure that I've done anything of lasting benefit. I still haven't got to the bottom of the trouble."

"This whole area is more peaceful than I've ever seen it before," Lyons said confidently. "In bringing that about, you've saved many lives."

"Well, we'll see what happens at the meeting tomorrow," Toby said, then grinned. "I hope your church doesn't get shot full of holes, Reverend Lyons."

The man laughed. "I'm sure it won't. I'll see you at noon tomorrow, Mr. Holt."

Toby shook hands with the man, then mounted and

turned his horse toward the main street. He had persuade most of the ranchers and homesteaders to meet and discus their problems. Once he had talked most of them into it others had quickly agreed to attend, not wanting to be lef out. With tensions remaining high, however, Toby was un certain about the outcome. If he could keep the meetin under control, it could be the breakthrough to peace in th area. If tempers flared, however, the meeting could spark range war. But with the trouble already spreading onto In dian lands, he had no choice.

He had settled trouble at other times and in many places and the cause had usually been obvious or had become clea with some investigation. Never before had he been so com pletely stumped as he was now.

As he pondered and rode through the town in the gath ering darkness, Pearlie called to him. At an hour when sh was usually in the saloon, she was on her way to the hote where she lived.

"I got an answer today to the letter I wrote to my pa," sh said happily as Toby rode over to her. "He's coming after me and I've quit my job in the saloon."

"I'm glad to hear that! I knew you were doing the righ thing when you wrote to your dad."

"You were right in everything you said," the youn; woman admitted, "beginning with the first day I met you I'm glad I finally listened to you."

"No, you finally listened to yourself," Toby stated firmly "You knew this wasn't the place for you."

"Yes, I did. I was never happy there. The worst part of it was having to deal with men like Rossiter. I just saw him, hi partner Steed, and a couple of other men going around to th back of the newspaper office, and I crossed the street just to stay away from him. Until my pa gets here, I'm going to sta in my hotel room."

"Why don't you stay at the M Bar B?" Toby suggested "Pack up your things and come back to the ranch with u tomorrow, after the meeting. Billy will bring the wagon."

"Do you mean it, Mr. Holt?" The girl was delighted "My pa knows what I've been doing, of course, but it woul be so much better if I met him at the ranch instead of in town."

"Then that's what you'll do."

The young woman thanked Toby, then went on to her hotel.

One thing had turned out right in Folsom, Toby reflected as he headed toward the ranch again. Then he suddenly reined up, realizing what Pearlie had said about the two land speculators. On several occasions when he had been in town, he had seen Rossiter and Steed pass Sloat, and they had acted as though they didn't know the man. Going to the rear of his newspaper office after dark suggested furtiveness and more than a passing acquaintance. Two other men had been seen with them. Who could they be?

Turning back toward the newspaper office, Toby weighed the implications of the secret meeting. The trouble in the area enabled the speculators to buy land at giveaway prices. But when he had been assured by several people that the trouble had started before the land speculators arrived, he dismissed his suspicions about them. Now he realized that they could be involved in a more devious scheme than he had expected, with Sloat as their partner.

The newspaper office was dark and locked. After tethering his horse, Toby walked behind the building. Four horses were in the alley, and a light was visible through a back window. Approaching slowly to keep from disturbing the horses, Toby peered in the window. Two gunslingers were in the back room with Rossiter, Steed, and Sloat, who were arguing.

"Let them have their meeting!" Sloat said loudly, his voice carrying through the pane. "Things could really heat up with everyone together, which would act in our favor. If they work the problems through, then we'll lay low for a little longer while everything settles down. Then Holt will leave, and we can go on with our plan, like before."

The land speculators shook their heads. "When everyone starts to town for the meeting," Rossiter suggested, "we can have the boys take shots at a few of them and burn some cabins and ranch houses. Before the morning is over, this whole countryside will be like one big hornet's nest."

"No," Sloat insisted heatedly. "We've already stretched our luck with Holt. If he had only wounded either the man with the Big Fifty or the man in the saloon, it would have been all over for us. You're asking us to take another big chance on his finding out about us. I say that we wait until he leaves."

"We can't wait," Rossiter said flatly. "This delay has cost us money and time, and Steed and I are about to run out of both. If we do it right, the ranchers and homesteaders will blame each other, like before. But it'll take all five of us to shoot at some of the men heading toward town, and to burn some cabins and ranch houses."

"I don't know anything about guns," Sloat grumbled. "We agreed that we'd hire men to take care of that part of the plan. Besides, if I'm not at that meeting taking notes, everyone will notice."

One of the gunslingers laughed sarcastically. "Sloat doesn't want his skin out in the open. He wants all the benefits but none of the danger."

The argument continued. Toby had already heard more than enough. Sloat, with apparently nothing to gain from trouble, had come to Folsom first and opened the newspaper office. He had hired gunslingers to stir up friction, then had his pals Rossiter and Steed join him.

In a rage, Toby moved a few feet away from the back door, gathering himself. He knew that it would be better for many reasons to have the marshal present, but now he had the five conspirators together, and the secret meeting might break up while he was going for the marshal.

He hurled himself at the door. It shattered and ripped off the hinges when he hit it with his shoulder. As Toby charged into the room, the men gaped at him in shock.

The two gunslingers reached for their pistols, and Toby threw himself to one side. One man was much faster than the other, so Toby drew his pistol and shot him first. The bullet hit the man in the throat. His bullet clipped Toby's hat and knocked it off his head as he turned his pistol toward the other man.

The second gunslinger leaped through the doorway into the dark newspaper office as he fired over his shoulder. The bullet hit the wall beside Toby's head. Toby snatched up his hat and crouched low, running toward the door. Behind him he heard Sloat, Steed, and Rossiter collide and stumble over boards from the door as they fled into the alley.

Knowing that the gunslinger would be waiting for him to be silhouetted in the doorway, Toby tossed his hat through it at shoulder level as he dived, then slid on his belly into the dark room. The man fired at the movement, and the hat flew back into the lighted room as the bullet hit it. Then the man snapped off a shot at where he thought Toby would be.

His guess was close, and the bullet plucked at Toby's shirt, then hit and shattered the lamp, as he fired at the red flash of his opponent's pistol and then rolled. The bullet hit the man, bringing an exclamation of pain. Then he fired at the flash of Toby's pistol. His bullet hit a type case, and a stream of type spilled out and rattled across the floor.

In the alley, Sloat and his two accomplices galloped away. The drumming hoofbeats faded, and quiet settled in the impenetrable darkness of the newspaper office, as Toby and the gunslinger each waited for the other to make a sound and reveal his position.

Placing his left hand over his pistol to silence the click, Toby cocked it. Then he slowly lifted a foot within easy reach of his left hand and silently worked to unfasten his spur buckle. He took the spur by the rowel to keep it from rattling and pulled it off his heel, then tossed the spur to one side.

The spur hit the floor, its clatter loud in the quiet. As the man fired at the noise, Toby immediately fired at the red flash of the pistol and then rolled. The man grunted in pain, then fired at where Toby had been. Toby fired and rolled once more. That bullet brought a scream of pain from the gunslinger.

Quiet settled tensely. The air was thick with gunpowder smoke. Toby silently opened the cylinder on his Colt and began replacing the spent shells with bullets from the loops in his belt. Hearing an empty shell fall to the floor a few feet away, Toby knew the other man was also reloading.

The man was making small, involuntary gasps of pain. He was a criminal, but Toby's sense of fairness asserted itself.

He spoke softly. "We don't have to keep this up. Slide your pistol over here, and we can get a doctor to see you."

The only reply was a blast of gunfire as the man shot three times in rapid succession. The second bullet ripped the sleeve of Toby's shirt. Then the man heaved himself to his feet and ran toward the plate glass window at the front of the office, looking over his shoulder, ready to fire at the flash of Toby's pistol. The gunslinger, hoping to escape, hurled himself through the air. But Toby, rising to one knee, took careful aim at his adversary's silhouette against the window and squeezed the trigger. The bullet blasted the man as he hurled through the window in a shower of glass. Shaking his head, Toby went to the window and stepped through it. The man was sprawled on the boardwalk in the shattered glass, dead.

The marshal, having heard the gunfire, was running across the street. When Toby explained what he had found out, Hubbard enthusiastically pounded him on the back. The two of them went down the street to Rossiter and Steed's office, where the land speculators and Sloat had apparently stopped briefly before hurrying out of town.

In the office a lamp was still burning. Papers were scattered, and the safe door was open. Hubbard looked around. "If I could catch them," he mused, scratching his head, "I'm not sure I could get a conviction for conspiracy. But I am sure that I would have a lynch mob to deal with, so I think I'll just let them go and say good riddance."

"It's up to you, Marshal," Toby said. "I've got rid of what was causing the trouble, so I'm satisfied." He looked through the papers on a desk. "There are a lot of property deeds here. It might be a good idea to get in touch with the folks who sold out to Rossiter and Steed and let the people have their deeds back if they'll return to their property."

Hubbard agreed. "I'll lock this place up for now, and tomorrow I'll go through all these papers and start contacting the people. Well, this certainly changes things for your meeting, doesn't it? You'll have something to tell everybody that will make them sit up and listen."

"I will, indeed," Toby replied, laughing. "I had my

doubts about that meeting before, but now I'm looking forward to it."

At noon the following day, the small church on the outskirts of town was packed. The side aisles were filled with those who had been unable to find seats on the crowded benches. The church was also silent; each person glared suspiciously at everyone else.

In the intense atmosphere of hostility, the young Reverend Lyons's voice quavered with nervousness as he stood at the pulpit, opening the meeting with a benediction. He finished quickly and moved aside in relief, turning the meeting over to Toby.

Toby stepped to the pulpit. "When I first came here, I went to talk with Elmo Lummas at the Circle S. He told me that John Hendricks at the Lazy H had put his brand on a calf that belonged to a Circle S cow."

"That's what he did!" Lummas barked from his seat on a bench. "He rustled one of my calves with his branding iron!"

"You're a liar, Lummas!" Hendricks retorted. "You probably put that brand on that calf yourself!"

"Then I went to the Lazy H," Toby continued, raising his voice over those of the two men as they argued, "and talked with John Hendricks. He told me that Elmo Lummas had ruined a Lazy H watering hole."

"He did!" Hendricks bellowed. "Me and my men followed the tracks from the watering hole to the Circle S!"

"You're lying, Hendricks!" Lummas roared. "I have more to do with my time than bother with your watering holes!"

As the two began arguing about that, other men muttered in an angry stir that passed through the crowd. Toby drew in a deep breath and raised his voice even louder. "Then last night," he shouted, "I found out that both Lummas and Hendricks were wrong! Someone else branded that calf and ruined the watering hole!"

Silence fell abruptly. Lummas and Hendricks sat open-mouthed, staring at Toby. He told the crowd about the meeting he had interrupted the night before, detailing the conversation and explaining the men's scheme. A muttering rose among the crowd. By the time Toby finished, the soft mutter had become a roar of outrage.

"Where are they now?" a man shouted over the other voices. "We'll fix them!"

A booming roar of approval rose. Lifting a hand for silence, Toby said, "They're gone. Two are dead. The others left town last night, and you won't see them again. But they had help from others."

"Who?" a number of men demanded. "We'll string up anybody who helped them!" shouted one man.

"Then you're going to need a lot of ropes," Toby replied, "because they were helped by every person in this room." In the sudden silence that fell again, men shook their heads and frowned. "I'm going to be very frank with you, folks," Toby went on. "You were too ready to be misled by the lies that Sloat printed, too ready to believe the worst of your neighbors. Instead of looking for a criminal conspiracy, you looked at each other. Rather than giving each other the benefit of the doubt, you believed the worst. So each of you helped them."

The men glumly accepted what Toby said. "Maybe so," one of them grumbled, "but we didn't know what was happening. Sloat and his partners hatched up a sly way of doing things."

"It was a crafty scheme," Toby acknowledged, "and it certainly had me fooled until last night. At the same time, they might not have succeeded if you had been less ready to hire gunslingers and more willing to trust each other. But that's in the past now. The task at hand is to keep new trouble from developing. To do that, you need to set up some kind of association to arbitrate your problems."

"A cattlemen's association," a rancher suggested while others nodded in approval.

"An Oklahoma Territory landowner's association would be better," Toby suggested. "There are both ranchers and homesteaders here, remember, each needing the other. The last thing you need is an association that will set you against each other."

A murmur rose as the crowd discussed the idea and gradually accepted it. Once that was settled, the issue of who would lead the organization came up. Toby remained silent until the man who was chosen by acclaim demurred. Then Toby spoke up.

"It's a community responsibility, Rob," he said cheerfully, stepping down from the pulpit. "Get up here and do your duty."

Rob smiled modestly as he stepped to the pulpit and took charge of the meeting. It lasted another hour, and suggestions were offered about the association. Then the meeting adjourned, with everyone agreeing to meet two weeks later at the M Bar B in a gathering that would include a social for families.

Outside the church, Toby shook hands all around, gratified by how events had turned out. While he had been in Oklahoma, he had made many friends among the ranchers and homesteaders. They could be stubborn and headstrong, but they were proud, independent people, the type who made his nation the free, powerful country that it was, and he was intensely pleased that he had been able to eliminate the friction among them.

Toby mounted his horse, while Billy hopped up behind the saddle on Rob's horse. They rode down the main street, where Sally had driven the wagon to the hotel. Billy helped to load Pearlie's belongings into the wagon, then took the reins. Toby and Rob rode toward the ranch, with Sally and Pearlie—who now asked to be called Rachel—chatting happily in the wagon behind them.

Rob smiled as he mentioned the stop that Toby had made at the telegraph office before the meeting. "It goes without saying that you were glad to send that telegram," he remarked.

"It does," Toby agreed emphatically. "Marrying Alexandra is my first priority. And I can't wait to see my kids and what the house looks like."

"Will you be married as soon as you get back to Portland, then?"

"No, we've decided on a large wedding," Toby replied. "It'll take some weeks to make all the arrangements. We'll have friends coming from far and wide, so we'll have to allow enough time to invite them and for them to get to Portland."

"Well," Rob said hesitantly, "I don't want to impose upon you any more than I have already, but if you could spend a few more days here, I would certainly appreciate it. Until the trouble we've had is completely in the past, people here are going to be hard to work with. You have a talent for knocking people's heads together without making them angry, like you did in the meeting, and that might be needed for a few days."

Toby laughed. "I'll stay for a few more days, Rob."

Rob grinned gratefully. "From everything you've said, Alexandra is a perfect match for you. I'd really like to be at the wedding, as would Kale. But with all that's going on here, I don't see how I can get things settled in time for us to come to Portland."

"I'd like for you and Kale to be there just as much as you'd like it yourselves, but I understand the situation. Edward will be arriving with the cattle from India before too many more months, and you should be here to help him."

"Yes, that's true," Rob agreed, then thought again about what Toby had said. "It's been a good while since you sent that money, so he probably left India some time ago."

"I don't know, Rob," Toby replied doubtfully. "With Brahman cattle being holy animals in India, Edward would have to make careful arrangements. The Indians in India don't scalp people, but they might make an exception with Edward if they caught him at it."

Rob pondered for a moment. "I don't see why he would have any serious problems, Toby. Holy animals or not, rounding up twenty-five head of cattle and loading them on a ship just isn't all that complicated."

As dawn broke over the shoreline of Bombay, Edward Blackstone was on the quarterdeck of the *Mercury;* the ship moved slowly toward the distant beach. He rested his weight on his right leg, since his left thigh occasionally still twinged with pain, and felt satisfied with how things had turned out thus far.

When he first heard about the arrangements that Edgar Dooley had made, Edward had expected the ship to be an old, barely seaworthy hulk commanded by a man whose disposition was dominated by a larcenous streak.

The *Mercury*, a square-rigged vessel out of Portsmouth, New Hampshire, was indeed old, but well maintained. While its patched sails and spliced rigging revealed that its profits were hard won in an era when the numbers of fast steamers kept increasing, it was as neat and clean as any warship. Its captain, Isaiah Sterch, a taciturn New Englander, was a skilled seaman and an earnest, hardworking man.

His preparations to transport the cows had been made carefully and methodically. The crew had assembled stalls in a hold, and while the other cargo had been loaded in Bombay, a large supply of fodder was brought aboard. As the ship moved forward, Sterch surveyed the beach through his telescope and gave orders to the helmsman, positioning the vessel to load the cattle as soon as possible.

He handed the telescope to Edward and pointed. "There's your shore party, Mr. Blackstone," he said, then shouted to the first officer on the main deck. "Mr. Gillis, reef the sails on the foremast and take soundings!"

Gillis roared orders, and sailors sprang into the rigging as Edward looked through the telescope. Edgar was sitting on a dune overlooking the beach, a dozen men in robes scattered around him. A large raft they had assembled for shuttling the cattle to the *Mercury* was floating in the water.

Scanning the shore, Edward saw no one else, but two large boats were beached no more than three hundred yards from where Edgar and the men with him were waiting. Mentioning the boats, Edward handed the telescope back to Sterch, and the captain replied indifferently that he had noticed them.

"Fishing boats, Mr. Blackstone. If the owners had intended to go fishing today, they would have set out at first light. However," the cautious New Englander added, "it wouldn't do any harm for you to be armed when you go ashore."

Having no intention of being otherwise, Edward went down to his cabin. He slung his Winchester over his shoulder and buckled on his pistol belt, then gathered up extra bullets. When he went back out on deck, the ship had slowed, and a sailor at the bow was casting a sounding line as he called out the depth.

At a mile from the beach, the depth was five fathoms over a mud bottom. The crewmen were poised to leap into motion when the captain gave the order to drop anchor.

The longer it took to shuttle the cows out on the raft, Edward knew, the more chance there would be to draw unwelcome attention. But running the ship aground while trying to get as close as possible would be disastrous.

The depth diminished to four fathoms, but Sterch still waited, his weathered face expressionless. At somewhat over a thousand yards from the beach, the depth was three fathoms.

"Mark three over sandy mud and shoaling," the man at the bow chanted, heaving the line and pulling it in. "Now a half off mark two over muddy sand and still shoaling. Coming up on mark two over muddy sand and shoaling fast. Two fathoms even over clean sand and shoaling faster."

"Mr. Gillis, let go the bow anchor!" Sterch suddenly barked. As the first officer bellowed and relayed the order to sailors, the anchor splashed into the water. The ship jerked to a stop, the stern began swinging around, and the port side of the ship came broadside to the beach. "Mr. Gillis, let go the stern anchor!" The second anchor plunged into the water, holding the stern of the ship steady. "Mr. Gillis, have a boat put over the side to take Mr. Blackstone ashore! Rig out a sling to haul the cows aboard, then mount the swivel gun on the port rail!"

Edward knew that a swivel gun was a small cannon. "Why do you want the swivel gun, Captain?"

"If any trouble develops," the captain replied obliquely, "please return to the ship immediately. We're here to get cows, not to harm anyone in any way."

"Yes, absolutely," Edward agreed.

"The sooner we're away from here, the better I'll like it." Sterch pointed toward the rail. "Your boat is waiting, Mr. Blackstone. Good luck ashore."

Edward went down the steps to the main deck. His left thigh twinged painfully as he stepped over the rail and jumped down to the boat, and he winced as he settled himself on a seat. The two sailors already in the boat rowed toward the beach.

A few minutes later, the boat bumped against the beach beside the raft. Edgar, a radiant smile on his round face, reached to shake hands with Edward as he stepped ashore. The sailors rowed back toward the ship.

"I told you there was no reason to worry about anything, didn't I?" the jolly Irishman said, pumping Edward's hand vigorously.

"So far," Edward replied cautiously.

"I want you to meet the man in charge of our cowboys. He's a tanner, so he keeps track of all the cows for miles around. Come on over here, Zofar."

Edward failed to share Dooley's enthusiasm for the unkempt little man. With coarse features that were marred by a wide scar across his left eye, leaving him with only one eye, Zofar fell far short of inspiring confidence.

"He's a tanner?" Edward asked, puzzled. "A Hindu tanner?"

"Yes. Their customs permit making goods from the hides of cows that die from natural causes," Edgar explained, then laughed. "But when he finds a cow that's pretty far gone, he helps it on its way, don't you, Zofar?"

Grinning and displaying the stumps of blackened teeth, Zofar nodded as he took a large hammer from under his robes and made a striking motion with it. The others gathered closer, and as Edward looked at them, he decided that Edgar's satisfaction with Zofar was a relative matter. He seemed to be the best of a bad lot.

Wearing grimy, ragged robes, the other men were the leavings of the dark, narrow back alleys of Bombay. They all had scarred, predatory faces and beady, malevolent eyes. Never had he seen such an evil-looking gang of cutthroats.

"Edgar," Edward said quietly, "what criteria did you use when you chose these men?"

"Whether or not they would do anything for money," Edgar replied in the same quiet voice. "I couldn't go to the rajah of Gujerat's palace and hire people from his staff to gather up cows for us, could I?"

"Well, I suppose it doesn't make any difference as long

as they'll do the job. That raft looks as though it'll hold about
five cows, and the sooner we get started, the sooner we'll
finish."

The Irishman climbed a dune and beckoned Edward.
"Take a look. All we need to do now is have the men raft
them out to the ship, so we'll be finished in very short
order."

Edward limped up the dune. At the top, Dooley pointed
to cattle in the shallow swale between the dune and the next
one. "There you are," he announced proudly. "Thirty-two of
them. Pick out the twenty-five you want."

Edward looked at the cattle in dismay. "But half of them
are bulls. I want five bulls with twenty cows," he said. "And
look at them, Edgar. Most are old and sickly."

A few of the men, understanding English, muttered in
Marathi as they frowned darkly. Several fingered knives under their robes. "Get your men in hand there, Zofar," Dooley
said. "I told you I didn't want any trouble."

"They say they bring cows," Zofar replied, pointing to
the cattle. "They say where is money."

"These aren't the right kind of cows," Edgar explained
with elaborate patience. "And the men must take the cows to
the ship on the raft before they'll be paid." He turned to
Edward. "Why don't you see if you can use any of the cows,
and I'll straighten this out with the men."

Edward went down into the swale as a furious argument
erupted behind him. Edgar spoke Marathi about as well as
Zofar spoke English, and they alternated between arguing
with each other and with the men, while the men bickered
among themselves in an overall bedlam of shouting voices,
waving fists, and flashing knives.

In looking at the cattle, Edward had found that, for the
most part, the bulls and the cows were as gentle as they were
stately and graceful. The large, sedate creatures sniffed at
him noisily as he nudged them apart and looked at them.
When he finished, Edward had found a bull and four cows
that were young and in satisfactory condition.

On the dune one man, who was holding a knife and
shaking his head stubbornly, was still arguing with Zofar and
Dooley. Edward climbed up the dune and ostentatiously

examined his Winchester and Colt. The man put his knife away and joined the others.

Four men remained behind to drive the five animals over the dune and pole the raft out to the ship, while Zofar and the remainder scattered, searching for more cows.

At the end of an hour, the men began returning, driving cattle and luring them with handfuls of grass. In general they were no better than the first ones, which started another argument, but Edward found four suitable bulls among them. One was the finest specimen he had ever seen—a huge young animal with wide horns.

It was also bad-tempered. With a casual toss of its head it sent Edward, Edgar, and two other men flying as they tried to push it onto the raft. Edward hit upon the idea of bringing fodder from the ship, which worked. The bull placidly stepped onto the raft and munched as it was taken to the *Mercury*, where it was hauled aboard.

The morning wore on, and the men brought more cattle. Very few were acceptable, and many were bulls. "We already have five bulls," Edward said to Dooley, annoyed. "Can't these men even tell the difference between a cow and a bull?"

Edgar turned on the men. Lifting a cow's tail and pointing, he bellowed in Marathi. Then the men slunk away, glowering and muttering, to search for more cows. Scores of cattle were wandering about on the beach and nearby dunes, and every time the cattle on the ship lowed mournfully from the hold, the ones on the shore responded in a deafening chorus.

Taking a swig from a bottle of bolabang, Edgar nodded as Edward mentioned the lowing. "Yes, it is loud, and when they all go at it, a man can hardly hear himself think."

"The lowing itself doesn't bother me," Edward said, "but others might hear it and come to see what's happening."

"Oh, I wouldn't worry," Edgar replied. "This is a very remote place."

Unconvinced, Edward waited anxiously for the men to return with more cows. When they did, he found a reason for even greater concern. Several of the cows had garlands of

flowers twined around their horns, patterns in colorful pastel
paint on their gray skin, and gleaming enamel on their hooves.

When Edward mentioned it, Dooley nonchalantly splashed
a handful of seawater on one of the cows. "See? It washes
right off," he said. "And that enamel on their feet shouldn't
hurt them at all."

"That isn't the point," Edward explained. "Hindus view
it as commendable to keep one of these cows and care for it.
That's what these are—they're pets."

"But they're handsome animals, aren't they?" Edgar pointed
out.

Several of the cows were young and in excellent condition, so Edward dropped the subject. He chose five cows,
bringing his total to twenty animals. Four men began taking
them out on the raft to the ship as the others left to continue
their search.

A few minutes later, Edward glimpsed a man on top of a
dune some fifty yards away. He shaded his eyes with his
hand, but the man quickly disappeared. "Edgar, I just saw a
man on that dune over there," Edward said, pointing.

"Well, he won't find any cows worth anything there,"
Dooley remarked, taking a drink from his bottle.

"He didn't seem to be scruffy enough to be one of our
men," Edward remarked, concerned.

Taking another drink, Dooley pondered, then grinned
tipsily. "It could be someone who's come to see why all of
these cows are squealing."

Realizing there was no point in discussing it with Edgar,
Edward cradled his rifle across his arm and watched the
dune. Meanwhile, the raft moved away from the ship, with
Gillis and six sailors on it, to take the last load of cows to the
vessel. As the raft touched the beach, Dooley greeted the
seamen in alcoholic good humor, warmly shaking hands with
each.

First Mate Gillis wore a worried frown as he spoke to
Edward. "Captain Sterch wonders if you can't get more of a
move on, sir. He remarked that he could fill a fleet of ships
with the cows standing about here."

Edward explained why the cows were unsuitable, and
the worry on the first officer's face deepened as Edward told

him about the man he had glimpsed. Then they fell silent, anxiously waiting for the men to return with more cows. Dooley began offering his bottle around to the sailors, who reluctantly declined a drink because Gillis glared at them warningly.

The men finally returned, this time with fifteen cows. They had apparently concluded they could obtain a better quality by raiding people's gardens for pets, for most of the animals had flowers on their horns and painted patterns on their skin. Edward found four young, healthy-looking cows among them.

As the sailors separated those cows from the others and drove them onto the raft, Gillis stepped over to Edward. "Mr. Blackstone, can't you find one more in this lot that will do? If we stay here any longer, we'll be asking for trouble."

Edward looked around, then pointed to a small heifer. "Very well, I'll take that one," he replied. "It's hardly more than a calf, but it looks strong and healthy enough. Edgar, you can go ahead and pay the men now."

Dooley took out a money pouch and handed it to Zofar, who opened it and began distributing coins among the men crowding around him. The Irishman ambled onto the raft, somewhat unsteady on his feet, and Gillis barked at the sailors to hurry and get the heifer loaded. Then Edward and Gillis joined the others on the raft as the sailors gathered up the poles.

Just then, the top of the dune overlooking the beach was suddenly covered by a mob of some forty men, howling with rage as they rushed down. Gillis roared at the sailors, who pushed frantically with the poles to get the raft away from the beach.

It appeared that disaster had struck. The raft moved very slowly, and the angry crowd splashed into the shallow water after it. Then the first officer and a sailor began jabbing at the nearest men with poles, making them stumble and trip up others, while the sailors poled the raft out into waist-deep water. It gradually picked up speed and drew away from the mass of furious men struggling in the water.

In the confusion, the small heifer almost fell off the raft, and Edward pulled it away from the edge. The crisis appeared to be over, and the sailors hooted in relief while they poled as rapidly as possible. Edward noticed that Zofar and the other men had escaped retaliation by simply melting into the crowd.

Then Edward saw that Zofar had joined the opposition with much greater enthusiasm than was necessary. Waving his hammer, the tanner shouted and pointed as he ran toward the fishing boats down the beach. The crowd streamed after him. "Now we're in for it!" Gillis shouted. "A boat will move much faster than this raft! Heave on those poles and make this raft move, men!"

Dooley laughed drunkenly. "Bend to with a will, me mateys," he called in a jovial imitation of nautical slang. "A Jolly Roger will be bearing down on us presently."

The men on the beach launched one of the fishing boats, and it began skimming toward the raft. Glancing at the *Mercury*, Edward saw that it was a beehive of activity; men were unfurling sails and hauling in the bow anchor. The swivel gun fired with a loud report, and smoke billowed from it, as the ball raised a splash in front of the fishing boat.

The cannon merely seemed to infuriate the pursuers even more, for their yelling grew louder as the fishing craft moved swiftly toward the slow, awkward raft. Zofar, in the bow, brandished his hammer and howled louder than any of the others. As he lifted his Winchester, Edward was tempted to try to clip the hammer out of the man's hand, but he aimed at the bow below the waterline, where none of the men would be wounded.

The bullets raised plumes of water and knocked splinters from the boards at the bow of the boat as Edward fired until the magazine was empty. Those at the bow danced about and pushed back among the others. The boat slowed as water gushed through the holes, but it still gained on the raft.

With its bow anchor raised and sails unfurled, the *Mercury* turned into the wind and began slowly dragging its stern anchor. Faced with the dual task of escaping from the fishing boat and catching the *Mercury*, the sailors poling the raft groaned in protest while they labored. Then the swivel gun roared again, the cannon ball raising a geyser beside the fishing boat.

The waterspout beside them startled the oarsmen as the water inundated those in the boat. When the men gathered up their oars again, the raft was drawing close to the *Mercury*. A sailor stood at the stern with a coil of rope, poised to cast it to the raft.

The rope snaked through the air, and the sailors on the raft shouted in glee as they caught it. The stern anchor was immediately lifted, and the ship edged seaward as sailors on the vessel hauled the raft alongside. Sailors began hoisting the cows aboard.

At last, the ship pulled away, the raft still in tow, and the boat turned back toward the beach, the men in it howling in rage. But as the ship picked up speed, the leading edge of the raft was pulled under the water. The small heifer almost fell off again, but Edward caught and held it.

The water was almost up to Edward's knees. The raft bounced through the waves and drenched him with spray. The logs thumped against the side of the ship and began separating as the sailors worked furiously to hoist the remaining cattle aboard. The heifer bawled in fright and lurched from side to side. Edward held onto it grimly.

He looked up at Sterch, who was at the rail, directing the work. "Captain, the raft is starting to break up!"

"It doesn't matter, Mr. Blackstone," the captain replied placidly. "The wood is rotten and worthless."

"It matters while I'm on it!" Edward roared.

"We'll have you aboard in a moment," Sterch assured him. "There's only one more cow to go, then we'll get that small one."

As the last cow was lifted off the raft, the heifer got a hoof stuck between two logs that were separating. Edward pulled it free, but the animal lashed about in fright and kicked him solidly on his left thigh. Searing pain raced through his thigh, and his leg almost folded under him. Clutching the heifer, he braced himself on his right leg.

The sling was finally lowered, and two sailors leaped down to put it on the heifer. They scrambled back up to the rail, but Edward knew his leg was too weak for him to climb. He held onto the sling as it was hoisted. Just as the apparatus was lowered to the deck, the animal kicked Edward's left thigh again, and he barely managed to keep from falling.

Edgar was at the rail, holding his empty bottle and waving to the men in the boat. He grinned blearily as he turned to Edward. "Well, we gotcher your cows!" he slurred cheerfully. "A bit of bother there at the end, but nothing compared to some of the fracases I've been in from time to time. So it went well enough, didn't it?"

Soaked with seawater and panting from the exertion of holding the heifer on the raft, Edward braced himself on his right leg. His left thigh throbbed with agonizing pain. Looking at Edgar, he pondered a reply, then decided that no reply would be best. He turned away and limped toward his cabin, urgently wanting a very generous drink of brandy.

Hermann Bluecher sat up in bed, glaring at the guard in the dim lamplight. "What did you say?" he demanded.

The guard, holding the garrote with which he had intended to silence Josef Mueller permanently, shrugged and shook his head. "The man is gone, Pasha," he repeated, apprehensive about being the bearer of bad tidings. "Disappeared. And," he added in a rush to finish with all the unpleasant news, "the woman Salima has disappeared also."

"Salima?" Bluecher erupted in astonishment. "Then call out the guard! Search the house and grounds! Search the city! Hurry, fool, hurry!"

The man salaamed and rushed out as Bluecher got out of bed. He wondered if Salima had learned the truth about her brother's execution. Doing without her would be a hardship, but not dangerous, as Mueller's disappearance might prove. The newspapers had reported the upheaval in Germany over the baroness's death, and an international incident of gigantic proportions would result if Bluecher, an official of the Ottoman Empire, was found to be involved. The full fury of Istanbul would fall upon him, and Mueller was the only one who could implicate him.

Bluecher went to his study, pondering what Mueller might do out of spite. Mueller's suspicious mind had to have been alerted to Bluecher's plans to kill him. Perhaps he and Salima had even met in secret and compared stories.

Bluecher reflected that nothing had turned out right lately. He had hoped to be promoted to provincial governor, for the incumbent had recently died, but instead of his achievements being rewarded, he was informed by letter that a new governor would arrive shortly.

Another recent directive concerned a payment of tribute from the slave traders to the government, an immense fortune due to arrive within the next few days at Izmir, whence it would be escorted overland to Istanbul. For the last part of the journey, Bluecher's soldiers would escort it, and he had toyed with the idea of taking the tribute and fleeing in retaliation for the lack of gratitude Istanbul had shown toward him. He had been unable to think of anywhere he wanted to go, however, but now, with Mueller's disappearance, it appeared that he would have to find a place.

A short time later, the captain of the guard knocked on the door. "The man Mueller and the woman Salima cannot be found, Pasha. They took eight horses from the stable."

Bluecher knew that the number included baggage as well as saddle horses and spares. Mueller had obviously planned carefully, so it would be impossible to catch him. In turn, that meant Bluecher himself had to flee. As the captain of the guard left, Bluecher looked at a map of the world on the wall.

The United States, more concerned with its own affairs than those of other countries, was one place where the reach of the Ottoman Empire failed to extend. It was also the home of Henry Blake, and revenge against him was still a burning issue.

Bluecher smiled. The United States, he decided, was a place to consider seriously.

XV

Eulalia Blake held up a lamp in the doorway of her guest room. "It's time to get up, Toby."

"It's only four-thirty!" he exclaimed, peering at his pocket watch, on the table beside the bed. "The wedding is at eleven o'clock!"

Leland shrugged into his robe as he stepped out of his and Eulalia's room. "You may as well get up, Toby," he called, laughing. "Your mother has been unable to sleep all night, and she's gone about as long as she can without company."

Toby laughed good-naturedly and got up. A few minutes later, he and Leland were sitting at the dining room table, and Eulalia had built up the fire in the stove and put on coffee.

Having a cook was a convenience, but Eulalia enjoyed doing things for her husband and son. She checked the dough she had mixed at about midnight, finding that it had finished rising, and divided it into pieces to bake rolls. In the quiet and privacy of the dark, early hours of the morning, she felt even closer to her family. As the rolls baked, she took special care in preparing the tray for the coffee and rolls, placing everything just right.

Her efforts were more than repaid by Toby and Lee's reactions.

Toby took a bite of a steaming roll. "No one makes these like you do, Mama, and I can't think of anything I'd rather have right now. But I do wish you had rested more last night. You've been working very hard on preparations for the wedding."

"Preparing for this wedding has made me feel twenty years old again. I'll admit I had my doubts at first, but I've come to realize that Alexandra is a fine young woman in every respect."

"I agree entirely," Toby commented. "And you've done a wonderful job in setting up everything just right. This must be the largest wedding Portland has ever seen."

"The largest by far," Lee confirmed. "And you and Alexandra have so many friends!"

"And I've found them all to be entertaining and interesting, including those who seem a bit unusual," Eulalia said. "That young Maida Oberg has the strangest accent! And Reverend Ezekiel Quint doesn't look at all like a man of the cloth."

"I met Maida and her family in Wisconsin," Toby explained. "She's German, of course, but learned to speak English by talking with an Irish family, which is why she has that accent. I met Reverend Quint in Kentucky, and he looks more like what he used to be—a boatman on the Ohio."

Eulalia listened as Toby continued talking about the guests. Representatives from the hunt clubs in Kentucky were there, as well as Toby's business manager in Chicago. Family friends had also arrived to swell the numbers.

Eulalia wished that Cindy, still in Paris, could have come. And through subtle hints in what Toby had said, she knew that he earnestly wished Henry Blake could have come. But because of the murder of his wife, he had gone to Germany. He had sent a telegram to Toby, telling him of Gisela's death.

Although her feelings toward her foster son remained painful, she acknowledged Toby's right to hold attitudes that were different from hers. Her own sentiments were less rigid than they had been, because years had passed since Henry had broken his engagement with Cindy. There was also the grandchild she had never seen, which distressed her.

The subject came up in an indirect way. Toby mentioned that Janessa had burst into tears when he read Henry's telegram aloud at a family gathering. "I wish I had known how she felt about the woman," he said, still troubled over the incident.

"It was no one's fault," Lee assured Toby.

"It was such a change," Toby said in wonder. "The last thing I would have expected was for Janessa to like the baroness."

"It was more than that," Eulalia put in quietly. "Janessa recognized the baroness's faults but still held her in high regard. That's a good definition of love, Toby." She sipped her coffee. "I understand there is a child."

"Yes, a boy named Peter," Toby confirmed. "Andy Brentwood mentioned the baby yesterday."

Eulalia eagerly turned to Toby. "What else did Andy say?"

"Nothing, Mama," Toby replied.

"Has he seen the baby? Now tell me everything, Toby."

"After he was assigned to Bern as the military attaché, he went to see if the baroness would invest in his family shipping company. He saw the baby while he was there. He said it was a fine-looking boy but didn't mention his color of eyes, hair, or anything else. All right?"

Eulalia nodded. The only way she would ever know enough about her grandson, she reflected, was by holding him in her arms. That realization created an aching sorrow within her, for she doubted that would ever happen.

"Speaking of Andy," Lee said, "something seems to be bothering him. He's just been staying in his room, which isn't like him."

"I believe it has to do with a romance," Toby said. "I saw a picture of a very attractive woman in his room and asked him about her. He said her name was Lydia, then changed the subject. I have an idea that she's married."

Lee frowned and let the subject drop. The conversation moved on to more cheerful topics. Toby talked about his honeymoon. He and Alexandra would leave on the San Francisco steam packet that evening.

Eulalia heard the cook come in the back door. With poignant regret, she knew that her quiet, close time with her husband and son had drawn to an end. She looked out the window at the rising sun. "It'll be cold but very bright and clear, Toby," she said. "A good day for your wedding."

With his blue Holt eyes that reminded Eulalia so much of his father's, he smiled affectionately. Reaching over, he put his hand on hers. "It's going to be a good day in every respect, Mama," he said, "because you've made it that way."

As the sun shone through the window into her room, Janessa Holt was sitting at her dressing table. She opened the small box in which she kept her treasures and took out the ring that Gisela had given her. In her struggle to adjust to the baroness's death, the ring was a comfort. It helped her to reach past her agonizing sorrow to the joy of having known and loved Gisela. Like the woman, it was exquisitely beautiful.

At a tap on her door, Janessa looked up. "Come in."

Alexandra stepped in, wearing her usual trousers, shirt, and boots. "May I take refuge with you, Janessa?" she asked, then noticed the ring and started to turn back to the door. "No, you'd probably rather be alone, so I'll—"

"No, no," Janessa cut in, putting the ring away. "Refuge from what?"

"From *whom*. Juanita," Alexandra answered, sitting on a chair beside the dressing table. "She's in a frenzy, packing, unpacking, and repacking the cases I'm taking on the honeymoon." She sighed and pushed back her hair. "I didn't sleep too well last night, so I need to collect myself."

"I could have given you something to help you sleep."

"No, I suppose I needed to think. A new chapter in life is a time for reflection. Regardless of how joyful the time promises to be, there is some nostalgia over what is being left behind."

"Yes, that's exactly how Cindy is about changes in her life. I may experience the same thing myself if I pass the college-entrance examinations."

"You'll pass," Alexandra assured the girl. "I've never had doubts about that." She glanced at the box where Janessa had put the ring, then looked back at her. "Dear, if you're not up to attending the wedding, your father and I will understand."

"No, I want to," Janessa said, a radiant smile wreathing

her face. "I want to make sure with my own eyes that we've got you so that you can't ever get away from us."

"Wild horses couldn't drag me away from this family now," Alexandra replied, patting the girl's hand. "And I'd feel that way because of you, even if no one else were involved. Amy probably has coffee made by now. Would you like a cup?"

Janessa and Alexandra went down to the dining room. Amy brought in breakfast as Timmy came downstairs. After the meal was finished and the dishes cleared away, Janessa and Alexandra were sitting at the table over another cup of coffee when the dressmaker arrived.

"I brought you something old, something new, and something blue in my case," she said. "You still need something borrowed."

"I'll take care of that, Mrs. Seeley," Alexandra said. "Could I ask you to stay in the church dressing room with me and make sure everything is in order before I start down the aisle? I want Juanita to be with the congregation in the balcony so she can watch the wedding."

"Why, certainly, Miss Woodling," the woman replied. "I'll go on up and take a last look at your veil."

"Thank you," Alexandra said, then turned back to Janessa as the woman left. "May I see your handkerchief?"

Wondering why Alexandra wanted to see it, Janessa took it out of her pocket. Alexandra plucked it from her hand, then stood. "There's my something borrowed," she said, winking.

"I have a new handkerchief in my room."

Alexandra leaned over to kiss Janessa's cheek, then turned to the door. "No, I wanted something from you, not from a store."

The girl smiled as Alexandra went out. After finishing her coffee, Janessa went to her room and changed into her blue gingham dress, then put on her coat and hat as she stepped down the hall to Alexandra's room.

The dressmaker was working over the veil while Alexandra, still in her riding clothes, was watching in tolerant amusement as Juanita rummaged through suitcases on the bed.

"I'm leaving now," Janessa said. "Is there anything at all that I can do for you?"

Alexandra smiled as she stepped to the door. "No, everything will be fine if I can keep Juanita from wearing out the hinges on my cases. And," she added as an afterthought, "the steam packet gets here on time."

"I'm sure it will," Janessa said confidently. "Well, we won't have a chance to talk again until you and Dad return from your honeymoon, so Godspeed and return safely."

Alexandra, knowing that attending a large, noisy reception would make Janessa extremely uncomfortable, hugged and kissed her good-bye, then the girl went downstairs and out the front door. An atmosphere of excitement gripped the ranch. After hurriedly finishing morning chores, some of the hands had left to see if they could help with any details of the ceremony and reception. The others were gathered at the bunkhouse in their Sunday best, talking and moving about restlessly. As Janessa was stepping into the buggy, a group of ranch hands passed, headed toward town. She exchanged a wave with them, then snapped the reins and turned the buggy toward the road.

The snow-covered Mount Hood loomed over the landscape, seeming very close in the cold, clear air. When she reached town, Janessa felt the difference in the atmosphere, for the wedding had taken on something of the proportions of a county fair for the townspeople. The streets near the front of the church were crowded with vehicles bringing guests, while the boardwalks were congested with people who had gathered to see the guests and watch the proceedings from outside the church.

Janessa parked the buggy behind the church. She smiled when she heard the deep, musical sound of a ship's horn from the river; the steam packet was on time.

As the packet approached its pier, Cindy Holt Kerr's view of Portland was partially obscured by the thick veil draped down from her hat. But that did nothing to dim the joyous excitement gripping her.

The society pages of the San Francisco newspapers had reported the preparations for the Holt and Woodling wedding in Portland. By reading them and checking the steam packet schedule, Cindy had found out that she could arrive in Portland just before the wedding. With the veil concealing her identity, she could avoid creating a flurry of excitement, which would inevitably take away something of Alexandra's day, and also fulfill her earnest wish to attend the wedding.

A wagon was waiting on the pier. Four workmen were sitting on the tailgate, and a man in a cutaway coat and striped trousers paced impatiently beside it. As soon as the gangplank was in place, the man in the formal coat dashed up it, pushing past the passengers filing off, and the workmen followed. They went inside and emerged with apparently light but large cardboard boxes, then ran to the wagon with them. The men repeated this task several times.

Cindy walked toward the baggage office on the pier, sharing the perplexity of other passengers, who wondered aloud what on earth the men were doing. When the wagon was stacked high with boxes, the driver's whip cracked, and the wagon veered around a corner and disappeared.

Others were still murmuring about the strange goings-on as Cindy stepped into the line in the baggage office and made arrangements to pick up her luggage later in the day.

She had wondered if her veil would completely conceal her identity, and she then found out that it did, because she almost walked straight into Calvin Rogers outside the office. He tipped his hat and stepped aside for her. Behind him were ranch hands with a huge mound of baggage, and none of the men recognized her.

Aware that time was running short, Cindy hurried toward the church. The town had changed since she had last been there, but most of the shortcuts remained. There was an atmosphere of celebration on the streets. When she reached the end of the block in front of the church, Cindy ran into an unforeseen obstacle: The street was filled with people who had come to watch from outside the church, and Cindy realized that ushers were probably ensuring that only invited guests were admitted to the limited seating inside.

But as a girl Cindy had sometimes been late for services, making a furtive entry necessary. Retracing the footsteps she had taken then, she went around the church to a small side door. She breathed a sigh of relief when she found the door

unlocked, then another sigh when she peeked inside and saw
no one.

The door opened into a narrow staircase leading up to
the rear of the balcony. Cindy tiptoed up the stairs. No one
noticed her; the ranch hands and townspeople on the crowded
benches were silently looking down at the altar. At the top of
the steps, she could see the altar herself, and she had to stifle
a gasp of admiration.

The window draperies were adjusted so most of the
church was relatively dim and the chancel flooded with light,
making it the focus of attention. The men scurrying about at
the steam packet, she now realized, had been collecting fresh
hot-house flowers sent from San Francisco. The choir stalls
behind the altar were a solid bank of red and white roses,
with a pattern of wide blue-silk streamers placed across them.
Blue baskets of red and white roses flanked the altar in lavish
profusion, the clusters of ribbons on the ends of the benches
in the same colors. It was a brilliant, dazzling display that was
both elegant and appropriate.

Cindy saw that Portland had finally become host to a
society wedding. The left front bench was filled with men in
riding costumes, with ribbons on the right sleeves of their
identical gray cutaway coats in the colors of their hunts.
Behind them were their families in rich furs and glittering
jewelry. Farther back—on Alexandra's side of the aisle for
some reason that Cindy failed to fathom—were the mayor
and the city councilmen of Portland, together with their
families.

On the right side of the aisle, Eulalia sat on the front
bench with Janessa, Timmy, Dr. Martin and his wife, then
Claudia Brentwood and her grandson. Stalking Horse and
White Elk sat on the next bench, and there were others
whom Cindy did not know.

Over the soft drone of the organ music, Cindy heard the
faint shuffling of footsteps ceasing, and the congregation fell
absolutely silent. Seeing a single empty seat at the end of a
bench near the front of the balcony, Cindy tiptoed along the
aisle toward it.

Abby and Amy Givens, sitting beside the vacant seat,

looked up as Cindy started to sit. "That is saved for Mi.
Woodling's maid, ma'am," Abby whispered.

A young, attractive woman with large, dark eyes sud
denly appeared at Cindy's elbow. "We will make room," sh
whispered in a Spanish accent.

The two sisters squirmed along the bench, crowdin
other people closer together. As she and Juanita sat dow
Cindy softly thanked the maid, who smiled and nodded. Th
whispering and movements having disturbed the quiet of th
church, Eulalia turned her head and directed a level stare u
at the balcony, then looked back to the front.

Janessa glanced up at the balcony and started to tur
away, then hesitated. Turning back, she gazed straight i
Cindy. A happy smile spreading over her face, Janessa final
turned back toward the altar. Eulalia glanced at Janessa cur
ously, and Cindy smiled to herself, knowing that the tacitur
girl would say nothing.

The vestry door opened, and the minister walked to th
altar. A moment later, Toby, and Andrew Brentwood as bes
man, came out of the vestry and stepped to their places.

Glowing pride swelled within Cindy as she looked at he
brother. Whether in the casual garb he wore when astride
horse or in the formal cutaway coat and striped trousers tha
he wore now, he always dominated the scene. His stron
features bronzed by the sun and wind, he was magnificentl
handsome. Andrew, tall and elegant in his formal uniform
stood beside Toby. The organ music suddenly stopped on
high, ringing chord that rose to a commanding volume, an
nouncing the bride's entrance. The congregation stood as th
high chord lingered, then faded into the opening bars of th
wedding march. The people below Cindy looked up the aisle
Over the stirring, majestic notes of the march, Cindy heard
collective sigh. A moment later, as Alexandra came into vie\
from the balcony, Cindy gasped in admiration.

Leland Blake had been asked to give the bride away
Alexandra was a vision of beauty in shimmering white as sh
walked down the aisle with Lee, who wore his formal uni
form. Alexandra's gown was of snowy mousseline de soie
trimmed with pearls and lavish yards of Valenciennes lace
The folds of crisp, white tulle carefully arranged over he

ead and shoulders formed a veil in front and draped down to
er long silk train in back. Her bridal bouquet, matching the
ecor of the church, was an arrangement of red and white
oses in a cluster of blue ribbons. Tears burned in Cindy's
yes, so overcome was she by the sight, and Juanita wept
ftly beside her.

Toby stood taller, a flush of deep color on his face as he
oked with love at his bride.

When Alexandra reached the altar and the congregation
as seated, the minister began the service. Cindy waited
xpectantly for her first glimpse of Alexandra's face at the end
the ceremony. When Alexandra's veil was lifted and she
rned to Toby, Cindy saw that the woman was radiantly
eautiful. But more than that, Cindy saw the deep love on
eir faces and knew that, as they kissed, her brother was
arried to the perfect woman for him.

The organ music pealed out again, joyous and trium-
nant, as Toby and Alexandra, exchanging smiles with those
n both sides, walked up the aisle to an anteroom. The
eople began leaving the benches in a rush to gather in front
the church, and Cindy stood in the aisle against the wall to
t them pass. When the balcony was empty, she stepped to a
indow.

Pulling the drapery aside, she looked down at the mass
people. The last few filed out of the church, and then Toby
d Alexandra came out. Pandemonium surrounded them,
d a cloud of rice fell on them as they ran to a gaily
ecorated carriage at the curb.

The carriage moved away, and the guests rushed to
her carriages and wagons to follow it. As Cindy had ex-
ected, the entire town was invited to the reception. She
ent back down the narrow staircase and reflected that the
me and effort required to get there were insignificant com-
ared to the pleasure she had just experienced.

Janessa, waiting outside the door, beamed. "You're not
e only one who's ever been late for church and had to
scover this door," she remarked.

Cindy laughed in delight. After hastily gathering up her
eavy veil, she hugged the girl tightly and kissed her. "I
ould have known that you would recognize me. The reason

I didn't want anyone to see me is because this should
Alexandra's day."

"Yes, I know," Janessa replied. "She would do exact
the same thing, but I don't know anyone else who would
that thoughtful. Come on, I have a buggy parked behind t
church."

Cindy followed Janessa along the path. It was characte
istic of the quiet girl to wander off by herself when any ki
of festivity other than a close, very small family gathering w
involved, so Cindy saw nothing unusual about her not goi
to the reception.

There was certainly nothing unusual about her smoki
until she mentioned it herself, lighting a cigarette. "Dad h
asked me to stop smoking, and I've been trying," she sai
"I'm not smoking nearly as much now, but I haven't bee
able to stop completely."

"Yes, I've heard that it's difficult, but please do kee
trying, Janessa. If you would stop, I would be just as please
as Toby."

During the drive to the docks to get Cindy's baggag
Cindy questioned Janessa about Alexandra, and everythi
she learned confirmed her initial impression. When they le
the docks, Janessa brought Cindy to a huge building und
construction.

"When it's finished," the girl said, "it will be the ne
charity hospital, the Reed Kerr Memorial Hospital."

Astonished and deeply touched, Cindy stepped out
the buggy and looked around. By questioning Janessa, Cin
learned that Alexandra was in charge of the project. It too
one more question for Cindy to find out the source of mone
for the enormously expensive project.

While she herself did not feel any animosity toward t
baroness, Cindy knew that Janessa had burned with hatre
toward the woman. At first she was perplexed when the gi
began talking about her trip to New York with the doctor. A
she spoke, it was obvious she was very distressed. The
Cindy finally understood.

"But there's nothing to explain, Janessa!" Cindy exclaime
"There's nothing wrong with your becoming fond of her. I

act, I'm pleased, because that's a far more worthy emotion
than hatred."

Still upset for some reason, the girl nodded and looked
away. "Well, I was worried, and I've been wanting to tell you
about it."

"Janessa, it's clear that you simply responded to a woman
who has a charming, generous nature."

"She didn't have a good nature," Janessa said. "She
could be very hateful, and she had a vile temper."

"Then how do you explain this?" Cindy asked, pointing.
"This is evidence of a large measure of generosity."

"The only reason she did it was because she liked me
and I wanted a hospital. She didn't care if sick people had to
die in the street. But there were other things about her as
well, things I just don't understand. I can't explain it, but
when she smiled at me, I couldn't help but love her." Bursting
into tears, the girl turned away. "And now she's dead,
Cindy."

Cindy was rendered speechless with shock. Pushing her
handkerchief into Janessa's hands, Cindy collected her thoughts.
"But you said that the surgery was a complete success."

"It was," the girl sobbed, wiping her eyes. "After she
went back to Germany somebody shot her."

Thoughts raced through Cindy's mind, but she forced
herself to push them aside. Janessa needed her.

By the time they were near the ranch, the girl had
recovered her composure and was listening as Cindy talked
about her work. Characteristically, Janessa had made no mention
of the house, and Cindy was speechless once more when
she saw the stately Victorian mansion where the ranch house
had been. The house was deserted, since everyone was at the
reception. They carried in the luggage, and Cindy found a
choice of a half-dozen guest rooms. Then Janessa showed her
around the house.

After the horse was unharnessed, Cindy and Janessa sat
and talked over cups of coffee. It was then that Cindy began
extracting the rest of the story of the baroness's death from
Janessa.

Janessa said that Henry had sent the telegram to Toby
from Dakota, not Germany. "He was stationed at Fort Aber-

crombie, near Fargo. The telegram said he was going t
Germany to attend to things, then he's coming back to b
assigned to the Seventh Cavalry Regiment, General Custer'
regiment."

Cindy sipped her coffee as she pondered. She intende
to visit family and friends in Portland for a few days, then se
out for Paris, to accompany the torch of the Statue of Libert
to Philadelphia, where it would be placed on display in tim
for the centennial year, 1876.

By then, she reflected, Henry would be with the Sev
enth Cavalry Regiment. Philadelphia was far from the west
ern plains, but somehow she knew that she and Henry woul
meet. Wounded pride still smoldered within her, but sh
knew she still loved Henry and always would. He had mad
another life for himself, and she was unsure of what hi
reaction would be when they met. She was even more uncer
tain about her own.

If you enjoyed **OKLAHOMA!**, the twenty-third volume of America's favorite historical series, **WAGONS WEST**, then you'll look forward to reading the next exciting novel of adventure and romance in this bestselling saga . . .

WAGONS WEST XXIV

CELEBRATION!

It is 1876, and America has achieved one hundred proud years of independence. From Oregon to New York, from Tucson to Philadelphia, Americans everywhere are bursting with optimism as they honor their nation's founding and look forward to another century of freedom and prosperity. But there are enemies of democracy, enemies of the intrepid Toby Holt, legendary frontiersman who stands ready to defend his family and his nation when they are threatened. . . .

Turn the page for a thrilling preview of the next book in this outstanding series, coming in fall 1989.

*In CELEBRATION!, Henry Blake and Cindy Holt Reed—
once betrothed—meet again for the first time since Henry's
marriage to Gisela von Kirchberg. . . .*

Henry rode up to Toby Holt's majestic Victorian mansion, tethered his horse, and knocked on the door. A
young, heavyset woman in a maid's dress and mobcap
answered.

"Good day. I'm Henry Blake," he said, touching his hat.
"Is Mrs. Holt in?"

"Miss Alexandra and Miss Cindy are both out in the
barnyard. They're refinishing a bureau. If you want to
come inside, I'll let them know that you're here."

Henry glanced at his horse, which had turned its rump
to the icy wind whipping its tail and mane. "I need to
put that horse in a barn, so I'll go around and find Mrs.
Holt."

It had occurred to Cindy that Henry and she would
meet again, and she had always hoped the circumstances
of their reunion would find her at her very best.

As the workshop door opened and Henry stepped inside, however, she and Alexandra were wearing old smocks
spattered with paint, and their hair was carelessly tied
back to keep it out of their eyes. Cindy knew she looked
like a laundrywoman at an army post. To make matters
worse, Henry looked as if he had just stepped out of a
bandbox.

"How do you do, Major Blake," Cindy replied coldly as he greeted her. "This is Mrs. Alexandra Holt. Alexandra, Henry Blake."

As he bowed, Alexandra placidly returned his greeting. Cindy reflected that Alexandra's Bradford and Woodling bloodlines gave her a social calm and stability in even the most humiliating circumstances.

"I've committed a grave discourtesy," Henry apologized. "I should have waited at the house. If you'll excuse me, I'll wait there. I would like to talk with both of you."

"Please stay here while I finish cleaning the brushes," Alexandra said to Henry. Turning to Cindy, she said, "Dear, if you'll go and tell Amy that we'll have a guest for lunch? . . ."

Cindy darted a grateful smile at Alexandra and fled toward the house, her cheeks burning with anger and confusion.

From all she had heard, Henry's wife, Gisela von Kirchberg, had been strikingly beautiful and highly sophisticated, as well as powerful and wealthy. Cindy had concluded that Henry had broken their engagement simply because she had been outmatched by Gisela. But Cindy knew she had changed since then, becoming cosmopolitan and successful. She had no wish to compete with memories of Henry's deceased wife, but she wanted him to know that she was no longer a naïve girl. Unfortunately, her appearance in the workshop had dealt her a devastating setback.

A short time later, when Alexandra and Cindy had freshened up and changed their clothing, they went downstairs together. Cindy had been savoring the thought of Henry left cooling his heels in the parlor. But as the two women stepped into the room, Henry came through the front door and explained that he had been admiring Alexandra's horses. Because nothing seemed to go wrong for the man, Cindy smoldered with renewed anger as they seated themselves in the large, lavishly furnished parlor, a warm fire blazing in the fireplace.

In a way, she felt that her anger was childish, but she also realized that her resentment was a form of self-defense. She still loved him with all of the intensity of years before. Her emotional wounds, however, had never truly healed, and she could not let him think he could walk back into her life whenever he pleased.

Edward Blackstone, meanwhile, is on a risky expedition up the Amazon River, hoping to destroy Brazil's monopoly on rubber. Assisted by explorer Teddy (Theodora) Montague and naturalist Cecil Witherspoon—and hampered by the ever-drunk Edgar Dooley—Edward plans to smuggle rubber-tree seeds from the Brazilian jungle. . . .

At a bend in the Amazon River a hundred yards ahead, a canoe came into view, a half-dozen Brazilian Indians in it. Edward Blackstone, standing at the rail of his steamer, gazed at the canoe indifferently. Natives had been sighted occasionally. They were curious about the launch and wanted to sell fruit and vegetables.

Teddy, standing beside Dr. Witherspoon, squinted intently at the canoe. Noticing Teddy's interest, Edward shook off his lethargy and looked at it more closely. The Indians were now lifting long, slender poles and putting the ends of them to their mouths.

Teddy and Captain Santos shouted in Portuguese while Teddy seized Witherspoon's arm and dragged him down with her as she fell prone to the deck. The crewmen scrambled for cover. Not understanding what was happening, Edward leaped to Dooley and threw him to the deck as he himself fell flat. Then he saw what the Indians were blowing—poisoned darts four inches long—into the wheelhouse and rails.

One of the darts found a human target, an Indian crewman, who screamed in terror as he stood immobilized, looking wild-eyed at the dart in his shoulder. Teddy rolled across the deck and kicked his feet from under him, then plucked the dart from his shoulder as he sprawled beside her. Panic-stricken, he struggled to scramble to his feet, but she gripped his long hair and rapped the back of his head solidly and repeatedly against the deck until he subsided, dazed. She took out a knife, opened the puncture the dart had made in his shoulder, and bent to suck the poison from the wound.

With the advantage of the current, the attackers' canoe was pacing the launch as darts continued thudding into the woodwork. Edward turned to Teddy, who was sucking blood and poison from the cut on the crewman's shoulder. "Teddy, tell Captain Santos to throttle down! I can't hit anything with my pistol while the vessel veers about!"

Teddy spat blood on the deck, then wiped her mouth with the back of her hand as she turned and crawled toward the cabins. "I will in just a moment, Edward! I'll get a gun and join you!"

Seeing her pistol in a holster at her waist, Edward wondered what she was talking about. He snapped off shots at the canoe in frustration, the bullets going wild. As he started to reload, Teddy, a dart sticking in the tall crown of her pith helmet, crawled up beside him with her elephant gun. Opening the breech of the gun, she seated two bullets the size of cigars in the double barrels, closed the breech, and shouted to Santos.

The wild hammering of the engine subsided to a murmur when Santos closed the throttle. The vessel stabilized, and Teddy shouldered the heavy rifle and fired both barrels simultaneously with a shattering clap. A huge cloud of smoke belched from the muzzle, and Edward, peering under the smoke, saw the bow of the canoe explode into splinters.

The canoe sank, and the Indians dropped their blowguns and swam toward the bank. "You see, that's far more effective than killing them," she explained as she and Edward stood. "They think more of their canoes than they do of themselves, and that lot will soon spread the word far and wide of what happened. We won't have that trouble again."

Edward nodded, then turned as Dooley exclaimed in despair. Thinking the Irishman had been hit by a dart, Edward rushed over to him. "What is it, Edgar?"

"I broke my bottle, and all and all," Dooley wailed in distress, looking at shards of glass in his coat pocket. The side of the coat was soaked with brandy. "My sainted father would disown me!" He continued lamenting, stumbling off toward the cabin as the launch started forward again.

Santos was shouting his thanks to Teddy in Portuguese, and Dr. Witherspoon climbed to his feet and appeared mystified as to what had happened. The crewman who had been hit by the dart, surprised to find himself still alive, tearfully expressed his gratitude to Teddy.

Shrugging off the thanks, she grasped a boat hook and stepped to the rail to fish the blowguns out of the river as they floated past the launch. "The curator at the Ethnological Museum in London will be very pleased to have a few of these," she explained to Edward.

He went to help her, reflecting that she had been the life of the expedition. When they had four blowguns out of the water, Edward and Teddy began pulling darts from the rails and wheelhouse. Laughing, he commented about Edgar's despair over having broken his bottle. She joined in the merriment, then grimaced. "I'll be glad to have a drink myself presently. Taking care of that crewman has left a horrid taste in my mouth."

"I'm sure it has. We're all very fortunate to have you as one of the party, Teddy, because you deal with situations very handily. That crewman in particular is fortunate that you're here."

Teddy laughed heartily, shaking her head. "No, he's fortunate that he got that dart in his shoulder. If it had hit his grubby rump, I'm afraid he would have had it."

Eulalia Holt Blake travels to Alaska with her husband, Lee. While he attends to army business, Eulalia is free to see the sights. . . .

It was another bright, warm day. Feeling energetic, Eulalia decided to go for a long walk. She set out down Sitka's waterfront street, which turned into a road leading around one side of the harbor.

A mile from the city, the water receded at the edge of a sun-dried mud flat studded with clumps of tough, hardy saltwater sedge two and three feet apart. She passed an abandoned logging camp across the road from old, decaying piers that reached far across the flat, where boats had brought supplies to the camp during high tides.

Glimpsing a distant movement on the flat, Eulalia looked toward it, shading her eyes. A short distance beyond the edge of the clumps of grass, where the mud was still damp, a gull was tangled in a fishing net washed in by the tide. She watched, hoping it would free itself, but after a moment she saw that it was too hopelessly entangled and exhausted. The poor creature was doomed to a slow, terrifying death when the tide came in.

She saw no one who might be able to help. The words of Dr. Sutton, a geologist she had met at dinner the night before, kept her from taking action: Potholes filled with quicksandlike silt peppered the offshore flats. Reluctantly, she started to walk away, but it was impossible for her to abandon the bird.

Thinking again about Dr. Sutton's warning, she looked at the flat. It looked the same as the many mud flats she had seen near the mouth of the Columbia River. Often, at the cost of a muddy dress and shoes, she had walked about to look at things washed in by the tide. Sutton had admitted that quicksand potholes in the mud flats here were very rare, and abandoning the bird on the basis of that slight risk suggested cowardice to Eulalia.

The gull was only about two hundred yards from the road. Eulalia stepped out onto a clump of grass, checking the footing. It proved as stable as the road. She stepped onto the next clump, then the next. The farther she got from the road, the farther apart were the clumps of grass, some separated by as much as four feet. Eulalia took long strides to cross the distance, taking a zigzag route to avoid wide stretches of bare mud.

Presently, she came to an expanse, ten feet wide, that she was unable to avoid. She cautiously stepped down to it. It was slick but firm. She crossed the gap, leaving deep footprints in the mud.

When she was halfway between the road and the gull, Eulalia heard a shout behind her. Balancing on a clump of grass, she stopped and turned. Two hunters with shotguns under their arms were on the road, and one was Samuel Claiborne, whom she and Lee had met during the voyage to Alaska.

"What are you doing, Mrs. Blake?"

"I'm going to free a gull caught in a net," she replied, pointing.

The men shaded their eyes with their hands, looking, then Claiborne stepped off the road. "I'll free it for you, Mrs. Blake. Walking around on the mud flats can be dangerous."

"Thank you, but I'm almost there."

The man nodded as Eulalia continued toward the bird. She reached the far edge of the grass; the gull was fifty feet farther, across damp, gleaming mud.

Eulalia hesitated, uncertain. Behind her, Claiborne called out again, offering to free the bird. Shaking her head and replying, she stepped onto the mud. It was less firm underfoot than the other areas, but it supported her weight. Holding up her hem, Eulalia left deep tracks as she moved toward the bird. The gull flapped and squealed in terror as she approached.

Eulalia held its wings against its body, then lifted it and the rotting net. When she freed the bird, it flew away. Eulalia wadded the net so no other bird would get caught in it and tossed it aside. Her attention no longer occupied, she realized her feet had sunk into the mud up to her ankles.

She lifted her right foot, her weight on her left. The surface seemed to give way, turning into a quaking morass. As her left foot suddenly sank into the mud up to her knee, she windmilled her arms to keep her balance.

Instinctively, she tried to free her left foot, but her right leg also sank into the mud to her knee. Fear gripped her as she felt herself sinking deeper.

Claiborne bounded across the clumps of grass toward Eulalia as soon as she began sinking and shouted to his companion to go for help. The man ran down the road toward Sitka, while Claiborne, slinging his shotgun over his shoulder, picked up the end of a long board the tide had washed in. Dragging the board, he leaped from clump to clump.

He crossed the bare mud cautiously, by following Eulalia's deep footprints. A few feet from her, he stopped and slid the board across the mud to her. "Hold onto this, Mrs. Blake," he said. "Rest your weight on it, and it should keep you from sinking deeper."

"Thank you very much, Mr. Claiborne. It appears that I'm in one of the quicksand potholes, doesn't it?"

"Yes, but don't worry. My friend will have some assistance here in a few minutes."

His tone was confident, but he glanced worriedly out at the Pacific Ocean, and Eulalia turned to look. The tide was coming in. "I'm very grateful for your help," she told him, feeling oddly removed from the situation and marveling at her calm, good manners. "And I regret causing trouble."

"People in Alaska always stand ready to help one another." He turned, looking down the road toward Sitka. "Look! My friend has sent some men already. I'll bet he's gone on into town to look for your husband."

Craning her neck, Eulalia saw a score of men wrenching boards loose from the old pier to lay a pathway across the flat.

Other men came from town, joining those who were pulling down additional boards. A few minutes later, the pathway of timbers was past the edge of the grass. Eulalia was in the mud up to her waist but sinking no deeper.

"That's good," Claiborne observed. "Maybe you're in a shallow pothole, Mrs. Blake. In that case, we should be able to pull you out easily."

Looking between the men who were dragging timbers to lay on top of the quicksand, Eulalia saw Lee, his colleague Captain Latham, and Samuel Claiborne's friend gallop up on army horses. Right behind them was Dr. Sutton, the geologist. The men leaped from the horses and ran down the path of boards toward her. Then the men laying timbers encircled her, covering the quicksand with boards.

Lee pushed through them, kneeling beside Eulalia in consternation. He and others took her arms and shoulders in a vain attempt to lift her. Her instant of relief faded; even though they tugged so hard she almost cried out in pain, she lifted barely an inch.

"You can't free her that way, General," Sutton said. "Glacial silt quicksand is very viscous, and the vacuum formed behind anything being lifted is much more powerful than the lifting force. Your wife's arms would be torn from her body before you could exert enough force to pull her up twelve inches."

"Then what can we do?" Lee demanded.

"Let's try to get the quicksand away from her so we can lift her out!" a man shouted. "There should be shovels at the Indian villages! Let's go!"

Sutton watched a dozen men race away along the path of boards. "I don't think shovels will suffice. I think we need to use the high-pressure hose on a fire engine to blast the quicksand away."

"I'll get the fire engine from town," Captain Latham offered. "I'll be back just as soon as I can, General Blake."

Lee frowned worriedly at the incoming tide, and Eulalia turned to look. The edge of the water was a hundred feet away. The milling men discussed and dismissed other means of freeing her.

The men who had gone for shovels returned and began scooping up the quicksand around Eulalia, but the effort was futile; as rapidly as they could dig it away, it flowed back in. The edge of the water finally reached the timbers covering the quicksand and began slowly deepening.

Accepting the consequences of the situation, whatever they might turn out to be, Eulalia maintained firm self-control. The men standing on the timbers around her were in ankle-deep water. She smiled up at Sutton. "I should have taken your advice. In freeing that bird, I got myself into the same fix."

"Well, no matter, Mrs. Blake," he replied, trying to smile in return. "We'll get you out directly."

"The water isn't nearly as cold as I thought it would be."

"No, ma'am, not at this time of year. We're in a phase of relatively low tides of short duration, with high tide lasting no longer than an hour. That makes the water warmer."

"But it will definitely get deep enough to cover me, won't it?"

The man nodded miserably, turning away. A moment later, however, he and the others began cheering wildly, pointing and shouting that the fire engine was coming. Eulalia glimpsed it between the men moving about in front of her. Its three teams of horses were pounding along the road, with Captain Latham and firemen clinging to the heavy vehicle as it jolted over ruts, smoke boiling from its stack.

The cheering faded when Latham and the fire chief joined the others surrounding Eulalia.

"I don't have enough hose to reach out here, sir," the fire chief said to Lee. "And the fire engine is much too heavy to bring out here. I'll send to Killisnoo for more hose, but it'll take about an hour for the man to get here with it."

A somber silence fell in the wake of the man's words, the last hope exhausted. Deep remorse and fear tugged at Eulalia, but she forced them back with her strength of will. Having confronted life with courage for almost sixty years, she was determined to face death in the same way. She also knew she had to be brave for Lee, because he was almost beside himself.

The water lapping around the men's boots as they stood on the timbers was nearly up to Eulalia's shoulders. She cleared her throat, taking charge.

"Gentlemen, I'm deeply grateful for everything you've done. I've seen for myself that Alaskans stand ready to help. You've worked hard and bravely, but fate is against us. Is there a minister present?"

A man took off his cap, stepping forward. "I'm a lay preacher, ma'am. Cletis Underwood."

"Mr. Underwood, please say a prayer for me and commit my soul to God. Then I'd like to be alone with my husband."

The men around Eulalia removed their caps and hats. Lee knelt beside her and held her hand as he took off his cap. He and the others bowed their heads, Underwood praying. Eulalia bowed her head and looked down at the water lapping toward her chin.

Alexandra Holt, seven months pregnant, had been warned by Dr. Martin not to travel from Portland to the Centennial Celebration in Philadelphia. She had not heeded his advice, leaving Dr. Martin to make arrangements with a colleague, Dr. Hicks, to accept Alexandra in Hicks's Philadelphia clinic should she go into labor prematurely. . . .

In their hotel suite, Alexandra called to Toby. When he came into the bedroom, she was sitting on the edge of the bed, a hand pressed to her stomach. "Would you get Janessa for me, please?"

He ran to his daughter's room down the hall. She immediately accompanied him to the suite.

"When did the pains stop?" she asked Alexandra.

"No more than a minute ago."

Looking at her watch, Janessa sat down.

"Abigail Schumann is such a pleasant, charming woman," Alexandra observed, thinking of Dieter's wife, who occupied another suite on that floor.

"Yes, she is," Janessa agreed nonchalantly. "I enjoyed staying with them in Chicago."

The two conversed as if nothing were happening. Toby, exasperated, interrupted. "Aren't you going to get Dr. Martin?"

"No, not right now, Dad. It's going to be a long night, and he isn't a young man. But we should ask the hotel to send a messenger to Dr. Hicks's clinic, so he can get everything sterilized."

Toby did as he was told. When he came back to the suite, he went to Alexandra and took her hand. "Can I get something for you? Would you like a sandwich?"

"Alexandra shouldn't eat anything now," Janessa said. "Her digestive system has stopped functioning."

Toby shifted from foot to foot as his wife and daughter continued talking. A few minutes later, Alexandra broke off and winced, prompting Janessa to check her watch.

"Isn't somebody going to do something?" Toby demanded in alarm.

Janessa turned to him, putting her watch away. "Would you like a spoonful of laudanum, Dad?"

"No, I don't want a spoonful of laudanum. I want somebody to do something. Shouldn't I get a carriage? When are we going to that clinic?"

"In an hour or so," Janessa replied. "Why don't you ask Cindy to come in here."

Fuming, Toby left. After sending Cindy, Abigail Schumann, and Tonie Martin to the suite, Toby met Marjorie White in the hall and sent her there, also. Dieter accompanied Toby to Henry Blake's room, where Toby paced the floor and puffed on a cigar.

After what seemed to be an endlessly long time, Cindy

knocked on the door and said it was time to leave for the clinic. Deeming the elevator too slow for him, Toby went down the stairs to summon two carriages. Alexandra came out, walking between Janessa and Dr. Martin, with the others trooping out behind them.

The clinic was in a large Victorian house on landscaped grounds overlooking the Schuylkill River. Catering to a wealthy clientele, it was luxuriously furnished and well staffed. Dr. Hicks led Janessa and Dr. Martin upstairs with Alexandra, while a maid showed Toby and the others into a drawing room, then brought refreshments.

The strong smell of phenol was strangely comforting to Toby. Still very nervous, of course, he controlled himself and sat down for the long wait that he knew was ahead.

★ WAGONS WEST ★

A series of unforgettable books that trace the lives of a dauntless band of pioneering men, women, and children as they brave the hazards of an untamed land in their trek across America. This legendary caravan of people forge a new link in the wilderness. They are Americans from the North and the South, alongside immigrants, Blacks, and Indians, who wage fierce daily battles for survival on this uncompromising journey—each to their private destinies as they fulfill their greatest dreams.

☐	26822	INDEPENDENCE! #1	$4.50
☐	26162	NEBRASKA! #2	$4.50
☐	26242	WYOMING! #3	$4.50
☐	26072	OREGON! #4	$4.50
☐	26070	TEXAS! #5	$4.50
☐	26377	CALIFORNIA! #6	$4.50
☐	26546	COLORADO! #7	$4.50
☐	26069	NEVADA! #8	$4.50
☐	26163	WASHINGTON! #9	$4.50
☐	26073	MONTANA! #10	$4.50
☐	26184	DAKOTA! #11	$4.50
☐	26521	UTAH! #12	$4.50
☐	26071	IDAHO! #13	$4.50
☐	26367	MISSOURI! #14	$4.50
☐	27141	MISSISSIPPI! #15	$4.50
☐	25247	LOUISIANA! #16	$4.50
☐	25622	TENNESSEE! #17	$4.50
☐	26022	ILLINOIS! #18	$4.50
☐	26533	WISCONSIN! #19	$4.50
☐	26849	KENTUCKY! #20	$4.50
☐	27065	ARIZONA! #21	$4.50
☐	27458	NEW MEXICO! #22	$4.50

Prices and availability subject to change without notice.

- -

FROM THE PRODUCER OF WAGONS WEST AND THE KENT FAMILY CHRONICLES— A SWEEPING SAGA OF WAR AND HEROISM AT THE BIRTH OF A NATION.

THE WHITE INDIAN SERIES

Filled with the glory and adventure of the colonization of America, here is the thrilling saga of the new frontier's boldest hero and his family. Renno, born to white parents but raised by Seneca Indians, becomes a leader in both worlds. THE WHITE INDIAN SERIES chronicles the adventures of Renno, his son Ja-gonh, and his grandson Ghonkaba, from the colonies to Canada, from the South to the turbulent West. Through their struggles to tame a savage continent and their encounters with the powerful men and passionate women in the early battles for America, we witness the events that shaped our future and forged our great heritage.

☐ 24650	White Indian #1	$3.95
☐ 25020	The Renegade #2	$3.95
☐ 24751	War Chief #3	$3.95
☐ 24476	The Sachem #4	$3.95
☐ 25154	Renno #5	$3.95
☐ 25039	Tomahawk #6	$3.95
☐ 25589	War Cry #7	$3.95
☐ 25202	Ambush #8	$3.95
☐ 23986	Seneca #9	$3.95
☐ 24492	Cherokee #10	$3.95
☐ 24950	Choctaw #11	$3.95
☐ 25353	Seminole #12	$3.95
☐ 25868	War Drums #13	$3.95
☐ 26206	Apache #14	$3.95
☐ 27161	Spirit Knife #15	$3.95
☐ 27264	Manitou #16	$3.95
☐ 27841	Seneca Warrior #17	$3.95

Prices and availability subject to change without notice.

Bantam Books, Dept. LE3, 414 East Golf Road, Des Plaines, IL 60016

Please send me the books I have checked above. I am enclosing $_____ (please add $2.00 to cover postage and handling). Send check or money order—no cash or C.O.D.s please.

Mr/Ms _____

Address _____

City/State _____ Zip _____

LE3—4/89

Please allow four to six weeks for delivery. This offer expires 10/89.